# A KID IN KEARLITH

Matthew Sanford

Artwork by Caitlin Dickens

*Dedicated to the kids who dream.*

*Especially when they're adults.*

ISBN-10: 0-692-94711-6

ISBN-13: 978-0-692-94711-1

Printed in the United States of America

First Printing, 2017

Kearlith Publishing
749 47th Way South
Birmingham, AL 35222

www.Kearlith.com

# <u>Chapter 1</u>

They were screaming again. The two twisting, devilish squeals were a few short wavelengths away from shattering Simon's eardrums. Angels in Hell couldn't have matched their pitch. His head pounded through the layers of dark and disheveled hair, leading to his explosive slam of the door. The idea backfired after the door smashed his toe in the shuffle. It was that kind of day. Again.

This certain occurrence reassured Simon of his choice to cover his basement room in whatever material he could find. Over eighteen long years of life, he had collected shirts, sheets, mattresses, felt, curtains, blankets, egg crates. He liked to describe it as "safety from the Sun". Light could rarely be found in this room, but it blocked out the noise pollution from the outside. Simon's personality matched this "safety from the Sun", another reason he felt the door needed to be closed. And there he sat.

On a bed in complete darkness other than the flashing lights on his various electronics. He still couldn't escape the screaming. He wished those two had been born without vocal cords instead of being born without parents. Their parents had a difficult enough time raising him, especially when he was never anything more than an inconvenience. Having heathen twins in addition to a nothing son would have completely ruined their exploratory lives.

They disappeared. His father's widowed mother was left to raise newborn twins and a nothing grandson.

This obviously was just shy of a failure, seeing as the ten-year-olds were currently fighting a vicious and most likely bloody battle about who the best Disney character was. His mind started drifting to the past again. Simon was used to this, thus his hands found the computer and started working their usual job of surfing the internet. He remembered a customer at the café earlier had mentioned a website of a guy that went on a two-week hike around the local mountains, some of the tallest in the Smokies, and shot nearly two thousand photographs.

With nothing else to do, he decided to check it out. Much to his surprise, the pictures were stunning. One picture in particular received a good ten-minute gaze. Golden leaves lined the ground of a path lit by fiery-red trees. Green and amber splashes dotted some, but mostly in focus were the three trees in front of the camera. The photo looked like an enchanted entrance. Simon wasted a few hours on the site that night. He couldn't tear himself away from photo after photo of the forest's complex color scheme. Finally, his squinted eyes glued themselves shut. He gave up and passed out.

Simon slept well. He had been dead tired from school and working eight hours; his body and mind easily remained asleep. He awoke in a panic the next morning thinking he was late for school but realized it was Saturday. His heart skipped another beat when he thought he was late for work but soon remembered it was his day off. He had all day to work on a couple of things for his Statistics class. Simon smiled thinking about how flawless this day would be. He took his time getting ready. Threw on his favorite CD and sang every word. Stunningly, he felt the light needed to be on.

The twins started their daily routine of fighting over morning cartoons, and Simon decided to head up to the café on his day off. Discounted coffee. Free internet. Nice place lacking screeching children. Nothing could hurt today. Even when Granny screamed, "You forgot the trash, jackass!" he just let it roll off his back, and intentionally forgot the trash. He was never anything more than an idiot, so he didn't give any more than expected. Simon wouldn't let anything affect him today.

Until he approached the counter at work. He ordered a simple cup of coffee to get started. He thought such a request was innocent, but apparently the coffee brewer was shut off after it started spitting coffee at the baristas. And then the customers.

Simon was to take full responsibility of it. At least, this is how his manager Kathy felt. She spat at him for his job of cleaning it the previous day. Her hundred-and-something-year-old wrinkled face scrunched into a knot as she warned him that the substitute latte might taste a little bitter because the grinder wasn't fully cleaned either. Her tone mocked subtlety.

More than anything he wanted to remind her that he wasn't alone the previous day. That the other two baristas sat and talked while he had to clean, stock, serve coffee, and ask them to help every thirty seconds. That in fact, he had asked only one favor of the other baristas. To clean the coffee brewer.

But the fangs were snarling. With his tail between his legs, he found a table far away from gunfire and pulled out his laptop and notebook.

Kathy wasn't done. She lurked and pounced on him a few minutes later, correcting his method of brewing the coffee. Again. Also for showing up late one day the week before because of a traffic accident. And for requesting off for his birthday last month. Not to mention the lack of effort she had noticed recently. Basically every reason why she wanted to fire him. He took it all in as his last shot at pleasing his boss to keep the checks coming in and Granny happy.

Fortunately, he worked the next day. He could prove himself. After a few minutes of torture, Kathy must have felt the amount of damage given was enough for this hopeless soul. She spun around and left Simon to ponder these revelations.

Out of the window he gazed upon a familiar sight. The rolling forest extended for miles up to a much taller mountain barely visible in the distance. Treetops blanketed the stretch from the café to the horizon, shadowed by the clouds overhead. Every layer of hill faded farther into fog. The overcast sky revealed a dim difference in the clouds just to the right of the mountain. Yellow lights with orange shadows occasionally swam along the surface of the hazy underbellies of the clouds. The hues faded and reformed.

He yearned to just up and leave one day. No warning. No notice. Simply get out and explore natural territory. Discover what these beautiful colors were up close. Strip out of society's uniform and live in complete freedom. His better judgment always got the best of him, though. The keyboard clicked and clacked again as his eyes returned to the computer screen.

Simon squeezed out enough motivation to finish four of the eight questions, but eventually he started doodling on the sides of his notebook paper. He was just wasting time at this point. Packing up his backpack, the pit in his stomach deepened. As expected, he was giving up. He ordered a double espresso to go and felt Kathy's cold stare on the back of his neck as he marched towards the front door.

*       *       *

"Home" hadn't changed; the twins were still arguing. Upon his entrance, Simon barely dodged a badly thrown teddy bear meant for his sister. He thought better of chucking it back. Instead, he ignored the attack and slipped past the demons into his "safety from the Sun." The light remained off.

Rock music drowned out the battle outside, but the yelling couldn't escape his head. The screaming voices took the image of his parents. Lying in his bed, the roaring distortion and gut-wrenching vocals of the music were merely dull murmurs. His head put, "You're just too much of a problem to deal with, Simon!" on repeat. The last words he heard them say.

Shaking himself of this disheartening state, he leapt up and grabbed his loyal laptop. The welcoming jingle distracted his rambling mind, but once the internet booted up, Simon drew a blank. He had nothing of interest to look at. Only interesting people used the web. Since Simon was not interesting, he had no right to browse. He was cursed. Dismal mentality tainted everything Simon touched. He could find depression in anything.

He had a job, at least. Kathy might take that away, too, but for now, Simon could find a small ounce of hope in his current career of making coffee. Despite Kathy's beliefs, Simon was proud of himself for his knowledge of the bean. He understood the science behind it and what makes a good cup of joe. In fact, he didn't hate his job. He could live without the favoritism and the abundant reprimanding, but he took pleasure in giving people a good drink, some caffeine, and a conversation. The café was his last shot at happiness.

# Chapter 2

The next day Simon required himself to stay cheerful. He worked from noon to eight. Eight hours to show Kathy he was good at something. Anything. Untouchable determination throbbed in his heart. He ironed his black outfit and grabbed a clean apron. This attention to detail air was rare, but he thought the occasion called for it. The iron almost burnt his shirt, but Simon managed to save it when it began sizzling. He wasn't going to let a single thing go wrong.

The twins tried him. He thought they were somehow still asleep, but as soon as he safely made it past their door, Max squeaked the door barely open and chanted, "Asshole! Asshole! Asshole!" Simon knew he shouldn't have turned around, but he did it anyway. The twins had him in their grasp. Max darted out of the door and tackled his knees, bringing him crashing down. The archer Alexis crept slower out of the room, using a backpack as a quiver to hurl various toys at Simon.

He knew he could only sit there and take it. The second he pushed them off, Granny would whip around the corner and consider all this his fault. Max repeatedly punched his defenseless legs, and his face continued to get pelted by little plastic action figures. Finally, he couldn't hold back, "Children shouldn't act like this!" to which Alexis's response was, "We're not children. We're brain-eating aliens!" She held the skin taut on Simon's face and bit her teeth into his cheek.

As expected, Simon shoved her off just as Granny crept around into the hallway and asked what in the hell was going on. Max turned on his puppy dog eyes and whimpered, "We were tryin' to hug Simon before he left for work, and he started punchin' us and… and… he called us a… asshole!" Simon had never seen his grandmother flare up like this. She strode over to him and gripped his bony wrist, ripping him up from the floor. "Who do you think you are? You consider yourself a brother? Why don't you go to your job and do something for this family. Asshole." And Simon left.

Her words couldn't hurt him today. He had given up on trying to please her and the twin demons ages ago, and he had enough to prove at the moment.

*     *     *

He arrived at work, and everyone seemed to pick up on his attitude. The regulars smiled and waved, genuinely pleased to see him. One picked up his coffee in a cheers-like fashion and tipped his hat. It was as if they all knew his mission, and they were in full support. Simon was filled to the brim with positivity.

As soon as he got on the line, the coffee needed to be re-brewed, a mountain of dishes was piling up in the back, the counters were covered in syrup, the milk was running low in the refrigerator, the baked goods needed to be stocked, and there were at least six people in line. He washed his hands and cleaned out the coffee urn, then brewed it the way he remembered Kathy telling him. There was no sign of her, though. *Oh well*, he thought. Hopefully she would hear through the grapevine of his competence as a barista.

The coffee grounds filled the measuring cup to the exact amount, and seconds later they were on the floor. Inches away from Simon's ear, Kathy screeched, "Did you clean the brewer correctly?" and the cup was then empty. "Yes!" Simon snapped back, huffing with wide eyes. He flew to the back to fetch a broom to clean up the mess. Kathy sighed, shook her head, and crawled back into her nest.

Simon hated that place. The only time he stepped foot in the office was because of some form of scolding. He claimed that's where Kathy performed ancient voodoo magic and ritualized the eating of lesser beings. Whether this was true or not could never be proven, but he trusted his gut.

The floor and counter were soon empty of coffee grounds, and Simon took a second crack at brewing the coffee. The brief episode with Kathy shook him up, though. He had to clear his head and get focused. He took over for the barista like a tag team match. Simon jumped in the middle of a drink and produced it without losing a precious second of time. In one fluid motion he filled a cup with the appropriate syrup, steamed a pitcher of milk, started an espresso shot, and delivered one of the seven drinks on the queue. No machine could work faster than he. Simon's eyes occasionally glanced over his shoulder to see if Kathy was watching, but she remained cooped in her nest. Until Simon made an error, of course.

He thought the cup said something about hazelnut, but as it turned out, the customer only wanted vanilla. The lifted attitude was unnecessary, but Simon understood it was his mistake. He apologized and remade the drink. The hand-off from barista to customer induced the appearance of Kathy, who just so happened to hear Simon's last apology for screwing up the poor customer's drink. She asked what happened, and upon his explanation she spat the two words Simon hated the most, "My. Office." He nodded towards the giant line that was growing by the minute, but Kathy turned about face and marched into her lair. Simon had no choice but to follow.

"I honestly thought the cup said-" Simon began to say as he shut the door to Hell, but Kathy's words overpowered his.

"Do you know what we pride ourselves on, Simon?"

He knew the answer, but he took a second to swallow his own pride.

"Perfection," he answered with half the spirit Kathy was looking for.

"Your performance is very short of that," she said.

"It was a simple mistake, Kathy. I promise I'll pay more attention."

"You keep saying that, and yet we're still getting displeased customers." Simon had so much to say, and yet no words came out. She continued, "No comment? You have nothing to say for yourself? You understand that the only one bringing down this company is you."

"I don't see how you can claim that," he blurted. A sudden burst of confidence shot into Simon's attitude. He wasn't about to allow this abuse. Kathy was using false facts against him, and she would not win this time.

"You're useless, Simon," Kathy responded.

"I make more and better coffee than most of the people in this place. Ask anyone out there."

"I don't have to. And your back-talk won't make me. All I know is no one else screws things up as much as you do."

"That's because no one else does anything to screw up around here."

"Simon," Kathy pronounced in her cutting, accusatory tone.

"I'm a good worker," Simon stated.

"Then show me," and the conversation was dead.

After a moment of tension passed, Simon spun around and strutted through the door to regain her faith. He didn't know how, but he had to.

He jumped back on the line, assumed the role of barista, and got into a flow again. A few drinks in, a man yelled at him for his latté being too hot. Simon shushed the man, which didn't decrease his temper. As an apology he offered to remake the drink to a cooler temperature. Luckily the man was happy with the second attempt, and he left before Kathy got a chance to hear Simon messed up again.

The next hour ran smoothly. Simon made every drink correctly, and no more customers complained. This streak ended when Kathy busted the office door open. He watched her sniffing and gazing, searching for an attack like a cat fresh from a nap. Her eyes met Simon's, and she scurried next to him.

"Have you seen the abundance of dishes back there?" she shouted.

"Yeah, I was going to –"

"Wash them right now? That's what I thought."

"Have you seen the abundance of people in this line?" he asked.

"I won't take much more of your lip, Simon. Now go wash dishes."

He obeyed. He made sure every speck of food was off every single plate, pot, and pump. Every dish was thoroughly scrubbed, dumped in sanitizer, and then put through a sanitizing cycle in the washer. Simon couldn't do much, but he was going to perfect the art of washing dishes. At least he was away from everything. He could cool off by himself in a stockroom with sinks and humming refrigerators.

Before he cooled off too much, Kathy showed her face again.

"What's taking so long?" she barked. "They need forks and small mugs up there."

"There are a lot of dishes."

"And it doesn't look like you've washed a single one."

"I just started," Simon said a little too heavily. "The small mugs are going in the next load."

"Do you like spilling coffee and dirtying up dishes so that you can waste time back here instead of up front on the line?"

"I've been back here for five minutes making sure your customers don't get dirty plates."

"Your tone is about to get you fired, Simon," Kathy spat.

"I don't know what you want me to do. I'm working as fast as I can."

"It's not fast enough."

"Well maybe you don't know what you're talking about," shot out of Simon's face before he could stop it. He meant to keep that all inside, but Kathy squeezed it out of him.

She stared at him for a second before she asked, "Do you like working here?"

"Yes," Simon announced with every ounce of devotion he could gather.

"Well that's too bad. Because you don't anymore."

Simon couldn't believe it. He heard the words, saw her mouth make the words, but it must have been something else.

Her pursed lips said exactly that, though. Simon didn't work there anymore. Kathy's talons extended, silently requesting his apron back. He untied it and threw it in her face as he passed her towards the exit.

Simon stepped through the doors and gazed across the miles of trees he could see from the patio. The sky was empty, save for a lone, perfectly circular cloud several miles out to the right of the mountain, exactly where the dim orange and yellow lights were yesterday. As if by instinct, Simon picked up his feet to leave the world behind and find something new to live for in the forest. The cloud would be a good direction.

# Chapter 3

To his surprise and relief, Simon felt at ease after his feet had treaded miles of endless trees and steep mountainsides. He had built up his endurance over the past few years when he found the tranquilizing effect and pure pleasure of walks in the forest.

The thrill of seeing the world in this light pumped his impulsion. Beauty filled every inch of the softly laid vines across suspiciously fallen branches, the oddly warped trees in positions that boggled what little he remembered from Biology, the boulders that stuck out to create adequate rest-stops, the dead leaves drenching the floor with burnt red, sheen golden, and vibrant amber colors, the rare splashes of the sun's rays, and the rest of the path Simon had been following for hours now. The forest was much cooler than the heat he was feeling from outside. The sun had started to set, and the nearly new moon was taking over. He took a minute to rest and watch the sun make way for the moon.

This clearing seemed eerily planned. For example, the stump he was sitting on was worn down and petrified like cold stone. It sat across from another stump coated with a thick skin of multi-colored moss and mushrooms. The surrounding trees formed a perfect circle.

Simon decided it was time to continue based on the theory

of momentum. He did not wish to end his hiking streak in a forest's courtroom. His mood shifted more towards frightened, but he journeyed on. Captured in the shadows were wisps of mirrored smoke. From far off it appeared to be foggy, but the area around him was constantly clear. He felt a brief chill like icicles floated amongst his blood cells.

The moon barely shed any light into the forest. Just enough to see a tree before he bumped into it. The trees were growing closer together, too. Only a few feet apart. And then a couple of feet apart. And in some areas a few that were only inches away from one another. The challenge of avoiding them became a kind of game to pass the time.

After what felt like hours, Simon noticed a kind of pattern to the trees, as if the entire forest were an enormous maze. Paths were lined out, ending and joining in clearings roughly five feet wide. He followed the paths in different directions, whatever direction that most moved him. He was already lost; maybe the maze would lead somewhere.

Simon stopped. He saw the tiniest flash of light in the distance. Very far in the distance, in fact. Despite the density of the surrounding trees, the source of the light seemed to be miles away. Simon wondered if he was close to a field of some kind. He walked on dodging tree after tree slowly closing in on this strange light. It now started to take on a blue hue. Simon's blistered feet brought a ping of pain with every step, but he kept on.

Just as he was about to take another breather, the light began to dim. Simon quickly picked up the pace. The light still seemed so far away, and he could barely see it now.

Finally, Simon lost the flicker in the dark. He wasn't even close. He thought he kept going straight, but soon he realized he had no idea where to go. He had no idea where he was. He couldn't walk anymore. He collapsed next to a tree with an odd bark pattern that he would have noticed or thought more about, but exhaustion bound him to the ground.

*          *          *

Not a single dream passed through Simon's head during the next two hours. The next thing he knew he was woken up by the brilliant blue light again. This time much brighter. The source was a blue, three-lobed leaf in the dirt a few feet away from him, no bigger than his outstretched fingers. It pulsed with radiant energy. Simon tried to move but couldn't lift a limb. He was forced to lie in the dirt and ponder this phenomenon.

He heard crunching and felt the strange chill again. He sensed he wasn't alone. He took a deep breath and painfully jumped up. Once he snatched the strange blue leaf the light dissipated, but he quietly ran in the opposite direction as fast as he could. Not without fully recognizing the bizarre bark pattern on the tree he slept next to, though. The markings were geometric. Dozens of different triangular shapes Simon had studied in Trigonometry were displayed on a grid with thin and thick lines. He mentally cursed himself for never paying attention in that class. They looked to form a kind of map...

He saw another blue light, much higher than the two previous. His growing fear did not stop his curiosity about this new light. After a couple of minutes sprinting, just when Simon thought the piercing in his calves would collapse him, he found the source. It was atop a gigantic rock at least twenty feet high, taking up most of the space in this clearing. The same blue leaf rested on the tallest point of the boulder. He had no idea how, but Simon was determined to climb up and gain more treasure.

As he approached he noticed odd holds sculpted into the stone like a spiral ladder. This convenience alarmed him, but nothing could halt his quest. Simon sidled the holds with every bit of energy he had left. He reached the top of the boulder but lost his footing and took a second to balance.

Suddenly, he heard a shrill screech and running following it. Something fast and terrifying was about to introduce itself.

A black blur darted out of the forest and leapt straight up to the leaf. The light from the leaf hit the animal for a split second as it snatched the light away – enough to give Simon a haunting image of the creature. Similar to a cat. Larger, but with the same sleek grace. Glossy black with glowing red marks running along its body. The face was strangely snake-like. The eyes shot directly into Simon's. Before he could pick up on any more anomalous characteristics, the creature was gone. Simon's eyes scanned the surrounding area. It had vanished.

Simon descended the rock with his lips pursed. He was stuck in another clearing with no idea what direction to go. He closed his eyes, rotated a few hundred degrees with his finger out, stopped, and opened his eyes again. This entrance seemed to be no better or worse than any other, so Simon marched on, hoping to get as far away from that speedy snake-cat as possible. As he passed the first tree into the forest however, he heard a woman's voice.

"You're not a very good Collector."

Simon stopped. He looked into the clearing and saw an impossibly beautiful woman standing in a glossy black dress with red markings that glowed. The designs reminded Simon of neurons in the human brain. Her blazing red hair sharply framed her perfect face.

"I'm not a Collector at all, actually," Simon responded after a few failed attempts at speech.

She chuckled at that. "I know. You couldn't steal Mizik from a Clauderban." Simon didn't know what to say.

"I'm not sure if that was an insult or a compliment," eventually came out of his mouth. The woman scoffed, and one eyebrow shot up.

"A Clauderban? The sluggish little bastards about this high?" She raised her hand roughly three feet off the ground. "They're pointless, but they eat enough Mizik to survive. Bloody Cuffersha, kid. You're not a very bright Intellect either, are you?"

"That's what I hear. But I have no idea what you're talking about." The woman's face dropped.

"Where do you come from?"

"I used to work in the café outside the forest."

"Oh no," the woman asserted. "You're coming with me."

And before Simon could protest, he found himself riding

the strange cat-creature from before, larger to accommodate his size. She had breathtaking grace. She flawlessly dashed through the maze of trees, taking the paths as if she were on autopilot. All she had to do was run.

She stopped abruptly, flinging Simon off her back. Before his consciousness caught up he watched a tree race closer to his face. He halted in mid-air, inches before his face met the bark, and he drifted down to the ground. His feet softly found the floor and a calming wave rushed through his body. The woman casually walked up beside him, and Simon thought he saw a wand flash back into her sleeve.

"Say nothing. Look at no one. Keep your head down." She grasped his arm and tugged him through a few more trees.

They opened up to a city unlike any other. Shacks were built out of rough boulders, broken planks of wood, twisted sticks, leaves, and vines woven into rope. Wooden signs with crude designs hung over entrances to different shacks. The buildings that bordered the tree line of the forest appeared to be abandoned, but in the distance Simon could see the salon, the jewelry shop, the hospital, the book store, and a sign that looked to resemble a potion. The woman led Simon down the less travelled roads.

The city thrived with a blooming society of animalistic beings. Strange magical creatures conversed and laughed. Firelight lit the dirt streets from lanterns and lamp posts. Despite the speed of this woman's swift lead, the view is what ripped Simon's breath from his lungs through a dropped jaw. Remembering her instructions on looking at no one, he snapped his head down.

Inevitably giving in to his curiosity's temptation, he looked up again. A block away Simon read a poorly drawn sign – 'The Mid-City Mizik Brew'. An out-of-proportion drawing of the same exact blue leaf that hid in his pocket rested on top of a coffee mug. He peered into the shack with wide eyes. Strange machines were clicking and clanking. Giant pots and urns were steaming as they brewed what looked to be blue coffee. The shelves in the shop displayed various scones, biscuits, even cakes. Simon was intrigued. Even more intriguing was the girl working behind the desk. Her face resembled that of a cheetah's with strange, twisted, black stripes running across her golden fur. Her long, green hair formed dreadlocks with beads woven into them. She fashioned a cute smile as she thanked her customer – a darkly dressed man with a fiery-red bold cut – for his purchase.

His leader must have noticed his attention because she gave him a slight tug and sped up.

Simon cheated again and glanced at the rest of the population of this hidden city. Brutish muscle men and women not unlike buffaloes walked these streets along with classy, tall and skinny men with enlarged craniums wearing large bottle glasses and tuxedos. Gazelles hopped and darted from shack to shack. Owls and eagles were sitting and chatting on rooftops, posts, and signs.

He saw another cheetah-creature similar to the girl he had seen in the blue-leaf coffeeshop, only with blue, spiky hair rather than green dreadlocks. The humanoid animal was on all fours swiftly dashing through the diverse inhabitants of this street. Simon suddenly noticed his eyes meeting everyone else's. Their conversations paused as their heads followed him and his leader. Simon snapped his head back down and continued on the unknown path.

One of the buffalo-men across the street yelled, "Hey Vezlin, when did you get back in the Enforcing business? Or is that your new date?" The woman continued on, picking up the pace.

"Not the time, Morolith," she shouted. The brute turned to his buddies and chuckled.

Tension transpired over the next few minutes until Simon couldn't take it anymore.

"Vezlin?" This stopped her. She did not turn around to face him.

"Yes. Vezlin is my name. I do not want to know yours. We will not know each other long." She started marching again after a tense jerk of Simon's arm.

"Just tell me what's going on."

"You escaped from the Outside. And somehow found us.

This is a problem."

"Found who? What is this place?"

"It doesn't matter. We'll find Lord Fyresk and solve it. Don't worry."

"Well we have a walk to wherever we're going. And I'm going to worry. Tell me something." Vezlin sighed. Simon thought he wasn't getting any more information out of her until she spoke up a moment later.

"You're Human. We are not."

"I gathered that much."

"We've been warned about you. About your kind. You fight wars amongst yourselves and kill your own brothers. Disgusting." Vezlin gave the last word extra emphasis as she glared at Simon down her pretty little nose. "I hear you come from a city of idiots."

"Yeah, I can agree with that."

Simon could now see a path leading up to a castle nestled into the foot of the colossal mountain. The massive palace resembled the hilt and cross-guard of a decorated sword with the blade, or the back wing, stabbed into the bottom of the mountain. Two towers on the cross-guard jut out at a forty-five-degree angle on each side, and above the massive main entrance a flat tower rose up. But the center of the sword where the blade, hilt, and cross-guard met was obviously the main tower. It rose hundreds of feet into the air, and on top sat a sizable sunroom – what appeared to be the only place in the castle that experienced sunlight. The rest of the mansion let in sunlight in hidden slits tucked into the corners and the designs running along the massive stone walls.

As they approached the castle, the atmosphere around them darkened tremendously. Even though the path was free of trees, the rocks looked black, the path looked black, the grass looked black. Some of the shadows even looked darker. He took a quick glance over his shoulder to see if there was a possible escape.

He could barely see the whole city from here. The marketplace was a small sliver to the left with dimly lit trails leading off to isolated neighborhoods of shacks to the right. A solid line of trees surrounded every inch of the city. No wonder this place remained hidden. Simon turned back around.

If Vezlin's arm had not been gripping his, Simon would have spun around and run away. They approached the ten-foot tall stone wall surrounding the castle. The spiked, iron entrance looked much too intimidating for his comfort level. Two nasty gargoyles stood solid on stone pedestals, guarding the gate on either side. Vezlin came to a halt and finally released Simon's arm.

She kissed the air as a tiny fireball escaped her lips and shot straight for one of the gargoyle's mouths. She did the same to the other. The mouths stayed aflame, and the gargoyles began to shake and awaken. The one on the right gruffly spoke first.

"Good to see you, Vezlin."

"Yeah, it's not often we get an awakening kiss from a pretty woman."

The two started to giggle.

"I think my legs are still a-slumberin'. Do you think I could get another just for good measure?"

"Yeah, that fire just really wakes up my wings, so one more would really help finish the job."

They seemed to be having such a good time chuckling, they failed to notice Vezlin's dress taking over her body, morphing her into a black cobra with the same red markings. She spat a line of fire at the gargoyles. She slithered forward, never taking a second to gather her fiery breath. After a while, she ceased her flames and transformed back into a woman.

"How's that for pretty?" she asked. The reddened gargoyles whined and coughed and waved them in as the gates creaked open.

# Chapter 4

Vezlin led him away from what looked to be the front entrance. A large staircase led up to giant, navy blue double-doors with a square tower rising above it. The hall past that extended straight towards the middle, main tower.

But Vezlin led him into a side entrance at the base of the angled right tower.

Simon never imagined walls more audaciously abrasive than the stark white bricks of the office at work, but these stone walls seemed to scream. The most frightening aspect of the long and tall hallways was the amount of blinding light surrounding everything. He could not even find his shadow. The hallways were wide and beautifully adorned with ancient rock and marble statues, but the whole place felt like an institution. Small and large doors made of dense steel led to many different sizes of staircases, more hallways, and tall and short rooms. The staircases were steep, marble steps that gave him too much of a work-out than he was used to. Many lamps that shone bright white hung down from the tall ceilings, on the walls, and even tucked away in corners. The halls were so bare and blinding, Simon thought he was close to insanity. None of this could have been real. This must have been a terribly long, intense dream.

When Vezlin jerked him around another corner, the pain in his shoulder proved that this was no dream. Simon was very much awake.

At the end of this hallway was a gargantuan wooden door. Vezlin stopped a few feet shy of it and bowed her head as if to prepare herself. A long sigh assisted her approach to the door. She knocked three dragging times. Simon could feel the cold echo in his heart. Suddenly a narrow, horizontal line of fire appeared on the door. Vezlin pulled out of her sleeve a thin red stick, raised it to the wall, and began writing as fiery ink followed its path on the door. She finished, and "Vezlin" written in flames sank into the wood.

They stared at the door for a few seconds until a bizarre symbol appeared, again in flames. In response, Vezlin raised her stick and wrote more symbols that resembled simplified hieroglyphics and Sanskrit. These soon sank too, and Simon heard several clicks on the other side of the door. Slowly it opened to a gigantic room not nearly as lit as the hallways outside. Long, crimson curtains hung over twenty-foot tall windows; golden rugs carpeted the floor; comfortable, cushioned furniture was positioned next to fireplaces. Ten intricate fireplaces lined each wall of the vast hall, in fact. This was the only place Simon had seen in this castle that possessed any semblance of peace.

He followed Vezlin inside. An old man, one of the tall and skinny types, was sitting in a chair discussing with a plump, burnt-orange cat the proper use of Cuffersha skin. Apparently you're supposed to allow them to soak for at least a day.

"Where's Lord Fyresk, Thimethian?" Vezlin asked.

The cat spoke in a regal tone. "In his office, I believe. Why?" Vezlin made a subtle nod to Simon.

"Oh, dear," was all that followed as Thimethian's eyes widened, and he returned to his conversation about the Cuffersha.

"Come on, kid," Vezlin barked. She didn't grab him this time, though. Simon quickly followed after her up another tall, spiral staircase.

Simon underestimated the true height of the castle. This staircase lasted for days. They seemed to be approaching the top, and Simon saw another ray of light up ahead. Just as he thought he was about to collapse, they reached the last step. He didn't want to move anymore, but this hallway was very short. He could try to make it.

They reached the end of the hallway, and it opened up to a round room. Another pathway was identically placed across from the one he just came from, probably leading off to hidden parts of the castle. The blinding light was coming from the door in the middle of the curve. The illuminated entrance was about three feet wide and ten feet tall.

Vezlin's hand turned to stone, and she punched the door with so much force that Simon felt the pound in his chest. He heard the clicking again on the other side of the door.

The door crept open, revealing the vast sunroom looking out on the city. The only source of light was the moon. A substantial wooden desk was shoved into the corner with hundreds of gadgets and half-finished projects strewn across and around it. In fact, that seemed to be the theme of the room- not dirty, but disorganized and cluttered.

The being named Lord Fyresk stood with his back to them. All Simon could see was a black cloak with a collar that covered his head.

"It's Vezlin. I'm here with the boy." Fyresk turned slightly so that Simon could barely see his hands and face.

His skin was as black as his cloak. He looked completely human, except his leathered skin lacked the trace of any descriptive hue other than charcoal.

"You come from the Outside?" His voice matched his appearance - burnt.

"I found him on Chirth Stone." Vezlin answered. Fyresk pondered a moment.

"You must be dealt with." Simon was frozen. If his legs hadn't locked up, he would have probably been on the floor. "Send him to the Cave." As Vezlin gripped his arm and began to walk away, Simon was surprised to find himself speaking.

"Where is the Cave? Why send me to the Cave?" he asked, desperation heavy in his voice.

"You must not escape again," Fyresk growled. Vezlin started to pull him away again, but Simon stopped her.

"I won't. Believe me. I have no desire to go back."

"You cannot be trusted." Once again, Vezlin gripped his arm to take him away.

"Please—"

"Do not beg!" Fyresk roared. He turned towards Simon to give him a better view of his enraged face. It followed the same skin pattern. Simon wondered if his heart could be blacker than his bald head. "You will not save yourself." Finally, Vezlin jerked Simon's arm almost out of its socket and began dragging him to another unknown location. But before Lord Fyresk turned away, he stared at Simon with the bluest eyes he had ever seen.

*     *     *

This was ridiculous. Simon was naïve and lost in this new world. He was surrounded by magical creatures, and no one would explain anything. He was certain of one thing, though. He hated Lord Fyresk. The few short words he heard from this beast shed no light on his future here. He could have at least listened. Simon could have convinced him to let him stay. Now he was being pulled to some cave without a chance of defending himself. He didn't know what he would have said, though. Something about being useful, maybe.

This idea diminished after they left the castle. He noticed the brutish men and the scoffing scholarly, monocle-equipped gentlemen walking the streets. He was useless in this society, the same as he was outside of it.

They passed the place with the blue leaf sign again, and Simon couldn't draw his eyes away from the cheetah-girl. She looked at him and smiled.

"Her name's Seskith," Vezlin said, giving Simon a little jump.

"She's intriguing."

"Yes, well say goodbye. Your love affair has ended. This way." She led him down a few more blocks of shops and ended up on another dirt road, but this one lacked business and people. The road was filled with empty, decrepit huts. Half of them were no longer shacks. Simply piles of wood, boulders, and debris.

Soon the shacks ended, and nothing but a dirt road leading to the Cave was left. Simon's insides twisted.

The Cave looked to be laughing at him. He could see teeth formed in the entrance as if smiling at his fate. Simon's legs suddenly dropped, but Vezlin did not slow down. With one fell swoop she picked him up and placed him back on his feet without losing momentum.

At last they entered the Cave, and the temperature dropped drastically as they descended the main passageway. To add to the daunting effect, the brutish buffalo-men were placed on guard every twenty feet with stoic glares. Intricate tunnels interlaced each other as they hugged the underground. He couldn't find a trace of any planned structure of this place. It looked like it was once home to a large family of gigantic ants. Vezlin kept leading Simon down the main passageway. Lord Fyresk must have wanted him deep enough to where he couldn't escape. She halted abruptly and pulled Simon back. He was so transfixed with this new world he didn't notice they had stopped.

Instead of a tunnel, he saw a large, oval rock resting on the wall that possessed an inscription of another bizarre symbol. Vezlin took out her stick again and traced the symbol. As the flames sunk in the rock, it slowly began to lift as if it were weightless like a solid balloon. Vezlin did not take a second to marvel at this magic. She continued on.

Simon's hopes for escape were close to none as Vezlin led him down these bewildering rights, lefts, downs, ups, overs, arounds. Some of the tunnels he passed through had open walls that revealed vast caverns and immense chambers with hundreds of tunnels that led to other parts of the underground. Even if Simon had the courage and the strength to knock his leader out, he would be running in circles and eventually end up throwing himself in a dungeon.

"I don't think I'm going to run away," he said.

"What?" Vezlin asked without looking at him. Simon made a quick jerk to break away from her tight grip. Her fingers slipped as he freed his arm just as the tattoos on her wrist and hand shone bright red and clung to him. His hand snapped back into her grasp. She looked at him confounded but decided he was right. She threw his arm back at his face and continued without attempting to pull his shoulder out of its socket. They descended to a dead-end passageway lined with oval boulders similar to the one with the symbol. These had small, square cut-outs, though. Iron bars filled the space. These were the cells, Simon decided.

Vezlin dropped down on all fours, and her body began to expand. Her dress overtook her head elongating her nose to a horn. She took the form of a black rhinoceros, still possessing the glowing red marks. She stomped over to one of the oval rocks and nudged it with her head. It screeched open revealing a dark, bare room. For a second Simon did nothing, but Vezlin's huff and gesture over to his new cell assured him of his next action. He hesitantly slumped in and turned around. Vezlin, the woman, stood in the entry.

"Look, kid. I don't know what will happen to you. You can't stay here, but Fyresk didn't think killing you was an option. I guess just sit tight until he figures out what to do with you. But be warned – any attempt at an escape might change his mind." And with that, Vezlin, suddenly the rhinoceros again, sealed the cell closed. Simon was left with a scarce amount of light through the iron bars and an empty dirt room.

He dwelled on the adventurous night, and the physical effects of his journey kicked in. He lay down and tried to fall asleep, but his head was spinning with pictures of this new world. The marketplace. The dense forest. Fyresk's castle. The blue-leaf shop. Seskith, the cheetah-girl. The buffalo-man Vezlin called 'Morolith'. Vezlin herself. Lord Fyresk. What was this place?

His questioning mind began to ramble on with theories of this land. Magic was obviously in use, and the people had an advanced technique about it. He wished so badly that he could catch on and learn how to transform like Vezlin or how to make whatever Seskith was brewing in the shop. Eventually, Simon's eyelids found each other, and he drifted off to sleep.

*     *     *

The episodes of that night played on in Simon's dreams. He remembered seeing Vezlin for the first time. The black, cat-like creature with the glowing red marks up her body. She dashed and darted through the forest with astounding agility. And what did she mean by 'Collector' and 'Intellect'? Why did she assume Simon was one?

Before he could resolve any of these questions in his dreams, a bashing of metal shattered Simon's sleep. He could barely make out one of the buffalo-men at his iron window slamming the bars with a hammer. He threw in a couple of blackened fish and continued on to the other prisoners.

Simon walked over and examined his breakfast. Wings took the place of fins on these once majestic fish-creatures. Their tails fashioned sharp and dangerous multi-colors. He had no other choice. He sank his teeth into the blackened teal scales and tried his best not to vomit. Surprisingly, it had a great taste. Like salmon, but sweeter and with a hint of citrus. He didn't care too much for the burnt taste, but all in all it was a decent meal. If only there were more of them. Two small fish were not enough. Simon was now angrily hungry.

In fact, Simon was now very angry. He had done nothing to these people, and now he was a criminal. Fyresk's blue eyes haunted his thoughts, and creeping hatred bubbled up to his skin. He tried to stay calm, but he couldn't hold back several wall-punches. He yelled as he pulled on the iron bars, knowing he did not have enough strength to even make them vibrate. After several minutes of failed attempts, he weakly crumbled onto the dirt.

He lay there panting, the blood pulsing through his bruised hands. He was trapped. His life would end in this dark room, and Simon was powerless.

He heard whispered laughter. It wasn't one voice; it was several small breathy chuckles all around him. Fear captured his body. All logical thought stopped. The laughter from the shadows invaded his brain.

The blue leaf in his pocket jumped into his mind, and in a panic he fumbled to pull it out. Still in tact, this beautiful blue leaf stared at him with its intricate veins still slightly pulsing with the blue glow. Trying anything, he bit off a piece of the side. It tasted of dry grass and dirt. Simon expected to be surprised like he was with the fish, but sadly the leaf tasted just as it looked.

A rush filled his limbs. He felt his blood pushing intensely through his veins. He was powerful. He felt the strength of ten men. Reaching straight to one of the iron bars, he wrapped his fingers around it and tugged. The bar gave a little, but remained wedged into the rock. With a jolt, Simon ripped it free and fell back onto the cold dirt. He heard the whispers again, not chuckling anymore. "That's it," he thought he heard them say.

His eyes found the iron bar in his hands. Reality sank in. This was Simon's work. With the help of this strange blue leaf, Simon had torn iron from a boulder. He shoved the rest of the leaf in his mouth and swallowed it in one gulp. Again, he felt the pulsing power from before. His fingertips tingled, and his heart beat at a galloping pace. He raised the iron bar in his hand and gathered up every bit of energy he could. He slung whatever force he felt towards the door in a fluent motion. He had no idea what to expect.

A burst of blue light shot from the end of the iron bar straight into the middle of the oval door. The rock kicked back a little, and almost balanced before it tumbled over like an oversized coin. He had no time to think, Simon bolted through the open cell door.

The turns in this cave were too confusing to get very far. Simon aimlessly ran through the interlocking tunnels opening up to more tunnels. Soon he came upon a dark room, and he heard the whispers again.

"This way," they said. The words seemed to come from every tunnel though, and he had no idea where the voices were coming from. Simon found himself spinning in circles.

"Stop," the whispers said with commanding presence. "Straight ahead."

"Where am I going?" Simon asked, not moving and without knowing the direction of the other speakers.

"Straight ahead," they repeated. Simon was hesitant but realized he had no choice but to follow the whispers' orders.

He ran through tunnel after tunnel barely hearing the

whispers anymore. He couldn't make out the words, just indistinct syllables. Simon's heart leapt when he turned a corner into the main corridor of the dirt dungeon. He could even see sunlight in the entrance a few hundred feet ahead. The buffalo-men were guarding this hall, though. On both sides of him. They grasped thick staffs with mysterious blue lines wrapped around them. More than a half dozen stood between him and the doorway. Simon still had no escape.

He crept along the shadows under the mounted torches on the walls, dashing from one to another. He was steadily getting closer and closer to the beasts. Simon's feet accidentally skid as he darted under a lamp. One of the buffalo-men snapped their head to his position. The beast began to clump towards Simon's hiding place, huffing in slight agitation.

A single, distinct whisper voiced "When I go, you go."

Simon didn't know what to say except "Okay", so he went with silence and nodded as a response. He had no idea what this meant, but he trusted whatever it was that spoke to him. The buffalo-man was now a mere few feet away. In an instant, the shadow he was hiding in leapt forward, covering the guard in darkness. The beast let out a fearful yelp, and the other guards began marching towards the incident. In another instant, the shadow flew from the creature to another beast as the darkness swathed another victim. Simon heard a long, breathy "Go!" and without another second of hesitation, he bolted towards the sunlight. The shadow continued to take more buffalo-men lives, but Simon's feet quickly passed the skirmish.

One of the creatures ahead bent over on all fours and charged at Simon. Using the same trick as before, he lifted the iron bar in his hand, summoned more energy, and shot another blast that knocked the monster on its back.

More buffalo-men charged, and more received a blast of energy from the end of Simon's iron bar. He took a second to marvel at his work but soon caught a glance of another beast up ahead flourishing his staff. A wave of blue light sent Simon flying back, pinning him to the floor. Any attempt to free his limbs was unsuccessful. He put every effort into raising his iron bar, hoping to cast a spell that could counteract the magic currently binding him to the ground.

Before Simon could blink, the wave let up. The buffalo-man hurtled past him towards the fighting shadow. Not one beast's eye was on him. He finally had a clear shot to the entrance. Simon dashed madly.

He burst out of the cave and felt the warm rays of the sun hit his skin. Relief swarmed his insides. Simon was finally free.

# Chapter 5

Simon's heart was beating almost out of his chest. The crisp air shot directly into his lungs. Everything possessed beauty. Wind delicately stroked the leaves of the soaring trees. An owl circled the sky as elegantly as if floating atop water.

His feet began mechanically running along the path, kicking rocks as he came upon them. The wind lightly brushed his grin giving him a feeling similar to the powers of the strange blue leaf. The buffalo beasts started to roar and bark from the entrance of the Cave, but Simon had plenty of space between them. He picked up the pace, and a burnt voice stopped him dead in his tracks. He instinctively raised the iron bar locked in his hand towards the source.

"How did you do it?"

Simon froze. He was facing a defenseless Lord Fyresk, black-skinned and fearful. His stature was one of static and dense menace. A full minute passed before Simon could respond. "With this." His eyes referenced the iron bar.

"Ah. And with absolutely no assistance?"

"Yes," Simon lied.

"Then they must be lying when they say the Gulverbruud are getting smarter," Fyresk answered, mostly to himself. He turned his attention to Simon again. "How did you get that?" he asked.

"I broke it off the cell window." Simon looked at the iron bar tightly gripped in his hands. "I can use magic."

Fyresk apparently found this amusing. His burnt insides choked up a single chuckle. "Of course you can with a little Mizik in you. You can put your wand down, boy. You don't need it right now." Simon obeyed skeptically.

"Mizik. You mean the blue leaf?" he asked.

"Yes. That blue leaf possesses magic. Humans can consume the leaves to gain magical abilities, but magical Creatures depend on it for survival. It's their food source."

"What is this place?" Simon couldn't take not knowing anymore. He finally had a chance to ask the question that dug deeper than the Cave he just escaped from.

"Follow me," was not the answer he was hoping for, but that's what snapped out of Fyresk's charcoal lips after a heavy sigh. He started on the path, and Simon obediently followed. A moment later he heard Fyresk's burnt voice again. "Okay, kid. You've proven yourself. Naturally escaping what I considered to be adequate security could not have been easy, but nonetheless you achieved it." Shame overtook Simon's face. He could feel his cheeks taking on a red hue. He didn't want to admit that he had received help on his escape. Fyresk continued. "Why did you flee here in the first place?"

"I don't have much to live for on the other side of the forest." Simon hoped Fyresk couldn't hear the humiliation in his voice. He must not have, since Fyresk's tone had shifted from frightening to damn near jovial.

"Feerthel Forest we call it. The only strip of land any of us ever see. I myself have not been farther than..." he trailed off. "Well, I have not voyaged too far from Kearlith. Let's leave it at that."

"Kearlith?"

"The city we're about to enter." They were approaching the empty shacks now.

"So Kearlith is the city in Feerthel Forest?"

"Exactly. A community of magical Creatures living together, working, and raising families. I'll give a better explanation once we find your home."

"My... home?" Simon asked, failing any attempts to sound nonchalant. Lord Fyresk hesitated. "Yes. Your home. This looks about as good as any other." Fyresk halted in front of one of the shacks that was still standing. He examined the structure to make sure the roof or walls wouldn't cave in. "It's not much, but it will do, right?"

Simon was elated. This piece-of-shit shack was his. He stared past the broken door into the inside of his new home. Torn planks of wood perfectly balanced on rough boulders. Dust covered the only pieces of furniture present – a cracked table and a broken chair sitting on three legs – along with the floors and walls. A rusty sink stood in the middle of the back wall. He could see the sun through large holes in the ceiling. But it was home.

"Tomorrow will begin your quest for a job," Fyresk stated interrupting Simon's internal montage of pictures he was creating of his shack once it was fixed up.

"What could I do?" he asked.

"Sit down. I'll tell you." Simon looked around for something to rest on. He decided the dust covered floor would suffice since it was almost his only option. Fyresk spoke again. "Since you're not bound by your race, you are free to choose your profession. There are Collectors, Keepers, Hunters, Enforcers, Builders, and Protectors.

"Collectors navigate through Feerthel and Collect Mizik – the blue leaves you have already found useful. Vezlin is a Collector, in fact. You've met her," Fyresk said. He appeared to jest, but Simon couldn't be sure. Simon remembered his first encounter with Vezlin. For the first time in two days, something was beginning to make sense.

"Collectors take their daily Collection to the Keepers who store it in the Mizik bank. Collecting and Keeping are noble professions. Only honest Creatures can be trusted to count for every bit of Mizik they Collect. I demand probity in my Collectors and Keepers. Thievery will not be tolerated." Fyresk's jovial tone turned stone cold for this last statement.

"Hunters roam Feerthel looking for lesser animals to kill and cook. They own and run the different meat shops around Kearlith."

"But I thought magical Creatures ate Mizik. Why do they eat the other animals?" Simon asked.

"The meats of both magical and non-magical beasts possess nutrients that greatly contribute to good health.

"Moving on- Enforcers are the police force. They report to the Intellects and uphold the law to the best of their ability. This was Vezlin's profession before she abused the privilege, and..." Fyresk stopped himself. "Now she Collects.

"The Builders," he continued, snapping back as if his hesitance hadn't happened, "are the mechanics around town. They are the gazelles that fix houses, furniture, weapons, boats, shelves, everything. You should talk to one of them about fixing this place up.

"Finally, Protectors are the owls who keep us hidden away from the Outside. They keep on the look-out to distract any wanderers who might be on the path to our city, like you. Speaking of which, I need to have a word with Voulderbrin..."

Simon tried to soak everything in, but this was all so new. He was bursting with questions. For some embarrassing reason, the only one to surface was, "What does Seskith do?"

Fyresk stared at him with an inquisitive eye. With a kind of smirk, he answered, "Collector. And her parents own the brewery so she helps out there as well."

"Oh," was all Simon could muster.

"Seskith is a Shintervah. The cheetah-people. Her kind are traditionally top-notch Collectors, although Seskith herself seems to be more interested in the Enforcing business. While we're on the subject, I'll give you a brief summary of the other Creatures.

"You've already met and apparently defeated some of the Gulverbruud – the beasts guarding Serlentos Cave. Most are dumb as rocks, but their physical power is unmatched.

"Vezlin is a Kyejoth. These half-bloods possess fire-magic. They are impervious to flame and are able control it at their will."

"Can all of them shape-shift?" Simon blurted out.

Fyresk took a second to respond, "No. Vezlin is remarkably talented in the ways of magic. The Kyejoth are mainly Enforcers, but as I've said, Vezlin abused the privilege and was forced to change professions."

"What happened?"

"She'll have to tell you herself. Moving on. The Gullen are the altered golden eagles. No Gullen in the history of Kearlith has ever been anything other than a Keeper. The Gullen are famous for their good-nature. No truer or more honest being has ever existed.

"The Biffleflenn are magical owls that live and nest outside of Kearlith in the trees of Feerthel. They're the Protectors of our society. They fly above the Forest, scouting any possible Humans who might be on the path to find out about us."

"How do they prevent it?" Simon inquired.

"A system of means. For instance, they cast a cloak over the treetops of Feerthel to protect it from the Outside's eye."

"That's amazing. So I just luckily slipped through their fingers?"

"Their talons, yes. Either one of them let you in or I underestimated you." Fyresk's eyes widened as he huffed. "What's your name?"

"Simon... Carter," he stuttered. After learning so many new names, he almost forgot his.

"Simon? Or Carter?" Fyresk asked with a confused expression.

"Both. My first name is Simon. My last is Carter."

"Ah." He made a small scoffing noise. "I think that's enough knowledge for today. I'll send Mortimer here tomorrow to give you another lesson."

"Lesson?" Simon's insides dropped a little. He thought he had escaped school.

"Yes, a lesson. What, did you think you could swing an iron bar around and call it magic? No, it must be learned."

"Oh. Okay." Simon wasn't much attracted to the idea of a lesson, but at least it was in the field of magic. "Who is Mortimer?"

"Oh yes, I almost forgot. Mortimer is an Intellect. They're half-bloods, but not quite Creatures. Very tall, experimental Humans. They hold all the information of our secret society.

Consider them the law."

"My head is still spinning with questions," Simon admitted.

"Save them for Mortimer. He can explain better than I. Now, I must head to Serlentos Cave and salvage the damage you've done," Lord Fyresk grumbled through a curt mouth, but his blue eyes were smiling. "Good day, Simon. And welcome to the city of Kearlith." With that, Fyresk turned on a dime and left Simon alone in his dusty shack to sit and ponder the ample amount of information he just received. The street noise a fair distance away was almost audible.

So many possibilities lay before him, and Simon couldn't put a finger on his next action. Clean the shack? Find some more Mizik? Explore Feerthel Forest? See what's in town? Introduce himself to Seskith...

He wouldn't know what to say. "Hi, I'm Simon. I don't know anything about you. Nice dreads. So, you're a cheetah..."

He couldn't make interesting conversation with any of that. He was in the mood for an adventure, anyway. He would meet Seskith later.

*          *          *

At last he decided to search for more Mizik. Simon stepped outside and observed his surroundings to get a visual image of his new address. About twenty feet square with a small window pane lacking glass just to the left of the door hanging off its hinges. Large and heavy rocks tossed into a lazy square prism. After a few euphoric moments, his eyes searched for an entrance into this "Feerthel Forest" that might lead him to more beaming blue leaves.

Leaves and twigs crunched and cracked as Simon crept through the web of trees. He didn't know if Mizik reacted to noise, but he didn't want to tempt it. The sun bled in little light through the limbs of the treetop ceiling.

Something flashed. Simon scanned in the general direction he thought he saw it and soon found the light again several hundred feet away. Remembering the limited time before the light would dim out, he took off as fast as he could dodge through the tight trees. The maze of the trees disrupted his focus as if they were intentionally drawing him away from the correct direction. He kept losing the light.

In his line of sight passed another tree like the one he slept next to his first night in Feerthel. It had the same geometric grid patterns carved into the bark. A solid dot sat on a line that very much resembled the path he felt he had been taking. This *was* a map. He memorized the odd angles he had to take in order to get on the straight line again and dashed off. He felt his Trigonometry teacher would have been proud.

Simon was getting the hang of this. He would reach a fork and swiftly take the correct route. The light began to slowly dim, but it was so close now. He forked left but lost sight of it. Flawlessly and successfully, he crossed over to a path he hoped was to the right. The glow wasn't quite gone yet, and Simon was yards away. He jumped and slid through the gap in the trees, snatching up the leaf at the last second. The pain in his knees quickly followed the rush of joy Simon felt.

In that moment, Mizik was the most beautiful thing on the planet. The light was gone save for the shining veins climbing up the stem. Simon's fingers traced the shimmering designs of this mystical treasure. His eyes were transfixed for a good five minutes. His heart beat assured him this is what he was meant for. He had to be a Collector. He laughed a little to himself as he remembered Vezlin's first words to him.

Surely Collectors accumulated more than one Mizik leaf a day. Snapping back to reality, Simon hoisted himself up still feeling the slight pain in his knees. His hunt for Mizik was on.

He hurried through the trees. His eyes darted from one gap to another searching for blue light. Minutes built up to an hour before Simon finally noticed another leaf of Mizik very far off in the distance. It looked too far, but he had to try.

The trees did not assist. Limbs whacked him; roots tripped him; Simon even thought a few trees jumped in the middle of his path. His hands and feet ached, and it took a large toll on Simon's dodging abilities. The light began to dim, and it was still very far away. He attempted to pick up the pace but slammed into a tree, knocking him back a few feet. With no hope, Simon watched the radiant blue leaf as it slowly faded to black. His optimism faded with it.

How was he supposed to be a Collector? Vezlin could turn into a cat and run through the Forest with beautiful ease. He hadn't seen Seskith at work, but he was sure a cheetah would have been much more suited for the job. Simon's total count for the day was currently one, and his body had already stopped functioning. Now he was lost in a magical Forest with no idea where Mizik or a way out could be.

A nearby tree caught Simon's collapse. He was fully conscious but unable to stand anymore. He remained planted in the dirt with nothing but his thoughts. And the single leaf of Mizik in his pocket...

Truthfully, he felt a tad mischievous for eating the leaf, remembering Fyresk's words about "thievery" and all that, but in his defense, it was magic. He couldn't help it. He only took a small bite. The similar feeling of pulsing power came back to his limbs. Strength and endurance revitalized his physical state, and to Simon's surprise, he was standing again. Boldly.

Checking his pockets, he found the trusted iron bar. He waved it around a little, acting like he knew what a magical spell looked like. His mouth spilled nonsense words he thought he remembered from one of his old fantasy books. Three zig-zagged shapes produced neither spell nor spark. Even the iron bar looked confused. Simon felt stupid brandishing a thick piece of metal as a wand. He didn't know the first thing about how to conjure a magical phenomenon. In a final attempt, he circled the air above his head a few times, gathering the same kind of energy from before. When he thought it was good enough, he discharged towards a towering tree, emptying his body of energy.

This time the nonsensical hand gestures worked. The tree burst into flames and completely engulfed the trunk, the roots, and every limb and leaf. Simon gawked at his work, amazed that this was really happening. He couldn't hold back a huge smile. He soon realized that the tree was still aflame and catching on to the surrounding trees. Luck couldn't help Simon counter a flame spell;

Feerthel and Kearlith would soon be ash all thanks to a stupid boy with an iron bar. His panic was not decreasing the size of the fire. In fact, it seemed to be steadily progressing.

Paws rapidly planting themselves in the dirt and leaves were like music to Simon's ears. Although he was sure to face a scolding harsher than Kathy could have ever given him, at least his blazing mistake would soon be extinguished. A girl's voice cried out a long, "Iceveral!" and a yellow blur made its appearance through the trees. In a flash Seskith burst out behind a tree, getting up on her two cheetah feet. She raised her hands to the disaster. Ice flowed from them like a water spout and plastered the raging fire. Without noticing Simon, she circled her arms and shouted "Kilito!" as she pushed her hands towards the giant icicle.

The thick blanket of ice shattered into millions of pieces, flying past both Simon and Seskith now standing sheer yards away from one another. Still without giving him so much as a look, she approached the tree and began rubbing it in a strange pattern. The bark was blackened from the debris, but after Seskith muttered a small chant to herself, it began to grow back its greens and browns until it fit in perfectly with the others. Simon stood frozen in utter astonishment.

Seskith quickly wheeled around to face Simon. She held a severe face as she approached him to get a better look. Suddenly her mouth formed a smile, and she let out a large laugh. Simon moved the muscles in his mouth to form words, but no sound came out.

"You need to be more careful," she said as her laughter died down.

"I had no idea what I was doing."

"Clearly. Apparently you had fire on your mind." Her eyes found the tree as if referencing it. A moment of silence passed before she spoke up again. "So, you come from the Outside?"

"Yeah, I worked in a café outside the Forest," he answered.

"A what?" Seskith questioned with an expression resembling Simon's during his lesson with Fyresk.

"A café. We brew coffee and sell baked stuff."

"Oh. Well, what is coffee?"

"It's a drink. A bitter... burst of energy," Simon stuttered, "most people drink to... enhance their daily lives."

Seskith's eyebrows quickly rose. "I do that," she said.

"Can you brew Mizik?" Simon asked, forgetting to sound intelligent.

"You can do anything with it. We brew it, grind it, bake it into cakes, weave it into sticks, stuff it into bars, powder it with sugar, steam it, grill it, and try almost anything to make it not so damn tasteless." Relief swarmed Simon's insides.

"That's great news. I'm not too fond of the freshly cut grass flavor."

"I'll make you a delicious cup of Mizik when we get back into Kearlith." Seskith said with an alluring grin. Was this a promised date? "I'm sure it'll beat your 'coffee'." She playfully took on a pretentious air.

"I don't know; I'm pretty talented," Simon countered.

"I sense a competition." A flash of blue light several hundred feet away interrupted the sprightly banter. Both of their heads snapped to see the Mizik leaf staring at them. Seskith gave a glance towards Simon. "Let's make it a race," she said with one raised eyebrow and a smirk.

"But I can't –" Simon started, but Seskith vanished before he could say anything else. He was alone again, and there was no possible way he could outrun a cheetah. He had no idea what to do. Try and fail, or not give in to this silly game.

A tiny, yellow ball of light aimed straight for Simon darted past the trees. Curiosity rendered him motionless. In three seconds the light hit him, exploding in a glorious wave of beams. He knew what he had to do. With a single push-off, Simon's legs propelled him through the obstacle course of trees with ease. In a fury his feet barely found land before they were aerial again, launching him closer and closer to victory. The Forest was not playing his game, however.

Thanks to Seskith's speed spell, in clear land Simon could have outrun ten cheetahs, but these trees gave his competitor a massive advantage. Although he was quickly learning how to navigate through the geometric grid, the occasional branch would jump in his path, slowing his speed. The Mizik began to dim.

Simon wasn't worried about reaching the leaf before the light depleted. After all, he felt faster than the speed of sound. His biggest fear was facing a goading cheetah. Just the thought of having to endure failure gave his legs an extra boost. He realized something; the light was still there. Seskith hadn't retrieved it yet. The goading cheetah might have to endure a jeering human. Hope found its way into Simon's heart.

When he leapt, he knew for certain he had won. The beam of light seemed to accept his hand's embrace as he landed on his chest, gripping the leaf in his tight fist. When his eyes regained focus, he noticed two yellow paws inches away from his grin. He looked up to a towering Seskith, and every piece of hope Simon had gathered over the last three minutes sank into his gut.

"I gave you that one," Seskith said finally. A trusting smile replaced her sneer. She held out a helping paw, and Simon accepted. He dusted himself off as she continued. "You're training to be a Collector, I suppose?"

"I think so," Simon answered, eying the ground. He couldn't bring himself to find her eyes.

"Well you'll need a load of training and knowledge. It's a profession, not a hobby." With this, Seskith started on a trail to the left. Simon couldn't tell whether it was back to Kearlith or not, but he didn't care.

# Chapter 6

"The Intellects' design of these trees is awe-inspiring. I've a book back at the shack about most of the growth in Feerthel." Seskith spoke with such passion. Every bit of devotion she had to this beautiful world spilled through her words. Simon grinned as he listened to her. "Different plants are used for different things. Collectors mostly Collect Mizik," she stopped to pick up a deeply crimson vine and snap it away from the ground, "but if they're smart enough, they realize some will pay money for anything." She pocketed the vine and continued on the path.

"Several different types of trees exist in Feerthel, but there are a few that you might find useful. The Giants are designed to grow fast so that the Builders can cut them down and use them to construct. Strings are the tall, skinny ones. They're strong and bendable like vines, so they can be woven into rope. Burners are a normal size, and they're extremely flammable. These make great firewood, if you can't put a name and use together." Simon saw a red vine Seskith missed. She walked right over it but didn't seem to notice. Behind her back, he quickly stooped down and snapped it off. Her voice electrocuted him, "The trick to making Burners burn is to find the right spell, although some plants will just burst into flame if you ask them to." He attempted to pocket the vine without attracting attention. Fortunately, Seskith continued as if she were oblivious to Simon's actions behind her.

"There are more, but I don't want to bore you. What you need to know is that all these different trees and plants make up a complicated structure. Ah, this will make it easier to explain." They approached another tree with the grid-map. "Pretty easy to understand once you see a map. Mizik needs a five-foot diameter of flat dirt in order to grow, so the Intellects placed Mizik spots at every intersection. A line is usually a foot or so wide, just big enough to see the beam of light, but much too small to fit through easily. The only way around is to follow the thicker lines – the paths – set at different angles. Every path is bordered by Markers- trees used for the sole purpose of navigating through the Forest. Your interest in Collecting will result in a highly acute knowledge of these."

"Can they move?" Simon heard himself ask.

"They've been known to. The Protectors talk to them. Some are trained to block off a line or a path to prevent anyone from continuing if they look like an Outsider. You've met some of them, I'm guessing." Simon huffed a small sigh of relief. Maybe his mind was still in tact after all.

"Collecting doesn't sound that difficult," Simon boasted.

"Wait until you get lost in the maze," Seskith said with a thin grin.

"I take it you know exactly where we are right now." This released a laugh from the charming cheetah-girl.

"In fact, I do. And I can tell you exactly where the Cave, my home, and the brewery are from right here. And roughly how far away."

"That's impressive," Simon admitted.

"You'll learn. Don't worry."

"How much Mizik have you gotten today?" he asked.

"It's been a slow day. Mizik grows best at night, but I wanted to get a jump start. I've only Collected about twenty so far."

"Twenty?" Simon exclaimed with more astonishment than he intended. Seskith giggled.

"Yeah, twenty. My quota for the day is seventy, though. I've still got a long way to go. Hey." Seskith stopped. Simon looked in the direction of her gaze and saw the blue light about a mile away. "Have at it, Human." She swiftly circled her paw a few times and shot the tiny, yellow light at Simon again.

He immediately sped off, not letting the Mizik out of his sight. He was gaining on it quickly. Half the distance was quickly traveled, and the light still shone. Simon occasionally got off track but stumbled to fix his mistake and get on target. The light just began to dim as he snatched it up. Now the Mizik in his hand was being lit up by his own beaming teeth.

"Nice work," made him jump ten feet in the air. Seskith stood behind him, arms crossed and possessing her own smile. "I'm Seskith, by the way. I guess I forgot to mention that."

"Simon."

"Good to meet you, Simon. I think I'm done for a little while. I'm going back into Kearlith if you'd like to follow and find out how to turn your two Mizik leaves into money."

Simon nodded before the words came out. "Okay. Yeah, that sounds like a plan." How lame. He could have shot himself right there. That sounds like a plan? What a most uninteresting thing to say. He imagined himself slapping his own face. Before he could recover, Seskith circled her paw and shot the tiny, yellow light again.

"Try to keep up," she said with a smirk, and she bolted off. Simon instinctively started making his best effort to "keep up", but she was much more knowledgeable about the layout of Feerthel. He lost her several times.

*     *     *

Soon they crossed the border into Kearlith, and Seskith returned to walking on two feet. "Every leaf of Mizik is worth five Duzuks unless it's damaged in some way. Before you ask," out of her backpack, she pulled out a bronze pebble, "this is a Duzuk. Fifty Duzuks are worth one Dillian. Fifty Dillians make one Doth. One hundred Doths are worth one Daxer, but I've never seen one of those. I'm not even sure if they exist anymore. Duzuks are bronze;

Dillians silver; Doths gold; and Daxers are black."

"So I've got about ten Duzuks," Simon said reaching into his pockets and grabbing the two leaves of Mizik.

"Yeah, after sneaking that little bit of Mizik before. You could have had fifteen. But…" Seskith trailed off and searched in her backpack for something. She extracted a handful of Mizik leaves, and thrust them into Simon's pockets. "This should be enough to get you started."

"You're giving me this? What about the head-start on your quota?"

"I'm an incredible Collector, Simon. Seventy Mizik leaves are nothing." She rounded the corner and stopped at a shack surrounded by beautiful golden eagles. The Gullen, Simon remembered. Their feathers were a dark, rusty brown, but the sun enriched the golden undertones. They shushed quick sentences to one another and peered their beady eyes at Simon and Seskith.

This shack was in better shape than the others, and significantly taller. The thick, rectangular bricks were lined with golden mortar that matched the colors of the bank's guardians. Mizik must need to be heavily guarded, Simon thought. The wide door was perfectly square and fit into its opening without the slightest slit. A strong, golden ring took the place of a doorknob encircling a black symbol engraved into the wood.

"Good day, Seskith," a young Gullen said as her wings opened, and she flew over to open the door.

"Good day, Terlinthia." The eagle bashfully lowered her head and took off.

"I think you have an admirer," Simon poked.

"I saved her when she was a baby learning to fly. She slammed into a tree and was too scared to try the air again. I just brought her back to her parents."

"What a hero."

Her humble grin faded. "I try to be," she said. Seskith's dedication to that sentence was undeniable. There was a fire in her eyes. They advanced to the front counter.

"Ah, Seskith. You're here early. And oh! What have we

here?" The Gullen was a delightful old chap, cheerful as morning sunlight.

"His name's Simon, Chrysaetos. He comes from the Outside."

"Oh," he coughed out.

"Don't worry," Simon responded quickly. "I'm harmless. Just an escapee."

"Well… Welcome to Kearlith, Simon. Have you any Mizik?" Simon moved to retrieve the leaves.

"He's been running his feet off out there. Right, Simon?" He was surprised to see her give him false credit.

"Erm, right," was all he added as he dropped the Mizik clumsily across the counter.

"Dear me, fourteen leaves!" Chrysaetos said with a smile. "So that'll be, let's see, a Dillian and twenty Duzuks. Not too bad for an Outsider. One moment, please." Chrysaetos fluttered over to a large basin covered by a thick, circular stone. He landed on it and rapidly flapped his wings. As he lifted, the rock lifted with him. "Aguila, could you claim the Mizik from the boy they call Simon?" he asked of another Gullen. An eagle sleeping in the corner awoke and obeyed the request. She flew over, gripped the Mizik in her talons, and threw it in the basin. "Thank you, dear." He let go of the stone, and it slowly slid through the air landing on the basin with a dull thud. In mid-air the two nuzzled one another, and Aguila returned to her corner with a peaceful grin.

Chrysaetos turned his attention back to Simon. "What was it? A Dillian and twenty Duzuks, right. I'm losing my memory in my old age," he squeaked as if the remark were a joke. Flying over to the counter, he plucked out a drawer to what must have been a kind of register. Hundreds of silver pebbles rolled out of the dark. Chrysaetos picked one up and slid it over to Simon and Seskith's position at the counter. "Do you have a bag, Simon?"

"No, I just have pockets."

Chrysaetos clicked his beak. "Oh, that will never do." He fluttered to a group of hooks on the wall and grabbed one of several leather pouches hanging there. He flapped back to the register and delivered the rest of the money.

After the Collection process, Simon and Seskith departed the Mizik bank, bidding the Gullen good-bye. They stood outside without knowing whether to depart each other or not. "That's not much, but it should help out." Seskith said, breaking the silence.

"Why did you do that?"

"You need it more than I do."

"You really are a hero," Simon admitted.

"Thank you," Seskith said, gazing at the floor. "I think I need to get back home to see if Mom needs help around the shack."

"Yeah, I need to get home and see how much help my shack needs."

"Stop by the brewery when you get a chance. I'll show you what a good cup of Mizik should taste like."

"Yeah… Uh, I will," Simon stammered without the ability to keep in a full-faced grin. They nodded to each other in a silent good-bye and made tracks in opposite directions.

*        *        *

Dust greeted Simon back at his shack. He opened the door, and the air circled as if it were surprised by his entrance. The bare room stared at him. He figured he had a couple more hours of daylight to get some work done but realized he had nothing to work with. He had nothing. A pocket knife and an iron bar.

A wimpy man's voice peeped, "Looks like you could use some assistance." Simon looked left and right but saw no speaker. "Down here." Simon gazed the ground. A gentlemanly gazelle stared at him with courteous eyes. "Name's Lagelle. And you must be Simon."

"You've heard of me?" Simon asked with astonishment.

"The Gullen are noble Creatures, but their beaks remain open. News flies faster than they do."

Down the road a fierce woman's voice squealed, "Lagelle!" The two darted their attention towards the source. Simon looked out of curiosity, Lagelle out of fear. A female gazelle came into a view, holding a piercing stare. She swiftly advanced towards the men, squaring her face a mere inch away from Lagelle's. "I have warned you not to take any more of my customers."

"I didn't know you knew about this one," Lagelle said. His eyes found the dusty walls of Simon's new shack.

"I did. Now step aside."

"It's my turn, Shalice!" Lagelle pleaded.

"The shack needs a lot of work," Simon interrupted. "You can work together."

"I will not share my wealth with this scoundrel," the lady gazelle hissed.

"It'd be ten Duzuks each," Lagelle said, dismissing her comment. He received a punch from the feisty Vanterslove.

"I'm sorry, how much?!" she wailed.

"What? He's new here. I'm sure that's all he can afford. Do you want his money or don't you?"

"I want *all* of his money. Twenty Duzuks would not pay for this place, especially not to be split. And *especially* not to be split with you."

"He's kind of right," Simon said. "It's twenty Duzuks or nothing." Simon scrounged in his bag for the pebbles and presented them to the gazelles, overlooking Shalice's protests.

"Shut your muzzle, Shalice. Working together wouldn't be so dreadful," Lagelle muttered as his hoof opened his own bag, awaiting the twenty Duzuks. Shalice's right eye twitched as if her brain failed to compute Lagelle's audacity. "Return in an hour, Simon. Your shack will be in tip-top shape." Simon nodded them off and headed back to town.

*     *     *

His brain was swimming with ideas of things to get for his shack. Bedding, a fluffy chair, some kind of light source, tools, soap, food, dishes, a wand...

Past the desolate wooden shacks that lined Simon's street into Kearlith, blotchy boulders housed abandoned shops. The first store that appeared inhabited held a sign portraying the image of a fire. He stepped inside the boulder hut, but no one greeted him at the desk. He began gazing down the aisles, hoping that he hadn't stepped into a haunted shop. The shop displayed curved lamps, elegant lanterns, lit posts, and bins full of tiny firewood. A golden, leaf-less tree reading "2 Dn" illuminated a corner. Its limbs shone a brilliant yellow that dropped Simon's jaw. As he continued, he saw a simple post with a bowl resting on top. The fire emitted an intense green color. His jaw remained open as he read the price tag. 5 Dn. This snapped his jaw shut.

A few feet away from the emerald lamp, a small stump about two feet in diameter held a healthy fire. It appeared to be made of wood, yet not an inch of it was charred. A simple, hand-written sign displayed "15 Dz", baffling Simon's brain. If that stood for Duzuks, he could afford this. If he could afford this, there was no question in his mind that it would sit smugly in the middle of his hut.

"A simple hex, really," said a large, scruffy voice. A hefty gazelle lugged down the aisle on two feet, breathless but giddy at the sight of a customer. "The stump's been enchanted to stay aflame without burning the wood."

"What's the spell?" Simon asked.

"Oh, just the sparking hex. Point your wand and say 'Flindervosa'. It'll spark right up and light a room in no time. Only fifteen Duzuk." The gazelle held out a bag pleading him to drop the money into it. Luckily, Simon was willing. He did not wish to disappoint an animal that could rip him in two. He grabbed the single Dillian out of his bag and caught a shining silver reflection in the robust gazelle's smiling eyes.

"Do you have change for this?" Simon asked.

"Yes indeed, sir." The gazelle heaved himself over to the counter and shoved the Dillian into a drawer. As he counted out the thirty-five Duzuks, Simon asked, "How does it extinguish?"

"Well you don't want to get too close for fear of flaming your trousers," he chortled. "Simply point your wand and say 'Extervoso'."

"Ah. Thank you." Simon took his change and bagged it. "Do you have anything to carry this?" he asked, eying the bulky chunk.

"A cart'll be an extra five Duzuk." The gazelle was smirking at the chance to gain a few more bronze pebbles. Simon counted out five more Duzuks as the beast wheeled around a cart. Simon thanked him and turned to exit.

He expected to simply walk through the open doorway, but it was quickly blocked by a hairy, yellow man with black spots covering a cheetah-like torso topped with bushy, green side-burns hugging a peaceful and gentle face. The Shintervah politely and awkwardly smiled at Simon as they both attempted to pass through the doorway.

After a you-go-no-you-go game, Simon successfully exited but instantly remembered the red vine Seskith picked up earlier. He searched his pockets for the one he stole behind her back. He found it and decided to ask the gazelle brute if it was worth anything.

He kicked the cart back in reverse, crashing into the Shintervah. After a painstaking number of apologies, Simon helped the cheetah-man up and dusted off his shoulders.

"It's fine," the man said after the fiftieth "I'm really so sorry."

With his head lowered, Simon approached the Vanterslove shopkeep. "Excuse me. Sir?"

"Oh! He's back!" The gazelle's eyes smiled with that same shining silver reflection.

"I was wondering if you bought as well as sold."

"What are you getting at?"

Simon presented the vine. "Would you buy this?" The beast gave the vine a stare deeper than the brick red covering it. In an instant, a vigorous laughter swarmed over the gazelle's robust figure sending him almost directly onto the ground. Taking this as a "No", Simon pocketed the vine again, turning to exit.

And was once again blocked by the cheetah-man. "Do you know what that is?" he asked pointing at Simon's waist.

"What... what is?" Simon said as he gave himself a look up and down.

"The Fyrovine in your pocket," the Shintervah said coolly.

Simon retrieved the red vine. "No. I've heard they're useful, though." The Shintervah held out his palm in a silent request, and Simon reluctantly handed over the vine for inspection.

"Quite." The Shintervah's eyes gazed upon every knot and

fiber in the vine. He squeezed different parts as if testing for ripeness. Finally, he spoke again. "I'll give you a Dillian for it."

"Gladly!" Simon's hand was still extended to regain the red vine, but he accepted the silver pebble with an equal amount of enthusiasm. He had no idea what he just sold, but he was eager to find out. "What are they used for?"

"They're a versatile tool. You should check out the book, *A Shintervah's Secrets Revealed*. The author discusses most of its uses. Some Creatures may disagree, but he was a mastermind of magic."

Simon felt it best to relieve the Shintervah of why exactly he had not heard of this book. He hoped this guy would think he was just a dumb Intellect. He went with, "No, I haven't read that one. I'll check it out."

The cheetah-man smiled. "Thank you for the Fyrovine, kid." The anonymous Shintervah gave him a calm smile and took to looking around the shop. As his business was finished here, Simon lugged his new lamp out of the Vanterslove's store.

Simon continued down the dirt street. The next sign he could make out looked to belong to a butchery, but the interior did not attract him. The meat was unlike anything he had ever seen before, and he had a fear of harming a brother or cousin to one of the Gulverbruud running the store. He remembered Lagelle's comment about the Gullen's quick skills in spreading news. Simon quickly scurried past before one of them recognized him as the boy who escaped the Cave.

Simon passed a few more shops he had no use for, eventually finding himself in front of a store home to blankets, shirts, pants, scarves, dresses, and many tall women working looms. Enlarged eyes stared at him through giant bottle glasses as he entered. He browsed the products in thick silence. He found a pair of baggy denim jeans, an interesting yellow scarf, a hat that he knew would make him look more threatening, and a dark green blanket with a Mizik leaf woven in blue. The material was thick and soft. An image of his shack flashed in his head: waking up in a cozy bed and pulling this blanket off him as he stretched and repeated "Flindervosa", illuminating his home. Warmth sent a sudden wave down his spine.

"30 Duz-" a woman began.

"I'll take it," Simon interrupted before the "uks" escaped her lips. The woman stood up revealing her true eight feet and marched towards Simon. She opened her palm, and he placed the bronze pebbles in her pale hand. A curt mouth pursed in skepticism. Without hesitation, Simon grabbed the blanket and escaped the shop.

He had a single Dillian left. He was sure this would not afford him much more, and still the shack lacked the complete picture of a home. Simon halted. A sign of a wand called to him. The poorly drawn picture ignited powerful attention and curiosity. He rushed inside. Shelves towered over him displaying hundreds of wands. Long, thick, thin, smooth, curved, cracked, colored, every type of wand Simon could imagine could be found somewhere in this shop. Each price tag cut a gash in his hopes. None of them were lower than a few Dn's. He was willing to spend the last bit of money he had, but that couldn't afford even a down payment on any of these.

Then he saw it- a simple white stick as thin as a pencil was gazing at him pleadingly. This wand must be his. Simon reached out to take hold of it. It fit perfectly. Slight finger holds were carved into the wood that tightly hugged his clenched fist. He gave the wand a test swirl and imagined himself in the Forest performing the same magic he saw Seskith pull off earlier.

A tall man whipped around the corner. "Hello there," he said. The man had bushy, black hair poofing out from under his top hat.

"Oh hello," Simon responded, returning to reality. He fixed his posture and stood strongly as if he had not been making use of his imagination. The man's smirk informed him that he saw his every move.

"I take it that wand suits you."

"Yeah, I think it's perfect."

"It's two Dillians." A sudden pain sliced Simon's insides.

"I only have one," he said hesitantly.

"Hmmm…" the man looked Simon up and down. "Are you a trustworthy soul?"

"I am!" he exclaimed. "I will pay you double when I can afford it."

The man let out a sound that resembled a short laugh. "That will not be necessary. What's your use with a wand?"

"I think I want to be a Collector."

"Ah. Well, you're right. That wand is perfect."

"It is. And in order to Collect I need a wand, right?" Simon tried to work his own magic.

"Indeed. For a Human, Collecting Mizik without a suitable wand is pure ignorance."

"Please," Simon begged. The man took him in with pensive eyes.

"Your logic is strong. Okay. You can pay half now, and half when you get settled. Deal?"

"It's a deal!" Simon exclaimed. The man extended his hand, and Simon dropped his last bit of his money into it.

"Do not disappoint me."

"I won't. I promise." The man exited the aisle.

Simon's joy was larger than any material product he had bought that day. He escaped custody, he made a couple of friends, and he independently earned trust that Kathy never saw in him.

He returned to the road and saw the sun begin to set over the trees in the distance. Simon thought the gazelles were probably done by now, so he decided to return to his renovated home.

They were bickering as he approached the shack.

"Simon!" Lagelle shouted attempting to free himself from the argument.

"Is the shack tip-top?" he asked.

"Not as beautiful as I had hoped," Shalice growled giving Lagelle a look, "but I think you'll be pleased."

"Well let's see it then." Lagelle opened the door hanging rightfully on its hinges to a sight that almost brought tears to Simon's eyes. Every hole was fixed, the sink shined, the floor was spotless, and the cracked table had been built into a bed nuzzled into the corner. It was home. "Thank you," he uttered. He could barely bring himself to speak.

"If you need anything else," Shalice began, "just let me know." She put emphasis on "me" and nudged Lagelle out of the room as she closed the door. Simon could only stand for the moment and take in the image.

## Chapter 7

Time was still. Simon was left with nothing but a place to sleep on and a stump.

But he was happy. He had made his place in this society. He escaped from prison and earned some respect from the Lord of Kearlith. Simon threw the new blanket on his bed. Thoughts of instant sleep due to deprivation and physical anxiety dashed into his head, and he still had to unload his new lamp.

He lifted the heavy stump of a lamp as close to the middle of the room as possible, although the weight seemed to outdo Simon's exhausted limbs at the moment. Very clearly off-center, the stump-lamp stayed where it was. It was good enough, he thought.

A fresh rush of exhaustion overtook Simon, and he slowly tumbled over to his bed. He made sure to pick up his new stick on the way. And there he sat.

On a bed in complete darkness save for a single tiny window by the front door shedding little light into his shack. His home had a hole-free roof now. After a bit of Mizik, he could light the stump and see more of his new shack. He wished he could gaze upon the white wand and see its beauty. Alas, he had to try and show off out in the Forest. Seskith must have thought he was an idiot after setting an entire tree on fire.

Simon's hands shot to his pockets. He didn't eat all of the

Mizik; he only took a bite before Seskith came along. The crunched up left-overs filled his palm, and he downed two pieces. The rush of energy came back and sent Simon to a stand. He felt around for the stump and shouted 'Flindervosa' with the wand pointed in hopefully the right direction. The lamp's bowl engulfed in flames, launching beams of warm light onto the walls of Simon's new home.

As if the sun itself was giving Simon's shack some kind of comfort, the stump lit the room with intense ease. He noticed smiling shadows given off by the rocks flickering in the firelight. A broom showed itself tucked away in the corner. It must have been a gift from the gazelles.

The tip of his wand rose, aimed directly towards the broom's handle. Simon shot his wand straight in the air and circled it like a lasso. When he felt a little bit of magic build up, he whipped the wand towards the broom.

A blue rope of light emerged from the white stick in his hand and captured the handle as it lifted in mid-air. He flew the broom across the room, making it crash and thunk on the stone walls and the wooden ceiling. The broom found Simon's hand as he flicked it back. Astonishment momentarily froze him.

His curiosity of seeing if he could ride a broomstick soon overthrew his disbelief, so he climbed aboard. It was unsurprisingly uncomfortable. With ease he shifted his weight to move forward, backward, up, and down. The broom was under his complete control. After enough practice, Simon began to wonder how to release the magical rope. He flicked the wand, and the rope came loose.

The broom remained in mid-air.

He had enchanted an object. Simon had successfully performed magic on his own. He threw his wand on the bed and sped off on his new vehicle. The door burst open, revealing an elated face holding on for dear life to a flying broom.

The cool night air kissed Simon's cheeks. For a few euphoric moments, he flew inches above the treetop blanket of the Forest. If a limb found its way in his path, it received a hard, flinging kick. Sometimes his balance wavered, forcing him to zig-zag back to control. His hands gripped the solid broom handle, and he zipped off to chase the horizon.

Thousands of trees gazed up at him from the ground below. They gave off a sense of satisfaction- like they were proud of Simon. He had never seen this view of the world before. It was as if the world were a massive globe that he could spin at his will. Out of the sheet of treetops, a quick blue flashed. The Forest was playing with Simon. It was begging him to dive in and catch more Mizik. He darted towards the light, although he could no longer see it. The treetops shifted to smirking thieves in Simon's mind. He had a vague idea of direction, but to find the specific location of a tiny, shining leaf in immense woodland would be impossible. He would have to search elsewhere. The moment had passed. He fixed his eyes on his next direction.

He noticed a glimpse of another blue light. Just a flash, but Simon was learning to instantly commit his surroundings to memory.

Instinctively, the broom shot down almost perpendicular to the earth. Simon's original intention was to simply descend, but the result was rocketing himself into the ground. Now the broom deeply penetrated the dirt a few feet away from the humiliated Simon. He remained collapsed and defeated on the cold earth. Several minutes later, he felt he had spent enough time in shame, and he achingly pushed himself up and heaved the broom out of its stubborn place in the ground.

Physical exhaustion tugged at Simon's core. He couldn't see the light anymore. His body was begging for sleep, and he was once again lost in Feerthel. He couldn't bring himself to attempt the air. The very thought of another plummet sent a shudder down his spine. Walking seemed out of the question since his legs could scarcely walk at all, much less travel an unknown distance through a maze he was sure to get lost in. He would have to pierce the air once more.

He hopped on the broom with a heavy sigh- the kind that doubled his weight. His feet kicked off the ground, and he was above the trees in no time. A sliver of Kearlith could barely be seen in the distance, not too terribly far away. Simon glided along the treetops slowly to his comfortable bed.

The second attempt proved successful, although he wished

he had stuck a more comfortable landing. He could not wait for the day when he would step off his broom instead of falling face first off it. With another sigh, he entered his shack and threw the broom in the corner. The stump was extinguished; the blanket was folded into make-shift sheets and a kind of pillow; and Simon's eyelids found each other.

The black cloak of sleep consumed his body instantly. No shifting positions or fidgeting; he sank straight into the depths of dreams.

*         *         *

A pulsing yellow blur painted a dense blackness. When Simon's eyes focused, he found himself in a starry sky- completely bare of surroundings save for the millions of constellations winking at him. He did not walk or swim, he simply moved through the air with no attention to gravity. These tiny bursts of light jingled as they lightly pelted his limbs and face. Simon could hold them, throw them, crash them into one another. But he could not touch the yellow blur.

It teased him as it raced around. His curiosity ached to discover this phenomenon. He lusted to touch it and feel its touch.

"Hey!" he laughed after it. To his surprise, it flew a little closer. "Let me-" a girl's giggle halted his voice in his throat. The lump stuck like ten thousand unspoken sentences.

He attempted to run after it. His body did indeed move but not nearly as quickly as Simon had hoped. He wished to sprint and experience the touch of the yellow catching him. The longing to feel this light left a vast, unfulfilled hunger in Simon. His emotions swirled into a twisted vine of an indistinct mood: fear, hunger, passion, joy, pain, humor, anger. Every sense was present and at its greatest strength.

The gap was closing in between the distorted smear of yellow hues and Simon. He felt he had to be close enough to touch this beauty, even if it were a mere graze. This was necessary. Making physical contact with this color was inevitable. He heaved his arm out, stretching farther than he believed he could reach. He was sheer inches away, and the blur sped off with a playful bounce.

A swarm of disappointment, discouragement, and unshakable determination devoured him. He would not fail this task.

Suddenly, the blur raced back keeping Simon's position as a direct target. A gasp escaped him. The anticipation burned hotter and hotter as long seconds passed. He was frozen in space, defenseless.

Just when he believed he was to be tackled by the playful yellow smudge, he locked his eyelids closed. His body tensed preparing for the worst. Or the best.

But nothing happened.

He was safe. Simon's eyelids slowly unfastened. He could not keep in a beaming grin exuding pure joy and affection. Her smile could not have been more than an inch away from his.

A loud crack ripped the picture of Seskith's strong and beautiful face out of Simon's head.

When he finally came to, he fumbled for his wand and illuminated the shack with an infuriated "Flindervosa!". Whatever had interrupted his glorious dream would be harmed or heaved out of the door. As the stump spat light on the last corner of darkness, a scratching shadow scurried behind the chair.

Simon's fear heightened. He knew how to shoot a large amount of forceful magic from the end of an iron bar, light a stump, and lift a broom, but past that he was ignorant.

"What are you?" he said. Only the quietest huff of breath answered him. "I have a wand!" he threatened.

The sound of leaves crunching startled him. He did not expect shadows to eat, let alone at a moment like this. Something was moving behind the chair, but his legs were too frozen to close in on the mystery.

Silence occupied the next few tense seconds before, "Then use it!" the Creature barked. The shoddy chair rose and threw itself towards Simon. He dodged it just in time, flicking his wand at the last second. A red jolt shot from the end and barely missed the flitting Creature. The shadow darted under the bed for cover, placing horror of the unknown into Simon's core.

"So you do know how to use it," a nasally voice whimpered after the spells had ceased.

"My wand? Oh… to be honest, no. I'm actually quite new to it," Simon responded. Maybe this wouldn't be a battle after all.

"Creature's peace?" the anonymous animal asked. Simon was boggled. Did this mean truce? He answered, "Yeah… sure."

"Whew. Good. Just please don't attempt the Kiliivna Curse again." With these words, a raccoon appeared from under the Mizik blanket-covered bed. He had a skittish quality to him. The smile was friendly and comforting, but the eyes smirked and mocked. The Creature stared at Simon for a bit longer than normal, as if he were calculating his strengths and weaknesses. Finally, the raccoon jumped on the bed and relaxed. "Now. Before we continue, I must ask what you're doing in my home." Simon's heart sank. He had no idea this shack might have been occupied before he moved in.

"Oh no. I'm so sorry. I –"

"Don't be like that," the raccoon interrupted. "In all honesty, I quite like the renovations. I simply was curious as to why you came to reside in my place of living." Simon was hesitant to admit he came from the Outside. He took some time to think of how to put it lightly. "Come on, it's not like you just appeared in the night, eh?" Simon's silence revealed his secret. The Creature's eyes went wide. "You're –"

"What's your name?" Simon asked to change the subject.

"Raelin. Yours?"

"Simon."

"Simon…" the raccoon repeated pensively.

"And yes. I come from the Outside." He knew he would have to face it eventually. Raelin took more time calculating Simon.

"Well, well. An Outsider in Kearlith. I'm surprised Fyresk didn't eliminate you on the spot. Or one of the Protectors."

"He attempted to imprison me."

"Attempted?"

"Yes. Unsuccessfully."

"You escaped?" Raelin pressed with disbelief. "Surely you don't mean from Serlentos Cave."

"I believe so, yes." To his surprise, Simon was beginning to enjoy the tale that he single-handedly defeated the Gulverbruud in the Cave. No one would ever have to know that he was assisted by the shadows. "Fyresk found me as I was leaving the Cave. I guess he changed his mind about me because he brought me back here and said I had to find a job."

"And he failed to assume someone might already call this place home."

"Look, I paid to have this place fixed up," Simon snapped with a little too much edge. He felt guilty for taking Raelin's shack, but in his defense, he did not want to lose his new home.

"Oh, don't get me wrong, Simon. I'm pleased with the restoration, and it does not surprise me that Lord Fyresk would place you in the Forgotten territory."

"Why not?"

"Look around you, sir. This place is deserted. Lord Fyresk made this neighborhood desolate years ago.

"Lord Fyresk?" Simon asked.

"Oh, yes. You haven't lived here long enough to see the true side of our noble leader." Raelin gave "noble" a good bit of sarcasm. "His selfishness is potent. Don't get me wrong; he can conjure a classic look of compassion when the situation calls for it, but eventually a lie is unmasked. Everyone in Kearlith is beginning to see him for who he truly is- a self-indulgent, destructive thief."

Simon knew the second he laid eyes on Lord Fyresk that he was evil. Despite his sudden change of mood earlier that day, he loathed Fyresk. His charred speech, his black skin, his dark demeanor, his honest eyes…

"I guess I can't say much," Raelin continued. "I'm a thief myself." Simon was taken aback by his blunt honesty. He had no response other than contorting his facial muscles. "Oh, don't be afraid. I'm not dangerous. Or destructive. Only sly. I'm not fast enough for Collecting or strong enough to kill a beast. Thievery seems to be my only gift."

"I think I'd like to be a Collector," Simon answered.

"Ho! You think you're quick enough? And how exactly do you expect to Collect enough to meet your quota?"

Shame bled into Simon's response, "I haven't really found a good answer for that."

"Well, magic makes all things possible, I guess. But you've

had no training."

"Fyresk said he'd send a guy named Mortimer over in the morning for a lesson."

Raelin scoffed. "Learning magic from an Intellect. I'll never understand that theory." He gave a large yawn for such a small animal. "It must be time for bed. You've got class in the morning, and I've had a productive day. I'm due for some hard sleep." Raelin scurried over to the turned chair and effortlessly lifted it right side up. "Bloody glad they fixed this," he said as he climbed on the seat. He placed his paws on the wood and whispered, "Flifferfin". After a flash, a cushioned green pillow dressed the seat of the wooden chair. Raelin curled up and dozed off.

Simon could not avert his eyes. His wonder fixed his stare on the resting raccoon. Shaking himself free, he felt the pull of sleep on his eyelids again. The stump was extinguished, and Simon slipped into sleep with hopes of picking up where he left off.

## Chapter 8

Unfortunately, the next thing Simon knew he was being greeted by a knock at the door- a slow, droning pound. Maybe Raelin had locked himself out. Was there a way to lock this door? And how could Raelin possess such forceful strength in a knock? This conversation occurred slowly in Simon's brain while he flexed his fingers and shook his head.

The pound became more alarming as he finally built enough strength to stand up. He lumped over and opened the door. Across the threshold stood a man roughly nine feet tall dressed in a classic and dapper suit topped with amazingly thick spectacles. The gentleman removed his top hat as a polite gesture. This revealed a crown of bare skin surrounded by shoulder-length, thin, grey hair.

"Good morning, sir. The name is Mortimer," the man hummed.

"Simon," he almost whispered.

"I know, Simon. You live in a shack surrounded by nothing. If I did not know who you were, then why else would I knock on your door?"

"Yeah, that's true."

"As Lord Fyresk might have told you, I am an Intellect."

"I assumed."

"I do not enjoy interruptions." Mortimer slithered out.

Simon nodded and chewed his cheek in a silent apology. "Sorry. Please, continue."

"Thank you. I serve as the Head Intellect on the Board of Advisors beside Lord Fyresk. I am among the many who Enforce the law in this city. Magic may be wonderful – especially to a new Human – but it must be confined. A darkness exists in every Creature. It's easy to witness their light, but no one expects corruption. Order must be set, and the Intellects create that order. We are the descendants from the Preeminents themselves; therefore, our word is law."

Simon prepared his mouth to interject, "And obviously descendants are immune to corruption," but thought better of it.

"Seeing as how this makes my word law, I suggest we migrate to a properly seated area. I do not wish to have a lesson over a threshold, Simon. Come with me," Mortimer said with a change of pace. The tall gentleman returned the top hat to his head and swung around, leading the path away from Simon's shack.

"Oh, yeah. Okay." Simon snapped out of his daze after a few seconds of stunned confusion. "Let me grab my wand." Mortimer stopped, tilting his head back and sighing in mock despair. Simon intentionally took a few minutes longer to get himself together along with retrieving his wand.

He closed the door to his shack and dashed to catch up to the Intellect. Once Mortimer was a few steps away, he turned around again and took at least thirty seconds to gaze Simon up and down. Simon squinted out of curiosity; Mortimer stared at him with dramatic disdain.

Mortimer spun on a dime again and strode down the path to Kearlith. His normal pace was speed-walking to Simon. Quickly they arrived at the buildings of the city. The shops on the outskirts of the center of town had larger yards with elegant foliage and strong trees. Some advertised their businesses by the upkeep of their yards. Other businesses apparently felt no need for advertisement.

As they approached the busier parts of the city, the buildings began connecting to each other. Some towered at five or six stories tall, others were tucked in between the alleys and pockets of the streets. Simon kept following Mortimer. He followed him all the way to...

The Mid-City Mizik Brew.

As intrigued as he was about the idea of a café in this city, Simon did not wish to experience his first taste of magic coffee under these circumstances. And Seskith might laugh. Nonetheless, he followed Mortimer into the brewery and found a seat hidden in a corner. The old Intellect looked a little confused as to why he would choose a spot so very far away from the bar, but he said nothing. Standing in line were four Creatures- two Gulverbruud, a Kyejoth, and a Vanterslove. The Gulverbruud were talking and laughing loudly to the woman who was taking their order- Seskith. She was talking and laughing right along with them, but she occasionally berated them about their order because the impatient gazelle and the furious, red-haired man glared at them.

"Speed it up, Krech, Rochi," Mortimer said as he got in line. The two buffalo-men halted their banter and creaked their heads to stare at the Intellect.

"Just a brew of Mizik," one of them said, then he turned to Seskith. "Please."

"The same," the other said. Then he looked at Seskith. "Please." Both of them gave a half second glance to Mortimer before they looked to each other and chortled. Mortimer simply turned forward.

Simon looked around the brewery. Giant, metal urns on the back bar were pouring steaming blue liquid into each other. Once one emptied out, they automatically switched places and repeated the process. The sleek metal reflected the lights from above. Hundreds of dull, golden lamps hung at various heights across the ceiling of the shop. The front counter, pastry cases, and brewing area ran to the center of the shack, then the bar started. It was an enormous hunk of wood, darkly varnished and sanded to a smooth curve on the edges. Simon counted seven Creatures in the nine seats.

Mortimer returned to their table with two steaming cups of the blue Mizik brew. Simon's excitement jumped. His was a lighter color than the old man's, though. He would have to wait to try the taste. The steam singed his nostrils.

"The Preeminents," Mortimer continued as he stirred some

pink and white liquid into his cup, "were the first to discover Mizik. They, much like you, escaped everyday society to create the city you've come to know as Kearlith. In 1801 this city was founded and they, along with the first Intellects, began reconstructing the surrounding forest into Feerthel.

"There were four of them, two married couples- Thomas Dirth the Brute and Eleanor Ocean the Beauty; then Nathaniel Lantern the Brain and Wendy Whisp the Brave. These four were highly acclaimed physicists, chemists, doctors, and veterinarians that tweaked and experimented with Mizik to learn all we know about it today."

"Is that what my lesson is?" Simon asked. Mortimer took a long minute to gaze and judge the naïve new citizen.

"One of many, yes," he finally said. "Thomas and Eleanor mainly focused on how to intake the Mizik. They were the chefs, so to speak. Nathaniel and Wendy experimented more with the magic of Mizik. Although all four contributed to the spells and curses, these two found and created thousands of defensive and offensive spells both with positive and negative effects."

Seskith flashed her eyes towards Simon. He was in the middle of blowing on his cup of Mizik to cool it off, but she turned away as Simon grinned wide.

Mortimer paused as he took a sip of his brew. "Pardon my brief obviation from the subject, but I find I must ask. Are you already acquainted with the Collector Seskith?"

Again, Simon's words got caught in his throat. Why would he ask that? "Yeah, I met her yesterday," he said.

"I inquire simply because when I was ordering your brew, she looked at you and winked at me. 'I got it,' she said."

Despite the freshness of his unbelievable surroundings, this statement was mind-boggling. Simon smiled wider and attempted to contain his composure. He could no longer wait to try Seskith's creation.

It was incredible. A perfect mix of sweet and bitter blended into a strongly satisfactory cup of art. A creamy taste of hazelnut and buttery almond captured and enhanced the typical grass taste. Simon did not undergo the pulsing power of the blue leaf, but instead a smooth calming sensation throughout every last one of his veins.

After a moment of blissful sensations with the brew, he looked up to Mortimer holding a slightly less disturbed scowl. This must be how the Intellects appear when they are amused, Simon thought. He droned on again, "Each of the founders of Kearlith prided themselves on their own magical race. Thomas the Brute created the Gulverbruud. Nathaniel the Brain was responsible for the Kyejoth. Wendy the Brave blessed Kearlith with the Shintervah. She snuck a few cheetahs over on one of her many safaris and raised them. She spent much time perfecting the race."

"They are beautiful," snuck out of Simon's mouth.

"Indeed. Wendy's work is highly recognized. The Shintervah hold a high place in our society."

"So what about the fourth founder?" Simon found himself genuinely interested in the history lesson.

"Ah. Eleanor the Beauty. She perfected the Serlentos. They inhabited both the area you escaped from and the region where you currently reside." Simon was beginning to lose Mortimer. The information was spiraling into a haze. The Intellect must have read his face. "Many years ago, the Serlentos lived underground in the Cave. Originally it was protected by Chirth Stone. Their Cave was built so that only they could enter, and but no one else."

"That's why the Cave has teeth," Simon interrupted. "And why Chirth has spiraling cuts." As soon as one question was answered, Simon would have five more.

Mortimer appeared to pick up on that. He quickly continued, "Indeed. They were scorpion-like Creatures as tall as Humans thought to be sons and daughters of the Sonx. The people and Creatures of Kearlith prayed to them. They would slip in and out of the Cave, and every Creature in Kearlith would give the Stone their magic as gifts to the children of the Sonx."

"The Sonx?" Simon asked, throwing Mortimer back.

"Yes…" he pointed to the ceiling. "The big light in the sky?"

"Oh!" Simon exclaimed as soon as he connected the "Sonx" to the sun.

"Right. The Serlentos were believed to be descendants of the Sonx –"

"But why would anyone believe that?" Simon couldn't stop the onslaught of questions now. They were spilling out.

"It's odd how lies can become truths, isn't it?" Mortimer asked as a rhetorical question.

"Eleanor lied to the people, and they believed her?"

"Mind what I said previously about my opinion towards interruptions." Mortimer warned.

"Right. I'm sorry."

"The story behind the extinction of the Serlentos is long and complicated, but in a nutshell- the city of Kearlith was once foolish and idiotic, and when she became wiser, the ones cursed with the lies had to be punished."

"But why is Chirth Stone on the other side of Feerthel now?"

"That answer lies in the elongated version of the story I just simplified. The point of the story is that the Serlentos are no more. We now use their former home as a jailhouse, as you've already witnessed."

"But you said they lived where I do now." He could tell he was running Mortimer's temper sky high.

"Yes. Once the truth of Eleanor's lie was discovered, Kearlithians rioted against the Serlentos. They attempted to blend in with society, but their eventual extinction was inevitable. Now, to continue the main story." Mortimer's aggravation seemed to speed up the pace of the lesson.

"Each couple had four children. Four were tampered with, and four were unharmed. Those who were unharmed continued their lives as Humans, leading the royal bloodline through a tempest of tragedies and heroes. The experimental Humans, for the most part," he paused for dramatic effect, "became the Kyejoth and the Intellects."

"Can I interrupt now?" Simon asked.

Mortimer inhaled through his nose with closed eyes. "It would appear you can."

"So there are other Humans. Other than me." For this, Mortimer took the longest pause of all. He couldn't tell, but by the look on Mortimer's face, Simon thought he might have just observed death.

Finally, the old man responded, "Yes. Only one other is left. He has been burned black, but his Human blood remains pure." He didn't need to say it. Simon might not have been the brightest kid in elementary school, but he could put together that he and Lord Fyresk shared something in this city.

Interrupting this revelation, Seskith entered Simon's life again. "Can I get you boys a refill?" she asked.

"I think I'm okay, Seskith. Thank you," Mortimer said.

"What about you?" She met Simon's eyes. "Did I disappoint?"

"Oh no, not at all," Simon squeaked. "It was delicious. Thank you."

"You're welcome, and now you've got enough Mizik to last roughly six hours. Enjoy your day, gentlemen." She walked backwards and managed to avoid crashing into all the tables and chairs in her path. She exited with a quick turn and a wave of her green dreadlocks. Simon was struck with awe.

"Your attention is clearly elsewhere. Should we continue at another time?"

"Um…" Simon didn't want to admit he'd rather be Collecting right now than listening to a droning old man.

"Meet me back here in a week at the first forty-five." Mortimer moved to leave, but realized Simon was too confused to ask what this meant. "The first time the Sonx is at forty-five degrees. Bloody Cuffersha, kid. Learn some geometry." The Intellect snatched his hat from the table and bid Simon good-bye.

Simon was empty on more potential conversations with Seskith. He could compliment her brew some more, but that might overdo it. Instead, he sipped the last bit of Mizik and snuck out the front door.

*       *       *

The city looked rather dry during the day. Whereas the streets were bustling at night, when the sun – or Sonx rather – could be seen, only a few Kearlithians wandered between shacks. Everyone must be working, Simon thought.

Raelin greeted Simon back at the shack. He was pulling various gadgets out of a little backpack fit for a tiny Creature. Simon's entrance sent him soaring four feet into the air.

"Holy Sonx! Oh, it's only you, Simon. You sent a fright into me. You see, my day was more productive than I thought. I barely scraped away clean. Could you keep a secret?"

Simon moved to protest, but he had no choice. "Yeah, I guess," he said. Raelin picked up one of his new toys and brought it to Simon. He never offered it to him. Instead, he jumped on the bedpost and shoved it in his face. The item looked to be a kind of locket. It was lacking a chain, but the locket itself was clearly priceless – the cover was a pewter sculpture of a beautiful woman in profile with her head bowed. She seemed to be alive and breathing, though Simon could not detect any movement in the picture.

"What is this?"

"A myth," the raccoon answered, snapping it back. "Legend has it that this particular locket belonged to Wendy Whisp."

"Why is it so legendary?" Simon asked. "Is it worth a lot of money?"

Raelin scoffed. "Not enough to make me part with it," he responded. He clicked the locket open exposing an illusion. After he had pulled out a coat tucked into a bundle with vines, three bars of Mizik, a cake, a jingling cloth bag, and a hammer, Simon found himself impressed. "This little beauty can store more than a tiny memory of a lost ancestor."

"That's actually impressive," Simon admitted. "Did you steal that today?" To his surprise, Raelin's face lit up with pride.

"Indeed. It was a heavy task that I've been scared of for months. But today promised success." The statement smacked Simon in the face.

"You're right, Raelin. In fact, I'm going to try my own luck at a little success."

"Oh yes, I almost forgot," he said as his paws unwrapped the coat bundle. "I thought you'd need a little help on your first day." He offered Simon a short blue rope of rolled Mizik, a few cookies with blue pieces, and a few grotesque chunks with shredded Mizik leaves falling out.

"Thanks, Rae. I'll take this as a house-warming gift," Simon said.

"A what?" the raccoon asked.

"You know, a—never mind. Thank you, Raelin. I think I'll go see Vezlin. Maybe she can teach me something about Collecting." The supplies were stuffed into his pockets, and Simon grabbed the broom and his wand.

"Be careful with that one, Si. She's litigious," Raelin said.

Simon shook his head as he opened the front door, not knowing whether to question why Raelin was warning him, or what the word litigious even meant.

*       *       *

Outside his shack, the fresh air filled his lungs with the promise of a new day, distracting the squirrels in his head. Simon took in every detail of his abandoned neighborhood. Despite the fresh and crisp air, the view contradicted the promise. Thick vines had fallen to the cold ground around the neighboring shacks. The vines had died off, but they clung to the rooftops as if they could not let go of the past. The Sonx was currently hidden behind a massive, fluffy cloud sitting atop the trees, giving a dreary, overcast air to the streets in his territory.

He continued into the city aimlessly hoping to bump into a Creature that could inform him of Vezlin's location. The matter was less than pressing, so Simon leisurely strolled along taking in more details of the city of Kearlith.

The marketplace was splotchy with random inhabitants. A ditsy gazelle hosted the counter at the lamp shop now. The hefty brute must have had the day off. The roof of the butchery nuzzled a slumbering Shintervah, though at the moment it was gazing at the sky attempting to will the Sonx to provide some warmth again. Her gaze must have worked for at that moment, the cloud hiding the sun shifted positions, and the city of Kearlith was again drenched in Sonxlight. The content Shintervah returned her head to her resting hands.

A small Gulverbruud chased an even smaller gazelle around

a beheaded black statue of a man resting his hands on the hilt of a fearful katana. An alarm went off in Simon's head when the gazelle suddenly smashed the Gulverbruud in the face with a swift kick, but the two burst into laughter, sending a sigh of relief throughout Simon's body.

He tried to get a better look at the statue. The man stood on a platform roughly six feet high. The statue looked as if it once had a head and appeared to be marked with designs of various colors and symbols. As more questions arose, Simon batted them away and continued.

A man sporting spiked hair the color of a new firetruck and a charcoal trench coat sat outside of the armor shop on a rickety bench. The man supported a helmet with his knees as he breathed little wisps of fire onto it. He tapped and tamped the helmet with a miniature hammer. Clanking and banging echoed down the streets. He must be another Kyejoth, Simon thought. Maybe he could have some information about Vezlin.

He didn't know how a proper greeting should occur. Hello there? What's up? How is it going? He went with, "Um… Hello."

The man stopped his fiery breathing and began tapping on the helmet again. "Ah, good day, sir."

"I was wondering if you could help me find someone."

"The city of Kearlith is small. I can most likely guarantee I'll be of service."

"Her name is Vezlin," Simon said, stopping the man mid-hammer. He turned to Simon with raised eyebrows.

"May I inquire as to your business with her? I ask mainly out of curiosity. She is not the type to receive guests." The man's skepticism was masked with a trusting smile.

Simon didn't know how to respond. "She er… I was hoping she might help me with my Collector training." The man's head bowed as his face softened.

"Yes, she has become quite a great Collector of Mizik," the man muttered. He returned to banging on the helmet. "She should be with the other Kyejoth. Her home mimics her dress- black with red markings." He lazily nodded towards a path leading into Feerthel.

"Thank you," Simon responded. He waited for a "You're

welcome" or a "Good day" or some other form of good-bye, but the man's manner notified him that this conversation was complete. Simon's feet resumed walking.

# Chapter 9

The Kyejoth's dwellings were much more elaborate than Simon's neck of the woods. Rocks atop wooden posts blazed the streets leading off to charcoal and boulder shacks. This was a bit overkill Simon thought. After all, it was getting close to midday. The Sonx illuminated the city well enough.

Tucked behind a group of shacks, Vezlin's home made its appearance. Shining red stones were placed sparsely amongst ebony boulders, and glowing red lines ran through some of the gaps, connecting them all together. Simon rested the broom against the wooden railing of the simple front porch. He reached for the doorknob, but there was no doorknob.

Instead a small, elegantly swirling symbol was imprinted into the door. As if a handle would appear, Simon grabbed for it. Just as expected, he merely grabbed the air. He gave up and knocked on the design.

"What bloody imbecile would knock on a door as if that were the appropriate way to mention someone's presence…" Vezlin continued to ramble until the symbol ignited, and the door opened. "Simon. How lovely. If you were educated in the ways of etiquette I might have just slain you. Seeing as how you are idiotic to proper introductions I shall let this time pass." Vezlin's arms crossed as a shield.

"What would be an appropriate way to… mention my

presence?" Simon agitatedly asked. He had been called an idiot far too many times to stand for it in this city.

"Trace the symbol. It will illuminate and alarm the resident of the home that someone is at the door."

"But this morning whenever Mortimer arrived, he woke me up pounding on my front door."

"Well, Intellects seem to think they are superior to magic. Acquire knowledge from them, not a sense of propriety. I must ask what your business is with me. I see Fyresk did not have it in him to dispose of you." Vezlin's tone was far too nonchalant. She was all business. Simon felt a tad bit of shame for bothering her.

"I was hoping you could help me Collect." With this, the corners of Vezlin's beautiful mouth formed the tiniest smile.

"How cute." She paused for a moment until Simon thought she had been frozen. "A Collector? Do you not remember our first conversation?"

"Vividly, but I didn't have magic then," Simon said.

"Ah, and you have magic now." Vezlin's playful sarcasm was beginning to sink in. Simon was fighting a losing battle.

"I do. If that's not enough for you I'll find other forms of employment." Simon sunk a few feet as he turned. Depression weighed heavy on his shoulders. "Maybe the Gulverbruud will hire me as a target."

"Wait, kid." Vezlin's eyebrows softened as she stepped a few feet closer to him. "I don't think even *I* could stand for that. Though I admit that might do the Gulverbutts some good, I think I might be able to lend a hand in your Collecting path. Come on. Let's go." She gestured for Simon to exit, and she followed past the threshold. Simon picked up his broom which ignited an insane fit of laughter in Vezlin.

After she caught her breath, she sputtered out, "You expect to catch Mizik on a broom? Oh, that made my side hurt. Whew. I can't remember the last time I laughed that hard."

She snatched the broom away from Simon's dishonored hands. "I couldn't think of anything else," he said. "I'm an idiot, remember?" This ended the fit. Vezlin could sense her words leaving too wide a wound.

"Too true. And the only cure for idiocy is good education. Luckily you will be following me. By the time I'm done with you, you will surpass anyone and everyone who ever claimed you bereft."

"Including you?" This time Simon's words left a whelp. Vezlin stopped smiling.

"Yes, including me." She set the broom against the railing and led Simon across town. The first few moments were an awkward silence. Finally, Simon found a question.

"So Vezlin, Fyresk told me magical Creatures already possess magic."

"That is true," Vezlin said to the air.

"Then why do you need a wand?"

"Wands do not possess magic; they are simply a way to better direct it. The thinner the point of the wand, the more accurate. The thicker the wand, the more powerful." Simon retrieved his. It caught the corner of Vezlin's eye, and a small gasp escaped her lips. "That's a beauty. I might have underestimated you. Nice choice."

"The wand shop guy said it was perfect for Collecting."

"And he was correct, which is not surprising in the least. Boffin is rather talented in the field."

"Of Collecting?" Simon asked. He had thrown any notions of sounding intelligent away.

"Yes. Unfortunately, the Intellects' destiny ends in intelligence. Though most of their noses belong in books, I've grown to like Boffin. He's assisted in my knowledge as well. He's afraid to admit this to his snooty family, but he's always dreamed of being a Collector."

"It sounds like a prestigious career."

"So it is," Vezlin said, although her tone did not match the statement. Simon expected more words to come so that he could change the subject to more questions, but he only endured a few more moments of silence.

When they reached the edge of trees, Vezlin spoke again. "When you collect five leaves of Mizik, come find me."

"Where will you be?" Simon had anticipated a lesson, not a test run.

"If you can find Mizik in daylight, you can find a woman in Kearlith." Vezlin swiftly spun around and left Simon with the challenge of proving himself.

*       *       *

This was a prescription for defeat. He had the magic and the wand, but no knowledge. The only spell he could think of was the yellow ball of light Seskith enchanted him with to chase after the Mizik.

Simon extended his arm away from his body with the wand pointed awkwardly at his chest. He circled his wrist a few times and threw the energy he felt at his torso.

Simon's limbs were sucked into a cyclone; his body spun like a top, trapping him in a rapid tornado that ripped through Feerthel Forest. Simon lost all control. He felt like a string puppet at the end of a chaotic mobile toy. With overexerted effort, he held out a hand to hold on to whatever his hand found first. A nearby limb offered assistance. He hoisted out to grab it but only ripped it from the trunk.

He continued flailing around the cyclone, smashing through the trees and creating his own paths, painfully fighting the resistance of the whipping winds. The air raged in his ears and ripped his cheeks from his teeth. He managed to find the branch with his other hand. Although the force of the cyclone weighed heavy on his shoulders, Simon was able to hold a steady position. He carefully planted both feet on the branch and rode out the tornado. It felt as if he were five hundred pounds heavier and falling from thousands of feet in the air, like he was skydiving into another dimension.

Slowly, the spell began to subside. After spindling down to a halt, Simon remained on all fours to catch his breath and sense of balance. The ground would not stand still. He collapsed on his side, heaving.

Simon was already out of ideas. He did not wish to send himself into another twister, so his one plan was dead. For now, he simply wanted to lie still. His limbs were glued to the solid ground.

Reality returned to Simon as he noticed the broken limb that saved him. It, too, felt glued to him and the solid ground.

Once Simon could feel blood rushing through his aches and pains, he sat up and tested the branch for flexibility. To Simon's best judgment, it was sturdy enough. He knew just how to Collect his five Mizik leaves. The wand was raised, the rope of blue light wrapped around the branch, and it found its way into Simon's hands, elevating him about a foot off the ground.

The bottom of the branch curved like a fishhook allowing Simon to stand at a comfortable position. He grabbed the jagged top and held it tight. In an instant, he sped off in search of more tiny, blue lights.

Sadly, Vezlin was correct about the difficulty of finding Mizik during the day. Not only was he still getting used to flying the fishhook branch, the Sonxlight drowned out any flashes from the magic leaf. After an hour of flying, Simon had only caught a glimpse of his imagination implanting a blue light into his mind. Simon cursed the mirage.

He needed a different perspective. He shot to the sky, high above the Forest to see the framework of the maze. Higher and higher he rose, several hundred feet from the tops of the trees. He committed to memory the main paths and Mizik spots, finding the patterns in the geometric shapes of Feerthel. Simon's eyes began to drift farther away from the Forest. The view transfixed him and kept him distracted. The trees waved a soft and steady hello. Simon felt the need to smile and wave back. It was only polite.

And the Protectors could be seen.

Owls starred the sky. Despite his height, they soared far above him and the Forest with beautiful grace. Some drooped low to speak business with the trees, but most of them kept watch from high above.

Once Simon looked back to the ground below, he noticed the absence of any recognizable patterns in the trees. Kearlith disappeared, too. He must have passed the cloak over the treetops. A prideful grin managed to surface on Simon's face as he gazed back into the sky. The owls were breathtaking.

In fact he gasped when he saw one racing straight for him. A tight tug yanked him back to the ground. All the air in his lungs escaped as Kearlith and the paths came into view, but just for a quick second. He swiftly approached the earth and smashed into the dirt. Soon the owl followed.

"Are you insane?" The Biffleflenn hissed. Simon attempted a response but only found that his mouth could not release speech. He was dumbfounded. He looked around his motionless body expecting a tiny crater, but the ground seemed untouched around him. He felt no pain. His arms and legs worked perfectly well, albeit a little shaken up.

"No," he finally said. "I was only looking for Mizik."

"I can guarantee it will not be in the sky. Do you wish to be seen by the Outside?"

"No. I never thought about that."

"You must. Thinking prevents you from doing something stupid. Like leading the Humans to Kearlith. Wait a minute…"

"Yeah, I'm a Human." Simon could see the realization overtake the owl's face. Although sore and bruised, Simon began to stand up again. "But I live here now. I don't want them to find me, either. I'll stay on the ground."

"That would be best for all," the Biffleflenn snarled. Then he quickly darted back into the air.

Several path patterns were still swimming around in Simon's memory. As vague and inconclusive as those images were, they were the best source of hope he could plan for. Simon remounted his fishhook branch and took a trail to the left.

The trees began to blur together due to Simon's lack of blinking. He took lefts, rights, kind-of lefts, quick rights, straights, hooks, and curves, but witnessed not a single hint of Mizik's shine. Directionless paths aimed him mostly everywhere around Feerthel. Simon felt he could have been miles away or spinning in a giant infinity symbol.

*     *     *

Eventually, just before the Sonx was tucked into sleep behind the horizon of waving trees, a cloud eclipsed, casting a temporary shadow of darkness over Feerthel.

A valiant blue light surfaced through the mass of dense trees.

The fishhook branch shot forward. After warming up to the effects the spell had on gravity, maneuvering the branch came easily in view of the fact that Simon had been crawling compared to his current speed. He barreled past corners with the same naïve ego. Simon tried his luck one too many times, and on the last corner of the trail, the fishhook branch caught a nasty tree root and spun Simon off in another cyclone.

With the Mizik still first in his mind, he lunged off the dwindling train wreck landing gut-first on the cold dirt. Down but determined, Simon thrust himself up and bolted as fast as his breathless body could towards the leaf just yards away. It wasn't until he noticed the brilliance of the blue beam as he freed the leaf from the earth that his alacrity might have been a tad unnecessary. After all, the blue light hadn't even started to fade.

A new kind of comfort filled Simon. This job didn't have to be a race. Next time he would exclude the crash, but he could do this. He was learning, after all.

One leaf down, he had four more to Collect before he could do anything else. This had to be some kind of easy. Vezlin wouldn't just abandon him for days…

Simon instantly changed his mind's subject to the remaining four Mizik leaves. The hunt continued.

The fishhook branch, although its fate was not planned, did seem to be his best source of transportation. His eyes began to gaze into the treetops eyeing out a decent replacement.

The Sonx scintillated through radiant pink and orange filters in the sky. The rare splotches of astounding colors were dispersed through thick and gigantic tree leaves. Strong limbs towered above Simon making him feel as though he were an ant trapped in a box of pencils.

Two separate events occurred simultaneously. A limb cracked and slammed into the ground directly in front of a path that burst into dazzling blue light. The Mizik leaf was far in the distance.

Simon's feet broke into a sprint, and he snatched up his new ride on the way. He enchanted the branch, jumped, and swung himself on the branch without the slightest give in inertia. The wind slapped at his face, every tree trunk gave Simon a slight heart attack as he dashed past them, and he hadn't the tiniest hint of where he was. But this was his training. He was going to astound Vezlin with his speed of catching Mizik.

*        *        *

Despite his slow start, the leaf was achieved along with the third and fourth after about an hour of riding around creating a kind of obstacle course out of Feerthel. Roots became platforms to jump off of to reach the branches. Trunks hosted vines that allowed Simon to swing. These trees built a gigantic playground for adults.

A local clump of boulders assembled a perfect ramp leading up to limbs that formed a curve back down to the ground. Distraction led to Simon's many attempts at this challenge.

Mizik leaf number five was the last to obtain, then he could hopefully get an actual lesson from Vezlin. It was time to continue the task at hand. He couldn't very well see Mizik in the dark while keeping complete focus on the trees he was hopefully about to land on. Simon grabbed his surprisingly agile branch and mounted.

Indistinct whispers made their return. Off in the distance, Simon could hear vague phrases and words, but he couldn't make sense of any of it. He followed it to the best of his ability, although there seemed to be dozens of voices that could have been coming from a number of paths. The whispers led him to the path hosting a brilliant blue leaf of Mizik awaiting his Collection.

After he retrieved the leaf and the light vanished from the minuscule clearing, Simon noticed a deeper darkness than the Forest surrounding Kearlith. The dim moonlight seemed to get trapped in the air as if it were wedged into the thick black.

His grasp tightened around the fishhook branch, and he bolted into the air.

As soon as his feet cleared the tops of the trees, talons found their way into the back of Simon's shirt. His body locked up, and he watched the fishhook branch drop back to the earth. He was being dragged through the air by another Protector.

The search for Mizik led Simon far away from Kearlith; the

Protector flew them for several minutes. Simon still couldn't see Kearlith or Fyresk's castle. Just a sea of endless treetops.

Suddenly, miles in the distance he could see Fyresk's castle beaming through the starlit sky nuzzled into the vast mountain. The sliver of the city slowly came into view along with it, but it seemed as if the city appeared out of nowhere. Simon must have traveled beyond the Forest. He attempted to scan the view behind him, but the talons clasped to his shirt held surprisingly firm. The Protector said nothing; he only picked up speed.

*       *       *

Soon, the two landed in the top of the southeastern tower of the castle. It formed the right cross-guard, jutting out over the castle grounds. The Biffleflenn's talons released Simon roughly ten feet in the air and dangerously close to a stone wall.

"What is going on?" Simon asked from the floor. He would have protested the landing, but he was begging for answers.

"You have voyaged beyond the trees of Feerthel. This is against Kearlith Law. You must speak with Lord Fyresk right away before—"

The door to the room flew open revealing the Kyejoth from the blacksmith's. His face fashioned a more charming suit upon this greeting, however. In fact, Simon noticed a hint of arrogance exuding from his grin.

"Hello again. I would tell you to follow me, but..." The man threw his hands out casting a lasso of pure flames. "... you'll have no choice." He nodded to the Protector, and the owl dashed back out into the night. He then started on the descent down a steep and narrow staircase. Simon remained unharmed in the circle of fire surrounding him. The flames danced around him and followed him. The man wasn't controlling it, but he figured he better not get distracted, or else the man would make use of the spell.

"My name's Caylo. I don't know if I mentioned that before."

"No, I don't think so. I take it you know my name."

"Yes, Simon. You're quite popular around town now."

"I'm sure the Gullen will be tickled about this new bit of

gossip."

"You escaped from Serlentos Cave, Si. Not only that, you were not instantly slain by Fyresk. It's worth discussing, even if you're not a chatty snoot."

"I watched a lot of TV and played video games as a kid. The Cave escape was just like a video game." Again, Simon chose to deplete the detail about the assistance from the shadows.

"I don't know what those words mean, Si."

"Right." Silence, save for the pounding echoes of their footsteps, filled the void until they reached an empty stone room. Simon tried to imagine a purpose for such a bare and cold place, but drew a blank similar to his surroundings.

The walls were long rectangular stones that matched the floor and ceiling. After Caylo released his fire circle, the blackness was splashed with a little hint of light from a tiny window fifteen feet high. The ceiling extended another ten feet past that.

Simon always felt so small in the office back at work, but that room was tiny. And the desk, filing cabinets, stacks of ancient paperwork, table, and Kathy's random voodoo gear all made mobility complicated. This room was huge. And absolutely nothing filled the space other than the two men. Now he felt like an insect. If Fyresk expected to lock him up in this belittling basement, he would go crazy.

Before he could calm himself down, an enraged Lord Fyresk filled the room with his presence. His burnt voice choked out an unsettling, raspy growl. "If you wish to be a Collector, you must follow Collection Law." Simon noticed Fyresk's blue eyes neglecting to meet his. He kept them focused on his collar bones. "This includes remaining in the perimeter of Feerthel. Any land beyond that is only seen if your occupation involves Protecting or Enforcing. Given that you've chosen a job finding Mizik that is located in close proximity to Kearlith, I suggest you keep close to home, kid." With this one packed word, Simon finalized his hatred for Fyresk. His grimace did not slow Fyresk down, though.

"From this moment on you will be taxed like a Collector. The city of Kearlith will take eighty percent of your earnings," the room gave a small gasp just after Caylo and Simon, "and if I ever catch you stealing a single bite of one Mizik leaf again, it will be back to the Cave with you. But be warned, some say I never quite killed the Serlentos off." In the dense tension, Fyresk's black skin sliced through the shadows and out of the dungeon.

Simon moved to leave, but Caylo's sleek sword swiftly prevented his path towards the door.

"You'll be staying here for a spell, Si. Someone will come and retrieve you eventually." Caylo's face was far from any others he had met here. His was the only one lacking malice or hostility. "You might be able to manage a bed and a desk before you run out of magic."

Simon silently bid him a silent good-bye, accepting his only choice of possibly spending the night in this hauntingly gigantic room.

He could swear he heard the echo of the silence. It was useless to try, but he had to find some way to light this place.

After a few balked attempts, the memory of lighting Feerthel aflame came back into Simon's brain. The wand shot in the air and began rotating, slowly building up energy. An inexpressible power coursed through his muscles, simmering in this new sensation. It was different than the caffeine burst from his beloved coffee. Every muscle in his body raged with life.

Although Simon was quite afraid of what would be discharged from his wand, he shot it towards the outside wall desperately hoping it would be fire. He let loose a roar as a massive snake of flames burst forth and attached to the wall, blazing the room in a deep, dancing gold. An intrepid attitude followed.

Simon made a quick circle in front of him and threw it across the room. Before the spell exploded into purple sparks, the wand was flicked to another wall sending a green electrical current to one of the stones. He attempted to rip it free but instead broke the current and the spell.

His brow furrowed, and the wand was raised to the stubborn stone. Simon could still feel a subtle pulse through his body. He focused his energy on the stone alone, trying to propel the magic through pure will.

Slowly, yet gracefully, a thin line of amber smoke emitted

from the wand. Simon's efforts increased tenfold, but the smoke remained at the same pace. Eventually it met the stone and captured it in an amber glaze. Though the surrounding stones followed, the enchanted stone twisted and turned in the wall depending solely on Simon's intentions.

A smirk appeared across his face. The stubborn stone was now under his complete control. Eyes transfixed, he firmly planted one foot behind the other in an attempt to pull the stone out. With great might and force, he did in fact pull it a few inches, but physical exhaustion eventually overtook his wishes of freeing the stone.

And the pulse fled from his muscles. Simon lay down in defeat but then saw the wall of flames that filled him with a little confidence. He managed to smile a little, then slip into an exhausted, half-conscious coma.

An hour passed, allowing Simon to rest his head and heartbeat. His anger with Lord Fyresk and the Protectors settled.

Then with propitious timing, a familiar face entered the room.

# <u>Chapter 10</u>

"Magic is pretty fun, kid." Caylo still fashioned an ounce of that trusting smile, but Simon let loose a tiny whence at the ranking of 'kid'. "Enticing," he continued as he held a strong stance with arms crossed. The iron door clanged against its lock. Caylo looked not at Simon, but the wall of flames behind him. "But it is powerful. It must be controlled."

"Don't worry. Mortimer's already tried to put the scare in me. I'll be careful."

"You've done some work here, Simon. I'm impressed."

"I didn't really do much," he said.

"Did you do that?" Caylo pointed to the blazing wall.

"Oh. Yeah," he said.

"Then you did something." Caylo took a few steps forward and smashed one of the stones in the floor square in the middle. His shoulder blades lit with green arcs of electric bolts. The current was sent to the stone creating the same galvanized force field around it, and he lifted the stone out of the ground to a make a suitable seat.

"Fyresk is a little greedy with Mizik, don't you think?"

Simon hesitated a second to carefully plan his answer. This fire-guy was an Enforcer. He could be working for Lord Fyresk to try and claim slander. "Not really. I understand that everyone has to pay taxes or whatever."

"Eighty percent is a robbery, kid."

"I know that." The response wasn't intended to sound bitter, but alas, the term "kid" pinched that anger nerve in his head every time. As cool as he could, he continued. "What else can I do? He told me my contract. I had no say in the matter."

"It's not like that in the New World." Simon could pick up on the extra time spent on "New World" as a begging to explain more.

"What's the New World?" he obediently responded.

"Hopefully the future of Kearlith – a realm where justice reigns and corruption fails." This speech was far too lyrical. Caylo had planned these words. But for what? Was he planning something? Caylo's gaze drifted to the sole window in the room. The firelight danced across his front half. "Fyresk has taken too much from us. His taxes are so high we can hardly live. If you do his dirty work you can make it rich, but the rest must give up a comfortable living because Fyresk demands Mizik. In excess. He was once a mighty and valiant leader of Kearlith, but he is no longer that man. We need a new Lord. One who could sacrifice for his kingdom." Caylo's speech was cut short for at that moment, the iron door clanged again. Vezlin stood in the doorway, fuming both in anger and her physical state.

"You, kid. Get up. What are you doing here?" The question was directed to a stunned Caylo.

"What? Oh, I came to check on the kid."

"Could you please stop calling me kid?"

"Could you please stop talking, kid." Vezlin's answer did not miss a beat. She continued in the same rhythm. "What were you discussing?"

"Fyresk is a little greedy with his money. That's all."

"Do not dishonor your Lord. He is your sovereign, and you have sworn your loyalty to him and the Board. What other subjects were involved in this little check-up, Caylo?"

"Nothing whatsoever. I swear by the Sonx itself I had only just arrived before you entered."

"Ah, so it was a late visit to speak with him when no one would be listening. Caylo, stay away from him."

This must have pinched the anger nerve in Caylo, for Simon

swore he saw sparks ignite within the furious red spikes of his hair. "He is a citizen of Kearlith, Vezlin. Pure coincidence could—"

"You may discuss business only. Any other matters are hereby forbidden by Enforcement Law."

"Vezlin –" Caylo attempted.

"Caylo –" she started again, but Caylo's swift face to face shut her up.

"I need not remind you," he said, "that *that* particular power belongs to Enforcers, and you happen to call yourself a Collector." His exit left a large darkness in the room despite the blazing wall just yards away.

"Simon," Vezlin snapped. "Follow me." Without another word, Simon kept a few feet away from his Kyejoth leader in pure silence until they reached the Forest just before the city.

The footsteps, flapping of wings, abrupt laughter, paws prancing, passing conversations, and Vezlin's dress ruffling were all dulled to Simon's ears. His brain was pounding with astounding velocity due to the cosmic amount of information that had been stuffed into it in the last three days.

Not to mention the last three hours. Simon was cursed to work for basically nothing, but if Caylo was victorious in whatever he was planning, that might not remain a problem.

Currently, he had a major problem with the formerly Enforcer and now fellow Collector, Vezlin. She sighed and took quick or deep breaths as if she were about to release some sort of conversation, but Simon suffered through more silence save for the muffled street noise. The city street dead ended into Feerthel.

"What's your count?" she asked as she halted. Simon scrounged around for the required five Mizik leaves. Much to his relief, Vezlin's pretty lips formed a flawless grin.

"Already? Great Sonx, I underestimated you. What did you use?"

"Okay, I know it sounds stupid," Simon began preparing himself for her cutting criticism, "but I found a branch that I can ride and follow the paths pretty well."

Vezlin scoffed. "You used a piece of tree to Collect?"

"Is that against some kind of law?" he backhanded.

"Not necessarily. Trees grow limbs back, so no major damage is dealt. I'm merely surprised you Collected five leaves in four hours with the Sonx alive for most of it… while riding a tree. I admit it, Simon. You've impressed me." Her eyes found the treetops of Feerthel. "Can you find a replacement?" Simon's eyes followed suit, scanning the limbs.

"Of course," he replied with empty confidence.

"Then do so. And be at my door in five minutes." Her hands swirled a thin, smoky yellow hula-hoop that gracefully jumped and found its way around Simon. "This is your next task. Five minutes." She gently tapped the circle and pounced off in her cat-like form.

As Simon desperately searched for another fishhook branch, he realized Vezlin's true damage on the circle still surrounding him. It was slowly deteriorating. Simply vanishing into thin air.

He saw it as a gauge of how quickly his calm temper would run. Once more, he was faced with one option- miraculously find a good fishhook branch, climb the tree, break it off, then find Vezlin before this smoky circle diminishes. The day could not come soon enough when he could do as he wished. Collect and enjoy Kearlith under his own orders.

All the same, he found a suitable branch two minutes later. Simon climbed the tree trunk at least fifteen feet to break off the branch, but it looked perfect. He remembered Raelin's snack from earlier which rejuvenated his magic, and he took off on his magically enhanced new ride. Simon basked in the return of the pulsing energy. The weightless freedom of the autumn air cooled his ego.

*    *    *

With plenty of smoke left in the time-circle, Simon smirked as he boldly banged on the door leading to her shack. As expected, a displeased Vezlin answered.

"What did I tell you about knocking?"

"Um… Something about how I should always knock first, and if no one answers, knock louder." She did not appear amused. "I'm an idiot, remember?"

She glared at him through dangerously thin eyelids. "Shut it, kid. Inside."

Simon halted once he entered. His astonishment at Vezlin's living room left him frozen with a slack jaw. The main room was surprisingly bright. Cheerful, even. Golf-ball sized orbs of light floated in the corners of the vast lounge; gargantuan planks of crimson-finished lumber spanned the floor, reflecting the vague glimmer of the orbs. Noticing his bafflement, she batted one of them towards him. It lightly pelted Simon's face and broke his trance.

"You want to be a good Collector? Here's the truth- I can't help you. Collecting is about luck and diligence. No matter how much I tell you, it will not increase your Mizik count. That task is for you alone to achieve."

"I have no idea what I'm doing, Vezlin."

"I know. Which is the only reason I'm helping you." She waltzed over to a strong, black armoire to fetch what looked like a frozen piece of red vine. Much like the Fyrovine that he sold to the nameless Shintervah in the marketplace. He finally identified it as the stick with which she wrote on the door at Fyresk's castle.

Simon's interest in the plant instantly skyrocketed, but he felt silence was best for now. He knew if Vezlin answered one question, she would have to answer five more. He took his seat on a wooden bench that displayed countless hours of carving labor. He would let her speak for a while before pelting her about the vine.

"Wand at the ready, Simon. Great Sonx, if someone's walking towards you with a wand and you fail to retrieve yours, then consider yourself an idiot and dead in a week."

He shot up. "Are you going to hex me?!"

Luckily, she laughed. "No, Simon. We'll just practice. What do you know so far?"

"Well, I don't know much, but…" Simon cast his wand, and the blue rope was thrown onto a marble black lounge chair. The pearly white cushion saved Vezlin's fall as Simon lifted her up. He did the same to an overly comfy armchair and hopped in for his own ride.

"I can't deny I'm beginning to like your little surprises, Simon," Vezlin said after all legs slowly found the floor. "Is this how you've been finding Mizik?"

"The branches make great vehicles."

"Very nice. Anything else?"

"No," he said with a bowed head. He decided to skip any attempts at the snake of fire for fear of his own safety and the amber smoke for the sake of potential embarrassment.

"You've got a good understanding of it, though. Basically, Mizik is the first physical form of magical energy. You can eat or drink the leaves and focus this energy to use at your will. The levitation spell requires little focus and no vocal counterpart which is why you've been able to cast it. As we've already discussed, wands vary based on how accurately you wish to focus your energy. Staffs, bows, swords, even rocks have served as perfectly adequate means of dispensing magic."

He had to ask. "Why did you choose yours?" This launched one of Vezlin's pencil-thin, ruby eyebrows straight up.

"It is made purely of Fyrovine. This specific piece was taken from the mother. I brought it back to Boffin, and he knew just how to craft it to serve as a wand."

"What's so special about it?"

The wand ignited as Vezlin's fingers exploded open holding the blazing, crimson masterpiece in mid-air.

"Fyrovine is best known for its ability to spark without a spell and stay aflame without creating ash. Some Shintervah use it to navigate Feerthel. I tend to find it most useful for various purposes. For instance –" She cast her fingers towards the armoire and retrieved another piece. She enchanted the new Fyrovine into a small circle and set it on a thick, flat stone. Her fingers flicked above the vine, and it flourished a neat flame. "Would you like a cup of tea?"

Simon was dumbfounded. "Tea?"

"Yes, Simon. Tea. To drink?"

"Oh yeah. Of course. Yes. I would like some tea." Truth be told, his attention was still very much drawn to the flaming red vine. A stone mug gripping a tea bag found its way above the flame, and Vezlin continued the conversation.

"It's a trick I learned from your little crush," she teased. "The Fyro Tree also has a legend attached to it." She paused as if expecting Simon to beg her to continue. He didn't, although his curiosity was screaming. She smirked before she continued, "She was discovered by the Preeminents just after they founded Kearlith. Lantern was the first of them to conduct tests and experiments on her to discover her uses. After his first son Jystik was born, he and Whisp decided to start—"

"The Kyejoth race," Simon finished.

She eventually smiled. "Yes."

"Where does she live?" he asked.

"Far northeast. *Outside* of Feerthel."

"Out of limits. Yeah, I get it," Simon said.

"For you," she picked up quickly, "it's best to educate yourself on the cultivation of Mizik. Our job as Collectors is to know when and where every leaf will spark at every second. You can find ways to navigate through Feerthel and Collecting will be easier, but if you wish to survive, you must know everything about Feerthel.

"It holds secrets that the Preeminents had damned. Banished. Creations that became so powerful, or pointless, they released them out into the world hoping they would never come back."

"What are you talking about?" Simon finally responded. Admittedly, he was rather lost.

"Your tea is ready." The piping hot stone mug found its way into Simon's hands. Vezlin picked up her own mug and migrated to a quaint breakfast nook in the corner. "Why else would we have made peace with the Fyro Tree?"

After a moment of a blank stare, Simon blurted, "I'm sorry, was that a rhetorical question? Because I have absolutely no idea what you're talking about." Vezlin's cute smile warmed the room. It allowed him to own up to his lack of knowledge of this world.

She picked up on that. "Survival. The Preeminents wished to show respect to the Fyro Tree. They had grand visions of expansion, and since the Tree is relatively close to the castle, they knew it was either peace or flaming destruction; thus, they chose the former." They both sipped their cups of tea in a quiet moment as Vezlin gazed out of her slim front window. Simon tried to soak in all the details of the previous story.

"During my session as an Enforcer," Vezlin picked up again, "a group of ruffians followed the trail of her vines all the way to the mother. They attacked her, and then attempted to attack us with her. For weeks it was a series of minor explosions and mild fire damage. Fyresk trusted me to face the flames and take them down."

"Is that when you..." Simon trailed off. He was a half inch away from asking about her termination as an Enforcer. "...got your wand?" Simon continued instead. Vezlin took a second to soak in her response.

"I did it. I spun a frozen disc at one of them. They dodged it, and I sliced a limb instead. After the battle, I picked it up and swore to repair my damage tenfold. I've long since returned the favor, and we've continued the peace."

"Congratulations," he said for lack of better words.

"My point being- Feerthel is crammed with menacing mysteries, kid."

"Vezlin-"

"Simon, I meant to say. I'm sorry. Look, just watch out for yourself. Okay, Simon?"

"Okay. I promise I'll contain my awesome magical abilities. But does that mean I can't continue to impress you with my Mizik count?"

"Watch it. That mouth will lead to a challenge, and you haven't quite shown me you're up for that," Vezlin said. Her tone and slight smile toyed with a more playful level of this beautiful, moody Kyejoth.

"The trick to Feerthel's navigation lies in those mysteries. For example, Fyrovine generally grows in the soil northeast of Kearlith. To the west, Rutroot can be found. The south is home to –"

Vezlin's red symbol shone bright from the door. She shuffled to answer it, but it crept open before she could rise. Lord Fyresk slipped past the door with a look that could kill a man. And he was looking at Simon dead-on.

"What gives you the right," he began, switching his attention to Vezlin, "to enter my castle and steal a prisoner? It has been a while since you had that power."

"I'm the one who arrested him and brought him to you in the

first place."

"You brought him to me on your own conscience. I did not ask you to act as an Enforcer. You are no longer in a position to take a prisoner out of Kearlith's custody."

"He asked me to help him. As your best Collector, I've taken him on as a trainee. I have every right to put his main focus on Collecting, Fyresk. You need me watching his every move."

Fyresk crept closer and closer to Vezlin. He looked her dead in the eye and stated, "Not this one." His look shot to Simon as he moved to exit. "You're coming with me, kid," he said just before the last bit of his blackness passed the threshold. Obediently, Simon followed. As the door closed behind him, Fyresk choked out, "grab your branch."

Not ten steps out of Vezlin's shack, Fyresk stopped to face Simon. "Do you trust yourself riding that?"

"Better than I do walking."

"Then follow me." The blackened Lord retrieved a striking navy blue wand with swirled designs of beaming Mizik lines dancing down it. He unsheathed a razor-thin katana that matched his own malevolence and tossed it to the ground. The steel never quite met the dirt. Fyresk stepped up to mount what appeared to be his form of transportation, feeling out a foothold on the cross-guard. Simon grabbed the branch and followed Fyresk on a distant path up the mountain.

# Chapter 11

Simon gazed below him to watch the paths in Feerthel disappear. As expected, the lines simply vanished into the chaos of wild trees. They were a short distance from the ridge of the mountain when Lord Fyresk halted. "If you haven't guessed yet, we are long past the trees of Feerthel."

"Yeah, I figured."

Fyresk's eyelids narrowed stopping Simon's quick mouth. "Of course you did. You more than anyone else here know there's more to the world out there. But you don't know this world, Simon. Take a look over the ridge."

As directed, Simon glided up to the peak of the treetops and gazed at the other side of the mountain. Other than the glorious view of mountainous emerald and jade hues, nothing appeared mystical or daring.

"What am I supposed to be afraid of?" Simon asked. Lord Fyresk rushed past him riding the katana, and Simon raced to follow. Lord Fyresk dipped into the blanket of treetops, but when Simon cut through the threshold, he was not fighting tree limbs or branches.

He was hovering over a glimmering, neon oasis carved into the trees. Under the cloak of night, the lake's magnificence would be overwhelmingly visible. Even lit under the evening Sonx, Simon squinted at the brilliance. Shimmering silver river lines pinched away from the lake to continue the current into other hidden worlds of the forest. Yellow and teal lines lit the dirt along the shore. Huge roots snaked up trees drooping large, elephant-ear leaves. The shore mimicked a beach with glittering sand and gravel swimming with the lake's movement. Simon knew that this is what true peace looked like.

A closer look at the lake exposed its unique movement. Quick ripples skidded along the surface, and eyes flashed occasionally just below.

"They're the Axolotls," Fyresk said.

"The what?"

"Enlarged Axolotls, similar to salamanders. The Preeminents thought they were cute, so they gave them the ability to speak and think. They never imagined them to be so lethal.

"Yes, they are quite dangerous," Fyresk continued, answering the question mark on Simon's face. The burnt man began to lighten as he spoke. He showed his eyes again. "The ability to speak and think gave them knowledge, growth, and progression. They excelled in the study of herbs and plants, and created venom that burns, stings, singes, and eats at your flesh."

"Are we friends with them?" Simon asked quickly.

"For the most part. They've agreed to keep our river lines clean. But take absolute caution around them, Simon. If they see you here, I cannot promise they will stay put." Fyresk's thoughtful blue eyes found the Creatures on the shore hundreds of feet below.

"I take it that's why the Preeminents dumped them out here?" Simon's question didn't seem to register in Fyresk's mind for a full minute.

"No one knows what's out there, Si," he finally said. "There are things that we all need to be afraid of."

It dawned on Simon the relevance of this outing. Not to show him the majesty and power of magic but to teach him a lesson about running off. He knew Fyresk feared him. One wrong spell could destroy the city. If Simon escaped, Kearlith and possibly the world would be ruined. The Axolotls could befriend him and turn him spy. He wished he had a mirror to see if he had 'IDIOT AND

DANGEROUS' written across his forehead.

"Right. Are we done here?"

Simon's sudden change of tone altered Fyresk's as well, and they lost eye contact. "You will stay within the trees of Feerthel, or you will find yourself dead or thrown in the Cave. Are we clear?"

"Yes, Fyresk. Now are we done?"

"In addition, I've decided to lower your tax to thirty-five percent. I couldn't live with eighty on my conscience."

"Thank you," Simon countered coolly.

"Your quota is set at fifty for now. Have it met every day by mid-day. Starting tomorrow. In one month, we will hold a review of your skills in Collecting, at which point your quota and tax will be revised." Fyresk looked to the sky as if sniffing out a direction. "Now we're done. Let's get back to Kearlith."

*       *       *

The windy ride home was colder than Simon had wished. He couldn't tell if Fyresk was trying to look out for him or put a leash of fear around him, but he refused to be a kid here. The Lord and ruler of Feerthel only needed to warn him once for the message to sink in. Why did he feel the need to bring Simon out here and show him exactly what he couldn't have? Those eyes must be the secret to his manipulative mask. Fyresk was a man of many tasks. Putting on a trusting face would be a back-pocket trick for him. As long as it got him what he wanted. The only reasonable explanation for this field trip was to give Simon an image to place with the warning. Now all he wanted to do was explore beyond the trees of Feerthel. Mostly out of spite.

These thoughts all brewed in the windy silence as the cool air transpired to a biting chill. Wind like this didn't occur in the trees. He could reach the swift speed he and Fyresk were now traveling as Kearlith grew closer, but it was difficult to manage the occasional gusts of twisting air currents. The shivering that followed became a bit comforting. It was the least of his worries.

Upon landing, Fyresk gave a short good-bye, and Simon was left to himself again. The bustling of Kearlith had begun. Chubby

Gulverbruud wives were roaring about oiled 'n' boiled Voxus patties for cheap. An older man sporting a worn red-on-black pinstripe suit was screeching as loud as his vocal chords could whistle about how sleek and strong his newest chain mail was. He begged Simon to upgrade today.

An uproar of laughter broke out in the middle of the street in front of Ziggokeif's Laugh-A-Day, which appeared to be a joke shop proudly displaying exploding rocks, chairs that would shatter themselves and then reassemble, and a massive amount of fireworks. Just past the amused citizens, Simon read *The Knowledge Factory* on a shack across the street.

His feet quickly found the entrance. Hundreds of books, thousands of facts, millions of secrets he could discover were haphazardly stacked on rickety wooden shelves running along the deep bookstore. He would have to trudge through feet of dust and dirt in order to read these books, but Simon was resolute.

"May I be of service?" said a sweet voice as she came around the corner. She was frighteningly tall like the rest of the Intellects but looked Simon in the eyes and not down her nose.

"I don't know. I was hoping I could learn something."

"Then yes, I can guarantee I can be of service. That's what books are typically known for- displaying information to learn about." Her slightly smiling mouth and direct eyes appeared to be making a joke, but her sarcastic tone failed to finish the image. Instead, Simon took offense.

"Thank you for clearing that up. I think I'll just have a look around." She clearly would not assist in any knowledge about defensive spells or attacks or Collecting hexes. He knew what a book was and what it was known for; he was guaranteed he could find one in this place.

He found *Larjo's Final Cut: What It Takes to Make the Lethal Strike* in the Hunting section; *A Bird's Eye View: Yintvin's Vision of Kearlith* in the Protector section; and *Stories of the Stone: The Secret Files of the Serlentos' Cave* in a section labeled "Kearlithian". The latter obviously required a good browsing.

Simon flipped through the pages and stopped once he recognized a familiar topic-

### The Lone Mizik Leaf

*The single leaf of Mizik that sparks atop Chirth Stone has refuted many of the past Mizik theorists. Before it was uprooted in 1976, the Intellect Karvayth was the leading academic of the properties and forms of Mizik; however, his hypotheses focused mainly on the Mizik leaf's dependence on light. He once stated, "The Sonx feeds energy to the magic in the soil, thus keeping it from sparking into Mizik leaves during the day."*

*Once the leaf started sparking on Chirth Stone, his theories were surpassed by a young Kyejoth- Grezev. At the age of thirteen, Grezev began writing extensive essays on Chirth Stone, claiming it was the key to discovering everything about Mizik. He continued his studies throughout his career, but his abrupt death in 1985 left his questions unanswered.*

"Did you find a book?" the sweet voice asked, interrupting Simon's wonderment.

"Yeah, it was pretty easy to spot once I really looked," he replied.

"Well, what did you find, dear?" Simon showed her the cover. "Oh my, you invade our city and go straight to the secrets I see." Her disapproving tone cut worse due to her honest eyes. Simon slammed the book closed and replaced it. He continued his search.

After an almost futile hunt through the outdated, damaged, or irrelevant titles in the Collecting section, *A Shintervah's Secrets Revealed* caught his eye. It was another book about secrets, but he remembered the anonymous Shintervah from the lamp shop. This was the "mastermind of magic". Lexandel. He checked around first to see if the old Intellect would spy her spiteful inquisitive eyes before flipping through the pages.

For a Shintervah, Lexandel seemed to know as much as the

Intellects about Kearlith. He took portions of the map of Feerthel and drew shapes and diagrams across them showing the patterns of the paths. He did this on several pages, but on others, he wrote articles about his findings. Some of the topics were headlined with "The Voxus-Hunt Will Forever Remain a Challenge" and "Kill Two Birds with One Hexed Stone and a String." The latter looked to be a type of weapon.

A spiked ball remained afloat in this particular illustration. The spikes' height ranged to an only threatening two inches but were placed in hundreds of spots surrounding the ball creating a vicious balloon. Attached to the side of this ball was a string leading to a ring, also drawn and detailed by Lexandel. The words "to slaughter and obey" inscribed the inside. The vigorous, volley-ball sized terror weapon could be used at the Creature's will, to wreak havoc and destroy anything within a three-foot radius.

Simon found no more information on how to find that device at present, so his search immediately dead-ended. All he could take from this page was the reminder that Kearlith was capable of marvelous things.

The sweet voice came squeaking down the aisles.

"Um... S... Sir? Um... Excuse-... Um... excuse me... Um, Sir, excuse me, but um, what are you reading now?"

His next move was based purely on escape.

"Nothing. I was just trying to find the exit." The Intellect was far too invasive for him to stick around. She quickly snapped her pointed finger to the door, but her eyes did not budge. Her disparaging stare singed Simon's skin. He only hid the book behind him in order to escape excess scolding.

With a wipe of his brow, Simon broke free with the book safely tucked in the back of his shirt, and he immediately ran home to see Raelin.

*     *     *

"Rae! Raelin!" he screamed once he busted into the shack.

"I'm right here," Raelin yawned out from the bed.

"Oh, sorry to wake you up. I'm just scared."

"Of what? Have the Gulverbutts sent a shiver down your fragile back?" Raelin mocked.

"I stole a book," he retorted, chucking the loot next to him on the bed. Simon sat in the newly cushioned chair. "I'm not a thief, Raelin. I was just terrified of the woman at The Knowledge Factory."

Raelin fingered the book with astonishment. "Lucky, lucky find, sir. Lexandel was certainly a genius; that much is certain."

"How much is uncertain?" Simon questioned. He received an inquisitive eye from Raelin.

"Much," was his only hint at the answer. "Look, Simon. You have nothing to worry about. If she had seen you, she would have caught you, right?"

"You're right. She didn't even know I was reading it. She only saw me reading *Stories of the Stone*."

"Haven't heard of that one."

"What's the story behind Chirth Stone?"

"That's what the books are for, Si."

"Of course." Simon humphed at the thought of the straining load of literature his brain would soon endure.

"Look, Simon. You're a good guy, and no one will miss Lexandel's teachings, I assure you; therefore, no harm has been done." He returned to his nap.

"Thank you, Rae," he said as genuinely as he could, although his gut still wrenched viewing this stolen book as cursed contraband. Nonetheless, he couldn't help but begin. He skimmed through the introduction and most of chapter one, but a note in the side margin caught his attention.

> *To Collect is to Hunt; to Hunt is to Protect; to Protect is to survive.*
> *To survive without Mizik is a Privilege.*

The collocation screwed up Simon's insides. The adjacent articles and headlines pointed to no further paths of explanation on the subject. He was stuck with a formless philosophy that made him feel quite uncomfortable.

He suddenly remembered he needed to be learning how to Collect through practice, since fifty leaves were due the next day. Earmarking the page, Simon scrounged around for Raelin's housewarming gifts. The pulse had fled from his muscles.

The energy bars Rae stole for him admittedly still tasted strongly of grass, but the sensation of magic returning overpowered his senses just before they bloomed and amplified. With Mizik, Simon felt fully alive.

He enchanted the branch and shot out the front door.

The slim moon lit little of Feerthel. Simon had no choice but to take it slow. The branch lazily lingered through the air as he scoped the blue light. Within minutes, Simon rounded the corner of a path hosting a bold beam and dashed to its location. It had just begun to dim, but he Collected it all the same. This process continued for a while; some leaves faded out before he could find them, but most of them were Collected.

He eventually found himself in a familiar surrounding – two stumps across from each other in an eerily planned perfect circle. With pride, Simon made the space a temporary office taking the stump not covered in moss as his desk.

Twenty-three leaves were counted, and Simon sighed a wave of relief. He was almost half-way, and the moon still stood tall in the sky.

The quick hisses of leaves shuffling returned.

"Who's there?" Simon intended to deepen his voice which only caused a cowering voice crack.

"No need to spell me, mate. I'm a peaceful Creature." The voice showed itself as a puny Shintervah with grayed-yellow C's spotted across his golden skin. His face formed a permanent smile like a constant, malicious laugh. "I know who ya are, Simon. You're one o' them 'umans. Fy tol' me to leave you be, though. 'Cause o' that, I only come to welcome ya."

"You're lucky you spoke. One more second, and…"

"I'd'a been gone, eh?"

"I've already learned the Kiliivna curse."

"Voxus droppings." The Shintervah let loose a cackle that matched his exterior- unsettling. "That particular spell I think you truly learned the name o' today requires many a year o' magic mastery to conjure."

"I did it once!" The truth knocked Simon's confidence down a few notches. He expected more hideous laughter but instead received an acquiescent smile that countered the previous malicious façade.

"Well, luck can lead to truly amazin' things, can't it?"

"I can, too." The statement struck like strong steel.

"So I've 'eard. I'd keep a good eye out for ol' Morolith, by the way. Dreadful chap says 'e's looking for ya. Says 'e 'as a few words to say about 'is brother Brobanarin." Frost crept down Simon's spine.

"Did he happen to be an Enforcer for Serlentos' Cave?" He wished he could stop time right then and there. He knew the answer.

"Indeed." The affirmation still cut gaping gashes in his fears.

"I'm dead."

"Maybe not. Not in the New World."

"Caylo's New World?"

"The same. Make a friend o' Caylo and ya might find yourself saved. Great to make acquaintances, Simon. Friziv's the name. I'll see ya around town." He left a full silence on his exit. It wasn't until several minutes had passed that Simon came to and snapped back into Feerthel.

He picked up his branch again and scouted for the remaining twenty-seven Mizik leaves. The hanging threat of an enraged Morolith gave his hands a steady shake. Fright filled his mind as he slowly reached his quota.

The fifty leaves were Collected, and Simon found his way home. All he wanted to do was curl up in his Mizik-leaf blanket and drift into a deep sleep. He hoped visions of yellow blurs would replace the terrorizing image of Morolith's fuming face.

# Chapter 12

To Simon's pleasure and disappointment, he awoke the next day fully rested with no remaining memories of the night's dreams. His hands lost their shake. If Morolith wished to make a scene, then he would have to do so in town, and hopefully someone would be there to take his side.

Raelin was nowhere to be found. This fact put a damper on Simon's comforting thought. His was the only non-vacant shack. It made a perfect target for any planned Brobanarin vengeance. He quickly readied himself and slipped out the front door hoping to make it to the Mizik bank unharmed.

Again, the streets were dry with life. Rare movement made the city picturesque as Simon found his way to town.

"Mornin', Si." Friziv was seated outside the joke shop chucking fist-sized rocks at buildings. After a few feet's hurling distance they exploded into black smoke.

"They're called Gotcha Rocks!" The Shintervah unfortunately fashioned the malicious laughter this morning.

"Good idea," Simon replied half-heartedly. He turned to exit hoping to slip past the distracted-by-laughter Friziv.

His success led him straight to the entrance of the

brewery. Her eyes met Simon's, and she smiled. Those eyes begged Simon to start his day there.

He painstakingly picked up his feet and continued past Seskith and her alluring gaze. His pace increased.

Chrysaetos greeted him with a humble grin as he approached the Mizik bank counter. "Hello, Simon! I did not expect you until well into nightfall." The harmless words bit at Simon's pride. "Have you your quota?"

"Yes," he muttered, retrieving the leaves.

"Glad to hear it. Lord Fyresk tells me your tax is set at thirty-five percent. Quite steep, if I may be so bold."

"I'm aware. How much does that knock off?"

"Hmmm… Let's see, fifty leaves of Mizik with a thirty-five taxer… one hundred sixty-two and a half, but we'll let the half stay in Kearlith." Chrysaetos beamed as if this were really in Simon's best interest. "I owe you three Dillians, twelve Duzuks." His talons gathered the silver and bronze pebbles and slid them to Simon. "Good day, Simon. Happy Collecting."

Simon gave him a quick smile, threw his pebble currency into his leather bag, and sped off to see Seskith.

*       *       *

Buttery, baked bread's aroma filled Simon's senses once he entered the brewery. The scent swirled with a sweet cinnamon bite and a slight hint of blueberries and hazelnut mocha. Few customers occupied the olfactory factory, and again Simon and Seskith's eyes met. She smiled as he took a seat at the mostly empty bar.

"How are you enjoying Kearlith?" she asked.

"I love it here." The mentioning of his slight displeasure at the threat of Morolith and his deep hatred for Fyresk remained locked in his throat.

"I'm glad." Her smile gave the room a similar sensation to the sweetened cinnamon and hazelnut. "What's your quota?"

"Fifty. With a thirty-five taxer, apparently."

"Wow. That's outrageous."

"What's your tax?"

"Twenty. Fyresk must have something against you." Her smirk softened the truth.

"He's scared of me. I know it. He thinks I want to take control of the city or something."

"Fy's changed these last few years. Hardened. Before the attack he was a completely different man."

"The attack that burned him?"

"Yeah, that's about as much as anyone knows about it. About seven years ago, he went out on a solo adventure 'to explore' he says, and when he returned, his skin and manner both were burnt. His only comment was that he was attacked."

"What do you think happened?"

"No idea. He's never told anyone. Can I get you anything? We have a special today."

"I'm not exactly sure how to order," and he was still hung up on the idea of a pre-demon side of Fyresk. "What's the special?" He felt the heat of embarrassment creep across his face.

"A Rutroot Scone and Sweet-Top Mizik brew. It's usually a Dillian, but I'll take care of this one."

"I can pay," he fired quickly as his hand shot to his jingling pocket.

"I don't doubt that. Don't worry about it." The enchanting Shintervah sauntered over to the counter and put her meticulous craft to use. She stopped a pair of the metal urns filling each other with the dark blue liquid, then poured some of the blue liquid into a porcelain mug. A sleek, pyramid pitcher was placed under a tangled chunk of angel-hair steel bars. Slowly, she poured the Mizik brew through the steel, catching bits and pieces of the dripping leaves. The pitcher and mug switched and the process was repeated.

So far, Simon related most of the work to his career at the café, but Seskith slid the steel bars through the air to the other side of the counter as soon as it stopped draining. Once they fully covered a bowl matching the pristine pitcher, she tapped each one gently to straighten them out and clean off the bits of Mizik. Her fingers were slightly larger than those of a female Human's, only slightly furrier, and the nails kept their cheetah-like qualities. Her palms were padded and were also heavier on the cheetah side. She swept the last of the Mizik bits into the bowl and set it down.

"You can thank Lord Fyresk for our clever techniques at conserving," she said as she returned to the brew. She dashed the remnants of the Mizik off her fingertips along with crystal white flakes across the top and lathered the surface with a golden syrup. A long and narrow spoon and saucer accompanied the mug upon Seskith's delivery to Simon's seat at the bar.

"What do you use that for?" he asked, nodding to the bowl of Mizik bits.

"Scones, muffins, snack bars, cookies, pretty much anything. The Mizik leaves still pack a pretty good magic punch, even after they're drained. You'll be having Rutroot, though."

She left Simon to enjoy his brew as she popped open the wooden saloon doors to the back. The taste was smoother this time. It was bolder, but creamy, and with a sweet bite.

Seskith popped the back doors open, wielding his Rutroot scone. Steam billowed off the top, and Simon could not wait to try the new dish. "Rutroot's a healer. It increases endurance and pain tolerance. And when executed correctly, it can be used to heal wounds and burns."

"I bet Fyresk has seen his share of that," Simon jested.

Seskith unfortunately took offense. "I'm sure he has. With a position such as his, he must keep himself strong." She pushed the butt of the bad joke to Simon. His intense grin burst with apologies and gratitude accompanied by an uninvited, high-pitched poof of laughter. It quickly faded as those golden eyes flashed and disappeared. Seskith grabbed the pitcher and went to wash it across the room. Simon figured her cold shoulder might have cooled off the Rutroot scone, so he pinched off a fresh and fluffy bite.

It tasted like dirt. Granted, it tasted like sugar and bubblegum flavored dirt, but the dirt flavor was definitely prominent. Simon changed the subject to give his taste buds a little time to recover.

"So we have to Collect every day?"

"Yes, Simon. Times are hard right now. If you want a day off, you better double your quota the day before."

"I'm okay with that. But Seskith, I'm lost in Feerthel.

Mortimer's putting me to sleep, Vezlin's just giving me mind games, and I need to know how to be a better Collector."

"You're the only one who can make that happen. The only way you'll get better is to get out there."

"I'll get lost."

"And you'll find your way back. That's the point."

"Isn't there a big map or an information center somewhere?"

"Of course there is. The Knowledge Factory is full of maps and information." Brief dread swept Simon with the mere mentioning of possibly stepping foot into that place again.

"I don't think the old lady there liked me."

"They won't help you anyway." She stopped and turned around to face him. "Simon, Feerthel Forest looks nothing like any map once you're staring at a circle of identical trees."

"They're not identical," he stated. "There are differences in Feerthel. I know that. Different things about different plants that can tell you where you are. I've figured some of it out, but I don't know what any of that means. And no one wants to help me figure it out for myself. Seskith, you've had your whole life to learn about Feerthel, and I've had roughly one week. If maps or books won't help me, would you please tell me where I can find any kind of assistance?" He started to huff.

Startlingly, the smile returned to Seskith's face. "Meet me next to the statue in Mid-City at Sonxdown. I'll show you how I Collect. But you'll have to keep up."

Her abrupt switch in manner threw him for a loop, but slowly his face matched hers. "Okay," he said. Before he could continue with a clever line or a charismatic come-back, a stubby Vanterslove walked in. The Mizik barista was forced to switch customers.

"Hello, Roibose." The gazelle's previously troubled disposition quickly brightened at the sight of her. Simon wasn't the only one Seskith affected.

"Good morning, Seskith. How's business?" he boomed.

"Collecting is great. Can't say so much about the brewery, though."

"Sorry to hear that, dear. Well, my usual should keep you all employed, eh?"

She let loose a cute chuckle. "Of course, Roibose. Let me get that for you."

The chunky gazelle found a stool on the bar. From a saddle-bag he pulled out a wand and notebook and flipped to a page filled with an empty rectangle. Simon couldn't help but watch him work. This "Roibose" drew a few simple, black lines roughly three inches long and stared at them for a full minute. With his fat hoof, he then scooted the lines across the page into a corner. After adding a square to the stack of lines, he must have felt the heat from Simon's wide eyes. He alarmingly looked up.

"Good morning, sir," Simon responded quickly. Roibose simply squeaked out a simple grin and returned to his work.

He sketched a long line across the frame of the piece and pulled three lines down to sit on it. He nudged them as if to get them all pointed to some specific center of the page. Finally, he grabbed the square to line it up with the center and set it on the three lines. Tapping the top right corner of the page's rectangle frame made the picture recognize the weight of gravity. It slowly toppled over, and the lines making up the square broke and fell amongst the thin abyss of the long, sketched line across the page. Roibose gave a slight huff as he scratched the long line attempting to save all seven of the others. He built the square again, and set the three sketched lines to a different specific center on the page. He continued this process for a while with no success.

Again he looked back at Simon, but this time with suspicious hostility. Before he spoke, however, he smiled.

"Good morning, Simon," he said as his eyes narrowed and his mouth formed a grin, fully recognizing who he had been sitting next to for ages now without the proper greeting.

"Morning, Roibose."

"Pleasure to meet you, son. Are you enjoying Kearlith?"

"For the most part."

"Shalice tells me you made her work with that half-wit Lagelle."

"My shack needed a lot of work." Simon was beginning to hate the guessing of whether Creatures in this city accepted him or not. Luckily this Creature bellowed a deep laugh, and the boom broke the tension.

"Believe me, Si, I thanked you as soon as she told me. Those two have been at it for years. It's about time someone forced them to settle it."

"Did they?"

"For the most part. They have agreed to disagree."

Seskith's hand gripped a mug upon her return followed by four floating plates. They placed themselves around the lip-licking Roibose. Simon figured he was showing bad manners by not feasting on his own meal. He sank his teeth into the bubblegum dirt and chomped off as much as he could shovel down. The quicker he ate it, the quicker he wouldn't have to keep eating it.

"The thing is, Simon," Roibose began again in between bites of his own Rutroot scone, "Shalice is always going to put a Dillian first. That little lady is a fiend for money. I had a chat with her, though. I think I may have helped diffuse the problem." Roibose almost bounced with pride. He took Simon's mouthful as a sign to continue. "I told her that there seems to be plenty to fix around Kearlith lately. She could still make a proper living fixing the rest of the town."

Simon stopped chewing. The view through the tattered window was a new one. Simon saw Kearlith for what it used to be and what it has since become. Most of the wooden signs on the street were missing corners; some hung slanted from rigged ropes. A few shops were poorly mended with rocks and wooden planks. Others fashioned different rigs to hold their structure up.

He could see a slim corner of the adorned plaza from here, where the streets connected past a few shacks up the street. Marble columns lined the circular court, but every single one was crumbled at the same height, just above the tallest shacks.

He gulped a gallon of trepidation along with the last bite of his Rutroot scone. Clearly, Kearlith was in dire need of change.

"She seemed to see the logic in that," Roibose continued after waiting several moments for a response. "She said she'll leave Lagelle alone if he gets to a customer first. Now, I hate to compare myself to an Enforcer," he obviously had no problem with it, "but I think justice was served."

"That's incredible," Simon faked. "Congratulations." The Vanterslove's arrogant banter began to bore Simon, and with the steadily deteriorating Kearlith staring him in the face, Simon couldn't sit still any longer. He had to get out and help this city. "It's been great talking to you, Roibose, but I have to leave now."

"It's quite alright, I understand. It has been a great chat, Simon. I hope to see you around town." A sincere smile followed, halting Simon for a second. It was full of self-righteousness, but it lacked skepticism.

"Can I get you a refill?" Seskith asked, returning to the bar.

"No thank you, Seskith. In fact, I'm about to go into town and see what trouble I can stir up." This time his jest was well-received. She smiled as she narrowed her eyes. "Thank you for the scone and Mizik brew," Simon said. "I'll see you tonight."

"See you tonight, Simon." Their eye contact never broke until he made it through the doorway.

\*       \*       \*

Simon halted mid-step past the threshold. No more than thirty feet away stood a beast fearful enough to slay every Kearlithian in that instant. Morolith's stare was dead still. Simon's first instinct was to run, but his feet were firmly frozen to the street.

"Hey hero!" the Gulverbruud roared despite the close proximity. "You know," he began to stroll forward, "at first I wanted to kill you. Yes, Simon, I wanted to find your dirty soul and rip it to shreds. But! I decided to go to Lord Fyresk and ask his opinion. And do you know what he said? He said to talk to you first." He couldn't tell if Morolith would attack or laugh or give him a big hug. Simon remained frozen, but his hand drifted toward his pocket to retrieve his wand.

"I promise I did not mean to—"

"Oh yes, I thought about that decision, too. The one about hearing what you had to say. But! I have decided that I don't want to know. You're clearly talented enough to call yourself a Kearlithian. You may have your own reasons for ripping a brother, son, and father from a family, but that's none of my business."

Morolith was dangerously close now. At this distance, he looked much more daunting. Not only because of what he said, but the way his eye twitched a vein in his massive cranium when he said it. His facial features were much more horrifying than his words. They were robust and chiseled, as if Thomas Dirth tried to carve buffaloes into resembling men. But Morolith's massive brow specifically seemed restrained, like he was far more in control of his gargantuan size than Simon realized.

"Because we're supposed to simply trust you, right? You Humans. Filthy thieves." He snapped to. His eyes shot to the passing citizens with matching open mouths. A few had stopped, and the fuming buffalo-Creature realized his words were approaching the point of no return.

"Happy Collecting, Simon. I'll see you around town." The beast's flared nostrils crept inches away from Simon's own as he passed him into the brewery.

Simon still stood frozen.

*     *     *

As if by an autopilot hex, his feet eventually began picking themselves up and aimlessly leading him around the streets of Kearlith. Morolith's manner offset Simon's brain. The Gulverbruud generally stood to a solid and striking seven feet tall, and yet he cruised through his revenge unscathed. Somehow, Morolith had drafted and signed their peace treaty, and Simon was to ask no questions. Bittersweet relief crept through him like subtle pins and needles. If no one asked him about what exactly happened in the Cave, he would never have to reveal the truth about the shadows. He could still claim all the talent and power it took to bring down half a dozen Gulvervbruud guards.

The sky unfortunately fashioned a gloomy gray. Low, grumbling thunder brewed several miles away, and its anger echoed. The wind snapped little bites of cold. Even a delightful looking lady Gulverbruud sported a coat as she stitched a leather helmet. She sat on a plain chair under a sign of what seemed to be crumpled brown paper. He knew her business must have involved more than that.

Taking a chance out of curiosity he asked, "Do you have anything for Collectors?"

She smiled as she noticed him. "Collectors, Hunters, Enforcers, Protectors, Keepers, Builders, and Humans. The name's Mathilda, Simon. Pleased to finally meet you." Despite her breed's natural dominance as evidenced by his encounter with Morolith, Mathilda smiled with softness. Her graying, matted fur was covered in aged leather armor. He followed her into a shop filled with leather backpacks, saddle-bags, coats, pants, vests, shoes, boots, gloves, everything Simon wanted to buy.

"Try this on," Mathilda said as she threw him a navy blue leather vest. Tan straps hosting clever hooks and pockets were sturdily stitched into an X across it. The cross-tie in the front took some time to untie. "You've got a place for your wand on the top left there, and below it is a line of hooks for money bags, snack bags, what have you. On your right is a place for your Mizik wallet, and below that is a spot for your canteen."

"This is amazing," he said. Once the stubborn leather ties were free, Simon tried on the attire.

"I kept it a bit big, seeing as how it's easier to trim than to add. I still need to put something on the back, too. I was waiting to hear your choice of weapon before I continued."

"Did you make this for me?"

"Yes, dear." Mathilda smiled as if the fact were obvious. "I heard you wished to be a Collector, and I've made plenty of these for the Shintervah."

"Thank you, Mathilda. I've only got three Dillians, though."

"That's fine. I still need to make proper adjustments. If you'd like it, I'll let you pay it off. It'll be five Dillian. How about one Dillian a day?"

"It's a deal!" He handed over the first silver pebble.

"Any suggestions for what you'd like on the back?"

"I don't know. What do people usually put there?"

A smirk and slight huff preceded, "Well, *people* don't normally wear them. But many Creatures store their selected weapons on the back."

"Oh. I haven't found a weapon yet."

"No matter. I'll take it in a few inches for now."

"Thank you," he said.

"You're welcome, Simon. It has been a pleasure meeting you." Mathilda gave a small head nod in a polite gesture, but Simon was transfixed on a friendly buffalo's face. He snapped back and bid his goodbye to the lady Gulverbruud.

The real and rare beauty of Kearlith became bright and apparent for the moment. Fyresk had his flaws, Vezlin viewed him as important as a dead roach, and Morolith wasn't easy to get along with, but people here- or Creatures, rather- trusted one another. That made the second citizen in Kearlith that trusted him upon their first meeting and made a deal with him.

Boffin being the first. Simon still had two Dillians left, and he was perfectly happy to pay his one Dillian debt to the Intellect who could actually teach him something useful. His eyes searched for that poorly drawn wand sign.

*　　*　　*

He could have found it quickly – it was right up the street – but Simon got turned around with his directions. Finally he found his way, and Boffin's humble smile hosted the counter. "Good morning, Boffin. Great to see you again, sir," he exalted upon his entrance.

"Ah, Simon. A pleasure to see you again as well. How is that wand treating you?"

"It's awesome. I haven't learned many spells with it, but it's got a nice feel to it."

"Marvelous magic can be achieved with that wand, Simon. If I may—" Boffin held out his hand in a silent request.

He held it delicately. With his fingertips rather than his palm.

He pointed the thin, white stick across the room and hoisted an old, broken box from under a pile of rubble. The box found Boffin's hands, and from it he retrieved a long and skinny limb. Boffin slowly nicked the top of the limb and began mumbling jargon. The wand scratched intricately detailed designs down a few inches, and brilliant blue lines lit the tracings.

After he was finished, he returned his attention to Simon, but the wand remained in his possession. "Some lucky Gulverbruud will be delighted to know that this wand will now send a path of ice and frost upon request."

"That's great. Can I have mine back now?" The magic was truly breathtaking, but Simon was beginning to feel rather attached to his wand.

Boffin gave him a long gaze before responding. "You have proven your word, Simon. If your wish is to be a Kearlithian, I think you have shown Kearlith without a doubt that you are worthy of that title. Do not," his face dropped, "abuse it."

Again, Simon found himself on the receiving end of a watchful eye. Boffin had managed to strongly compliment and offend him in seconds.

"Oh, I won't disobey you, sir. Sir Boffin the Great and Wonderous Wand Master. From this day forth I shall do no wrong." Simon felt overindulgence would be his safest response. To follow, he knelt down on his knee and presented the Intellect with his single Dillian debt. Boffin hesitated before accepting the silver pebble but did not speak. Something in Simon forced Boffin to endure roughly thirty bows coated with apologies, compliments, and thank-you's before his exit through the door.

After a few moments of walking the calming streets of Kearlith, he realized he couldn't blame Boffin. It wasn't his fault. It was everyone's. Although admittedly Simon had found a few friendly faces, the majority of the city's population gave him looks dirtier than the debris filled street gutters. He was useless to them. They studied him and saw his thin limbs as signs of weakness; his lowered eyes as cowardice; his viciously unkempt, short black hair as an indication of evil.

The marble-grey sky robbed Kearlith of color and life. An invisible sludge plastered Simon's feet. His limbs began to tell him he had spent a week out in a forest and needed rest. In honor of his aching arms, feet, back, legs, knees, and neck, he took the quickest path home. Maybe Lexandel could teach him something that would impress the rest of the chary Kearlithians.

## <u>Chapter 13</u>

Indeed, Simon learned much from this mystery Shintervah Lexandel. His race was known for its speed and agility making them the best Collectors, but Lex had mastered that craft early in his career. Among numerous tidbits of Collecting knowledge, Lexandel shed light on Protecting, Building, Enforcing, and predominantly Hunting.

Hunting seemed to be his specialty. Simon was surprised to find himself both thrilled and appalled by the weapons Lexandel thought up to kill animals. Crossbows with fire, ice, magnetic, explosive, and telekinetic attachments; gigantic bear traps; and a simple bow were among the many. But this was only a hint at what Simon was in store for during the next few hours.

Raelin must have been out pick-pocketing, for he didn't show up at all. Simon filled the silence and gloom of the dying society with the words of the first half of *A Shintervah's Secrets Revealed*. He began memorizing the notes in the side margins, which he learned were Lexandel's Teachings. This was a theme early introduced in the book. Lexandel's genius was undeniable; thus, he spent an ample amount of time explaining every detail of everything he covered. In the side margins were his most important pieces of information that would, as he stated in the prologue, "… directly relate to survival as a Creature." Included in the various examples of his mastermind were, "Speed is a test of skill. Magic is a test of thought. Hunting is a test of courage," and "Your power can only be seized by you," but the one that still dug at Simon was, "To Collect is to Hunt; to Hunt is to Protect; to Protect is to survive.

"To survive without Mizik is a Privilege."

Lexandel referred to the Privileged several times throughout the book. During Simon's lesson of the Preeminents' creation of the races, he came to understand that term as anyone not born of magic or reliant on it, i.e. the Humans and the Intellects. A harsh tone was present in Lexandel's feelings towards the Privileged, but he couldn't quite place it.

He continued reading on, learning spells to lasso Mizik, hexes to place lacing vines whenever an attacker passed through them, and maps and maps and maps of Feerthel. To fit Feerthel's full roadmap of paths into one page would prove to be chaotic, Lexandel admitted. Accordingly, he provided a section of the map on which he focused for the next chapter. Random mini-lessons were thrown in throughout the book, allowing Simon to learn how to deflect a magical attack and redirect it, how to set an instant but weak shield, and how to rapidly juke from side to side. Raelin's absence led to Simon's ability to act like a complete buffoon. He tested Lexandel's attack spells, defense spells, redirecting spells, and every other off-hand trick at making something magical happen in the shack.

After a few successful attempts at the metalling spell, Simon rested on his newly reinforced bed. Freshly forged steel now grasped the posts and weighed it down. He found the lesson on how to use Fyrovine as a marker in Feerthel.

"Find a Mizik spot located deep in Feerthel. Retrieve the leaf, but replace it with a stick of Fyrovine. Step back and cast a levitation spell to keep the Fyrovine suspended roughly twenty feet in the air. Light it, and keep it lit as you take one path (and only one path) to the next Mizik spot. Use this as a way to backtrack to your starting point. When you meander from the Fyrovine's path, remember your steps or set another Fyrovine ablaze."

Simon read on for another hour, finally coming to a mini-lesson on how to brew tea with Fyrovine. The spell perfectly mimicked the technique Vezlin said she learned from Seskith. Lexandel sketched a rough etching of what Fyrovine would look like rolled into a circle four inches in diameter. It was a simple trick, one that could easily be thought up by the simplest of Creatures, but Simon found throughout the rest of Lexandel's lessons that this simplicity involved a great deal of understanding.

Lexandel's mind was that of a painter's. Although Kearlith rarely saw use for paint or art, he used magic as his color scheme to create masterpiece spells rich with the multifaceted arches, curves, hooks, swirls, corners, and angles of a classic artist. He used fire when burns were not the objective; he used water when dry climate was required; he molded matter when dense solidity was the endgame.

He thought with an eye for the unnoticed.

Simon's wincing eyes gave him the sign of the Sonx's departure from the sky. Outside the window, the clouds released a brief good-bye of the rays' light that cut through the bleak streets. It was almost time to meet up with Seskith.

*     *     *

Fire began filling the bowls of the posts lining the roads of Kearlith. As soon as the darkness settled in them, they would spit sparks and ignite as if to fight off cold sleep. Simon glided along the streets of the city, still catching every last glimpse the shadows would give him. Some Creatures cracked their shutters open and bellowed that they were open for business.

Simon soon arrived at Mid-City. In the middle of the marbled plaza that he could barely see from the brewery's window, the streets intersected into a single point – the ebony-black statue lacking a head, resting his hand on the hilt of a sword. As Simon approached, he saw that the plaque had been vandalized. All he could make out was LORD FYRE-. The rest was rubbed out and filled with the odd symbols. This was Lord Fyresk.

But for some reason he was unrecognizable. Maybe it was because of the absent cranium; maybe it was because this man stood with purpose and pride, when the Lord Fyresk he knew hung his shoulders low as if to create less of a shadow.

He was trying to decipher some of the bizarre symbols when he heard, "Hey hero! You got a hot date?" She smirked as she approached.

"What made you change your mind?" he asked. He was smirking, too.

"Well," Seskith's eyes glanced around to the various Mid-City shacks, "you understand Feerthel. I pictured your kind incapable of such an innate knowledge, but you surprised me. Plus, standing up to me always scores points."

"Really? That has never worked in my favor. And I don't know if I really understand Feerthel. Humans from my hometown don't really visit the trees much," he meekly admitted.

"Nothing personal," her full alluring smile returned as she looked back to Simon. Her golden eyes met his. "Your race is not well received here. Clearly we were wrong in your case. You must be the exception." She bit her bottom lip and looked back to the trees. "The point is- you know what you're doing. You came to me for help, and I decided to assist. So let's get started."

This meant dashing off on all fours down the street, forcing the sparse Kearlithians to jump out of the way.

"Follow me," he heard her sing, or probably scream pretty loudly and unladylike, but Simon definitely heard a melody. He bolted off as fast as his Human legs could sprint. Fishhook branch in hand, Simon leapt into mid-air and landed cleanly on the hook.

When he got to the Forest, he split through the trees' entrance like a razorblade. The path seemed fairly straightforward. Seskith was venturing deep into Feerthel. His flow never faltered despite the thick and skinny trees zooming past him. Trust allowed him to take every corner with the full belief of a safe recovery.

Seskith guarded the Mizik leaf in the clearing. This clearing was different- it had a rock gate on the left-hand side. The gate served no purpose since he could easily walk around it through the trees to the other side. There seemed to be no path leading to that direction, though.

"Just as a precaution," she said, "these are the End Marks. These gates mark where you can't go past. Either it's to other parts of the world we don't know about, or to, you know, the Humans. Take it." She gestured to the Mizik.

"Thanks. So these mark the end of Feerthel. Are there paths that go that way?"

"Yes. Only a keen eye can find them; all of them involve a specific path. Most Creatures have to be told where they are. But for you, there are not. Collectors stick to everywhere on this side of these gates. I'm not assuming you're going to run off or anything, I'm just telling you so you can avoid jailtime."

"Thank you, Seskith."

"You're welcome. Nice flying out there. Where did you get the idea?"

"Necessity, I guess. Being lost in Feerthel."

Her smile increased. "Stick to that, Simon. I've heard legends and parables of Humans trying to find other ways to Collect, and they all failed."

"What were their ideas?"

"Bad ones."

"I don't care. I'm just curious."

She hesitated but eventually melted. "They would hex themselves. Make marks on their legs to give them speed, agility, endurance, and brakes. To cast a spell is to simply control the beam of magic from your wand, but to hex is to mark with magic. The object, or in their case- legs, will always respond with the imprinted hex. This makes the object rely on magic to stay alive. Without recharging, the magic and whatever it was living in will die out."

"I'll stay away from that, then. So could I hex the fishhook branch?"

"Of course. Since an object can't really die, the hex can always be recharged."

"But the branch is still alive when I break if off."

"And then it dies. And becomes a lifeless tree branch. Just as your legs would."

"My legs would become tree branches?"

"Yes, Mr. Literal."

"Oh." The shame settled into his mindless curiosity. "How do I hex it?" he asked, attempting to save himself and acquire practical knowledge.

"You'll have to look that one up. It takes practice, and we're here to Collect. So come on." She led him into a path opposite the rock gate, this time at a walking pace.

"Every gate in an End Mark points directly to Kearlith," she continued. "Some of them have a path that points straight to the city."

"So I can use the gate kind of like a compass."

"Quick learner." She turned her head to look at him just as the Mizik burst a couple miles down the path. Simon used the opportunity to impress. He mounted the fishhook branch and whooshed around Seskith. The possibility of clipping a root or catching an untrimmed tree limb increased as his speed picked up, but the thrill of winning over the Shintervah put his inhibitions to bed. He had the lead, but the Mizik leaf was still far in the distance.

Her paws began to drum behind him, rapidly and in rhythmic spurts. His complete focus was on the shining blue leaf. The trees blurred past almost whistling a warning. He was hundreds of yards away now, and her drumming paws were still behind him.

The idea of stopping flashed over him, complete with an ice cold grip on the fishhook branch. To win, he still had to slow to a halt and retrieve.

Without a chance to plan, Simon spun around and let the direction of the magically enhanced branch work against the force of inertia. His calculations were luckily correct, and he jumped off just inches behind the blue treasure.

Seskith was seconds in his wake. She arrived panting with a look of defeat.

"I gave you that one," she tried to say.

"Of course you did. That's why I'm giving it to you. Take it." He smirked, and so did she as she snatched the Mizik out of the ground.

To his relief, Simon recognized the section of Feerthel they were in from Lexandel's lessons. They were about halfway from Kearlith. He tried to imagine the course back, but Seskith was leading him on a path in the opposite direction. Simon identified a nearby Tywyre tightly clasped around a low limb. As Lexandel foreshadowed, the limbs of all the trees were twisted and misshapen. Tywyres were jade, vine-like worms that were known for their ability to relentlessly wind and grip whatever they found. Fortunately, these lethal snake vines only populated a small, southern circle of Feerthel. These trees looked like they were screaming.

"Careful of those," Seskith said as she led him west. "They'll—"

"Attach if I stand still near them, and their grip will probably kill me," he butt in.

She spun her head around just to give him a smile. "So you've been studying, I see." Her eyes found the dark path again. Simon wondered how she could even see the path, but she seemed to move by instinct and not by vision.

"Yeah, I've learned a lot," he said.

"From a book?"

"Yes," he simply answered. The name and author of the book remained in his brain.

"What's that?" She pointed to a gargantuan, violet, jellyfish-like animal descending from the limbs high above. Its countless tentacles dug out a clear path through through the tree limbs. Out of everything Lexandel had taught him so far, these Creatures were anonymous.

"I don't know," he said.

"It's a Flervana. They're very electric, so—"

"Be careful, yeah."

She dropped her jaw to retaliate, but she bit her bottom lip instead. She continued with a smile. "They were raised in the Axolotl Lake but were bred to breathe oxygen. When the Preeminents released them into trees, that's the last time they had control of them. They lived and populated in the treetops around here. The Flervana are known for their ability to kill at will. In their eyes they show us mercy as long as we don't steal the Mizik they're eyeing."

The tentacles of the Creature swam down through the thick treetops slowly and effortlessly. It did, in fact, appear to be on a straight line landing on the Mizik spot at the end of the path. The spot and their path exploded with blue light. The Flervana remained at the same speed.

"The winner gets the next five Mizik leaves," she said, halting and spinning. Her smile was unfair. Simon was forced to take the dare.

"Okay," he said. She pulled out of her backpack an inch-sized street rock and threw it in the path in front of them. They stared for seconds before it popped.

Both of them were off. Simon was now in a race with Seskith and an electric death. The grip on the fishhook branch tore the color from his knuckles. Her quick lead swiftly dwindled as Simon grew more accustomed to the map of Feerthel. The Markers were passing in flashes, marking the rhythm of his heartbeat more than his route. The Flervana noted the couple's race and swam faster through the leaves. Simon was inches away from Seskith's heels. Pulling a trick out of the book, he aimed his wand at a Marker about halfway to the beaming Mizik. He shouted "Zapatta!", and as practiced, a lime green vine shot out of the end, vaulting Simon to the midpoint Marker. Full concentration prevented him from a gloating glance back at Seskith.

His eyes focused on the illuminated treasure hundreds of feet ahead. The Flervana loomed dangerously low, but his wits wouldn't quit. In a desperate attempt to win, he tipped the fishhook branch almost parallel to the ground. He could probably catch a bullet at these speeds, he thought. A tentacle lunged out toward the leaf, but Simon held tight. He was yards away before...

The blinding blue light quickly faded, and the world went black.

*     *     *

"It's taken me years to realize that Creatures really only care about themselves. They develop friendships, but when they're faced with losing themselves, they always fold. Friendships are just ways to use each other. Camaraderie is a con." Seskith led him on a path located dead north of Kearlith. They had traveled through half of the circle around the trees of Feerthel. The trail had been long, zig-zagged, disconcerting, and frankly impossible if he didn't have his fishhook branch. He was still suffering from a decent amount of pain.

Simon now fashioned a few vicious flesh wounds. The Flervana's tentacles first slapped him off his fishhook branch, and then grasped his entire left leg. Then it tossed him into the treetops, pulsing him with paralyzing jolts of electricity.

Seskith filled him in on the story as they made the long trek around Feerthel. His fingertips lightly touched his new scars – a gnarly smile gashed just below his rib cage on his right side; several thin stripes sliced the left side of his face, barely missing his eye; and a swirling line of blistered skin surrounded the entirety of his left leg, making evidence of the Flervanas' tentacles' controlled power. Seskith fortunately prepared herself for a little first-aid for this lesson, but she had to break out her wand and perform some quick mini-miracles. She managed to revive him, and they continued to Collect. Seskith's handy work had a catch, she said. He was now a hexed man. He was to charge his scars every day or else the saved skin would die off and become permanently dead.

"You think there's no escaping ego?" he asked.

"I think it's theoretically possible. Maybe where you came from. But in Kearlith it's every Creature for himself."

"Especially if you're Human. Then that rule increases tenfold."

"You need to give Fyresk a break. He's a mysterious man I'll admit, but not dishonest. And he's never given me any reason to identify him as egotistical." Either she was blatantly blind or omnisciently intelligent.

"He originally taxed me with eighty."

"Ouch," she said. "But he knocked it down to thirty-five, right?"

"Yeah. He was just mad that I ventured past the trees of Feerthel. I didn't mean to. It wasn't even my fault. I was..." Simon trailed off. Again, the secret of the whispers couldn't escape him. "... just curious."

"And ill-informed."

"Exactly. Now that I know to stay inside the trees, I won't try it again. I don't really want to talk to any Protector or Lord Fyresk again anyway."

"You stick to that and all other general do-goodery, and you'll see Fy in a different light."

"He showed me the Axolotl Lake."

"Isn't it gorgeous?"

"Yes. It was like a visual insult to Kearlith."

"Well, you don't want to be anywhere near the Axolotls. They're—"

"Dangerous. Yeah, I know. And I'll keep my curiosity in check. But still."

"It's gorgeous," Seskith sighed.

"How have you seen it? Fyresk said only Protectors and Enforcers could leave the trees of Feerthel."

"That's true, but my father has a good relationship with the Enforcers, granting me little special privileges."

"Sounds like conned camaraderie, if you ask me." Simon looked to Seskith, expecting her smirk and a witty retort, but Seskith had no chance to comment.

A deafening screech singed the airwaves. Furious pounding followed. Simon instinctively halted, and Seskith crouched to a pounce position. The two were transfixed for seconds before Seskith bolted off. Simon followed without the slightest hesitation.

She halted at an empty Mizik spot, drastically larger than most and with several more paths; her eyes gazed the area to determine the path from which this monster would reveal itself. Although the owner of the terrible tumult hid behind the dense trees, Simon pictured a beast with 8,000 fangs, ten paws, and X-ray vision. It released its auditory terrorism once more, and Seskith dropped to her defensive position locking her eyes on a path.

Paws still pounding, a startling Gulverbruud emerged from the opposite side of the circle.

"Step back!" he roared.

"Sounds like a Rog," Seskith said.

"Indeed. Two. I've been tracking them. I may need your help, Seskith."

She closed her eyes and clapped her hands together. They

sank into a deep violet as she mumbled incoherent syllables. The Gulverbruud tipped his staff towards the path's entrance. Feeling foolish, Simon unsheathed his white wand from the pocket in his jeans and circled the air.

Silent anxiety synced the three in defensive harmony. Within seconds, two fuming Red River boars dashed into the Mizik circle, met with an explosion of colors. After the initial spells died off, Simon noted the bold redness of the boars' skin; their long, wispy ears attempting to grasp the limbs of the Kearlithians; their huge, snarling black and white faces. They lacked the thousands of fangs and paws, but their true image was comparatively petrifying.

One of them charged the anonymous Gulverbruud and sank its teeth into the rock-solid skin underneath the mat of thick fur. The buffalo-man took the opportunity to smash its face in with a strong fist. The Creature was knocked back but continued to blindly bite the air with a fury. He narrowly missed Simon, who somehow succeeded in producing yellow sparks from his wand. The sparks landed on the beast erupting another deafening outcry.

Before his triumphant smile could form, Simon realized he had just revealed his location. Sure enough, the Rog then charged. Simon shook, flicked, and waved his wand without another successful spell. The Rog tackled him to the ground but soon vaulted backwards as Seskith lassoed him. She placed her hand on his snout and shouted "Craesoffe!" The beast's head detonated.

The Gulverbruud managed to distract the other Rog, but he was taking damage. Seskith circled her hands to build up another spell. She was too focused to see the Gulverbruud kick the Rog back, punch him to the ground, raise his staff high above his head, and let loose his full force. The beast burst like his brethren.

"Curse Crysis! I hate it when they fight." The Gulverbruud took a knee and wiped his face of the Rog's skin and blood. "My wife demands a clean steak."

"Watch your language around this one," Seskith said, but there was no need. Simon had no idea what it meant.

"Forgive me," the Gulverbruud started but immediately stopped once he realized whom he had just saved. "Simon," he concluded as his face melted to a scowl.

"Thank you. Both of you. I can't even --" Simon failed his attempts at illustrating his gratitude. He meekly smiled at the seething buffalo-man and bowed nervously.

"Happy Collecting," the Gulverbruud barked through gritted teeth. He huffed and found his exit through a path in the Forest.

"Seriously, Seskith, thank you," Simon repeated as he sighed.

"You owe me," she said with her smirk.

"I know," Simon said. And he did know. He knew that he owed her his life, and he was willing to put his life on the line in return.

# Chapter 14

"So why do you want to be a Collector?" Seskith asked as she led Simon on a path toward the city.

"I don't know. I guess it makes me feel like I contribute." He felt that if he brought up how fun it was to jump off stuff, he might appear a bit childish. "Like the city has to depend on me, even if it's for a fraction of a whole."

"Those words are truer than you know, Simon. Do you think you can handle that?"

"I hope I can. There really seems to be no other options left. I'll never fit in with the Gulverbutts." Seskith couldn't keep the giggle trapped in her throat. "I don't really have what it takes to be an Enforcer, and I don't think I'd make the best owl. Collecting seems to be the only thing I may possibly be good at."

"Well you know you have the freedom to choose. You could be anything you want in Kearlith." Simon would have instantly attacked since he knew the truth of her desired profession, but her hostility in the "you's" of her words gave Simon enough reason to try a different angle.

"Do you want to be a Collector?" Simon emphasized his "you" as well.

"Of course. I'm great at it. It's easy. It's fun if you can make games out of Feerthel." Simon's heart slightly siphoned. "I want to do it. It will be a great…" she reluctantly finished, "… calling."

"What do you really want to do?" Instead of responding, she knelt down and pocketed a Fyrovine.

"I want to be an Enforcer," she announced finally.

"Then be one."

Seskith unleashed an exaggerated laugh. "It doesn't work like that."

"Why can't it? Look, back home—" the Shintervah whirled around with a very stern face, swinging her dreadlocks in a wave. The rapid transformation was unsettling.

"Kearlith is your home now. Simon, none of the Creatures here know anything about where you're from, and the same amount of Creatures don't want to. You live here. And this is the way it works here. The Kyejoth are the Enforcers."

"And the Gulverbutts," he added. She didn't laugh this time. "Seskith," he continued, "I'm not trying to change the city or force my Human ways upon you. I'm just saying you could be a damn good Enforcer."

"Kearlith doesn't work like that, Simon. The Shintervah are Collectors. We always have been. It's what we were made for," she sighed.

"If Vezlin can be a Collector –"

"I'm no Vezlin."

"Yet. Vezlin has some years on you. Think of where she was when she was your age, and think of where you'll be when you're her age. Then, tell me you couldn't Enforce this city just as well as she did." With that, the pair moved in pure, unbreakable silence until they reached the outer city streets of Kearlith.

Several blocks away, the chatter and laughing of Kearlith could be heard. The hustle and bustle of the nocturnal town invited Simon to stay awake, but his body ached for rest. Although the fishhook branch received the bulk of his travel, his limbs were still verging on immobility.

"Pretty soon, fifty Mizik leaves will be an easy task. Then Fy will raise it so that you can get more money. But you did well for your second day." Simon grabbed the middle of the branch with his free hand and jumped off to endure the painstaking tempo of steps. The relaxing strides were intertwined with fierce flashes of fire down his entire left leg. Seskith admired strength, though.

"Thanks. And thank you for saving my life and all that. Twice." Simon quickly assisted her side. He enjoyed the ability to actually look at her when she spoke instead of at the knotted and beaded dreadlocks draped down her back.

"Don't thank me. I started it the first time. You would have done the same for me, right?"

"Of course!" Simon bashfully recovered from his rapid response. "If I knew anything about magic I could have saved myself."

"Your knowledge is growing, Si. How else could you have Collected fifty Mizik leaves?"

"But still. In the heat of a battle I'd like to be prepared."

"You don't have to worry about a battle." Seskith turned towards the bank once they reached its street beside Mid-City. "Fyresk and the Board keep things safe around here."

"The Board?" Simon asked.

"Each race has a representative that is called upon for city meetings. To determine laws and the like."

"I thought the Intellects were the law around here."

"They like to think so," Seskith spat. "But anything you think Fyresk might be up to would be known and accepted by the Board. So keep your nose out of their business. You Collect, and they'll Enforce and Protect."

"Got it." Simon was so very sick of this message no matter what form it took.

"All the same, Feerthel does require a certain amount of self-defense. The Rogs were a good example of that. Maybe when you're not with Vezlin and I'm not at the brewery, I'll teach you a few things."

"That would be fantastic. I want to know all I can about this place."

"You're not alone. Not a soul has existed that knows every detail of Feerthel. Many have tried but... failed in the process."

"Not even the Intellects can hold that much information?"

"The immense amount of information is the smaller issue. Acquiring it is the killer." They neared the bank. For the first time, he could not wait to bid his good-bye to Seskith. It meant he was one step closer to falling fast asleep. Possibly for days.

Chrysaetos mentioned how pleasant it was to see them both and managed to redden Simon with compliments of resilience. Two Collections in one day were rare apparently. Simon mumbled his way through the small talk and gathered his earnings. One step closer. He and the Shintervah awkwardly halted outside the threshold of the bank.

"Thank you again for... well, everything," he said.

"And again, you owe me," she retaliated with her smirk. "Kearlith could use a Collector like you, Si. You're clearly devoted to us, and you're resourceful. With magic, you could become very successful here. I'd like to see that happen."

"Where's my warning?"

"The dangers of gaining success and," her grin widened, "ego... should be obvious. But there's no warning here, Simon." Seskith playfully thumbed a wooden bead in a dreadlocked bang. "I'm saying I see a great future for you in Kearlith."

"I hope I don't disappoint. I had a habit of doing that back home."

Seskith huffed and rolled her eyes. "The Outside isn't your home anymore, Simon. You're a Kearlithian now."

*       *       *

Slow pins of pressure impressed the feet, calves, thighs, waist, and finally chest of Simon's unconscious body. Though his awareness of them was distant, his attention became alarmingly acute. He observed the flowers as they began sprouting from the pinpoints and plucking themselves out. Irises, daisies, marigolds, lilies, tulips, daffodils. He begged his body to move, to stop the flowers from sprouting, but his limbs failed to respond. Simon could only lie back and observe the colorful floral fireworks. Once the trail of bouquets reached his shoulders, it ceased.

Incessant tapping on his right temple brought his

consciousness swimming back to life, gasping for reality. His awakened eyes scanned the blossomless bed. Then the quiet room of his shack. All was still. The flowers were just a dream. But the tapping was very real.

Although Raelin had already retired by the time Simon returned from Collecting with Seskith, the cushioned seat was vacant. The rest of the room remained motionless. Thieves work best at night, Simon thought. Breathlessly reassuring himself with one final scan of the room, undetected danger allowed Simon to slip back into sleep.

Not five minutes after the ordeal, the tapping returned. This time he snapped awake. But the room remained empty. As did his bed. He saw nothing to disrupt his slumber.

A stifled titter sounded to the right of Simon's chest, and he noticed two shallow indentions in the Mizik blanket. The air above the indentions rippled as Raelin materialized, removing a delicate chain around his neck. Wendy Whisp's locket was the pendant.

"I truly tried," Raelin attempted, "to keep quiet. But your face—" The laughter consumed him once more. He made several attempts to reenact Simon's reaction, but he broke into fits halfway through.

Although he was profoundly annoyed at the disturbance of his sleep and the exaggerated ridicule, curiosity got the best of Simon. "How did you do that?" he asked.

"I found the chain," Raelin beamed. "This locket stores thousands of magical trinkets, although most are fake decoys. Wendy Whisp found a way to gain invisibility by linking the chain to the pendant. Knowing this power was too much for most Creatures, she hid the chain in the vast storage space of enchanted garbage."

"Hence why you were so proud to steal it."

"That, and the fact that the mission was mostly impossible. I had to…" Raelin cut himself short. "Work my own magic."

"Any chance you'll part with it?"

"Do you sincerely want that answer?"

"No. But it was worth a shot," he sighed.

"Maybe if the situation calls for it," Raelin responded. Simon shook his head and returned to his slumber.

*       *       *

Simon finally awoke the next day in a state of comfort. He could sleep in since he had no pressing responsibilities. If Raelin was here, he was wearing Wendy Whisp's locket. He tried to silence the questions of how he obtained it. Or how Wendy crafted it. As soon as he forced his eyes closed, they would pop open at the thought of another mystery. He decided to compromise and continue reading *A Shintervah's Secrets Revealed*.

In the second half of the book, even Lexandel himself admitted the contents of the mini-lessons were for mature minds only. Modest few could manage some of the spells, hexes, objects, locations, and other secrets created or discovered by this Creature. Simon assumed he was just fulfilling some kind of legal treaty with whoever published the book, seeing as so far it featured several things only mature eyes should see. He learned the warning was painstakingly essential.

Lexandel's halfway mark was the Protection spell. Four complete three-sixties with a wand flipped backwards while chanting this disjointed collection of syllables created a cloak that would cover and cling to the caster. This cloak weathered against blades, heat, frost, and fists. The catch was correctly chanting the spell. The accuracy and steady speed of the four three-sixties determined the strength and longevity of the cloak, but if one letter of the spell was mispronounced, the cloak turned to eternal stone and continued the process. If the Creature were witty, they could counter this mishap. The Privileged, Lexandel made a specific note explaining, would instantly die with failure.

Simon quickly flipped to the next lessons.

The Axolotls were found within ten pages of the Protection spell. Fyresk was right to warn him; they held a vicious reputation. Aside from perfecting the art of herbs and potions, they compensated for their size by spitting poison and lava at their opponents. Simon shuddered as he kept flipping through the pages.

More areas were discovered; none lacking lethal attributes.

He made a specific reminder to steer clear of the Southeast. In dangerously close proximity to Chirth Stone lived a species of cursed Black-Footed Cats. These adorably small kittens hosted an intensely hostile attitude to recompense for their height at just above eight inches once matured. If their eyes met yours, they possessed your full attention. Even the worst aiurophobic would melt in their presence. They used this to draw victims in with their mastered technique of allure. Once within slashing distance, the Creatures would pounce and most assuredly claim victory.

The naiad cats inhabited a circumference of about one hundred feet just east of Chirth Stone. They burrowed nests in the roots of the trees thereby hiding any signs of their territory. Consequently, the Intellects demanded that the trees surrounding their homes be marked with golden yellow skin. The bark remained the usual brown, but when caught in the right light, the golden skin would glint, warning anyone who approached of the surrounding threat. These trees were added to an ongoing list of places Simon would be on the lookout for.

Earlier in the book, before he began filling Simon's mind with imminent nightmares, Lexandel wrote a lengthy history of the man named Crysis. Simon had skimmed through before, but he now decided to revisit the article. Mainly because at the end of it, there was an expertly sketched blueprint of the Scythe of Crysis.

One of the first direct descendants of the Preeminents, Crysis was the younger brother of Jystik, the next heir to the throne, and Kyo, the first of the Kyejoth race. Their parents frequently had more problems with "covetous Crysis". They feared he would at some point use extreme means to gain the throne, thus they banned him from the castle at the early age of fifteen. His hatred of them burned and boiled. Revenge was naturally impending, but he would have to throw the royal family off guard with years of patience.

While leisurely building up a strong and secret assemblage, Crysis spent his extensive free time perfecting hexes to augment his weapon of choice- the Scythe. The final product of thick black steel could pierce stone just as easily as paper. As an indication of its depravity, the blade was consistently ice cold. The same effect of licking a metal pole in dry snow. To further improve this effect, he etched a hex of magnetism. To everything. He could deliver everything or one single thing in the room right in front of him as if he were a giant magnet and objects were scraps of metal.

Hundreds of hexes filled the inches of this six-foot Scythe. Crysis could attack, defend himself, light a room, morph matter, translate inscriptions, build temporary bridges, and perform numerous complex spells with heavily increased ease.

The climax and conclusion of the story were skimmed again. Simon had to find this Scythe. More about his trusted minions. Something about an attack during which Crysis loses the Scythe. Then a brief history of the possessors of the Scythe. In the last paragraph, Lexandel admitted to finding the buried Scythe and relocating it out of respect for other adventurers. He bid his hopes of good fortune to Simon.

*       *       *

*A Shintervah's Secrets Revealed* hardly plopped onto the Mizik blanket before Simon was out the door. He knew he had to get some Mizik and pay his daily Dillian to Mathilda before adventuring. Mathilda was closer, he thought.

He briskly found her shop and paused at the closed door. Knock? There was a doorknob. No emblem to ignite. He knocked.

"Come in," she soothed. "Ah! Simon, you're early," she said as he entered. She flipped through a few scraps of leather before retrieving his vest. "Let's see how it fits," she said as she crossed to him.

"I have a question," he said sheepishly. His idiocy signal was thriving, but he had to ask, "Do you know anything about the Scythe of Crysis?"

Her hand was in motion to pass the vest to Simon's awaiting hand, but she froze. She stared into his eyes for several seconds before time began to pick up again.

"I know of the Scythe. Why do you wish to?"

"Because it's awesome!" he declared as he accepted the vest. "And you said I needed a weapon."

"I could fashion you a hold for a scythe. Although I cannot

accept to create anything that assists a terror weapon of that caliber."

"I probably won't even find it. Do you know where it is?"

"I know where it's been. But no, I am not aware of its location currently. Hopefully it will die there." She slowly became the gentle Mathilda once more, although a hint of disgust lingered from her frozen state.

"The vest fits perfectly," he said in hopes of ripping the tension in the room.

"Thank you," she sincerely hummed. "Will it be a scythe clip on the back, then?"

"Yeah," he said. "I'll be riding a scythe whether I find this one or not."

"Riding a scythe?"

"Like the fishhook branches. I break them off the trees and enchant them to fly. But with this, I could ride along the back of the blade and keep hold on the handle."

Her pensive gaze lasted for quite a while, but it concluded in a smirk. Finally, she said, "A scythe clip it is."

"Thank you. Here's your Dillian."

"Thank you, Si. Tomorrow you'll have a spot for a scythe. I beg mercy you don't have one by then. At least not the one mended by that monster." Simon returned the vest and exited Mathilda's shop.

He strolled along the streets looking for any stores that would provide Mizik. After he passed the training gym, the hardware store, and a window filled with shields, Simon found the sign proudly displaying a beaker of potion.

"You must be Simon," said a smooth voice as soon as he passed the threshold. A smiling man stood behind the counter with both hands resting on top. He was a Kyejoth that looked to be about six or seven years his senior. The man's chin-length, espresso brown hair swayed in the windless shack. Countless mason jars, vials, beakers, and glasses lined the wall behind the counter from floor to the tall ceiling. A reading nook was tucked under the front window. Next to a mauve leather chair stood a sleek, cedar bookshelf packed with books. Some looked to be centuries old. Simon stood in the doorway struck dumb with awe.

"I am," was all he could say.

"I'm Thrax. You mustn't fear. I happen to be pro-Human, but regardless of that fact- you mustn't fear."

"I'm not afraid of you!" Simon retorted.

"I did not say you were, but you reek of fear." Though the words were harsh, this Kyejoth calmed the tone.

"I…" Simon began. He couldn't place his next words. "I'm afraid the people here hate Humans and therefore me," spilled out. "I'm used to being hated for no good reason. I thought things would be different here."

"Creatures," Thrax corrected with heavy emphasis, "respect people. Darkness, fear," his eyebrows rose and fell, "exists in everyone. Man or Creature. Humans are simply more prone to hide in that darkness."

"That's a lie," Simon stated with almost intended hostility.

"Believe what you will. But to a Creature, Humans are the weaker race," the Creature cooed as if this were a fact and not a radical opinion.

"And to a Human—" he stopped. He couldn't claim the reverse of that statement. "I need some Mizik. Will the Creature help the Human find something he can use?"

"The Creature will." Thrax arose from his stool and scanned the hundreds of vials behind him.

A deep breath allowed Simon to take in the situation anew. Thrax was merely discussing ideas, albeit radical ones. His attention was genuine and his opinions grounded. Simon was the one feeding from the darkness and allowing his anger to surface. The Kyejoth met a cooler Human on his return to the counter.

"This vial will give a good week of magic. Two sips a day."

"How much? I'm still kind of poor."

Thrax smiled. "We all are; I took that into account. It's two Dillian."

The Duzuks weakly clapped at the loss of their silver brothers.

"Thank you," he said.

"Remember my words. You mustn't fear."

"I will." Simon half-smiled and exited. He sipped the tiny

bottle. A sip was all that was needed; the power flashed through him again. He eyed the trees to see his best entrance into Feerthel.

Of course he couldn't find a possibly buried scythe by searching every inch of the Forest, but it had to be unearthed somehow. Maybe he could search through Lexandel's favorite areas. Or the most dangerous. Although some of those were happily unbeknownst to him. He decided to try the favorites first. A northern location slightly veering west was home to chameleon squirrels named the Tobbly. They would be a safe target.

# Chapter 15

The Tobbly were described as playful Creatures. They kept a keen sense of humor and were fond of physical banter. Complete control of their skin pattern allowed them to both hide themselves in any terrain and boast about their abilities with loud and dashing colors. They preferred the latter. As Simon slowed his approach to hide in the surrounding trees, he saw gold ones, polka dotted ones, metal-and-bolt ones, sparkling ones, and hairy ones.

All of them seemed uproariously involved in a severe game of tag. Instead of one leader, seven or eight chased around the dozens of others. One lunged from the tall lower branches, crashing into another on the ground, and they both rolled a few yards. They recovered from the fall, but not from their inexorable snickering. One with silver fur landed on the ground and proudly sauntered over to one disguised as a rock, facing the other direction. The tiny little Creature didn't prepare before his fist left his side, and he bashed the unsuspecting rock roughly ten feet into the clearing. Once the disguised Tobbly arose, he did not return to his original spot with a look of deceit; he was in a fit of squeaky hilarity. It was, as the victim Tobbly put it, "a really good one". He tried to tag his opponent back, but she jumped back just out of reach. Their laughter was infectious.

Until Simon stepped foot into the clearing. Then their

manner was infected. The atmosphere was poisoned by an instant awareness of him. Every eye was on Simon. The previously cheery Tobbly were now sinisterly staring at him, some approaching with a slow and droning crawl. Their skin became a collective crimson pouring the spot with what looked to be blood in the low light. As he began to inch backward, a few lunged and sprinted in pursuit. Simon had to run. With a gimp leg and a nagging right side.

Limbs laughed from high above. None seemed even remotely obtainable here. He kept sprinting. The leading Tobbly were swiftly gaining distance; at this point they were barking at him. Shrill little barks, but they were profoundly ferocious given their size.

His leg seared with pain. Every other swift step was like jamming thousands of nails into every cell. He looked back. They were feet away. He tried choking out, "Creatures' peace?!" but the barkers began giddily laughing.

Rapidly, he remembered the trick he had used earlier to cling to the tree limb in the race with Seskith and the Flervana. His scorching leg pleaded to be free of excess steps. With a painful complaint from his torso, Simon thrust his wand at a designated angle and shouted, "Zapatta!" The green vine shot straight into the air and fell just inches from reaching the branches. Sadly landing amongst the grass, the green vine vanished. Simons gasped through a sandpaper-dry throat

He didn't need to turn around. Their barks and intermittent hilarity gave away their position inches from his heels. A strong sense of desperation purified another bolder "Zapatta!"

This time the trick worked. Simon was launched towards his anticipated tree. Upon landing, he quickly scanned his surroundings.

As expected, the Tobbly began effortlessly traveling through the trees. They quickly ascended to his level. They hopped and leapt across the branches; their mirthful barks and hilarity increased to sporadic insanity.

Simon stood still out of spite and cast another lasso of the anti-gravity blue rope. Seconds before the Tobbly attacked, he heaved forward and snatched a lucky shot off of a neighboring tree. Falling encumbered his judgment, but he successfully fought off gravity with a few feet to spare. The new fishhook branch shot out of sight of the wicked Tobbly. He could hear their mirth morph back into roars.

His scars still burned. Although his right leg now supported most of his physical exhaustion keeping balance on the branch, the Flervana's marks felt scorched. Even his face singed. Every pulse of blood brought a new wave of pain. This ache was in excess of overexertion; he had played soccer as a kid and knew how to run out of breath. Those hard learned lessons were nothing to this recovery.

Slapping his face didn't help, but Simon realized he hadn't charged his scars today. They were probably dying. He traced them just as Seskith had taught him, repeating the spell over and over. The pains immediately subsided, and Simon comfortably eased through the trees of Feerthel. The other areas of interest were a moderate distance away, so he dazed through the trees studying every knot, root, and vine. The rest of the random Creatures Simon discovered did not institute a stampede of assassins, but he had remained hidden for the most part so he was less impressed. He had lost count of how many new environments and Creatures he found.

*    *    *

Simon Collected seven Mizik leaves over the next few hours while he met plenty of new mysteries. He wasn't on the job, but their convenience egged him on. Not long after Simon felt the anxiety of being lost would he eye something that put him back on track. He traveled a wiggly east; Lexandel showed an unusual admiration with the areas out there. Simon was on a bare trail when he pocketed the seventh leaf.

Far off in a path adjacent to the one from which he just travelled down, he saw something blocking the trail. The fishhook branch crept down the path, and Simon unsheathed his wand. The Creature did not appear to be threatened by his approach. As he crept closer, he could tell it had its back turned. Its horns were stony black, straightened S-shapes with a slight hook sitting back on a long curve. It was a Vanterslove with a backpack that had armrests and a device sticking out of its open pocket, extending far into the treetops. Its ears twitched as Simon drew near.

"Hey," he said as Simon tensed in defense.

"Oh, hi. Sorry if I scared you creeping up like that."

"I didn't see you, so you were no threat. I still don't see you, and you don't sound like a threat. So no worries." The gazelle's distracted tenor and smaller size suggested adolescence.

"I'm Simon," he said.

"I figured. I'm Dagrio."

"Do you care that I'm a Human?" Simon was sick of the games. His bluntness was a result of a hunt for substance.

"Nah," Dagrio said. "If you wanted to take over, you'd be doing that. And you're Collecting. So all you're doing is feeding Fyresk."

"You're a smart kid."

"I'm sixteen!" Dagrio blurted, finally turning himself to face Simon. A patch of brown fur on his snout offset the surrounding white with a bold stripe bordering it down to his chest. His face emanated innocence. Shadows were marked under his eyes and extended down close to his nostrils.

"I'm eighteen. Don't you hate that word?"

"Yes!" Dagrio agreed. "All the Creatures in Kearlith call me that. Even the kids. And the adults think they can't give me anything to handle. So I have to walk around Feerthel all day and weave the treetops to cover the spots of Mizik."

"What good does that do?" Simon asked.

"The Sonxlight shining on it is supposed to energize the magic in the soil, so it makes it harder to grow the Mizik."

"Because there won't be much of a build up of magic once it's energized. It could easily escape the traps in the roots."

"Smart kid," Dagrio repeated. Simon tried to glare menacingly, but he laughed instead.

"Is that why you have a telescopic backpack?"

"Yeah." He started reeling it down." There's a hand on the end of it that grabs the branches for me. With these," he pointed to the joysticks on the armrests, "I can control all of the arms' movements."

"That's pretty awesome," Simon admitted.

"I guess. So I've explained what I'm doing out here. What's

your excuse?"

"I'm Collecting," he said perplexed. He thought they had already established what he was doing.

"Not out here. Come on." Dagrio started on a way he knew was straight to Kearlith. With a sigh and a heave, he followed. "How long have you been at this?"

"I don't know. Three, four. Maybe two hours," he said.

"Are you hungry?" Dagrio asked.

"I'm starving."

"Well look, I have to come clean. I know about you, Simon. My dad is Roibose, the guy you met in the brewery yesterday. And he has not shut up about you. I'm sure my parents would love to have you over for lunch."

"Wow, thank you. That would be great."

"Who knows? Maybe they'll start to think I can do something." Simon didn't need to see Dagrio's face to envision it. He knew exactly what that face looked like.

"They will, Dagrio. I promise, this world is about to change. And you'll be a part of it."

"You speak like you know secrets," he said.

"I don't. But I want to. Do you know about the Scythe of Crysis?" Simon was begging to find a hint of its location at this point. The Vanterslove did not respond. They kept walking, but half a minute passed before Dagrio finally said, "Yeah. Anyone who knows any history of Kearlith knows about Crysis and his Scythe."

"It sounds like a great treasure."

"It's not," Dagrio snapped. "It's a treasure, but it's far from great. Do you know who Crysis was?"

"Yeah, he was some whiney Human who was jealous of his big brothers. He wanted the throne, and he didn't get it. But I want the Scythe!"

A long sigh preceded, "Crysis wanted to enslave the Creatures, Simon. He felt the Creatures needed to be controlled and... limited in population. He wanted the throne because he viewed Humans as the stronger race."

Half-jesting, Simon tried, "And of course, Humans are the weaker race."

"Ha, right," Dagrio flatly retorted. "Fyresk is no man to cross."

"So you like him, too?"

"I think he's no man to cross. He's been Lord for most of his life – over thirty years now; he has to have plenty of tricks up his sleeve. He's far from weak."

"I don't trust him," Simon admitted.

"I'm still deciding. He could easily pass for a virtuous saint or a patient demon."

"I can't picture him being a saint."

"That's because you're not the Lord of Kearlith and Feerthel. Or anywhere near his position. And you never saw him before the attack. I mean, he's no King Kowlakro, but the possibility of his sainthood remains indefinite."

"True," was all Simon could spit out. "I'll keep the Scythe buried." Just as he would the questions about King Kowlakro.

"Thanks," the Vanterslove said. Simon was struck with the memory of Mathilda's shop. Her reaction bothered him. She seemed terrified of this one mystery of Kearlith. Her race was built for the dangers of the Forest, but this one story haunted her. Because that look haunted him.

"I don't want to kill any Creatures, Dagrio. Ever. I hope I never have to."

"I believe you, Si. I do. But do you really want to Collect? You have the ability to be anything you want, and you choose to run around all day?"

As if trying to put a verbal puzzle together, he said, "It makes you need me."

"How?" Dagrio asked.

"In a small way. Everyone contributes here. But because of what Collectors do, the supply of magic can be increased or decreased. And I want to make Kearlith prosper."

"And knock off plenty for yourself on the side?" Dagrio accused.

"Not really, no. I can't stand the taste. I'll stick to buying cooked and brewed Mizik."

"You're either a really great liar, or a blessing to the

Collecting team."

Simon laughed. "Definitely the latter, Dagrio. I hope."

\*        \*        \*

"You know, I could craft you a scythe," Dagrio said a little farther down the path.

"You could?" Simon asked, attempting and failing to conceal his excitement.

"Sure. It probably won't be able to enslave Creatures, but—"

"I don't want it to. I want to protect myself. And ride the blade."

Dagrio spun his head to sneak a peek at the fishhook branch. "Wow, you really are a smart kid," he said as he looked back towards the path ahead.

The two traveled the distance to Kearlith within the hour, chatting about different mechanisms Dagrio had thought up to help around the house. His inventions astounded Simon. He had a Lexandel-like brain. A scythe created by this genius would crush Crysis. Simon felt the bond of a very valuable friendship building.

The Vanterslove's homes were gorgeous. Their profession in various styles of architecture was illustrated by their skyline decks with lower floors of houses underneath. Some of them peaked at just under the tallest trees. The more elegantly designed homes were the ones fashioning decks. The rest possessed their own collection of architectural wonders- bold, looming columns; intricate, gigantic gazebos; floral archways; delicately detailed trim clinging under rooftops.

Dagrio's house had an immaculate yard sampling one of everything.

"So let me be clear," Dagrio said as he slowed his pace. "You *really* impressed my dad yesterday. Don't be alarmed by his over gratification."

"Um, don't worry about it. I didn't think I was doing anything that great."

"Honestly, me neither, but my dad seems to think otherwise," Dagrio confessed as they approached the front steps. He opened the door using a wooden doorknob with an imprint of a gazelle's hoof set inside.

"Mom? Dad? Kellabane? Soiko? Bentavi? Is anyone home?" He received no answer. "I never know where they all are."

"Are those your brothers and sisters?"

"My sisters, yeah. They're probably working. My little brother is still out training right now." Down the hall a booming voice could be heard outraged at an unknown source. "Sorry, don't mind them," Dagrio mumbled once he realized the rumble belonged to Roibose. "My dad's always stressed with work. They're not fighting or anything."

"I didn't think they were. Kearlith is facing hard times for everyone."

"Too true," Dagrio said. "Mom! Dad!"

Roibose and his lovely wife emerged from the back as if the preceding argument were a quiet conversation over tea. His mom, introduced as Alencia, was politely verging on overindulgence, but Simon didn't mind the overexerted attention. Alencia fashioned a pearly white front half; she too had the long line-shadows under her eyes.

"You seem like a hungry boy," she said. Simon had to fight the pang of anger that shot up his spine. "Dagrio is always complaining of an empty tummy, but you look like you need it."

"Are you saying I'm fat?" Dagrio asked in resistance.

"No, I'm saying Simon's bone skinny," Alencia declared as if the statement were the mentioning of his hair color.

"I just have high metabolism," he said. "My body burns food faster so it doesn't build up fat and make me bigger," he continued so that he cleared the gazelles' quizzical looks. Simon swore he heard Alencia mumble "Must be one of those Human things..." but he couldn't be sure.

"Sounds like a body fit for a Collector," said Roibose. "Although Kearlith could never have too many Builders."

"I heard the field is getting crowded," he said.

"Oh, Voxus droppings. Don't let Shalice get to you."

"Nah, I'll stick to Collecting. I like riding the branches."

"Terribly understandable, my boy." Out of his peripheral

vision, Simon looked for and sadly glimpsed a slight wince from Dagrio. He wondered if that term had ever applied to the Vanterslove prodigy.

Simon addressed Alencia, "Not to press, but," to change the subject rather, "you mentioned lunch?"

"Yes, yes! I was just finishing up. Have a seat at the table, dear. Looks like it'll just be us four. The girls are working- as usual," a weighty pause followed as her eyes found Dagrio, "and your brother is –"

"Still training. Yeah, I know," Dagrio finished. "What's for lunch?"

"You know his review is coming up," Roibose butt in, completely ignoring Dagrio's attempt to change the conversation.

"Yes, Dad. A week from tomorrow. And he has to design and build THREE DIFFERENT BUILDINGS." Dagrio's eyes widened; his jaw dropped to finish the effect of true astonishment.

Simon again decided to step in and save the conversation, "So Alencia, what's for lunch?"

Fortunately, she understood the situation completely. "Voxus stew and Guaraberry salad. Come on, let's have a seat at the table."

*       *       *

"Your parents are really nice," Simon admitted a few paces down the path after he and Dagrio said their good-byes to his parents. Dagrio had agreed during lunch that they would continue the adventure afterward. Scythe of Crysis or no, Simon would not return to his shack empty handed. Dagrio said that an adventure might ease his boredom, so he consented.

"They can be. I never seem to impress them. Kellabane's got the looks; Bentavi is a mathematical mastermind; and Soiko is a master Builder. All of them think my gadgets are toys."

"They're not. Your nailgun and saw table ideas were fascinating. Nobody wants to help you make those?"

"I think they're trying their hardest to prevent it," Dagrio said.

"That's insane. You're a Vanterslove. You're supposed to be

Building."

"That's still a puzzle I have yet to solve. I'm supposed to Building houses. Not tools."

The distant sound of wood snapping accompanied a muffled flash a few shacks down from Dagrio's home. The two shared a look of questionable advancement, and wordlessly agreed to proceed. Dagrio informed him that the flash came from Nighfall's home. Nighfall was the aged Building member of the Board, so any trespassing needed to be heavily guarded. Nighfall's rumors gave justice to the Vanterslove's clever ways. The short description was cut even shorter as they approached the front window. Hooves and boots scratched against wooden floorboards. Simon crouched and slyly sidled the house, stretching his neck to its capacity.

"Look, we're not here to—" he heard Caylo say. Then another muffled flash, this time indigo blue, followed a lunging yell.

"You're here to convert me," he heard a higher pitched, reedy voice assert breathlessly. It must have been Nighfall who lunged.

"We're not here to inflict harm or damage by any means," Caylo said. "Your involvement with the Rebellion is an intellectual matter."

Simon and Dagrio could barely catch a glimpse of the interior to the house. It too had a high deck on the back, but this conversation was in a front living area. Strong, thin planks of mahogany held the exterior walls. He could only see a wooden rail on a high loft above, but most of the interior was blocked by the windowsill he was hiding behind.

"Excuse me, Caylo," another voice said, deep and smooth, "but we are no longer alone." The voice must have referenced the window. Simon heard footsteps creep toward their direction.

Simon's veins froze; he was stuck in a hunched position with an ear as strategically close as he could place it pointed towards the window. Simon had just decided to run for it when the footsteps stopped, and he felt a rush of coldness. The increasing drop in temperature within his body forced his face to whence, and his body followed.

When he opened his eyes, he and Dagrio were curled up in the fetal position in the middle of Nighfall's living room. It was modernesqe, with squared lounge chairs at strange, exotic angles to parallel some of the frivolous lines of the high, sheen wooden walls in the living area across from the loft.

Four Creatures were glaring at them. Caylo fashioned a mischievous half-smile. Friziv sported a look of quiet curiosity. An ancient-looking gazelle with strong black stripes running down his muzzle glared with disdain mostly pointed towards Dagrio. A brown owl with black flecks in his feathers and large, piercing black eyes shook his wings, recovering from the teleportation spell.

Simon decided to speak first, "Nobody fear us! Please don't lock us up or tell us to run along. Nighfall, you need to join the Rebellion. Fyresk's evil is plain to see, and if other Kearlithians don't see that yet, he will gain more power and take over." The words were erupting from deep within. Simon had no idea what his next word was going to be, but he felt it, and it was verbalized. Caylo and the Protector shared a raised-eyebrows expression.

"Ha! The Human thinks he can address Kearlith business," Nighfall mocked.

"I'm a Human who lives in Kearlith now," Simon corrected. "I've seen Fyresk's good side, and it's fake. I've seen through the cordial mask. His objectives are contaminated by a selfish drive."

"But who's to say you're no different, eh?" The lean, elder Vanterslove said, scoffing. "Your race appears to be tainted with egotism." Simon took a second to muster a witty retort, but Nighfall stopped him short. "Save it, boy. Your lack of words is enough."

"Nighfall, the Rebellion will –" Caylo began, but Nighfall waved him away with a hoof as well.

"Caylo, your many words are enough." Nighfall's eyes found the ground, and he sighed. "Fyresk does seem to be a bit sick these days. At first I thought he was just pulling a fast one, but it's been long enough with no answers." Nighfall looked up to Caylo. "You've yet to prove your worth as a leader, but that man has more than proven his failure as one."

The room remained quiet. Nighfall continued, "Maybe Kearlith needs a new Lord. Who do you see taking his place, Simon?"

The question put Simon out of place. "Any person other than

Fyresk," he finally answered. All of the Creatures, even Dagrio, laughed and cackled like his statement was the punch line of the greatest joke he'd been telling them.

Slowly, Dagrio came out of the fit. "Any *person* other than Fyresk," he said as he cut back to his laughter, "would be you."

Simon was again hit with a mouth coma. His replacing the position of Fyresk would be rather laughable, but these Creatures were hysterical.

These Creatures.

Right. Any *person* other than Fyresk meant any Human other than Fyresk. He began to find the humor.

"Okay, let me rephrase that. Any *Creature* other than Fyresk,"

This again erupted another wave of chortles, but at least Simon was included in it this time.

After the laughter subsided, Caylo spoke again, "In the New World, Simon, Nighfall – I will be King."

"An' I'll be first-hand," said Friziv.

"And I Sergeant-at-Arms," said the Protector.

"We three will govern in a new era. One not afraid of the world Outside. One that protects its own. One that flourishes in its own economy."

"One that fails at the first sign of disagreement," Nighfall interrupted.

"I have been Lord Fyresk's right-hand man for almost three years now, Nighfall," said Caylo. "I will not take the throne lightly."

"But you'll take the throne," Dagrio piped up with a hint of fear. "You plan to kill Lord Fyresk?"

"Sadly, murder is the only option. But I will not be killing a man. I will be releasing a suffering man from his demons."

Nighfall snorted. "You're not a Creature free of demons yourself, Caylo."

"I'm aware," he snapped. "But I will justly grant disciplines and honors, and with these two and possibly you by my side, corruption is avoidable."

Nighfall contemplated as he gave Caylo, Friziv, and the Protector a long glare. "My involvement with the Rebellion will give you four on four," he finally said.

"Hence why we've come to you. Morolith is our next major target, although his participation will be more difficult to obtain," Caylo said.

"You expect to use our immunities to the castle to go in and slay him?" Nighfall started to sound nervous.

"Yes," Caylo said. "With five on three we can easily get past most of Fyresk's protection spells. We'll overthrow the law," he ended with a smirk towards Simon.

Nighfall continued his pensive glare, longer this time. They all watched him sit and size Caylo up for a few minutes. "Morolith will never convert."

"In the case of that," Caylo began, "we will be four on four. Which will only strongly hinder our attempts, but it will not prevent them. However, Morolith is pro-Creature. We could possibly play to that."

Nighfall chuckled. "Every Creature is pro-Creature. But I'm still anti-murder," he said switching back to a cold gaze.

"So am I, Nighfall. Believe me, were there any other options, I would take them. The death of Lord Fyresk is inevitable."

"How much is Mizik in your New World?" the old Vanterslove asked after one last long pause.

"Free," Caylo answered in that suave way.

"I'm in," Nighfall said with a nod and a cold gaze.

"Excellent."

Caylo smiled and sat up to standing. He motioned for the four of them to leave.

"Your involvement will not end in regret, Nighfall. I assure you. The New World will be a better one," he said, and they all exited.

## <u>Chapter 16</u>

Up in the sky, the Protector directed the relaxed triangular formation- Friziv on a pop-out pogo stick; Simon on a fishhook branch; Dagrio clumsily balancing on a broken branch of his own; then Caylo riding a sword in the fashion of Fyresk, only his sword was backwards and had a much bigger hilt.

Caylo popped up behind Simon and Dagrio. "What do you know of the Rebellion?" he asked. Dagrio almost tumbled, but found his grip just before his footing slipped and caused him to flail back to a safe position. He took several minutes to find his legs and a comfortable speed.

"Nothing. Obviously, I know you're running it now," Simon said through intermittent giggling, "but I haven't heard anything about it until tonight."

"You've got drive, Simon," Caylo said, recovering from their entertainment of the night as well. "The Rebellion might see use in you."

"I want to help. If the goal is to bring down Fyresk's reign of terror, then I want to assist."

"I'm afraid most of the spots are filled for the government of the New World, but much would be rewarded to a mighty leader of the Rebellion. The spark that will ignite the flames of peace in

Kearlith for ages."

The remark had a very impressive ring to it. "I would say I'm in, but that would just be copying Nighfall's moment," Simon joked.

"Excellent," Caylo said smiling. He looked like he was about to continue, but Dagrio butt in after finally finding all four grips on the branch.

"Where are we going, Caylo?"

"To a spot I think we are all acquainted with- the Torn Trees."

Dagrio gave an exaggerated "Oooo..." with the required hand motions, consequently causing him to lose his balance on the branch again. He spun off on another tangent to gain his center of gravity. Simon was begging to know more about the Torn Trees, but he had to know something first. He quickly took advantage of Dagrio's absence.

"What are your plans for Lord Fyresk?" he asked.

"Not here," Caylo said tightly, looking to the trees below and to the sky above.

"Oh, I said, 'water your plants for... Fyfith.' It's a holiday I made up in honor of... shrubberies," Simon said a little louder, catching on. Caylo laughed loudly.

Dagrio returned a little shaken, but more at ease on his transportation.

"Are you guys laughing at me?" he said a little hurt.

"No," Simon barely made out.

"Then what's so funny?"

"Fyfith."

"You should water your plants," Caylo said, bursting the suspended bubble of laughter. The Protector shushed them from up ahead. "Sorry, Voulderbrin," he quietly called.

Of course the owl was Voulderbrin. The Lead Protector and third Rebellion member of the Board. He was half responsible for Simon's access to the city...

"Why the Torn Trees?" Dagrio complained. "Why not somewhere dangerous and off limits? This is a Rebellion, after all."

"Clearly your trainer skipped a few history lessons," Caylo said, switching his manner to that of a chaperone.

"Yeah, they used to be the center of conflict like a hundred years ago," Dagrio moaned. "But now it's just two stumps."

"Those stumps remind many Kearlithians what conflict is like."

"What happened?" Simon exclaimed. He had hoped they would be arguing about details, but he hadn't caught a clue on the origins of his provisional office.

"Nearly one hundred years ago," Caylo began, "the Creatures —"

"The Creatures were really mad at the Humans," Dagrio interrupted, "because the Humans thought they were more powerful. To prove it, the Humans planted a tree that could withstand any of their magical curses. Of course the Creatures tried to destroy it, and of course they failed. In a final attempt of vengeance, the Creatures planted a tree that could withstand any of the Humans' attempts right next to it, and the Humans tried to do the same. How's that for a history lesson?" Dagrio eyed Caylo.

"So which is which?" Simon asked.

"The mossy one is the work of the Humans," Caylo answered taking his glare off Dagrio.

"They're stumps now because after many botched attempts, the Humans finally hacked down the Creatures' tree, so the Creatures did the same to the Humans'. After that, they were just stumps," Dagrio said with a smirk and an eye still on Caylo.

"We're nearing the Trees," Voulderbrin muttered in a distant, channeled way as if to shush them again. He slowly started the descent, and the rest followed into form.

*       *       *

Oddly, Simon felt a bit at home in view of the eerie clearing. It somewhat led him to Kearlith before he knew the power of the shining blue leaf. And he was there when he met Friziv. In the air the creepy Shintervah was second in the line-up, but the Trees seemed absent of any Rebellioneers. Voulderbrin was gone, too.

With Kearlith a fair distance away, the inaudible murmur resonated a calming quiet into this small circle of Feerthel. He couldn't hear her, but he felt her rhythm like a second heartbeat.

He hopped off the fishhook branch with intentionally impressive finesse as Dagrio smashed into the ground and slid, flailing an embarrassing distance. The juvenile Vanterslove rapidly recuperated to all fours. "I'm okay," he said. Caylo flew in, snapping his sword up and routinely sheathing it and landing flawlessly. Simon's astonishment blew a fuse. He stood for a moment rewinding the occurrence in his head. He came to just in time to see Friziv fly in on his pogo stick, kind of park it, hop off easily, fold it up into a two-foot cylinder, and snap it to his hip.

"Dagrio," Caylo began, delving into more of the broody man Simon had seen at the blacksmith's shop, "how uncomfortable are you with killing Fyresk?"

Simon wished his adolescence wouldn't spark a senseless riposte. Luckily, the Vanterslove pondered the question. "Why kill him?" he asked.

"Fyresk is a powerful man, Dagrio. To lock him up would be senseless, especially if we use his own prison. We need to make sure he will no longer threaten the heart of Kearlith."

"By murdering him? How?"

Caylo huffed a slight sigh. "We have begun plans to permeate through the castle, find Fyresk, and slay him."

"But he has protections!" Dagrio declared. "Spells! Guards! Strongly devoted Kearlithians!"

"Strongly devoted Kearlithians wouldn't attest to the New World," Voulderbrin peeped up from out of the shadows of the Trees. "Without Fyresk, Caylo can bring order back into Kearlith."

"Hence the plans. We're not attacking tomorrow, Creatures," Caylo hesitated, "and Human. Dagrio, you know too much Rebellion knowledge. Naturally, and this is to all of you, this knowledge is to remain secret. Whether you're with us or not, dismissal of this information could warrant *dire* consequences. Is that clear?"

"Yes, your highness," he answered.

"Are we still in disagreement on the fate of Fyresk?"

Dagrio paused again to reflect on his response. An eerily more mature gazelle answered, "No. He is no longer the man who once ruled Kearlith."

"Good," Caylo nodded. "Every individual in this clearing is under the protections of the Rebellion," he said, slightly tapping his heart. His chest quickly glistened with tiny, sparkling lights. The same sparkles formed at the heads of Simon and Dagrio, sinking to the ground and into the dirt. Simon was fascinated, but the rest of the Rebellion gave no notice to the spell. "This means every individual here is a member of the Rebellion. This detail pilots a decent amount of responsibility and duties. Nothing you boys can't handle."

Simon didn't like this darkened Caylo as much. His affability ended immediately once they landed.

"We wish to build a small army," he continued as he began to pace like a drill sergeant. "Most of it will be planted at the gargoyle's gate leading to the castle to protect us from the strongly devoted Kearlithians." Caylo eyed Dagrio. "Several Creatures will continue on to take care of the guards and claim their positions. A handful of the craftiest Creatures will infiltrate the castle. The Rebellion is already one hundred thirty-seven members strong and growing. Within the next month the Rebellion will attack.

"Over the course of that time, part of your responsibility will be to gain other members. The challenge, of course, is to recruit without revealing your true loyalties."

"How do we recruit, then?" Dagrio asked. "Give them a helmet and a sword and say 'You'll know what to do'?"

"The Rebellion is to remain anonymous in an open setting. Although Kearlith is facing troubled times, very few Creatures would initially sign up for a plan as insane as this. If you happen to meet one of those few, discuss their inner criticisms of the city. If their problems lie in our Lord, hook them. But trust them. If you don't trust them, you're just another pissed off Kearlithian, and they're just another oblivious citizen that will be saved by the Rebellion when the time comes.

"Let me emphasize-," Caylo continued harshly, "you *must* trust them before any mentioning of the word Rebellion enters your mind. We're running on a thin line with enough obstacles to keep us occupied without any assistance from a spy. End your initial conversation without a word of the Rebellion, and pass them by me at the next meeting. We'll discuss the possibility of their joining us."

The Kyejoth returned to where he landed and threw the easily unsheathed sword onto inches off the ground in Fyresk-like fashion.

"Dagrio," he continued as he turned around, "do I and the Rebellion have your trust?"

"Yes. Even if Lord Fyresk is using all this Mizik for a good reason, he'll never be the same."

"So Fyresk used to be good guy?" Simon asked.

"'e used to smile," Friziv butt in. "Kearlithians never seen 'im much, but if they greeted 'im, 'e'd 'appily wave back in gra'itude."

"But then the attack…" Simon added.

"Since the attack, Kearlithians never see him," Voulderbrin the Protector said to the sky. He put much more aggression into the "never".

"'arder to see 'im when 'e's black as a shadow," Friziv retorted.

"And he's clearly planning something," Simon entered as his two cents. "If he doesn't trust the Board to know what he's doing, it must be something he knew some of you would refuse." These words were powerful. And they were his. This wasn't Mizik, but the wave of confident energy was becoming a strong competitor. "He must be stopped." The last word was an accident, and the others hurrahed him, but that certain phrasing ironically stopped him.

Lord Fyresk needed to be stopped, but Simon didn't want to kill those eyes.

Allowing him to continue ruling Kearlith under crooked tyranny was no longer the lesser of the evils. It was time for a Rebellion.

"Meet us here after two days," Volderbrin appeased. He had been hovering around the Creatures' tree, but he took higher to the sky. "We will discuss our progress. As of now, this meeting is adjourned."

"Agreed," Caylo said. "I have a separate target in mind, but I must see if he will be willing to join at all. For the best defense, I have been doing my share of research. I plan to speak to him soon. Maybe by the next meeting."

"No targets in sigh' for me," Friziv blurted, "bu' I'll keep slashin' my tongue around."

"As will I," Volderbrin seconded. The Shintervah and Biffleflenn pounced into the air.

"Simon, Dagrio, the Rebellion will be stronger thanks to you two," Caylo said, and he pounced as well.

An odd silence overtook the clearing. No Rogs; no Flervana; no other Creatures; just the Torn Trees and Dagrio. To soothe his burning curiosity, Simon drifted up to the treetops just above the blanket.

He saw no signs of other life save for Kearlith's dull glow in the distance. Past that, Fyresk's castle could not even be seen. He quickly scanned the sky to see if any on-duty Protectors would bash him back into the ground. Then he willingly descended back into the clearing. Dagrio had disassembled his branch by the time he got back.

"Why did you do that? It took forever to find you a good branch!" Simon exclaimed.

"Watch, imbecile," the Vanterslove spat. He depressed the trunk of the branch onto the Creatures' bare stump with one hoof and grabbed the sliced limbs piece by piece to reattach them. His symmetrical placement allowed an easier hold, and the hexed joints allowed limited rotation for more acute control. Simon possessed a skeleton of a scythe; Dagrio a skeleton of a mini-cockpit.

The suddenly nimble gazelle took hold of his new ride and said, "Maybe we should continue our adventure in the city."

"That's true," Simon agreed. "We better get back and start recruiting."

*       *       *

Dagrio led the way back to Kearlith. Simon alone could have most likely doubled their time, but Dagrio fumbled a few turns. Once, he saved the gazelle from the same twisted disaster that had introduced him to the fishhook branch. Dagrio shamefully thanked the new Human and remounted the branch's convoluted arms.

"My sisters would have let me torpedo into that tree," he confessed after a few minutes of flying. "That's one of the reasons

I've avoided the air. I could never get used to it."

"You're getting the hang of it," Simon retorted. "It took me a little while to feel out how the magic alters the gravity. It's not easy. But couldn't you build something that made it simple for you?"

"I've tried, but my body and my family and most of Kearlith seem to want me on the ground. I'm supposed to be Building houses. Not attempting flight."

"That is Building!" Simon exclaimed. "Why would they want to limit you?"

"Your guess is as good as mine. I'm sure they won't be giddy about me crafting a scythe for you either, but I've been done with trying to get in their good graces."

"You don't have to, Dagrio. I don't want to cause any trouble."

"No, it's no trouble," Dagrio snapped. "It sounds like a great challenge."

"I promise I will never enslave the first Creature with it."

Dagrio laughed. "You might make use of some of the lesser Creatures in the Forest. A few can come in handy when called."

"Well I might befriend them, but that scythe will be for self-defense. If I had one when the Rogs attacked me yesterday, I might have been a threat."

"You defeated a mad Rog?" Dagrio's reaction surmounted disbelief.

"Not alone. Seskith and a Gulverbruud did most of the defeating."

"Oh. Well, that makes sense. For a Collector, Seskith can fight."

"She said she would help me learn to defend myself."

"I would take her up on that. With her lessons and my scythe, the Creatures in Feerthel will bow down to you."

*       *       *

Before long, the boys found the edge of Kearlith. Dagrio continued to lead him.

"Where are we going?" Simon finally asked after passing

through Mid-City.

"Flarehva's Trinkets," Dagrio answered. "I need to pick up something."

This street was fresh to Simon's eyes. He had passed many shops along many roads, but somehow he had missed this one. Golden posts grasped long, red, flowing ribbons around the edges of the road. The ribbons appeared to disregard gravity like feathers in the wind. Atop the posts were miniature bowls meant for fires at night. Simon paused, transfixed by the dancing of the ribbons, and the two posts in front of him spit to life followed by the pair behind them, followed by the pair behind them, until the entire street was unnecessarily illuminated.

"What did you just do?" Dagrio asked as he turned to face Simon.

"I don't know... I—" and then he heard it. Laughter. Muffled and shushed at first, but soon a few Kyejoth erupted from the first few storefronts. "His face!" and many attempts at "his face" were passed between howling neighbors.

"Flarehva!" Dagrio barked, halting it all.

"What?" The youngest of the three asked. She was a dangerously attractive pixie-haired brunette that looked fit enough to be just as flat out dangerous. Her shack looked thrown together with random wooden planks, steel bars, and sheets of aluminum. "Kid, it was just a joke. Lighten up, Daggy," Flarehva replied. The title of "kid" struck a little harder, seeing as she looked barely older than Simon.

"It wasn't that funny," Simon entered.

"On the contrary, it was hilarious. Daggy, do you need something or are you just giving our guest the grand tour?" Flarehva cooed.

"I was hoping to find something," Dagrio sharply answered.

"And I'm not a guest," Simon added.

"My apologies, Simon. But you must admit it was kind of funny."

"Not really... No," he said honestly. The joke was, in fact, getting old.

"Well, come on, then. Into the shop. I'll let you pick

something out to show no hard feelings. Deal?"

"I guess. Deal."

"What were you in the market for, Dag?" Flarehva asked as they passed the threshold into the store. Clearly, Flarehva fashioned the layout of her shop to match the unorthodox angles and shapes of the Forest.

"I'm not really sure yet. I just wanted to look around and let Simon meet a good friend of mine, which seems to have been a terrible error in judgment."

"It was in jest!" Flarehva defended. "Simon, I really do apo—"

"It's okay, guys. Really. So I can pick out anything I want?" Simon asked.

"Within reason. Most of the junk I have in here is cheap, so it shouldn't be much of a loss. Have a look around."

Simon started gazing at the mismatched shelves along the walls, then the various kiosks and items for sale on the floor before the bookshelves. Set up in an extravagant battle scene on a small, marble chess table were armor-plated figurines of knights wielding swords, warhammers, battle-axes, maces, and even a boomerang.

"Psst," Flarehva whispered from behind him. "Yell 'fight'."

Simon did as told and the scene burst to life. The knights swatted at and bashed each other all across the black and white checkered table. No damage was done since the figures were metal, so for several minutes Simon witnessed numerous deadly blows, and the knights recuperated to continue the undying battle.

"Rest,' Flarehva called.

"That was pretty awesome," Simon admitted.

"There's plenty more to see," she said, motioning to the rest of the crammed space. Dagrio was pilfering through the "Bins of Random Odds and Ends" as they were named by a nearby sign. Behind him, dozens of mismatched racks and bookshelves shoved themselves together creating a haphazard layout of aisles. Flarehva had curiously placed a creepy golden statue of a stoic Gullen just at eye level on the closest bookshelf. Simon shook off the stare and traveled down the first aisle.

Tiny signs displayed the names and descriptions of a few of

the more arbitrary devices like the Extinquisher – a gyroscopic, neon blue sphere that acted as a high powered, fully rotating sprinkler – and the Resonator – a keychain-sized cone that could amplify the speaker up to twenty times. All the gadgets and gizmos were of interest, but nothing jumped out at Simon. He didn't *need* any of this. It was all just really, *really* cool. He was just finishing up the last of the wall shelves when he saw a thin, metallic blue case no bigger than his hand. He unclasped the hinge on the side to pop it open. Tabs were placed on both sides to hold down... minuscule paperwork?

"It's a hexed Mizik wallet," Flarehva answered from the counter. "You can fit an endless amount of Mizik leaves in there."

Without hesitation Simon decided, "I'll take this."

"Fair enough," she said. Dagrio must have found something as well; he was just finishing up his transaction.

"What did you get, Daggy?" Simon asked which caused a furious and deadly look from Dagrio.

"Do not call me Daggy," he said with every bit of menace he could assemble. Flarehva stopped herself from giggling a retort.

"Sorry, Dag."

"I bought a mask," he said. Sure enough, he held up a decorated steel, sinister gazelle mask. The horns protruded from the side elegantly and severely.

"For what?" Simon asked.

"Like you said- self-defense."

"Those horns are nothing to mess with," Flarehva said, "but the real beauty behind this piece is its indestructibility. This will be here until the end of days."

"Thanks, Flarehva," Dagrio said.

"Never a problem, Daggy. And really Simon, it was only a trick in jest."

"It's completely okay, Flarehva. I'm kind of used to it," he answered. And surprisingly, he really was okay with it. The comedian Kyejoth turned out to be in the miniscule population of Creatures that trusted Simon so far. "And thank you for the wallet."

"You're welcome. Glad to have you here, Si," she said with a grin. Not in jest; genuinely.

# Chapter 17

The day outside had not quite turned to dusk, but it was threatening. The autumn air chilled Kearlith to a biting temperature. Simon would have to Collect in that tonight. First, he had to make a pit-stop.

"Do you want to stop by Mathilda's?" he asked Dagrio.

"Sure. I wouldn't mind looking around. She's usually got great stuff."

"She's making me a vest," he said.

"Seriously?!" Dagrio asked.

"Yeah, it's costing me five Dillian, but she's fitting me for it."

"I would love to have some of her work. She always manages to put everything you need into all of her pieces." Dagrio gazed into the treetops appearing to be deep in thought. "She used to have bracers that lifted things for you. So when you started lifting boulders, they would feel like pebbles. Her mark was stitching tons of hooks all over them for hammers, nails, screws, screwdrivers, levels, everything. They were stitched for the Builders. I still wish I knew who bought those, but…" Bashfully, Dagrio trailed off.

"Why didn't you just buy them?" Simon asked.

"Parents," was the answer. The practiced and repeated

response to most of this Vanterslove's problems.

"Oh," was all he could say in return. Simon wanted to offer more comforting advice, but he knew very little about parents. Plenty about grouchy and abusive grandmothers along with heathen siblings, but nothing about the kind of Creatures Roibose and Alencia were. He would have loved to call them Mom and Dad.

\*     \*     \*

Mathilda's humble shop welcomed them with an open door despite the dropping temperature. Inside, Mathilda sat rocking in her wooden chair, sewing the buckle onto an impressively dressed utility belt. She grinned when they entered.

"Good to see you again, Simon," she said. "And it's always a pleasure to see you, Dagrio."

"Thanks, Mathilda. Same goes for you." Dagrio's usual abstractedness stopped at the front door. Every bit of his attention was on the amiable Gulverbruud.

"Mathilda, I think an apology is very much in order," Simon admitted. "I had no idea that the Scythe of Crysis was used to enslave Creatures. I promise, I never want to harm a Creature just because I can. I want to defend myself, but—"

"Simon, dear, it's okay." She smiled with her astoundingly understanding eyes. "The story of the Scythe is interesting, there's no doubt. In fact, it's the main reason my late husband went searching for it himself."

"Did he find it?" Simon asked.

Mathilda's face dropped before she responded. "He did. But rest assured, that blade always finds itself buried deeper into the ground with hopes of never surfacing again."

"Well, I don't need it now." Simon gave Dagrio a friendly shove. "Dag's gonna make me an even better one."

"There's a clever idea. Dagrio's potential is undeniable."

"Really?" Dagrio exclaimed, jumping a little. He quickly corrected his zealous response.

Mathilda chuckled. "Yes, Dag. When are you going to put some of your machines to work and start fixing Kearlith?"

Simon answered for him, "Oh we've got plans for plenty of new machines. Some of them could probably be used to chop down some of the overgrowth."

"And the others?" Mathilda asked with that disapproving grandmotherly look. "What will they be used for?"

Both Dagrio and Simon were speechless. Finally, Dagrio saved them with, "Saving Kearlith, of course."

Mathilda kept her gaze, but some of the ice chipped off her shoulder. "Make sure of that. I'll not let another Crysis cross me unscathed."

Deep down around Simon's gut region his insides twisted and coiled, but his curiosity took control and spoke up. "Do you mind if I asked what happened?"

She sighed but said, "You mean with my husband?"

"Yeah."

Dagrio quickly glanced at all the walls trying to find something to be distracted by. "I'm... I'm just going to... look around," he said as he did so.

Mathilda lingered before releasing, "You may."

She returned to stitching the leather and began, "Shastlin was a Shintervah. He was a beautiful Creature that lusted for adventure. He chased it like a cat to a mouse. For a long while I was his target, and I ultimately submitted."

"Did anyone care that he wasn't a Gulverbruud?" Simon asked.

"Everyone," she answered. "Technically he wasn't even my husband. The city forbade it. Both he and I were all but exiled from this place. By that point I had built up a decent reputation as a leatherworker, so my customers fought for me. And there were a small few that admired him like I did. He promised me we could convince the staggering majority of those who did not.

"I had always grown up as an outcast of the family. The idea of forbidden love just kind of fit right into my story line. I was thrilled to fight for it. We argued with the Enforcers, Intellects, Protectors, and Lord Fyresk for years in defense of our citizenship. Finally, we settled on no marriage in return for our slots in this society.

"That Creature could not be tied down, though. He continued testing the Enforcer's limits by sneaking out of Feerthel to find the Preeminents' secrets. He searched for the Scythe, the Rogue Project, Wendy Whisp's locket," Simon's heart dead halted and his eyes widened, "and Kowlakro's Harness, just to name a few. That Harness of Kowlakro's was the one that did him in, though."

"What happened?" Simon blurted.

Mathilda sighed again. She relaxed her hands and gazed into something out the window. Perhaps a memory. "I was the problem this one time," and for the first time, Simon saw a vulnerable and more pained Gulverbruud. "Every other quest and adventure, I was the one who kept him safe. I kept him grounded and out of death's grasp. But because Morolith had a certain attachment to this quest, he stopped at nothing to end Shastlin. It pains me to share the blame."

Simon was dumbfounded. He expected her to continue, but he ultimately had to ask, "Why would that matter?"

She looked at him in the same perplexed manner. "Morolith is my younger brother, dear."

As Simon's brain clicked the stories into place, he twisted his face accordingly into a number of odd arrangements. His only response was, "Oh. I would have never guessed that."

She giggled a little. "Yes, it made things much more difficult to choose sides. And in addition, Kowlakro was in our bloodline."

Simon could finally speak. "So Morolith wanted the Harness more than your husband Shastlin."

"Morolith felt it was rightly his. Shastlin simply wanted the treasure. As much as I love both men, I had to side with my brother, and he spared me."

"Did he kill him?" Simon asked.

"I have been told so, but I know my brother. He'll shamelessly kill any beast with enough debt to pay, but I think he spared him. I think they made a deal. I still feel him out there."

"Do you think he'll come back?"

"It would be foolish to think that. If he's alive out there, my best hopes would be that he plans on returning, at least for me. But do I expect it? No," Mathilda said as she returned to her sewing.

"So... Brobanarin was your brother, too," Simon said bashfully. "I'm sorry about what happened in the Cave."

"Brobanarin was a thug," Mathilda said with slim eyes. "No Creature in Kearlith deserves death, but if there were any exceptions, he would have been at the top of the list," she said as Dagrio turned the corner.

"How much for the lifter back there, Mathilda?" he asked.

"7 Dil."

"It's just a lifter..." he said in slight protest.

"Yes, but that particular lifter could lift up to forty of my biggest brethren fifty feet into the air."

Dagrio's eyes widened, "I'll take it."

"That's the spirit. You know better than to think me greedy."

"You never disappoint me, Mathilda," he said as he went to retrieve whatever a 'lifter' was.

"Thank you, dear."

Simon tried his best to approach this question lightly, but the best he could come up with was, "So everyone hated that you loved someone... another... kind of Creature?"

"Everyone," she repeated.

"What about now?"

"My reputation has saved me. Creatures may harbor their opinions, but no one will publicly deny my contributions to Kearlith."

"I think Dagrio admires you more than he lets on."

"Really?" she asked with a sarcastic scoff. "That's the great thing about my fans. The Creatures who really know what I do love me and trust me. All the rest can—" Again Dagrio turned the corner, ending her sentence.

"Thank you for this, Mathilda," he said. "It's really great work. The design in the support beams seems flawless."

"Thank you, Dagrio. It is."

"I better get back home," he said as he paid up. "Mom will have a list of things for me to do, I'm sure."

"Best of luck to both of you, boys."

"You too, Mathilda," they said, and they left.

*       *       *

Outside, the Sonx had begun to die. It took less than a minute for Simon to start shivering. He made it one block as a sudden, brisk breeze blew in from an alley between the archaic rocks of Brudo's Butchery and the sleek steel of Zekel's Staff Shop.

The latter always stood out on this street. It was run by an Intellect Simon had only seen at a distance and in quick glimpses, but he never heard anyone in town talk about him. His shop was a masterpiece. Gothic in style, but updated to an almost futuristic fashion trend. The whole place resembled a darkened jester's hat.

Simon slowed to take a longer look, but the wind seemed to be waiting for him. The instant he crossed the plane of the outside wall of the shop, the wind raged. Summer was ending, and autumn was furiously stepping in. He made a mental note to pick up warmer clothes before he Collected.

Dagrio skimmed along beside him riding the lifter he enchanted with a similar method to the blue rope. He, too, was shivering.

"Hey Dag, who exactly was King Kowlakro?"

"You would have liked him. He was the first one to restore Kearlith to peace after the Creatures took power."

"And he was a Gulverbruud?" Simon asked, attempting to hold back his astonishment.

Dagrio nodded. "A good one. He was purely loyal to Hunting, a master at it, but after enough people asked him, he accepted the throne. For fourteen years, the Humans and Creatures thrived together."

"What happened in the fifteenth year?"

"He was assassinated. By a Human."

"Ah. I'm starting to see why peop— Creatures were so skeptical of me now," Simon sighed.

"His Harness was awesome. It was just a few straps that stretched out and bound to its target. It was so hexed, it could bring down any beast that it touched. He would just set a hex and throw it or shoot it, and his enemies had no chance to escape."

"I bet Morolith still has it."

"He does," Dagrio said. "I've never seen it. He keeps it locked up somewhere."

"That's a shame. Have you asked him to let you see it?"

"Yes. But you've met him."

"Very true."

A couple of streets over, Simon caught a glimpse of the store where he bought the Mizik blanket and eyed the warm coats in the tall, dusty windows. He tapped his pockets although he knew full well the contents. A few pointless Duzuks. He would have to endure the biting cold of Feerthel without the warm assistance of a jacket tonight.

# Chapter 18

Three short weeks had flown by since Simon and Seskith's race with the Flervana, and again his adrenaline was pumping at outrageous levels. The Axolotl Lake rested mere yards from Thrax and him. They were safely out of sight, waiting in one of the pockets of the Forest just off the shore.

"I know you'll hate me asking, Simon," Thrax whispered, "but do you remember the spells Seskith taught you?"

"Like the back of my hand," he boasted. Seskith had in fact taught him much in the field of self-defense over the past few weeks. Every few days they fought the Forest together. Or rather, she fought many of the horrifying Feerthelian Creatures and Simon would watch, then she would explain what she just killed or ran off.

"Good," Thrax answered, gulping. "These little critters are terrifying."

"I thought this was why you became a potions master, so that you could adventure and collect rare ingredients."

"I used to thrive in it," Thrax answered bashfully. "But I've stared at death so many times and lived to tell the tale, I'm starting to wonder when my luck will run short."

"It's not luck. It's skill," Simon answered. "And we've got plenty of that. Now let's go get some Liriwi!" he declared in a whispered yell.

"I like you, kid," Thrax said. "Simon," he corrected after a fierce look. Simon nudged his head for Thrax to lead the way, and the Kyejoth did as ordered.

Thrax crouched and crept past the last few trees, his eyes darting to every nook and cranny. Simon followed suit. His legs began to ache after they reached the line of trees, but he muscled through the pain. Thrax was clearly a veteran to this. He was pin-drop silent as he stepped through the bed of stiff and dead leaves. He saw it, but just as he was about to mention it, Thrax snapped his wand at the curly, teal vine hiding ten feet away. It snipped away from the ground and into his hand. He quietly pocketed it and eyed the ground for more.

Simon could see Axolotls scattered about in random places. They were located at a dead end bank that they hoped would be less conspicuous. Although the Axolotls could see far better than Humans at close range, their vision was near blind after forty feet.

The two were betting on those forty feet. The closest was only pushing sixty, but he seemed far too enthused in testing his limits running up a tree and flipping off of it to notice them.

Dusk would not arrive for a few hours, but moody clouds covered the Sonx today. One advantage to looting the Axolotl Lake was the luminescent environment. Without it, the Liriwi would remain unattained. Thrax had an eye for them, and Simon was catching on. They tended to point to each other. Simon almost always found one on either end of the line of the vine; he just had to search for it. It was like mapping the trees of Feerthel on a tiny scale.

The added task of perfect silence kept his blood pumping. The nearest Axolotl occasionally checked back to see if any invaders were approaching, but he swiftly started running and jumping off of the trees again. Simon and Thrax remained tense, knowing at any moment one of them might patrol the area and break that forty feet.

Just as Simon spat a whispered "Anahvy", the Liriwi jumped into his hand, but a handsomely dressed, ghostly gray salamander crossed the threshold of the trees roughly thirty feet down from the looters, the feelers around his face seemed to sniff out danger. Thrax and Simon immediately stopped; their eyes both locked on the

Creature. He was profile with his head directed down the opposite side of the shore. He kept walking, auspiciously in the other direction.

Simon spotted a Liriwi by his foot, but he couldn't move even if he wanted to. The unfamiliar terror of the Axolotl took hold of his body and petrified him. Thrax took advantage of the situation and pocketed it himself.

"That one could have been yours," he whispered.

And the Axolotl heard. He snapped his head to the trapped two on the shore and hit a pitch strikingly close to that of Alexis and Max at their best. Within seconds, fifty Axolotls rushed in from every pocket of the Forest.

Seskith's words rang in Simon's ears, "Stay calm, and you stay alive." He routinely unsheathed his wand from the notch on his leather vest and enchanted a vast, thick circle of fire around them. The Axolotls barked and roared.

"Nice," Thrax noted.

They bolted towards the nearest entrance into the surrounding forest, only to see roughly ten of them leaping and sprinting down that path. They were trapped.

Thrax threw out his palms and began working a spider-webbed ball into the air. The Axolotls were giggling like little kids; childlike voices and all. Simon hoped this trick of Thrax's would stop them. He knew a few spells to back them off, but with targets so tiny, he could never outmaneuver them. Lexandel wrote about their primary attacks- at long range, spitting fire or poison; at close range, gripping body parts with their sticky fingers and bending them to break.

The front line contained an indigo Axolotl almost red from fury, a sneering green one, and a dull golden one that would have been beautiful had it not been for her haunting grin and mischievously shaking feelers. They jumped into positions to pounce, and Thrax threw the ball of spider-webs, hitting them mid-stride.

It stretched out spanning dozens of yards wide and equally as tall. The invading Axolotls were caught in the wall of webs, but the ghostly Axolotl and his guards on the opposite side of them were quickly advancing. He and the others had extinguished a path in Simon's ring of fire and were again on the chase. The indigo Axolotl spat flaming lava at Thrax in between bites he was taking of the spider-web wall to free himself. Thrax threw up his palm again, freezing the lava in the air, and shot it back. A hole was cut into the web due to the blast. Thrax dashed for it. Simon followed, but he hesitated just for a second outside the hole to check for ambushers. Thrax continued unscathed, so Simon tore through the wall and made up his distance.

The attacks anything but ceased. The spider-webs were diminished to ashes within seconds, and the Axolotls were gaining on them. This time was too close for comfort. Peril chased inches behind them, spitting globs of lava and poison merely centimeters from their ears.

A fishhook branch occupied the slot where his scythe would soon live, but Simon's full attention was pumping his legs as fast as they could run. Any movements not assisting his aerodynamics or avoiding the onslaught of deadly attacks were ignored. His focus allowed him to pass Thrax with ease, but he couldn't say the same for the vicious Axoltols. They were a mere few feet away from the looters.

One of the youths – an odd appearance for a race of enlarged, premature salamanders – leapt out of the pack and latched to Simon's shoulders. His blades snapped back, and pain shot through his collar bone down to the small of his back. A deep roar erupted from his throat, but his shoulder blades and most of the pain were instantly released. Thrax raced next to him with a smug smile.

"Thanks!" Simon tried to say.

His side and leg screamed. He had charged his scars earlier that morning, but the fearful Axolotls were taxing every muscle available to sprint faster. Blindly, Simon kept shouting Seskith's random attack spells and waving his wand behind him.

Beside him, Thrax reached out and grabbed the fishhook branch from the back of Simon's vest. Simon instantly caught on and grabbed it as well. The branch was enchanted, and the pair sped away from their doom. The creepy little critters were still spitting, but Simon's flying had quite improved.

They were free.

*       *       *

Their expedition and escape had taken them far north of Feerthel Forest. To head straight back to Kearlith would land them right in line of the castle and the Kyejoth's neck of the woods. Thrax wanted to avoid the Enforcers, and he needed to return to his shop to drop off their Liriwi loot. They continued west, curving around the circle of the city, clinging to the shadows with their eyes peeled to avoid any confrontation with the law.

Simon was automatic. He systematically chose directions based on their endpoint without hesitance or even realizing it. Kearlith's silent voice called to him and pulled him like a magnet. They pit-stopped to get Thrax his own fishhook branch and continued to the city. Both spoke very little to decrease their attention to passers-by; also because neither of them could muster the amount of words it would take to comment on their past hour together.

The past few weeks came rushing back to Simon. For a moment, he felt fresh and almost foreign. He stared at the trees, at his ride, at his friend, at his hands. An overwhelming wave of reality rushed in like he was new to his own skin. Memories of the cheetah-girl were the first to surface.

Part of Seskith's charm was her adorable grin and playful laugh. The other part- her ruthlessness and skill in the Forest. She could interrupt a very funny joke to destroy a Creature twice her size and land the punch line like she planned it. Truthfully they hadn't encountered such a Creature on their adventures into Feerthel yet, but Simon could dream. As if by coincidence, he found himself on the exact path he traveled down two days ago in another race with Seskith. That time, they met a nasty Kratikoi – a race of enlarged, grotesque praying mantises – and the charming cheetah out-slashed him to his death. Simon kept a keen eye on anything resembling a long, green blade. However, he had since stitched a few tricks up his sleeve. Any sign of a Kratikoi on the offensive would not end well for the Creature this time.

His real reason for this particular adventure flooded in after Seskith's face faded. The Rebellion was moving forward, and one of the leading men pulling the strings was about to catch another bite. At the previous meeting, Simon had mentioned to Caylo a conversation or two in which he and Thrax ragged on their noble Lord. Thrax's words were light and only slightly offensive, but Simon could tell he wanted to dig deeper. Caylo agreed that Thrax would be a fine addition to the team. When Thrax asked Simon if he wanted to join him in collecting ingredients, he immediately signed on.

"Why were we so afraid out there?" Simon began.

"Are you serious?" Thrax gawked. "I hate those monsters!"

"Yeah, but after we got away from the Axolotls. On the way back – we were still afraid."

"The Protectors' eyes are always on us out here."

"As they should be," Simon agreed. "But we're not afraid of them."

"What are you getting at?" Thrax asked, suddenly skeptical.

"I'm just saying- why aren't you able to acquire ingredients under the protection of the Protectors rather than the eyes?"

"Lord Fyresk wants us in Feerthel, I guess."

"Exactly."

"Ah, I get it. This is all Lord Fyresk's fault. If he let us venture past Feerthel, all would be well. Right?"

Simon knew he was losing him. He had to stay ahead, "That's not at all what I'm saying. I'm saying – hypothetically – if someone else were in power, they could work out a better deal than under the table."

"Someone else? Who?" Thrax asked.

"I don't know. Me," he jested. Thrax nearly lost himself and toppled over. Simon joined in on the laughter.

"That was good," Thrax said as he wiped his eyes.

"Okay, so not me. Who do you think?"

He pondered for a moment. "Out of the current population of Kearlith- I'd have to say Vezlin."

"What?" Simon exclaimed. "Her world would be chaos! I mean, she's incredibly intelligent, and damn good with a wand, but she would enforce Fyresk's legacy tenfold. It needs a brand new start."

"Well then, honestly, who would be your pick?"

Now came the moment of truth. As calm and cool as he could, Simon faked contemplation and answered, "Caylo."

He didn't receive a laugh or a titter, but instead- "Now that's an odd choice."

Simon quickly picked up, "He's already an Enforcer. A good one. He's had three years' experience on the Board. And I hear he's terrifying with his sword."

"True. Caylo would be a wise choice. But I always see his smile. I think you need to see a man's frown before you can know him. And I've never seen his frown."

Simon thought back to the beginning when he first met Caylo at the blacksmith's shop, then the drill sergeant side that kept recurring at the Torn Trees. He knew that frown.

He sighed before admitting it. "He has one."

"You've been here just shy of a month, and you think you've seen more of that man than I?"

"Yes," he said. "And you can see it too, if you'd like." Thrax's face twisted into a fit of confusion. Simon knew he was dancing around daggers now. "Thrax, you'd trust that I would never reveal your secrets of where you get the ingredients for your potions, right?"

Slowly, he answered, "Right."

"Then promise you won't share a secret of mine."

"The Rebellion is real, isn't it?"

This time Simon was flabbergasted. Finally, he asked, "What have you heard?"

"Nothing definitive. I knew it was only a matter of time before someone took action and decided to change things around here. And I've heard quick whispers about something bubbling under the surface. I never imagined Caylo would be the boldest to step up, but I stand corrected. Is that why you were so eager to adventure with me? He has you as one of his henchman?"

"He doesn't make my decisions," Simon snapped. "The adventure was a double whammy. I got to see the Axolotl Lake and escape death again, while simultaneously making the Rebellion stronger and saving Kearlith."

Thrax lightly huffed. "Caylo will save Kearlith."

"The Rebellion will save Kearlith. We'll all play equal roles in our own right. Caylo isn't planning on total rule. We will all have a say in his government."

"We have a say in Fy's government," Thrax refuted.

"We-- You used to. But Lord Fyresk doesn't listen anymore."

He let out a single laugh before asking, "What do you know of the old Fyresk?"

"Little," Simon answered, "and I don't need to. I know the Kearlith and Fyresk of today."

Kearlith's glow bled through the trees exposing the darkness that had ascended on the trip back. They arrived at the city, but Thrax stopped him once they dismounted.

"So what was your plan, Si? I'd like to see it through."

"We're meeting again tomorrow. The Torn Trees at the last forty-five."

"I'll be there." Thrax took full attention of Simon's eyes. This was no frown, but an absolute statement of candor. "And Simon, regardless of the outcome of the meeting, you have my word- the Rebellion's secret is safe with me."

"Thank you," Simon answered trying to match his gaze. "See you tomorrow. And good work today. I think you'll be plenty stocked on Liriwi for a while." Thrax simply nodded with a small smile and made his exit. Si kicked off on the fishhook branch for the ride home.

His mind began to wander again. In just five days' time, he was to face Fyresk for a review on his Collecting abilities. Based on his performance, his fair and selfless Lord would grant him a raise. Simon audibly huffed as he thought about how well that would pan out.

Despite her original hostility towards Simon, Vezlin had recently made it her priority to kick his skills up to spectacular Collecting quality. In fact, she reacted with pleasure when he told her about racing up and down the dead trees in their first lesson. She made him repeat the process and others like it time and time again.

On top of that, she had him slaloming and swinging through most of the paths now. He could effortlessly fly the fishhook branch on a straight line, so her challenges now involved much more intricate footwork.

She would also set a Collecting quota within five, ten, or twenty minute increments. Simon really had to plan his paths ahead of time. He would rarely make the quota, but it didn't matter. The method was working. He was picking up on the schedule of the Mizik leaves and when they would spark. Some areas of Feerthel were quicker to regenerate Mizik than others. Sometimes he would nail the challenge; most of the time he had no such luck. Even when he had Mizik leaves to spare, Vezlin only displayed a look of minimal satisfaction. Still, Simon had to admit she was making him a damn good Collector.

*       *       *

After Simon's debt to Mathilda was paid off and he had built up a healthy cache of magic, he was finally able to somewhat furnish his shack. It popped into view a few paces up the street marking his final destination.

He smiled at the handsome new window Dagrio built. He dreamed about the interior- his fully dressed bed, his entirely too comfortable couch and two chairs circling the stump-lamp, his strong cedar armoire. The shack was becoming his dream home. Raelin left for the day's thievery early that morning, so he would probably be napping right about now. Simon tiptoed through the front door.

He was greeted by two raccoons when he entered. The fire was lit, and Raelin sat in a chair across from another raccoon on the couch who had a few more gray whiskers on his cheeks.

"So you're the new Human?" the new raccoon said.

"Yes. And you're... in my home. Who are you?" Simon still couldn't rid himself of his edge when called 'the new Human'.

"Tormos. I'm Raelin's big brother."

"Tormos was just about to come to his senses," Raelin said with a heated glare at his brother.

"I'm saying nothing, Rae," he said, defensively. "Mom and Dad are just a little crazy right now."

"They've always been crazy. And your being there isn't helping," Rae said.

"Would anyone care to include me in the conversation?" Simon butt in.

"Sorry, Si," said Raelin. "You see, back in our pocket of Feerthel, our family is rather—wealthy. Our heritage traces through some of the greatest magical raccoons in Feerthel's history, so our family has never had to ask for much. I explain this to say- our parents adore spending their time wasting it. And Tormos here was just explaining how frustrating it can be to spend any more than a few hours there."

"I love our parents!" Tormos exerted. "I do. They're real life-lovers. You know? But they can be kind of a handful," he admitted on a sigh.

"Simon, you're the rightful owner of this shack. What say you- does Tormos have a second home?"

It took a moment to respond. He tried to say "Yes" or "Maybe", but the words got caught in his throat. He had many more questions about Tormos, some of which he would feel much more comfortable knowing before he agreed to have another roommate. But he finally answered, "Sure, I guess."

Raelin punched the air. "Come live here, Torm! Mom and Dad will always be crazy."

"How will I make it on the streets of Kearlith?" Tormos asked. "I need money to be here, and I doubt Mom and Dad will hand any of theirs over."

"And Fyresk is cracking down on crime on the city, so we don't need another thief." Simon had a strong gaze on Raelin. By this point, Rae knew everything about Caylo and the Rebellion, but naturally he knew to keep quiet. "He knows something is brewing in town. He's got his nose in everything."

"Neither Fy nor any Enforcer could catch me," Raelin said, answering Simon's glare with one of his own, "but you have a point, Si."

Simon thought back to his dinner with Dagrio's family.

"Roibose said the city always needs Builders." He stopped mid-thought once he took in Tormos's size. "How are you with magic?" he asked. Tormos lowered his brow. Behind them, Simon's bed with the heavy iron legs smoothly lifted into the air and started to spin. It accelerated faster and faster. His new sheets and blanket whipped in the wind. After he had made his point, Tormos calmly set his bed down and made it up.

"Decent," he answered. Simon pursed his lips in speechless defeat.

For the next few hours, the boys watched the fire burn and crackle in the wooden bowl and shared story after story of mischievous misdoings. It felt good to laugh like this again. Simon had been spending an increasing amount of time in the Forest fighting for his life with Seskith, reaching astounding speeds with Vezlin, or debating arrangements for the Rebellion with Caylo. He could really relax now. The Rebellion was brewing, but Caylo made sure Fyresk was following a ghost trail. He had no idea what was being planned. The anxiety still existed, but Simon could cool it off for the night. He had to admit Tormos was proving himself to be a necessity in the shack.

Eventually all three pairs of their eyes began to feel heavy, and Simon had the bright idea that they should retire. The raccoons mumbled in accord, the fire was extinguished, and Simon soon found sleep.

## <u>Chapter 19</u>

It felt as if he had just closed his eyes when a small but steady "shhhh" next to his ear awoke him.

"Follow me," the whispers said.

"How?" Simon whispered back. A cold sensation over his right hand was his answer, and he silently obeyed. He followed the cold air pocket out of his bed and out the door of his shack. Only until they were under the dull glow of moonlight did Simon realize he was following nothing but a small shadow on the ground. The anonymous presence led him into the woods. He lost sight of the shadow, but the chilling sensation in his wrist stayed.

"Where are we going?" Simon whispered. Nothing was whispered back.

After a while of walking, Simon stopped them. He snatched a new fishhook branch and charged his scars. He couldn't tell if the shadow was surprised, impatient, or simply waiting, but finally he said, "Okay, let's go." He didn't feel the cold pocket anymore besides the chilling temperature outside, but the fishhook branch took off as if on its own accord.

They traveled a few minutes before the shadow kicked up the speed on the fishhook branch. Progressively. The trees started whirring, then blurring past him in the long stretches like a drum-rolling vertigo. Barreling past fifty miles an hour at times, Simon had no idea how far they had come from Kearlith. Definitely miles. Although the shadow was not holding back on testing Simon's ability on the branch, the journey still took nearly half an hour. He lost their place on the map the first time he topped at fifty, but he did catch one thing. East.

Finally, the trees parted into what Simon assumed was a clearing, but in the center of it, darkness radiated like a miniature black hole. Autumn's biting cold snipped almost every leaf from the surrounding trees. The full moon shed just enough light to notice the absence of any in the middle of the massive space. As his shadow chauffeur and he approached the black hole, the vicinity started to take on somewhat of a shape. Asymmetrical spikes in several separate clusters shot out of the ground; some had curves or corkscrews. They all varied in size, although five thick columns in the center of the clearing towered over the rest of them, their peaks reaching inches above the blanket of treetops. The duo appeared to be heading straight there.

But they stopped. The shadow moved out a few feet and began to rise. The shadow formed the feet, legs, torso, and finally face of a man roughly Simon's age. He smiled as his form finalized. The vibrant moon allowed Simon to barely see the man's image – a three-dimensional holographic blackness. He couldn't exactly tell where the being began, but a man lacking light and matter was obviously standing three feet in front of him.

"Hi," he said with a velvet voice.

"Hi," Simon answered with a blank stare.

"I'm Zahti."

"Si-" he started.

"I know. We all know you, Simon."

His disbelief was paralyzing. Confusion only fed his fear, and all-knowing, yet indifferent time kept telling him a shadow just formed and told him that all the other shadows knew… what about him? Before the questions built up and burst, Zahti continued.

"I'll tell you a few things, but that'll be on the way to the Elite. He's our Fyresk, if you will." Zahti waved the fishhook branch forward. Simon simply glided along the path, squinting at his surroundings and trying to make sense of the layout of various spikes. Without Zahti's magic, he would have perched there in midair until the spell wore off. He still hadn't grasped his current reality. It was like discovering Kearlith all over again, only overwhelmingly darker and with a genial shadow dragging him along instead of a ferocious woman.

"No one makes it as far as you, Si. Most of the Humans get tired or turned around and head back to town well before you did. They never even smell Feerthel. But you stepped right into the city. And Fyresk didn't slay you. You're remarkable, Simon."

"How much do you know?" Simon interrupted. The shadow's obsequious air was the final straw. Something about his overexerted admiration made Simon vocal.

"We were all ecstatic to hear Thrax has shown interest in the Rebellion."

"What?!" Simon exclaimed. "And who is 'we'?" The words left his lips, and the ground started to ripple in response. Hundreds of shadowy avatars began shooting up from the ground, taking considerably less time to appear than Zahti.

"Shadows!" Zahti shouted throwing his hands up. "Do you want to scare the man to death? That was a terrible introduction!"

"Sorry, Zahti," a small boy's voice said.

"We're the Vevra," Zahti said, returning his gaze back to Simon.

"You're the ones who saved me in the Cave."

"Yes. I am," he said, bringing his hand to his chest.

"You? But it sounded like there were hundreds of you!"

Instead of an instant answer, the slow howl of whispers captured the sky. "I can do that," they said, but Zahti's only facial movement was a holding a smug smile.

Despite a shattered mentality, Simon managed to ask, "So… Why?"

"Shadows!" Zahti turned around and shouted. "You've now seen Simon. Hopefully soon you'll have a chance to meet him, but for now, return home. This man has a meeting with the Elite."

This man. Zahti was the first Creature in the Forest and Kearlith to acknowledge him as an adult rather than an adolescent boy.

"Sorry about stalling back there," Zahti started once a path cleared between the shadow people. Most of them shrunk back to their two dimensional forms and wandered into the surrounding shadow spikes, but some stuck around in their avatars to gaze at Simon like he was an art piece.

"The Elite will have to answer your question of why I saved you, but I can tell you this- he's thrilled you've kept us a secret."

"I didn't really think anyone would believe me. How they can believe I did it by myself is beyond me, but…"

"Could you do it now?" Zahti asked.

"Yes," he said without hesitation.

Zahti smiled. "I bet. The truth is, Si, we've been watching Kearlith. Your Lord is indeed corrupt, and your attempts at an assassination will end in victory."

In a quick glimpse of a memory, Simon caught those blue eyes again, and his guts slightly pinged in remorse. But the rest of his demeanor was just mysterious enough not to trust. His end must come soon. At the end of his scythe. "I'll admit I'm confident in my skills, but what makes you so sure?" he asked.

"Seskith is challenged now. Before, she was teaching and toying with you, but now she's truly scared every time you duel her."

"I've never seen Fyresk battle," Si started.

"He's good," Zahti interrupted. "Very good."

Before he could finish, they entered a clearing within the forest of inferior spikes. In the middle of the space stood the five shadow towers, all rising taller than Simon could see. The Vevran territory seemed to suck the light straight from the moon.

They approached the middle shadow tower placed within the four on each side, and Zahti halted them. "There are a couple of things you should know before you meet the Elite. First and foremost- you must keep in mind that at any point, under any circumstance, the Elite could slay, slice, sting, split, and/or destroy you in seconds. He is a terribly respectful Creature, but he demands the same of those in his presence.

"Second, having said that, this is in no way a threatening inquisition. This meeting is purely in peace. So, relax."

And Simon did, somewhat.

Zahti turned to the spike and whispered an unintelligible scream. Within seconds, the Elite materialized from the massive spike – in full color – holding an amiable grin. His steel, full body armor squeezed in biceps and calves that were the thickness of Simon's entire self.

"I've been looking forward to the day I could finally meet you, Simon," he said.

"I'm sorry to admit I can't say the same, but it is an honor to meet you now, sir. How can I see you, and not the others?"

"I'm a master of magic and light, Simon. I apologize if any of this has frightened you," the Elite began.

"I'm starting to be desensitized by surprises," Simon interrupted.

The Elite gave an amused huff. "But we must keep ourselves secret. Naturally this meeting is to remain sealed as well. Zahti has brought you here to discuss an alliance. One between you and the Vevra."

"I am the Rebellion," Simon stated. He received a raised eyebrow from the Elite.

"As you shall remain," he said. "But this information is limited to you only. Your Rebellion will not be needed."

"They'll ask questions."

"And you'll answer them. Without so much as a whisper of the Vevra." The Elite kept a cool composure, but Simon was beginning to see the reasoning in Zahti's first and foremost rule.

"What are you offering?" He felt it was best to keep it blunt. He wasn't here for games or a crooked deal, but additional support in the deposition of Fyresk piqued his interest.

"An absolute guarantee of the assassination of your Lord," the Elite said as if answering the question of the forecast.

"And I'm supposed to agree to this without the Rebellion – namely Caylo – finding out?"

"That will be part of your deal. Your plans are to infiltrate his castle within two weeks' time. It's simple – lead the Rebellion there, find Fyresk, and slay him. Or we will do it for you." He gave a two-second smirk as a closing.

"What's in it for you?" Simon asked.

"The trust that Feerthel will remain pure. Without a power-hungry parasite."

It took a moment for Simon to carefully plan his next words. The guarantee of success was enticing, but could he really trust this guy – this Creature? He had no other choice.

"Deal," he said.

"Excellent," the Elite said. "And we sincerely apologize for the invasion of privacy. We've been impressed by you, ever since you stepped into Feerthel." He started to sound too much like Zahti.

A burning question found itself in his mouth, "How did you get me here?"

"We didn't," he said with an honest look of astonishment. "The Protectors did, I believe. Or one of them did, at least."

*Voulderbrin,* Simon thought. "Oh," he said. "Well could you please back off on the invasion of privacy?"

The Elite smiled wide. "We could tone it down, yes."

"Thank you. It's been a pleasure doing business, but can I go?"

"Indeed. We will be watching enough to ensure our agreement remains secret, and we will speak again soon. Happy Collecting, Simon," he said.

Simon mounted his fishhook branch, and Zahti raced him back to Feerthel Forest.

*   *   *

Simon awoke late the next morning as though his exhausted body had just hit the mattress. His head was still spinning. Three months ago he would have easily thought last night was a dream, but the twists in his stomach assured him of the truth. The shadows, the Vevra, were willing and ready to assist Simon in assassinating Fyresk.

He groggily threw on his shoes, pants, shirt, vest, jacket, and an extra jacket for the biting autumn he expected outside. Rae and Torm were still in deep sleep, both finding positions only lithe raccoons can pull off. Simon didn't need to sneak, and he didn't try.

The world felt heavy today. The Elite's words, "Slay him. Or we will do it for you," were set on repeat in his head like a bad but catchy pop song. He had said it plenty of times to Caylo, and thought it many more times to himself.

But now he found himself walking like a man who would kill Lord Fyresk in two weeks.

Fortunately, autumn kept the Kearlithians inside. Simon was free to stroll the streets without having to give a half-assed hello to someone and pretend today was just another happy day in Kearlith. He decided to walk instead of ride the branch. His scars screamed at the exercise, but Simon wanted to take his time and get warmed up.

The brewery had become his kick-start to a good day. Seskith and something that resembled coffee – but instead allowed him to cast magic – was his perfect combination of life. If anything could wake him up and bring him back to himself, it was her smile and the first sip of Mizik. The more he imagined the warmth of the steaming mugs of blue liquid, the more he ached. He craved that place.

But he slowed down. Facing Seskith today would be rough. She remained completely oblivious to the Rebellion, and Simon wanted to keep it that way. He had to act natural. He shook his hands. Stretched his back. Pumped his fists. Tried in any way to regain his normal composure. Finding a normal stance was impossible, though. How did he usually swing his arms?

This was far from natural. With a hefty sigh, he turned the last corner on the route. The fog-filled windows gave a translucent glow to the place, almost like a mirage, but the paradise at the end of the street was very real. Simon bucked up and continued.

"Catch!" Seskith said as soon as he entered. He did, but not gracefully. She tossed him a twisted hunk of Rutroot the same width as his scrawny torso.

"Seriously?" he exclaimed.

Over the past couple of weeks Seskith had allowed Simon behind the line to do some of the work in the brewery. She had him making Mizik brews and prepping some of the ingredients for the food. His favorite task by far was chopping the Rutroot. Although he didn't care for it in taste, he loved slicing it up.

"Yeah," she said, "Flecter brought it in last night."

"This is going to take hours," he said.

"Maybe." She sneered. "I can do it if you—"

"It's already in my hands. I got it. Gimme the knife." He sneered, too.

Her dreadlocks whipped around as she did as told. She carefully handed him the knife necessary to cut through the root – a foot tall and roughly three inches thick on top to give it extra weight. This knife could chop through the thickest root out there, but this was a tangled jungle gym of them. This would take work. Simon pumped his arm again to get loose.

Seskith seemed to like standing a safe distance away, watching him. At first, she was monitoring and protecting both of their safety, but she stood now with a hint of amazement. Knife in hand, Simon slashed down to make the first slice. The knife awkwardly bounced off the side of the stubborn root. Seskith softly chuckled. Simon tried again. He cut into it on the second slash, but only halfway. On the third chop the metal blade finally hacked through to the cutting board. He looked to Seskith for approval.

"Would you want that in a muffin?" she asked, nodding to the pieces of Rutroot. Three pieces had broken off, each one the size of a scone. He huffed and pushed them off to the side.

"You know," he said as he took another slash, "you'd think that," he slashed again, "given the limitless abilities of magic," another slash, "you could come up with an easier system," a final, full slash, "than this." Five pieces broke off this time, half the size of his previous attempt.

Seskith raised her eyebrows as she unfolded her arms and walked across the bar to find a hammer that was hanging underneath. Without a word she strode over to him and took the knife. Simon took her position on the wall. She laid the knife flat on top of the Rutroot and held the hammer two feet above it.

"Gravro-rull!" she shouted. The hammer crashed down onto the knife, smashing the Rutroot into all its pieces. She handed the knife back to him and returned the hammer to its place under the counter.

"You always amaze me, Seskith," he said, staring at the cutting board. Dozens of easy roots were sprawled out now.

"I try," she said, handing him a brew of Mizik.

"Thanks." He meekly smiled and returned to chopping the bigger pieces of Rutroot. She smiled back and sat on the bar.

"So what are your plans for the day?" she asked.

Slightly off-kilter, Simon answered, "Um... I have to train with Vezlin after this. And then nothing. Until Sonxdown," he added a little too quickly.

"What's at Sonxdown?" she asked with an eyebrow raised.

"Collecting, of course," he recovered. Luckily, she took it.

"Ah. Well I want to show you something. Can you come by the brewery after your training?"

"Definitely," he said. "What is it?"

"No hints," she taunted, skipping to the back kitchen.

The thought destroyed him. More secrets. How would he be able to effectively Collect with everything on his mind? He took a large sip of the Mizik brew, and Seskith's father, Vranzic, stumbled in.

"The biggest cup of Mizik we have, please," he said, taking a seat at the bar. His short, bronze hair looked disheveled. "Hello, Simon," he said.

"Hello, sir. Having a rough morning?" Simon gave Vranzic his full attention and blindly poured him a cup of Mizik.

"You could say so. I've been in business over twenty years, and I'm still clueless as to how I'll keep this place running." Vranzic's days were hit and miss. Sometimes he would walk in bursting with energy and a glass half full – or filled to the brim. Other times he lazily flopped in similar to this, but never to this hopeless extent. The glass was near empty.

Simon always felt it best to keep his questions to himself with Vranzic's mounting problems. He could in no way cheer him up, and the thought of losing his favorite place in Kearlith stung him with a similar empty feeling.

"Mizik always makes me feel better," he said, offering him the mug.

Vranzic gave a slight sigh that resembled a laugh. "Customers that had money to pay for a good brew of Mizik. That would make me feel better."

*       *       *

After the last drop of the brew was sipped, Simon felt fresh and alive. It was time to face Vezlin. He bid his good-byes to the Shintervah and started on the long path up to the Kyejoth territory. A familiar Intellect stepped out of one of the last shops on the street, though.

"Hello, Boffin," Simon announced. He hadn't seen the wand-master since he paid off his debt, and the way that meeting ended ate at him.

"Hello," he answered.

"Listen, I'm sorry for my childishness last time. I don't know what came over me. It's just--"

Boffin interrupted, "No apology necessary, Si. Lord Fyresk has us all on edge." His face didn't match the statement; it was bright and thoughtful.

"I guess so," he said. "It's just that everyone keeps telling me to be careful here. As if I'm not already terrified by everything already."

"Terrified?" Boffin asked.

The correct term for his emotions was hardly that simple. Kearlith twisted fear, adrenaline, astonishment, and ecstasy into one inexpressible wave of sensation.

But he answered, "Yeah. So far I've battled Flervana, the Axolotls, Rogs, and Kratikoi. Plus, I've learned about dozens of others I never want to meet. Not to mention, I've met our Lord."

"Indeed, Feerthel can be treacherous," Boffin said. "But with that wand and your mind, you shouldn't worry."

Simon's eyes found his for the first time. They were golden; darker than Seskith's, but they, too, emanated sincerity.

"I'm still learning," he said, breaking the stare. Boffin's words cut him down rather than lift him up. He had no idea of Simon's approaching challenges. "So why do you think Lord Fyresk is stirring up such bad emotions in town?" he asked pointedly.

"I can only wonder," Boffin said. "It's my personal belief that," he stopped to check the street for eavesdroppers, "whatever attacked him did more than skin damage. In Kearlith's past, men and women have attempted immortality, although it took a great deal of knowledge, cunning, ruthlessness, and Mizik. All of which—"

"Fyresk has plenty of." Simon finished. This theory was fitting into his perfectly. "I agree," he added. "Wholeheartedly."

"Those bastards scared the life out of him." Boffin continued, gazing off down the street into nothing. "He left for that venture a man full of burning curiosity and fearlessness. He returned a spineless mediocrity of a man thirsty for more magic. More life. More power."

The urge to mention the Rebellion yanked his attention, but Simon kept it suppressed. He had to pass it through Caylo first. Boffin was, after all, an Intellect- the law.

"Something has to change," he said, staring off down the same direction.

"Indeed. Any suggestions?" Boffin asked as he returned his attention to Simon. The yanking increased tenfold.

"None," Simon choked out.

"Well if you think of any, run them by me. I think everyone around here is beginning to get a little rebellious," Boffin said with a small wink.

Simon's heart dropped along with his jaw. The Intellects were identified by their knowledge, but how much did Boffin know? Before Simon could answer, the tall half-Human was gone.

The fuse connecting everything together in his brain nearly overheated and sparked. Boffin must have known something of the Rebellion. Seskith had something to show him. And shadows could take form and guarantee his quest of murdering his Lord. Now he had to Collect with Vezlin.

As always, his feet picked themselves up without Simon telling them to.

Vezlin believed, as Fyresk did, that there was indeed an unnamed traitor in Kearlith. Vezlin strongly accused Caylo of owning that title, but she had no hard evidence yet. She was blind to Simon's involvement. Today would be hard to keep up the façade. Though their usual training time was during the dark of night, today his mentor wanted to test his skills against the Sonx. Simon learned early on that this was far from the prime time to Collect Mizik leaves, but usually he enjoyed the additional lighting on the daylight training days.

Except today. He cursed the additional light. The shadows would have hidden his grave image. He made a few wacky expressions to try and replenish his scowl back to somewhat alive.

He stopped outside her door, sighed, and lit the symbol.

"I'll be right out," she called.

He took one more deep, calming breath.

She opened the door and said, "Take this." She handed him a short, thick tweed rope.

"And do what with it?" he asked as he accepted it.

"Just wear it as a keepsake," she sarcastically poked. "You'll be using it in training today. Follow me." She took off to South Feerthel.

Simon followed in heavy anticipation of the Creatures they would meet in the South. He remembered Lexandel's lessons. He kept an eye on Vezlin, but he mainly stared at the rope in his hands. It was a bit heavier than he expected. He wondered how he could possibly make use of a useless piece of debris.

Vezlin halted after a few minutes.

"Obviously today's lesson will not be focused on the amount of leaves you can Collect," she began. "Rather, it will test your memory and geometric skills. Your instructions are to build eight triangles into an octagon with the rope in your hands. Each side of the triangles will be three Mizik points deep."

"What?" Simon finally asked. In the dirt, Vezlin sketched an octagon and connected the intersections to reveal the eight triangles. She then marked two equidistant places on each of the inside lines.

"Those are Mizik spots," she said.

"Oh," he said. She still hadn't answered the question of how she expected him to do this with a ten-inch piece of tweed. He looked down at the rope in his hand.

"It will work," she said through a smirk. "I'll be watching from above to monitor your process. You have twenty minutes."

"What am I supposed to do with this?!" he yelled, but she rapidly transformed into a massive black hawk with glowing red feathers and took to the sky. Simon found it remarkable how Kearlithians could make such quick exits.

He plopped down in the middle of the Mizik spot and willed the rope to show its worth. He snapped it a few times to check its elasticity. It twanged tight every time. From the treetops, he heard a hint of laughter. He snapped his head up looking for her, but he couldn't even be sure it wasn't the wind or the shadows. He had to figure out the puzzle and end this.

Seskith was waiting.

His attention returned to the rope. He tried using it as a wand, although, as expected, the tree that he was aiming it at did not double its limbs. He tried a simpler spell, but it failed to turn blue. After several attempts he dolefully leaned up against the nearest Marker. To prove himself, he unlatched his true wand and made sure the tree across from him was blue. He latched it back with a small smile of satisfaction.

The calm in the Forest reminded him of one of his only good memories of his parents. He was seven, and they had taken him out to an enormous lake to go fishing. Only a few clips and images remained in his head, but he could still hear both his parents cheering him on as he reeled in his first catch. It ran in slow motion like a PowerPoint presentation, and Simon found himself casting the tweed rope like a fishing rod.

That's when he felt the rope extend. The harder he cast it, the longer it grew before it returned to its original size. He took both ends of the tweed and slowly pulled. It worked like a seat-belt. He could pull it out farther than he could reach, but as soon as he tugged, it caught. The puzzle pieces clicked into place.

He quickly tied the rope around the tree he was leaning on and grabbed his fishhook branch. This challenge was going to be a breeze. He just had to go straight through two Mizik spots and tie the rope off on the next. In no time Seskith would be revealing her something-to-show-him.

After the octagon, Simon drew a star, a torch, the head of a Voxus, and a convoluted Gulverbruud. Every new illustration decreased in time. He had just released the rope before he heard Vezlin announce that his five minutes were up. Despite himself,

Simon smiled wide as he let loose a large sigh.

"Decent work, Si," Vezlin said as she descended into the clearing.

"Thank you," he said. "It's beginning to feel second nature."

"Good. Unfortunately, Feerthel's trees are rarely this geometric. The Intellects created this area specifically for training. But now you can better handle the paths and traps of the Forest."

"So are we done for the day?" He couldn't hide his eagerness.

"We are. You've done well today, Simon. Keep performing like this, and Lord Fyresk will be amazed at your abilities." The compliment was masked with tight, curt lips.

## Chapter 20

Simon could not get back to the brewery fast enough. As skeptical as he was about learning more secrets, the thrill of another adventure in the Forest with Seskith always overpowered any other emotions.

"Hello, Seskith," he said on his entrance.

"Hi, Si," she said, smiling.

"Ready to get going?"

"More than ready. Just one second," she said. She ran to the back and not a minute later reappeared without her apron.

"So where are we going?" Simon asked.

"I can't tell you that yet. It will ruin the surprise. And I want to see your face."

Simon sighed an exaggerated "Harumph," but followed her out of the brewery. Seskith perfected the art of teasing. As if to prove it, she stopped once they reached the trees and offered him a blindfold. He pursed his lips and did not accept it.

"I want to race," he said.

"I would have the advantage since you don't know where you're going. And I don't know if they will want anyone else to know their location."

"They?" Simon asked. Seskith just smiled. Reluctantly, Si

ripped the blindfold out of her hand and tied it around his eyes.

"Grab your fishhook branch," she said. He did so. "Now hold on tight." Although he saw nothing but blackness, Seskith and her smirk became clearly visible in his mind. She wasted no time. Simon blindly bolted into the Forest. His apprehension halted his breathing, and then a flood of anxiety pumped through his veins like a river breaking through a weak dam. Seskith zoomed him through the curves and quick hooks of the paths. He couldn't catch his breath, and when he finally did, it froze his lungs.

When Seskith finally slowed him down, the color had drained from Simon's already pale skin. He collapsed off the branch and tore the blindfold off.

"Never... do that... again..." he managed to say. Just as he had imagined it, Seskith and her smirk appeared over him.

"That was only half the fun part," she said. "When you want to get up, you can see the rest."

His curiosity got the better of him. With a grunt, Simon vaulted himself up. When he looked ahead of them, he saw nothing but a thin and shallow brook. The current lightly trickled past the smooth rocks on the banks. The peaceful sight was pretty, but he did not believe it justified the roller coaster Seskith had just put him through.

"Get in," she said. Simon climbed down into the middle of the river and found it to be only knee-deep. Seskith followed in line behind him. "Keep walking," she said, as if it were obvious.

Simon did as directed. A few hundred feet down the river, the rocky bottom began to sink deeper and deeper until Simon was swimming and shivering in the chilly water. After his body temperature dropped far below comfort level, he heard a small waterfall up ahead. Not a deathly drop, but beginner-level rapids. He wondered if the other half of the surprise was placed past them.

Before he could find out, he was ripped under the water. The river plunged into his lungs. Pain and a strong taste of death coursed through his body. He flailed attempting to gain some amount of control. He shot down much deeper than he thought the river was. Hundreds of yards later, Simon splashed into another river.

When he sputtered above the surface, he found himself in an

enormous underground cavern. His eyes focused, and an oversized oak leaf floated against the current towards him. His arms were giving out, so he thrust himself into the bowl of the big leaf. He looked back up to the mouth of the waterfall with hopes of finding Seskith, but he remained alone. Despite being far below the sight of the Sonx, the long cave was plenty illuminated. Up ahead, a gargantuan tree inhabited the bank. It emanated a green-yellow glow. Its roots stretched across the dirt until the longest of them were barely breaking the water's surface. Its branches crowded the lofty space between Simon and the earthen ceiling, and they pierced into it and the dirt walls.

Before he reached the bulky tree, a branch full of lively jade leaves jutted out from the opposite bank and blocked his path. He tried to steer the boat-leaf away from it, but the current of the river only pushed him closer. He ducked as low as he could go just in case the leaves were infused with poison or electricity. There was an unsettling life to this barren cavern.

He was mere inches away from the branch before it exploded. Every single leaf shot away and zoomed all around him. The blurs were too quick to catch their true appearance. Simon sensed a trap. He gripped the branch and hoisted himself ashore. Soon the zipping lights settled back onto the branch and revealed their true forms- fairies. Hundreds of them like oversized, humanistic butterflies. Some were a metallic teal or jade or cobalt blue, others shined golden or silver. Some bodies matched their wings, some wings were complimentary colors to the body. Collectively, they looked like an Impressionist oil painting in motion.

"Tverey oleck?" one questioned.

"Ah, oleck vruskyr wonta," another one said.

To themselves, they caught and pitched this jargon with intermittent chuckles before another splash interrupted the scene at the bottom of the waterfall. Seskith easily took hold of another giant leaf and joined them on the bank.

She also entered the conversation of nonsense. "Lyfro thrunk ovrousi kyr. Ano greez tithy," she said. Each fairy felt inclined to give an enraged response all at once. Finally, one of them spoke to

Simon in a language he could understand.

"What is your name, Human from the Outside?" he said in a surprisingly deep voice despite his tiny size. He had golden wings with a body of smooth bronze.

"Simon," he answered.

"Simon," the fairy repeated pensively. "An Outside Human in our hidden realm."

"Take it easy, Blirbeck," Seskith said. "He's fragile." She held her smirk, and every single fairy erupted with giggles. Simon's face dropped. He was obviously the opposite of a threat. The fairies zipped off again and landed on his limp arms, lifting them up as if to prove their frailty. Simon shook them off.

"I'm not so weak with magic," he said. His hand instinctively found the wand on his chest, but Seskith's hand stopped him.

"Don't prove yourself here," she whispered. But the damage was done.

"He wishes to prove himself, does he?" Blirbeck said.

"No, Blirby. Don't do this. This is not how I intended this meeting."

"But alas, this is how it will go." Blirbeck shot his hands out in front of him. Simon's feet left the ground, and he floated to a wider spot on the bank. Blirbeck softly set him down. His heart leapt into his throat.

"Are you familiar with duels, Simon from the Outside?"

"It's just Simon. And no. Not in Feerthel. I've watched plenty of movies about them, though."

Seskith charged in. "Stop it, Blirbeck. He means no harm."

"Relax, Seskith. No real harm will be given or *taken*," Blirbeck said. "Simon, Xivian will count down from five. On her 'go', you are free to use whatever spell you wish. Mine will be a harmless paralysis spell." He turned his attention to Seskith. "See? I gave him the advantage. I'll take it easy on him," he said with his own smirk. "Ready Xivian?"

A teal fairy with luminescent, white wings nodded to him.

"Five," she started. Simon drew a blank.

"Four." After everything Lexandel and Seskith taught him, he could not think up a single attack.

"Three." It didn't have to be a powerful attack.

"Two." Just any attack would do. He had to think.

"One." Quickly.

"Go!" Xivian shouted. Reflexively Simon dove out of the way of Blirbeck's paralyzing blast. He cried "Iceveral" in midair to freeze the fairy's wings, and Blirbeck dropped like lead. The ice shattered once he hit the ground, but when he recuperated, he was staring at the end of Simon's wand. Simon beamed at Blirbeck's blank expression.

"The Human has learned," he said with astonishment.

"He's got some power in those skinny arms," Xivian tittered. Simon ashamedly looked at his lack of arm strength, but just as he huffed his discontent, he noticed the white wand gripped in his fist. He felt the pulse of magic again. What he lacked in physicality, he more than made up for in his mentality. Kearlith was molding him into a powerful thinker.

"Now that you boys are done playing games, Simon, I'd like to introduce you to the fairies," Seskith said with a sigh and curt lips.

"Hello, Simon," they sang in unison.

"Hello," he said.

"We rarely have visitors, Simon. Forgive us if we're slightly astonished," Blirbeck admitted.

"You're forgiven, I guess."

"Don't worry, Blirby," Seskith said. "Simon has been surprising all of us."

"Ah. Welcome to our realm, Simon," Blirbeck said, widening his arms as if in presentation.

"Why are you hidden down here?" Simon asked.

"We have no use for what's upstairs. Our mother Lahdavehr gives us everything we need." He referenced the bulky green tree across from them. This close, Simon noticed the green lines running throughout its – her – limbs, trunk, and roots. She was a marvel, and although she stood perfectly still, she radiated vitality and life.

The fairies all scattered to various places on the large tree's knots and limbs. Lahdavehr's green lines instantly gleamed. She was no ordinary tree.

And though Simon picked up on the fairies' mocking fits of

hilarity, he wasn't discomfited here. His soul laughed with the tiny leaves that dashed to life and circled around Lahdavehr's branches.

One single voice – a crisp, captivating alto – cut through the chatter of hundreds of jargon-gabbing fairies. Another few matched the melody, and they all began to settle down. Soon, more fairies harmonized with the leading alto, adding flavors of soothing soprano and luscious bass, sending the song into a complex web of connected noise. The fairies began playing with different notes and stringing them together into a chaotic and wonderful chorus. Thousands of pitch-perfect tones echoed off the walls, pulsing in the same rhythm, as if they were all in sync with a silent metronome. Their vibrations flooded Simon's heartbeat with a subtle, overwhelming sense of joy and wonder as if he were a newborn watching cartoons for the first time.

*        *        *

For hours, Simon and Seskith witnessed a spectacular show bursting with music, dancing, some form of an abstract story, and hundreds of unclear emotions that bubbled to the surface. Eventually, Seskith called the fairies down.

"Sorry to ruin the fun, everyone, but it's almost time to start Collecting. We've got to get back to Kearlith."

The fairies sighed and frowned and protested as they descended from Lahdavehr's branches. They all swarmed around Simon, covering him from head to toe. His limbs dropped in response to the calmly pulsing flow of the fairies' effect. He felt energized and alive, but on the opposite end of the spectrum from his blood-pumping adrenaline rushes in the Forest. The fairies seemed to sing through his veins.

In an instant, they flitted away back to the safety of Lahdavehr, and Seskith guided him to the exit – a waterfall that absolutely contradicted gravity. At the end of the underground river the water rushed into a massive collection of boulders, then the current defied the laws of physics and shot up to the surface.

Simon prepared for the ride this time. He jumped into the water, locking his hands to his side. He held his breath and trusted the current to take him above ground. The river still managed to jostle him, though. The sensation was surprisingly the same as falling, despite acting against gravity.

After the fall upwards, Simon emerged to a slight drizzle in Feerthel Forest. Fortunately, he had just traveled through a river so the moisture was less of a burden. The temperature above ground severely dropped once he came to his senses. He almost didn't notice the Sonx setting.

"The fairies are…" he failed to find the right word, "fantastic," he said for lack of a better one.

Seskith smiled as if she knew the right word he was looking for. "They've been kind of a second family to me. You have to swear you will keep them a secret."

"I promise, Seskith. I won't tell another soul about them. I would never want that place to be compromised."

"Thank you, Si." She started on a path back to the city.

Simon's next lines hurt him, "I'm actually going to break off and start Collecting, Seskith. Thank you for introducing me to the fairies. I'll see you later."

She skeptically said, "Okay," but Simon made an exit quicker than the Kearlithians.

He truly wanted to spend all night with Seskith, but he was late for the Rebellion meeting. Assassinating the Lord would have to take priority.

Five minutes later he found himself lost in the trees. He should have asked for directions before he bolted off like a frightened rabbit. The Protectors were hovering above, and Simon was in no need of being noticed. The treetops were beginning to grow bare. Streams of the setting Sonx's rays were bursting through the holes as light rain drizzled through the sparse leaves. Normally Simon gawked at the beauty, but the rays of light looked like lasers of the owls' gaze today.

*       *       *

After some time, Si recognized a patch of whipping grass. According to Lexandel's maps, he was in the northernmost part of the map. He would have to dart around half the Forest to make it to the Torn Trees. The Sonx was already bidding goodnight. If Vezlin hadn't taught him to cut corners like a pro, he would have been more worried. He dashed past the hundreds of Markers fearlessly, and soon he found himself staring at his brothers in the Rebellion-Voulderbrin, Friziv, Caylo, Dagrio, and now Thrax.

Caylo was the first to notice. "Good of you to finally join us, Si," he said.

"Sorry, I was... distracted," he answered breathlessly.

"Distraction will eat you in Fyresk's castle." He was in drill-sergeant mode. Simon straightened up accordingly and attempted to slow his wheezing.

"So the plan is to best the beast in his home?" Thrax asked.

"Yes. If we tried to ambush him any other place, he would naturally retreat there anyway. The plan is to infiltrate the castle and slay Lord Fyresk. He will most likely be located in his office."

"That sounds like an easy enough task." Thrax smirked at his sarcasm. Caylo did not.

"Listen, we've spent months preparing for this attack, and we will not take it lightly. If you think—"

"I think you know what you're doing." Thrax lowered his half-smile to full sincerity. "I'm curious as to how you plan to infiltrate."

Caylo unlatched his wand and drew a diagram of the castle on the non-mossy stump. He spent a full five minutes explaining every detail of everyone's purpose and specific place. Simon had now heard this speech countless times, and although he was no specialist on battle strategies, he had yet to find a flaw in the plan.

"Why do you want me on the front line?" Thrax asked after a few moments of mulling it over.

"We need a healer. Fy's castle is full of traps and tricks, and we will need more vials than you can carry. There's no doubt in my mind- plenty of us will be harmed. You'll be there to fix that and prevent us from forfeiting."

"Hm," Thrax muttered in agreement. He opened his mouth to speak again, but no words fell out. He kept staring at the diagram on the stump.

"Are you up for it?" Caylo asked. He received no answer. "Thrax?"

"Yes," Thrax said as his eyes focused back on Caylo. "I apologize – the reality of it all is a little daunting. You have my full support and cooperation, Caylo."

"Splendid. The Rebellion welcomes you, Thrax."

"Thank you. All of you," he said looking around at his new team. Each member cordially bowed their heads with pleased grins.

"In addition to your responsibilities on the day of the attack, I require one more task of you," Caylo said. "You're now acquainted with our talent of recruiting."

"Indeed," Thrax hummed. Everyone snuck a quick glance at Simon who bashfully found his feet. "Keep any mentioning of the Rebellion out of our mouths until we run it by you, I assume?"

"Exactly. You're well aware Kearlithians can catch on to rumors quickly, but as long as no Creature can trace the rumors back to us, they're simply hearsay."

"You have my word, Caylo. Potential Rebellion recruits will only be invited after you and I have discussed it first."

"Thank you. Now on to the rest of you. Dagrio? Do you have any possible recruits yet?"

"No, sir," he answered with a small grumble. Simon felt a sting of sympathy. While he and the others were bringing in multiple suggestions to every meeting, Dag had yet to find one potential new Rebellioneer.

Caylo sighed. "Well, keep thinking. Simon, who is your next target?"

"Okay, I already know what you'll say to this, but hear me out. I was talking to Boffin yesterday…" As expected, there was an uproar amongst every single one of them. Simon shot out a palm to cease the murmur. "I said hear me out!"

They grumbled but conceded. "Boffin seems just as displeased with Lord Fyresk as the rest of us. He asked me if I had any ideas on how to change things around here, and of course I said no. But he winked and told me that if anything came to me, to let him know. He's an Intellect, guys—"

"Exactly!" Caylo and Voulderbrin shouted.

"So, surely by this point the all-knowing half-Humans must have caught wind of some sort of Rebellion. Who's to say Boffin will not be willing to assist us?"

Caylo was quick to shoot him down. "I can say it. Kearlithians can barely be trusted; least of all the Intellects. They seek power and use knowledge to attain it. Any information handed over to one of them will assuredly be used against you."

"How do you know that?" Simon asked a little too heavily.

"Because I was raised with them!"

"He's right, Si," Voulderbrin butt in. "We've worked with Mortimer for years now, and if I've learned anything from the all-knowers, it's that they only act in their own interest."

"Boffin seemed different than Mortimer," Simon said.

"He's still an Intellect," Caylo said.

"Well..." Simon tried, but it was no use. Boffin would have to be marked off the list.

The meeting continued and adjourned after all the Creatures had discussed their possible Rebellion recruits. Caylo gave a short speech on the value of trust and brotherhood, but Simon barely listened. His brain was circling with ideas on how to test Boffin. Although the others had every right to doubt the Intellects, Simon just knew that this particular one was an exception. Even Vezlin had picked up on it. For now, he'd have to let it go. He would not disobey the Rebellion.

"Wait up, Simon," Dagrio said after the other Creatures took off.

"What is it, Dag?" he said.

"When is your review with Fyresk?"

"In three days. He said to meet him at his castle at mid-day."

"Good. You should stop by my house early tomorrow. I still have a couple of hexes for the scythe, but I hope to finish it tonight."

Simon beamed. He was afraid he would have to prove himself to their Lord on a humble fishhook branch, but after two days of practice, he would be a scythe-riding master. "That's great!" he said. "I'll be there first thing in the morning."

## Chapter 21

Whereas the previous day he awoke with heavy anxiety, Simon shot out of bed and giddily got dressed today. Within the hour he would be marveling at the brilliant Vanterslove's newest masterpiece. For three weeks Dagrio had kept it from his eager eyes, which only escalated Simon's anticipation. Would it be cold and black like the Scythe of Crysis? Or would the hexes illuminate it like a psychedelic rave party on a stick?

He hopped out the door with one shoe on. The other could be applied and tied on the fishhook branch. Fortunately, the Vanterslove's neighborhood was adjacent to the Forgotten territory, so after a few minutes Simon was passing through the entrance- a giant arc of twisted gazelle antlers. Dag's home was easy to spot; it was the tallest on the right side. He dipped the branch a bit to pick up speed. The gazelles were all early risers, so he slalomed through the yawning and stretching obstacles on the dirt roads.

Finally, Simon found the door. The Vanterslove were knocking Creatures so he pounded on the door until Roibose groggily answered.

"Good morning, Si," he said before he yawned. "Why the excitement at this early hour?"

"Um, no reason." His brain raced with possible excuses.

"Just a day to love life, you know?" He mentally cursed himself, but Roibose joyfully bought it.

"That's the spirit, my boy!" The obese gazelle said, perking up. Simon smiled and rushed around him, not giving him a chance for excessive conversation. He whipped around the halls and practically toppled into Dagrio's room.

"Where is it?" He exclaimed before the door closed.

"Shh!" Dag hushed from his bed. "My parents are still unaware I've been building a fearful weapon."

Simon bounced on his toes as he apologized. Dagrio was taking too long to get out of bed. "Come on! I want to see it. I want to ride it!"

"You will. Just hold on a minute. And shut up!" Dagrio was not one of the early rising gazelles.

He took his time getting dressed as if to torture Simon. Three pairs of shorts were pondered over before he found the right ones. After two vest options, Simon took it upon himself to start the search. He checked under the bed, tested the floorboards for a loose one, then ran to the large armoire.

"Finally," Dagrio said, chuckling. Simon almost ripped the doors off, but his face dropped. He saw nothing but clothes.

"Come on!" he yelled.

"Keep it down. Do you want my parents to come in and confiscate it before you've even ridden it? Just have a seat." Simon huffed, but obeyed. "Now, close your eyes."

"Dagrio!" Si could tell Dag was enjoying himself just a bit too much.

"You won't see it until you close your eyes," Dagrio said, failing to hold back a giant grin.

"Ugh. Fine." His palms covered his face. "Okay." He heard rustling and was dangerously tempted to peek, but he remained blind until Dagrio finally said, "Alright, you can take your hands down."

It was beautiful. The newness gleamed like cellophane. The wooden staff had a coffee-colored stain but displayed etchings of red, blue, green, white, yellow, and black. Both sides were tipped with the gazelle antlers from the mask he bought in Flarehva's trinket store. The blade was a cold grey, but with similar markings. It was strange how an inanimate object could scream threats of vicious malice. Dagrio began to twist the staff holding the blade in place.

"The staff twists off to become a bow. Without the blade, it can be quicker and even more deadly if used correctly."

"I... It... Thank you," Simon said. "It's magnificent."

"Do you want to try it out?" he asked.

"Are the Gulverbruud stupid?"

Dagrio laughed. "Okay," he said, "but we'll have to wait for everyone to leave for work. In the meantime, you can look through this." He chucked a thick notebook at the awestruck Simon. "Those are all the spells and their calling words."

"Cool, but hand that over first."

"Oh, yeah."

Simon heard a choir of angels' harmony as he received the scythe. He could feel the life pulsing through the wood and steel. He twisted the two pieces back together and gave it a few practice swings. Dagrio leapt out of the way.

"Careful!" he shouted, but Simon was in another world. In his imagination, he was slaying dragons and foul beasts, all cowering under the power of his weapon. After a few whirling strikes and near misses of his friend, Simon came back to the room.

"You're an astounding Builder, Dag."

"Thank you," he said, flinging the handbook at Simon's face. "Read that to prepare yourself. You have no idea what that scythe is capable of."

Simon nodded in agreement and began flipping through the pages. The master Builder had covered everything- defense hexes, paralyzing hexes, fire hexes, frost hexes, explosive hexes, the magnetism hex. This blade could destroy anything in its path, even the Scythe of Crysis.

An hour passed, and Simon had only made it halfway through the handbook. He practiced the scythe's levitation hex to the point where it became second nature, along with a few attack and defense spells. They heard the front door open and close enough times, and Dagrio calculated that all of his family had left. The coast was clear. Dagrio picked up his make-shift branch cockpit.

"I hope you can keep up on that thing," Simon mocked.

As soon as they passed the threshold of the doorway, Simon mounted his new ride and bolted off to the city. Wind whipped his disheveled hair. The scythe felt just as ecstatic as his new master to be free. It seemed to vibrate its praise.

"Where should we test it out?" Simon asked Dagrio after they arrived in Kearlith.

"The Torn Trees?" Dagrio suggested.

"It's only appropriate," he said with a smile.

The two boys took off yipping and hollering as they picked up speed and tricked off the treetops. Simon toggled between Tarzan and Tony Hawk using one tree branch to grind and hooking the scythe onto another to swing for speed. A fall from these heights would have broken a fishhook branch to pieces, but the scythe was indestructible. It laughed at the challenge. Simon did, too.

An almost-too-close encounter kept Dagrio on the ground. He narrowly missed the branch he jumped to and crashed through the branches below. Just before a devastating landing, he tugged up on his branch, and the levitation spell fought against the force of gravity. Simon could have the treetops all to himself. Dagrio said he enjoyed the sport better from a safe distance.

Soon they arrived at the Torn Trees, and Simon shot out of the treetops into the open clearing with an elongated "Woooo!" He effortlessly bounced to a safe recovery on the other side of the circle.

"That," he wheezed, "was fantastic."

"I'm pleased to know my work is appreciated," Dagrio said with a grin as big as his muzzle.

"Fyresk will have no chance against this beast." Simon couldn't take his eyes off the scythe.

"Oh, yeah." Dag said, his smile fading. "He won't know what hit him."

"Dagrio, are you still scared of bringing down Lord Fy?"

"I'm not scared!" he cried.

"Then why haven't you brought anyone to a Rebellion meeting?"

"I don't know. I truly have been thinking, but as soon as I have an idea, one of you says it before I get a chance to."

"Do you have an idea right now?"

Dagrio kicked the dirt before, "No. I'm sorry I'm not much of a Rebellioneer."

Simon thought back to all the times he himself ashamedly answered that he had come up short of everyone else's expectations. He couldn't help but sympathize with the young gazelle. "You don't have to be sorry, Dag. You're Building skills are top-notch. Who cares if you don't bring in the most recruits? You are still essential to the Rebellion."

"Well, I did have one idea. Not about anyone to recruit, but about the plan."

"What is it?" Simon asked with excitement.

"Do you remember the lifter I bought from Mathilda? I wanted one anyway, but I mainly got it because I think while the rest of the Rebellion infiltrates the castle, a few Creatures could ride up to the office on it and flank Fyresk from another side."

"Dag, that's genius! You should bring that up to Caylo at the next meeting."

"You really think so? I've been altering it so that it could reach up to Fy's office. I'm just scared that Caylo will shoot down my idea."

"No, Dagrio. I think Caylo would love that. We need every trick out of every nook and cranny we can find. And you've got thousands stored up there." Simon knocked on Dagrio's skull. The gazelle evaded it, but grinned.

"Thanks, Si. Maybe I will mention it next time."

"You should. But for now, what spell should I try out first?" Simon gripped the scythe and took an offensive stance.

"Oh! Try the slicing spell."

"Perfect." Simon smiled as he looked around for a target.

"Here," Dagrio searched around in his backpack and pulled out a little figurine mannequin. Simon's face dropped.

"My accuracy is decent, Dag, but—"

"Invosis!" Dagrio shouted. The miniature mannequin's size increased to lifelike proportions.

"Yet another handy gadget." Si smiled again. He gripped the scythe, focused on his target, and swung the blade with full force. He successfully slashed the air, but the wooden man remained completely intact. Dagrio chuckled, and Simon tried again. This time he calculated correctly, and the mannequin sliced smoothly in half. Simon's fist punched the air. "Now what?" he asked.

"Again," Dagrio demanded. He walked over to the wooden dummy and pieced it back together muttering a short string of syllables to bind the sliced torso. He ended with a yell Simon understood. "Activate evade!"

The mannequin instantly backed away from the two and circled the clearing. It came back around, and as soon as Simon jumped in to block his path, it changed course. Simon bolted into pursuit. It was much quicker on its feet than he, so he jumped on the back of the blade to catch up. When he was inches away, he lunged off and flipped the scythe in mid-air to land the blow. This took several attempts. Finally, Simon let out a blood-curdling "Yah!" as the blade made contact and smashed the wooden man to bits. Dagrio gave him a standing ovation and uproarious applause. Si tried to bow out of respect, but the weight of his body and the exercise doubled him over. His lungs burned, but every quick breath in brought waves of joy and relief.

"My turn!" Dagrio fixed the mannequin and set it to evade again. Streams of ice and fire shot across the clearing as he perfected his aim. He wasn't looking to destroy, just to damage. Almost every spell shouted landed and either froze a limb or melted the ice and caught fire. Simon sat utterly amazed at the Vanterslove's skill of ranged attacks. Eventually, Dagrio collapsed next to Simon to catch his breath.

"It's all yours," he panted.

Once again Simon was back on the blade. His attacks fried, froze, paralyzed, and shocked the wooden evader until the impassive puppet appeared terrified. The maneuver of dismounting the blade into striking mid-leap eased into his muscles' memory. His full attention was on his next attack. Time after time he struck with a lethal assault.

The mannequin eventually keeled over just before Simon followed. One more air-strike and his aching legs would have buckled under. He sprawled out on the ground and felt the adrenaline pump the blood through his veins. His teeth gleamed towards the sky. Across the clearing he heard Dagrio heal his heavily wounded gadget and stash it back in his bag.

Simon's attention switched to the descending dot falling towards them.

"Oh boy. A Protector," he said.

Sure enough, the dot developed into a silhouette of a Biffleflenn shooting down to their exercise space. Only after it had passed the plane of the treetops, Simon recognized the friendly face- Voulderbrin. And the friendly face was accompanied by a friendlier smile. The first one he could remember from any Protector.

"Fyresk may think himself a powerful Human," he said as he perched on the mossy stump, "but he will meet a serious challenge on the day of the attack. You've progressed far beyond our expectations, Simon."

"Thank you, sir," he said with a nod.

"You as well, young Dagrio. We may require you in the castle rather than holding down defense at the gate."

Any mention of the Vanterslove's youth seemed to pass right through. Dagrio gratefully grinned and nodded. "You give me too much credit, Voulderbrin. Only the best should be saved for the infiltration."

"Voxus waste," the owl scoffed. "Don't be modest. I've witnessed every attack of the last hour. The best of the Rebellion would include you. I assume only one with your genius could craft such a blade." Voulderbrin's full gaze was on the scythe.

If a gazelle's coat could blush, Dagrio would have been ruby red. His eyes found the treetops to save his mouth from an inferior response.

"Keep at it, boys. Less than two weeks' time and the New World will be in order. Until next time," and the Protector shot back into the sky.

"See you soon!" they called out.

"Two weeks," Dagrio said.

"Less than," Simon noted.

"The reality of it all is starting to set in."

"I know what you mean." The previous morning's weight pulled at Simon's shoulders again. "Do you think you could handle the castle with us?"

"I don't," Dagrio admitted. "I'm all for defending the gate, but up against Fyresk… I would freeze."

"Don't worry, Dag," Simon said, nudging his shoulder. "You'll be the best defense on the line."

"Thanks, Si. I'm confident I can keep off any loyal Kearlithians, I just wish I could reduce that number. I need to find some recruits. One, at least."

The outline of an idea landed in Simon's mind. "Maybe you can. Come on, let's see." He jumped up and offered a hand of assistance to his friend. Dagrio's hoof skeptically accepted it.

                              *        *        *

Caylo instantly declined Simon's scheme about inviting Boffin to the Rebellion, but if he could convince Dagrio, maybe the two of them could influence him to reconsider it.

They reached the street with the wand shop, and Dagrio caught on. He halted and rapidly waved his hooves. "No way, Si."

"What?" Si feigned, playing dumb.

"You want me to help you with Boffin. Caylo put it plainly- do not trust the Intellects."

"I don't trust them, as a whole. But I'm telling you, Boffin can help us."

"What makes you so sure?"

"That's what you're here for. We'll talk to him, and you can see for yourself. I'll tell him I'm in the market for a more offense-oriented wand—"

"Aren't you forgetting your destruction-oriented scythe?" Dagrio said.

"I'm not going to buy anything. It will simply be the conversation catalyst."

"If you mention the Rebellion, Caylo will hang your head on his throne when this is all over."

"That's why I won't mention the Rebellion. Come on, if I say anything out of line, you can tattle on me to the new King."

Dagrio sighed. "You know I could never do that."

"Yup. That's why I brought you along."

"You realize what you're risking here," Dagrio heatedly pleaded.

"Yes," Simon responded coolly.

"Not only the exposure of the Rebellion, but your involvement—"

"Yes," Simon repeated with a little fire of his own.

Dagrio slumped and started the way. In the depths of Simon's imagination, the chords of the Death March began ringing. Slowly they approached the wand shop.

Boffin warmly greeted them when they entered.

"Hello, Boffin."

"As always, a pleasure to see you, Simon and Dagrio. Si, have you thought any more about how to change things around here?" Boffin asked right out of the gate. Dagrio shot him a squinted glance.

"Um… Yes, sir. But I've come up short. What about you?"

"Nothing worth mentioning. I have only the mind of an Intellect, after all," Boffin said with his smiling eyes glancing at Dagrio. His muzzle snapped open, but he clamped it shut to conceal his astonishment.

"I actually stopped by for another matter," Simon jumped in. "My white wand is perfect, but I was hoping to find something a little more…"

"Lethal?" Boffin asked, grinning with raised eyebrows.

"Um, yeah. Some of the beasts in Feerthel have shown me quite a bit of menace."

"Well," Boffin turned and led them down one of the aisles, "You'll need to play on weaknesses. A Creature's weakness depends on his or her dominant element. The Gulverbruud, for instance, are infused with rock and earth; therefore, they are strong against fire and air, but weak against water. As well, the opposite is true. The Shintervah, being dominant in the element of air, can put out fires and evade water. However, they are weak against the Gulverbruud's earth abilities."

"I'm not looking to defeat any Shintervah."

"Of course not, Simon. But the theory of elements is still

important. Now, probably the most useful tip I can provide is a Human's weakness. Humans succeed in psychology and can excel at all the elements, but they cannot escape their weakness for the elements themselves. No matter how great a Human gets at controlling water and defending against fire, they will be burned if licked by a flame and drowned in a flood."

"I'm not looking to kill any Humans, either." Si could feel Dagrio's burning eyes.

Boffin simply smiled. "Of course not. But you should know your own weakness. Just in case. Ah, here's a fierce one." Boffin picked up a thick, charcoal black wand from the shelf. "It's designed to shoot exploding mines. Tap the back of the wand, and they detonate. Ten Dillians."

Simon took the wand and held it up to the light. "Intriguing. Ten Dil is a little steep, though."

"Believe me, the sight of one explosion will make you think twice. And this wand has an unlimited supply."

"I'll keep it as a possibility. What else have you got?"

"An abundance of options." Boffin continued as he led them down the aisle.

Several more wands were discussed and inspected for longer than Simon had wished. One thing he could not deny was the Intellects' pride in knowledge. Boffin spoke for what seemed like hours. Fortunately, his speeches were delivered with passion and excitement, opposed to Mortimer who spoke as if every single word uttered were painful.

Still, Simon had neither the money nor the will to purchase anything from him. His scythe would suffice as his destructive weapon.

Eventually, Dagrio attempted to end their lesson on wands. He made it seem like it were dire for Simon and him to help his mother with lunch. Boffin humbly understood and sent them on their way.

But as they bid their good-byes, they were greeted outside the shop. "The Intellects," Caylo stated with fiercely folded arms, "are off limits."

## Chapter 22

Caylo led the path to the Torn Trees silently. He raced around the curves and hooks as if to reprimand the young Rebellioneers for disobeying orders. Simon knew this would not be their only penalty. They reached the Trees, and sure enough the chastising and condescension began before he could even dismount.

"I would expect this from Friziv, Simon," he screeched, "or Voulderbrin. But from you…" Caylo's head dropped on a sigh. "You two are much too young and ill-equipped to supersede a direct order from me." His eyes found the sky and then Simon. The stare cut gashes into his insides.

"In our defense," Dagrio squeaked, "We didn't mention the Rebellion at all. We didn't even hint at it. And for what it's worth, I believe Boffin would be beneficial for us. He seems to be on our side."

"Dagrio, I don't want to hear it," Caylo said without so much as a glance toward who he was talking to.

"Well you're going to," Dagrio stated. "You're going to have to listen if you want to rule this place better than our present Lord." This got his attention. Caylo's slit red eyes soon shifted; they admitted defeat.

"I'm listening," he said.

"Boffin was... well, he seemed like," Dagrio tried, but he couldn't complete one sentence.

Simon saved him, "He told me subtly, but specifically, how to overcome and use a Human's weakness. We are physically defenseless against the elements, but our psychology allows us to shield against them. As long as we alter our spell's element to counter that of the attack or defense."

"Yeah, he told us all about that," Dagrio added. "Plus, he really did seem like he was hinting at Simon. I think he knows all about us, and he wants to get involved."

Caylo appeared to actually take all this into consideration. He blindly looked around at the trees and the sky. He chewed the side of his cheek and nodded his head. "Having Boffin on our side would be greatly beneficial for the Rebellion, but I will not lead the Rebellion into an Intellect's trap. If Boffin knows about us, then he knows about me. Let's let him come to me, and I will consider it. In the meantime, we have a new potential recruit. You should focus on him."

"Who is it?" they both asked.

"A Creature all of the leading men are focusing on." Caylo must have known the anticipation was killing them.

"Come on, Caylo," Simon demanded.

"... Morolith," he finally said.

"That's impossible." Dagrio's nostrils flared as he let out a laughing whinny. "Morolith is Fy's best Creature besides you."

Simon knew he had to object, too, but his fear of the beastly Gulverbruud paralyzed him. Morolith thought through a lie that he had enough power to blindly slay his brother and plenty more of his race. But he had to respond. "He's not a very big fan of me, either."

"That's a piece of the challenge," Caylo said. "One part of being in the Rebellion is we have to deal with you, which is fine for the rest of us. Morolith, however, has much against you."

"I'm aware."

"Somehow we all must find a way to convert him. If we have him working with us, we will be relentless in that castle. Currently, we have four members of the Rebellion that are on the Board, against three that are loyal to Fyresk. If Morolith joins our ranks, we will be able to overthrow the power present in the castle."

"Especially since Fyresk will be left with Chrysaetos and Mortimer," Simon added.

"Exactly," Caylo said. "There are certain quirks about that place that are only accessible to members of the Board. Some are specifically built to let anyone else pass through. Lord Fy has filled the entire place with traps and challenging chambers. We need as many Board members on our side as possible."

"So basically we all have to find a way to convert him before we attack next week," Dagrio said.

"You're smarter than Creatures give you credit for," the Kyejoth said. Dagrio's brown eyes brightened.

"Caylo," Simon butt in, "what if Morolith completely rebels against the Rebellion? He could go running straight to Lord Fyresk. Surely you've taken this into consideration."

"Of course I have Si," Caylo said, frowning again. "If it comes to that, we will be four against four, which is still destined to succeed. Think of the four Board Rebellioneers against Mortimer, Chrysaetos, Fyresk, and—"

"Morolith," Simon spat. "What makes you think he'll convert?"

"We had a Board meeting last night. Lord Fy failed to state it plain, but he made indistinct comments that suggested an issue with the Preeminents. And Morolith did not take it well. Thomas Dirth was his main target, and he is a god among the Gulverbruud."

"What did he say?" Dag asked.

"Simply that some of the Preeminents were not as perfect as we think they are. Not all of their experiments were as successful as, say, us." The Kyejoth and Vanterslove both looked at themselves before Simon. "Some, according to him, would make even the strongest of us weep. He wouldn't explain much more.

"Naturally most of us were appalled that he doubted us. He's supposed to be Lord, and he thinks that because he's Human..." Caylo stopped. His jaw locked, but eventually the gears starting turning again, and he finished it, "he thinks he's stronger than we are."

Both Creatures were dead staring at Simon. He sighed and

retorted, "Please do not associate me with Fyresk. We're the same race, okay? But I'm not evil. Caylo, the first of your own race tried to destroy most of what the Preeminents built."

"Kyo was a different kind of Kyejoth," Caylo snapped.

"My point exactly."

"My point," Caylo said, "is that Morolith would side with the Creatures over the Human, regardless of his loyalty to Lord Fyresk. We can use that for our benefit. Simon, do you object to that?"

Simon gulped, but countered as if it were an order, "Absolutely not, sir."

"Look, Si," Caylo lost the frown, "that war has been waged since long before our time. Humans are powerful in their own right. And anyone who can't call a truce on the matter is blind and idiotic."

"But Fyresk is speaking against his own people!" This time it was Dagrio becoming outraged. "The Preeminents were icons of the Humans' power."

"But he was speaking against Creatures' power, Dag. He shows little faith in us."

Dagrio darkened. "He's a traitor to the throne."

"Do you have any ideas on how we can go about converting Morolith?' Simon asked.

"Not many that would come to anything."

"Okay," Dagrio said, "not to beat a dead Rog, but maybe Boffin can help us convert Mortimer instead of having to—"

"Maybe," Caylo stopped him. "But we need Morolith first."

"Count me in," Simon stated. "Let's find a way to win this war."

"Good." Caylo grinned. "I like your scythe, Si. Where did you find that?"

"Where Crysis left it," Dagrio said with a mischievous smile.

Caylo's face dropped three feet. "How in Lantern's name did you discover that?"

"He's kidding, Caylo. He crafted this for me," said Simon.

"Fine, fine work, Dagrio," Caylo said, switching back to his swagger.

"Thank you, sir." Dag bashfully looked away.

"With our amount of talent, the Rebellion is sure to succeed.

May the Rebellion rise against." Caylo nodded at Simon and Dagrio. "Until next time, gentlemen." Then he mounted his sword and shot to the sky.

"So now what?" Dagrio asked. "How exactly are we supposed to convert Morolith?"

"I have no idea, Dag. But we might know someone who can help us."

"Oh no, Si," Dagrio tried, but Simon already on the scythe. "Don't say—"

"Mathilda," Dagrio finished, but Simon barely heard it.

*       *       *

After enough of a head start, Simon decelerated. He looked back through the path in the Forest and listened, but there was no sign of his friend. He was relieved; he could panic freely.

Morolith.

The Rebellion.

Shadows.

Lord Fyresk.

The Scythe.

Seskith.

Fairies.

Vezlin.

There was no end to the onslaught of thoughts that pounded through every single neuron in his brain. Every short breath brought reality closer, and he couldn't escape it. He was isolated yet completely exposed out in the Forest. He felt like all of his secrets and insecurities were tattooed in script on every inch of his skin.

He dreamed of the New World in Kearlith. A city that wasn't afraid of itself. A city that thrived and prospered in magic and honor.

Once again he focused on his goal. Morolith. Somehow he had to find his weak point. If this were a duel, Simon had no chance of besting Morolith, but this was a psychological battle. And Humans were known for their psychology.

Simon set his route toward the city and made it within minutes. Regardless of the outcome of his discussion with

Morolith's sister, he knew he needed a nap after this conversation. The world was weighing heavy today. The few citizens he passed on the streets received a half-hearted hello or an insincere head nod.

When he turned the corner to her street, he dismounted and clipped the scythe into place. Then he stood there like a child begging for more allowance. This discussion had to be thoughtfully planned and untraceable to the Rebellion. He gathered the words and sentences in his head and started walking.

The court room debate in his brain was rioting.

"Say this!"

"That won't appeal to her ethos!"

"She'll know something is up!"

"Not if you say it this way!"

He shook his head to free the flies. On a heavy huff, Simon knocked on the door.

Dagrio answered. "Hi, Si. Mathilda and I were just talking about you." He smiled as he gestured for Simon to enter.

"Oh, I was just here looking for—" Damn. Out of all his brain's babbling, it hadn't come up with a good excuse for his presence.

"I told her, Si. About the new harness we want," Dagrio winked.

"Yes. Right. We want one of our own."

"I wish that stubborn brother of mine would let you kids at least see Kowlakro's," said Mathilda. "It's a magnificent treasure. But Morolith keeps it locked up tight."

"Does he ever make use of it?" Dagrio asked.

Mathilda seemed to wilt before she spoke again. "He's used it before."

Enough of an awkward silence passed, and Simon decided to jump in. "Morolith is a very proud Creature."

"Yes, dear."

"Would you consider that a weakness?"

Dagrio's eyes widened, but there was nothing he could do. Mathilda looked Simon up and down before subtly smiling. "Pride is not the weakness. Too much of it is. And yes, I think my brother has too much of it."

"I don't think that will ever be my weakness," Simon admitted. "I'll be lucky if I have pride one day."

"You should be proud, son. You're one of the finest Kearlithians I've ever met." Her eyes meant every word. She ended the last bit with a wink that pinched his chest.

"Thank you, Mathilda."

"So, do you have any harnesses available?" Dagrio dug in.

"Right this way, boys." She led them through an aisle filled with dozens of harnesses, nets, and saddles.

"So how do you overcome too much pride?" Simon pried. Dagrio nudged him.

"With defeat," Mathilda said simply. "Ah, here we are."

She showed the harness to Dagrio and Simon, but Simon wasn't paying attention. The words 'defeat' and 'Morolith' associated together jumbled the other thoughts.

Mathilda presented them with more and more options of harnesses and various other alternatives. Dagrio really wanted to sell their lie so he asked question after question. Luckily Dagrio sold their lie because Simon was barely in the room. He couldn't escape the dread of defeating Morolith.

Soon, Mathilda sent them on their way. Dagrio gave a hearty "Good-bye, Mathilda!" while Simon nodded and muttered a couple of unintelligible words.

"Are you okay, Simon? You look peaked..." Dagrio said.

"Yeah, I'm okay," Simon lied. "I think I'm just tired. I think I'll head home and take a nap before Collecting."

"Alright, Si. I hope you like the scythe," Dagrio said bashfully.

"I do, Dagrio. It's beautiful." The Vanterslove gave a small nod of thanks and left Simon alone outside of Mathilda's shop.

With a heavy heart, Simon trudged through the streets of Kearlith to his shack. As soon as he opened the door he collapsed on the bed and quickly fell asleep. For the night.

# Chapter 23

The sound of Fyresk's grilled voice wasn't the greatest wake up call, but that's what Simon received the next morning.

"You've missed a Collection," he barked the second Simon opened the door. "You're in debt to the Bank. If I remember correctly, tomorrow is your review. This is quite honestly the worst timing."

"I'm really sorry, Lord Fyresk," Simon protested. "I meant to only take a nap last night, and—"

Fyresk threw up his palm. "You're not under review yet, Simon," Fyresk spat. "But I must ask, what has gotten you so fatigued?"

"Kearlith!" Simon yelled. "Collecting! Surviving out in Feerthel Forest! Fitting in here! It's not easy, Fy."

"Being Human?" he asked, his blue eyes giving in to his honesty.

"Exactly. We're the only ones left. And it seems like the Creatures are winning some war I've never been a part of, but now I'm half the army."

Fyresk sighed. His blue eyes lightened as he tried to find his next words.

"That's a persistent war in the city of Kearlith, Si. The story comes and goes. But have no fear, the Creatures are not winning. I'm still Lord, and this is still my city."

"I… have faith in you, Lord Fyresk," Simon choked out. Fyresk's black lips barely formed a slim grin.

"You will not be late tomorrow. And you still have two days' quota to Collect before tonight." the grin vanished. "Good day, Simon. The next time you miss a Collection, you'll see me again, and I will not be this nice." Fyresk was full on scowling. He mounted his sword and found the door, slipping out as if he had never been there.

"Rae? Tormos?" he called out, but there were no raccoons present. He shoved his pillow over his face and cried.

He let out everything he was hiding out in the Forest. All the ties and knots in his stomach were throbbing. He twisted and turned as if he were having a nightmare, but he was wide awake. Fyresk made sure of that. Tears wouldn't stop pouring and his chest burned. He had to stop. He had to handle it. He had to breathe.

Finally the inhales swept in easily, and Simon was able to simply lie motionless on the bed. His tear-soaked pillow was still plopped on his face, but he didn't have the will to move it. He was only just beginning to feel normal again.

He had two days' worth of Collecting to do. Maybe riding the scythe alone in the Forest wouldn't be such a bad way to spend the day. No Rebellion; no Fyresk; no Caylo. Just the ride. In fact, he felt it wouldn't be such a bad idea to test his own limits. If Lord Fyresk wanted him under a microscope, he was determined to prove the cells in his skin were forged with pure talent.

This got Simon out of bed. With a fresh new stance he got dressed. Even before his first sip of Mizik he felt stronger. His fingertips sizzled, restless for another challenge. He learned early in Vezlin's lessons to warm up his limbs before Collecting. Riding the fishhook branch and now the scythe took a surprising amount of physical strength. He usually limped home sore after her lessons. He did his rounds of push-ups, sit-ups, jumping jacks, and calf stretches. He jumped on and off the scythe to practice, then switched the scythe from riding position to wielding in one jump.

He took a break on his bed to catch his breath. He leafed

through the pages of *A Shintervah's Secrets Revealed* and took his first sip of Mizik- one of Thrax's famous potions. Collecting before the Sonx set was madness, but he had to hone his skills before the review. He would Collect until the next morning if that's what Fyresk wanted. The Collectors would bow to his speed and dedication. They would praise his name, and their noble Lord would have no other option than to double Simon's pay.

Even if it wouldn't matter when the New World took control next week.

Again, Simon shook the flies away. The New World could wait. Today was for Fyresk. Scythe in hand, he left his shack a refreshed man. He would not return until he had at least doubled his quota. He would face whatever beast or Creature he came upon in the Forest. He had no more fear.

He had given plenty of attention to the East of the Forest, so he decided to tread in more unfamiliar territory. The West would be the perfect starting point for this particular adventure. He slipped through the empty streets of Kearlith and found a good gateway into Feerthel.

Not far into his journey, Simon met with an expected Creature- the Zelph. These snakelike lizards were wise and quiet, remaining calm unless startled. And Simon burst through their domain like he was the star of the party. Dozens of several-foot-long lizards stopped and stared at him for seconds before they hissed and spat in pursuit.

He laughed as he raced them around their clearing to prove his elusiveness. He had much too far of a lead, and the Zelph realized it. They tucked their tiny legs into their bodies and slithered to their true speed. In seconds, Simon was side-swiped by three elongated lizard heads. Their fangs teasingly floated inches away, desperate to down the intruder.

But Simon's scythe was quicker. He set the blade to burn and leapt to slice the three heads. The leading Zelph reeled in pain, and the others in pursuit seemed to take the hint. He snuck a glance behind him, but they had all slunk away.

Simon sped into the nearest path of the Forest and never looked back. He cursed himself. Out of everything he remembered of Lexandel's lessons, he managed to forget the Zelph's advantage of speed. How many times had he read that chapter? Five?

Regardless, he found himself out in the Forest alone again. The trees had grown quiet. Silent, in fact, which was odd for Feerthel. Usually some animal, insect, or Creature was chirping or singing or barking somewhere off in the distance, but Simon heard nothing but a slight whirr of the wind. It was unnerving. He had grown accustomed to the busy city or the noisy Forest.

*       *       *

After several hours Simon found a branch high enough to sit and eat his dinner. He was officially lost out in west Feerthel. Kearlith was nowhere in sight. Simon could only see the Sonx setting. The magnificent oranges and mauves and lavenders and crisp golden lines. The boldest red Simon had ever witnessed. The rays cut through the smoky mountaintops with picturesque quality, far superior to his old HDTV.

He munched and gazed upon life's glory well into nightfall, but Simon was confident. He was beating Feerthel. He had already attained thirty leaves, more than half of a regular day's quota.

The Zelph were only a warm-up compared to some Creatures he had faced already. Fearsome zebra-lions, a pair of devious aardwolves, and some friendly penguin-swans were others. So far none of them had matched Simon's skills with the scythe. Every battle ended with him as the victor.

His pride squashed his hunger. He was eager for more adventures, and the night was young. Lord Fyresk and the Bank would have their Mizik plus more leaves than they could count. Simon slid off the branch and landed easily on the scythe. His knees automatically accounted for the change in inertia, and he was soon just as easily gliding through the trees.

Just before the next clearing, he stopped and gazed around at his surroundings, recognizing the trees. He knew what was next – the Goyliguin. Creatures fused with both iguana and grizzly bear. Simon knew their weaknesses- sound and distraction. The scythe for once was ill-equipped for either, but he had to pierce through. Their realm entangled much of Feerthel, and any bypasses would take him too long. Additionally, he was dead-set on being Simon the Brave. Or Simon the Fearless. Or Simon the Feerthel Conqueror. Whichever the Kearlithians preferred.

His face tore into a threatening scowl, and he continued into Goyliguin territory. They were somewhat peaceful Creatures. Homes built with earth and clay held finned grizzly bear families. Individually, each happy family noticed the Human waltzing down the street like it was an easy Sunday morning. Their faces found the windows. Every furry reptilian head in the vicinity stared with their beady eyes.

A guard shouted underneath a fire-post.

"Halt, Human! What is your business in Feerthel?" he demanded. His teeth snarled as if they were hungry for dinner.

"Just passing through, sir. I'm just a kid in Kearlith that needs to get through."

"There are several major Mizik paths close by, boy. What exactly led you here?"

Simon tried to suppress it, but his anger flooded in. "I was just exploring the Forest. I'm new here."

The Goyliguin's bear blood bled through, and he approached Simon with a heavy fighting stance. "You come from the Outside?" he exclaimed.

Simon instinctively wielded his scythe. "It's a long story, but yes. What of it?"

"You do not belong here!" the Goyliguin bellowed. He stretched out to slice Simon, but Simon deflected the attack and froze the beast in place. The surrounding guards that had gathered throughout the discussion all thrust at once to take him. He was already on the scythe and on the way to his next location. The Goyliguin's image alone was enough to haunt him.

Taking the street was the wrong decision. Simon thought he could cut through the back alleys and end up on the other side of the territory, but the Goyliguin's tactics were stronger than anything he had met in the Forest. A strapping Goyliguin guard in pursuit shouted, "Fles Kivizik!" and the two lampposts five feet in front of him built a wooden fence in one second that landed him flat on the ground. His face and hands were pulsing in pain, but he gradually recovered from the collision.

The Goyliguin guards were shouting behind him. "Take him! Catch that Human! Bind his flesh!"

The adrenaline kicked in, and Simon's pains vanished. He tossed himself onto the scythe and started slaloming and singing, "Mary had a little lamb! Little lamb! Little lamb! Mary had a little lamb…" The attacks were missing him by inches, but he was safe. He jumped up occasionally to detonate the scythe to explode, and he landed like it was some cool trick. As long as he kept up the theatrics, he could flee the Goyliguin's treacherous territory.

But a blast from behind knocked him off his scythe. From the ground, he scrambled to grab his scythe and deflect the storm of spells that flew at him. By the time he rose to his feet, three Goyliguin were swinging maces and axes at him. He bashed their blades back in defense, but these Creatures emanated power. Simon could never take them all down. He jumped up and spun 360 degrees, creating a cyclone that swirled the Goyliguin away from him.

Simon leapt over the huts and shacks in the Goyliguin's territory, losing the mob of iguana grizzly bears. He still heard their shouts and hollers, but soon enough, he dashed into the safety of the other side of the Forest.

Finally, he was able to breathe. Feerthel's calming trees sent him into an instant state of relief, and he could shake off the intimidation of the Goyliguin race.

*       *       *

Night had fallen over the Forest. Simon had lost track of time, but the moon stood tall in the sky. Other than a few nasty enchanted rats, Simon finished his Collecting unscathed. He didn't bother counting. He knew there were plenty more than a hundred leaves in his backpack, and he wanted to be astonished along with Chrysaetos when he turned them in. He was heading there now.

Terlinthia, the youthful golden eagle, was her usual shy and cute self. She greeted Simon with a giggle, and he entered the Bank.

"Ah, the new Collector returns," Chrysaetos said. "I hope you have enough for two days' worth."

"And more to grow on," he backhanded, dumping the Mizik leaves on the counter. As expected, the golden eagle's black eyes widened to the width of his face.

"Great Sonx, this is quite a Collection." His talons touched every leaf before he finally announced, "One hundred thirty-seven leaves. Fyresk will be rather pleased at your review tomorrow."

"Thanks, Chrysaetos. How much money is that?"

"Let's see, after the thirty-five tax… eight Dillians, forty-five Duzuks," he said. "Not too shabby, eh?"

"Not at all. Thanks, Chrysaetos. See you tomorrow."

"I hope so," said the Gullen.

The Dillians and Duzuks were nice, but the best part of his night was next on the agenda- the Mid-City Mizik Brew. Simon bowed to Terlinthia as he left and boarded the scythe. Seskith was sure to be proud of his adventures in Feerthel. He fought snake-salamanders, aardwolves, the Zelph, penguin-swans, and the Goyliguin, then managed to Collect one hundred and thirty-seven leaves of Mizik.

He quickly arrived on her street. The brewery's welcoming door was lit like a luminescent mirage. Every Kearlithian was awake this time of night, thus Simon spent more time greeting Creatures and small-talking than actually moving. He never idealized himself as famous, but he had to admit – all the Creatures wanted to talk to him. Simon was improving Kearlith's collective opinion of him. After the third "Great to see you, too!" he threw the door open to the brewery and slammed it closed like he was escaping a pride of lions.

"Hello, Simon." Seskith said from behind the bar. One eyebrow was skeptically raised.

"Hi, Seskith. Can I have a cup of Mizik, please?" he said.

"Of course. What have you gotten into tonight?"

Simon noticed his torn sleeves and singed pants. He couldn't come up with a witty excuse. "I beat Feerthel." He beamed and sipped the molten lava of Mizik brew. His virility couldn't be burned.

It did, though. The liquid ripped through his food pipe. He

knew his esophagus would be in pain for the next three days, but he didn't care. Seskith was smiling.

"And how exactly did you conquer that?" she asked.

"I outran the Zelph!" he shouted with pride. "Even when they were all snakey! I talked my way into some of the Sengli family, and I fought off the Goyliguin!"

Seskith's shine stopped. Her smile grimly turned to a frown. "The Goyliguin are noble Creatures, Simon. Why would you want to hurt them?"

"They called me Human!" he shouted.

"You are Human!" she struck back.

"They wanted to kill me because of it." The truth pinged when he admitted it aloud. "I was just exploring Feerthel, and I needed to get through. Their territory is huge, and if I went around it, I would have probably lost my direction. Which I did anyway."

"So how did you succeed?" Seskith asked.

"I just hopped on the scythe and sang a song to distract them. Lexandel says that if I—"

Seskith's full fury lit up. The sight of her instant change in manner sent a shock of chaotic fright through Simon. She hissed her next words, "What do you know of the demon Lexandel?"

Simon could only pause. He didn't know how much to admit about his hidden mentor. "He wrote a book."

"Burn it!" she screeched. "If you have any love for Kearlith or being Human you will forget Lexandel and everything he had to say."

"Who was he? He actually taught me a lot about surviving out in Feerthel. Lexandel—"

Her golden palm halted his speech. Seskith sighed and calmed herself before speaking again. "His name is hated now. You speak his name, you bring up terrible memories. For all of us, especially your Lord."

"I'm very sorry, Seskith," he admitted and sipped more Mizik. He, too, calmed himself. "He wrote a book that had a lot of lessons, and I had no idea who he was. So could you please inform me?"

"He beheaded Lord Fyrethold, Fyresk's father."

Simon gasped in astonishment and waited for her to continue, but he finally just asked, "What happened, Seskith?"

"Lexandel was a prodigy Collector. He mastered it by the age of nine. He took on every other profession after that to prove himself, and every Kearlithian loved him for it. When King Hithry died, he was unanimously the city's next King.

"Three weeks after he took the throne, he built up enough Creature courage to kill off every Human in Kearlith." She let that sink in for a minute. Simon tried to breathe. "He almost succeeded, save for Fyrethold and his infant son, Fyresk. Lexandel searched for them himself, and when he finally found them, Fyrethold was prepared. He set hex-nets around the entrance to the room they were hiding in. They bound to Lexandel's skin and set fire, just when he got to see Fyrethold's face. Fyrethold explained that if he came within five miles of Feerthel, the hex would remain ablaze.

"After his heroic victory, Fyrethold took the throne, but he took the name of Lord, and he ruled all of Feerthel rather than just Kearlith. 'King' had a bit too much bite to it, he said. He ruled this city and the Forest for Creatures and for the two remaining Humans alike. He was a pure Kearlithian and listened to his Board and his citizens.

"Lexandel didn't return for ten years. No Creature knows where he went during that time, but when he came back he had more hexes on him than skin. He had attempted to counter the fire-hex, but he had difficulty getting through the streets of Kearlith. Out of psychotic physical pain and hatred, he sliced the statue in Mid-City, then ran to do the same to our Lord. None of the Enforcers could stop him. I'm sure he used many of the so-called lessons you've learned from his book.

"He dashed through the castle and up to Fyrethold's office. By the time he found them, he was mad and out of his mind. In a fury he made Fyrethold match his statue. He then turned to Fyresk, who was already wielding a sword. Lexandel moved to strike, but Fyresk instantly plunged the sword directly into his heart.

"There was much debate, but Fyresk was named our new Lord at the age of twelve."

Simon stared without blinking. "Wow," he said. "That

explains some of his—"

"Darkness?" Seskith interrupted with a raised eyebrow.

"Yeah," he said.

She almost smiled again. "That's not all. When Lexandel was exiled, he had many fans that followed him. What happened during those ten years is a mystery for the most part. All the rebel Kearlithians vanished after Fyresk stabbed their leader. But a few years into his exile, both of Lexandel's sons showed up here. Delezi at age five, and Vranzic at age three."

The puzzle pieces clicked into place. "Vranzic, your…"

"Father. Yes."

His insides twisted again into viciously tight knots. "I'm so sorry, Seskith," he finally said.

"It's okay, Si. Next time you should just do your homework on who you're learning from."

"I thought I was," he muttered. "I could tell he had something against the Privileged, but I didn't know it led to that."

"He probably published that book while he was getting famous. I've heard he was a great Creature before he was King. Polite, charismatic, tolerant, and insanely brilliant."

"Was he the one that came up with brewing the Mizik?" Simon asked.

"He was," she said, "insanely brilliant."

"But he killed off every Human? How?"

"How do you think, Simon? He walked around singing deadly lullabies so the Humans peacefully died in their sleep."

"That would be a great tactic. In fact, that would fit Lexandel's style."

"He didn't actually do that," Seskith said, rolling her eyes.

"I didn't actually think he did." Simon kept sipping his Mizik and hoping the magic would help him deal with the news. He had seen many of the weapons Lexandel had designed. He didn't want to imagine some of the worst ones torturing or killing his own kind.

"So what happened with Vranzic and Delezi?"

"Vranzic is petrified about our history. He's always felt in debt to Lord Fyresk. But Delezi was loyal to Lexandel. He tried to rise against Lord Fyresk when he was about fifteen, but Fyresk proved his skills with magic and his blade."

"Why does everyone want to kill that guy?" Simon joked.

"I wish I could tell you, Simon. If Creatures truly listened to him and trusted him, Kearlith might actually be happy again."

Simon couldn't speak. He bit his tongue and acted as if his gut wasn't exploding.

"How do you feel about Lord Fyresk?" she asked after an awkward minute.

This was the question he was squirming on his bar-stool to avoid. "I… think he's a lot nicer, and a lot kinder than everyone gives him credit for. And he's clearly brilliant."

"But how do you feel about him?" she dug.

"I don't trust him," he admitted.

She scoffed but found humor in his truth. "After a month here, and everything you know now about Fyresk's history, you still don't trust him."

"I'm not claiming that he's *definitely* up to something evil, but I think he's hiding something. And the fact that he's hiding it makes me suspicious."

"You shouldn't question your Lord," she sliced.

"Why not, Seskith?" Simon could not hold it in any longer; the words spilled out. "Why are you stuck in this old-fashioned vision of Kearlith where you don't do anything unless you're told, and you don't speak unless spoken to? I'm not accusing Fyresk of anything. I have no idea what he's doing with all our Mizik. But I'm free to wonder."

Seskith sat shocked with her mouth pursed. "Old-fashioned vision of Kearlith?" she hissed. "You, Human, have no idea what Kearlith used to be."

"And why have things changed?" he demanded.

The gears were working in her brain. She carefully selected her next words, "Something happened to Fyresk. The attack changed him. It's been seven years since the attack, but I remember the golden-haired Lord with a dazzling smile and a solid stature. I still see the same Human behind the darkened skin and manner, but he's much colder now."

"Do you think he's working on something?" Simon asked.

"I think it's none of our business," she snapped.

"That's not what I asked."

After a fierce gaze, she answered, "Yes. I don't care to know what it is, but I doubt he's using all the magic for his own benefit. If he's keeping it from us, there's a reason."

"He scares me," Simon said. "I want to believe him and trust him, but all I've seen is post-attack Fyresk. And with Outside eyes, he's grade-A evil."

"Sometimes I see that," she confessed. "I feel like he's losing his old reputation, his old image. His old self. He barely leaves the castle anymore. I never see him in Kearlith. His eyes used to light up when he saw me, but now it seems he only speaks in business. His eyes are empty."

Simon sighed. "I know I never saw it, but I miss the old Kearlith. I wish it was the same city today, but it's not."

"It will be," Seskith stated.

"And I can't wait to help."

The Shintervah finally smiled again. "I'm glad you'll be here with us, Simon."

"Me too," he said with a humble grin.

# Chapter 24

The day of dread finally arrived. Today, Simon would face Lord Fyresk and hopefully increase his quota and his pay. The Sonx mocked from outside. Its cheerful rise only made Simon sink deeper under the covers. Seeing a man he was looking to kill in a week was far down on his list of priorities.

Alas, the review would move no smoother if Simon was unprepared. He ripped off the sheets and groggily got dressed. He envied the slumbering Raelin and Tormos; he had half the nerve to wake them up just so they could join him in his frustrated state.

He thought better of it and quietly warmed up. In roughly three hours, his flying skills would be judged and picked apart. He had to be well practiced and at his peak performance. He challenged himself to a race around the outer circle of Feerthel. Its circumference was around eight miles, and his current record was fifteen minutes.

Simon checked the pocket-watch he had borrowed from Raelin, and off into the Forest he went, slicing past the hooks, bends, curves, and turns. He had full faith in his path. When Vezlin first gave him this challenge, he bumped into plenty of Feerthel's fun little Creatures. His first attempt took nearly forty-five minutes to complete. Now he avoided every obstacle and route that would sacrifice seconds of his time.

South, East, then North were quickly conquered, and only when Simon reached the West did he feel winded. He knew his time was great, but this race always exhausted him.

Finally, Simon found his shack and checked the pocket-watch again. Thirteen minutes, thirty seconds. "Yes!" he yelled to himself, his mouth wide with a smile. He threw the door open and practically crawled to his bed, flopping on the Mizik blanket. The intrusion awoke Raelin and Tormos, who were notoriously late risers.

"What's all this excitement about?" Tormos spat as he wiped his eyes.

"Give him a break, Torm," Raelin defended. "He's got his review from Fyresk today."

"Thanks, Rae. And I just raced around the edges of Feerthel in… Drumroll, Rae."

"You're insane," Raelin said, yawning.

"I raced it in thirteen minutes, thirty seconds," he said. Both raccoons sparked up.

"That's impossible," Tormos said. "Jahravel was the fastest Collector Kearlith's ever seen, and her time was just under fourteen."

"Actually," Raelin butt in, "Her time was beaten. Lexandel cleared it in thirteen."

Simon's insides burst with a wave of pride. He was second best to Lexandel, Kearlith's best Creature.

"He wanted to record it," Raelin continued. "He got a group of Creatures to bring their own clocks and watches to prove no foul play. I'm positive it's in a record book somewhere."

Soon, Simon's roommates were awake and lively, and all three of them talked about Kearlith's history until the time finally came. He was grateful for his raccoon friends; their conversation calmed him and rid him of his nerves.

But now, on the way to castle, panic settled in. His throat was dry, and the squirrels and flies in his head were rampant. Ego, modesty, agitation, anxiety, and self-doubt all battled, and Simon could not shake them this time.

He greeted the gargoyles guarding the gate, and they let him pass with no questions asked. Fyresk never told him exactly where in the castle to meet him, but all questions were answered once he reached the main doors. The Lord's thin sliver of an appearance seemed taller up against the ten-foot, navy blue entrance.

"Thirteen minutes, thirty seconds," Fyresk said pensively. "And one hundred thirty-seven leaves of Mizik in a day." Simon expected a smile or some satisfied smirk, but Fyresk plainly spat, "Not bad. Now follow me." The Lord unsheathed his sword and dashed towards the entrance of the castle. He threw the sword ahead of him and landed on it just as the enormous front doors burst open. Once he passed the threshold, he flashed out of sight.

Simon slightly hesitated, but he was soon on his scythe and gaining on Fyresk.

"You almost lost me!" he scolded from up ahead.

Simon stayed silent. The walls in the castle were blindingly bright, and the corners were sharper than in the Forest. His full attention was ensuring he didn't slip up and end his review before it began. Or was this it?

This was definitely a challenge. After passing through the Hall of Kings for the third time in a different direction, Simon realized Fyresk was trying to lose him. They were clearly going in circles, and both Humans were increasing their speed. But Simon knew this game. He and Seskith raced almost every day. If Lord Fyresk intended to outrun the scythe, Simon was more than willing to wreck his plans.

He took a deep breath and let the scythe fly him for a moment. The curves and hooks were automatically programmed into his physical memory, and he could focus all brain activity on calculating how he could close the gap in the pursuit. Fyresk was fifteen feet ahead of him. In the long hallways he tipped the scythe to reach ear-splitting speeds. Ten feet. He caught the scythe on some corners to swing him around and save him from loss of momentum. Five feet.

Not once did Fyresk look back or give any recognition that Simon was close behind, other than his swiftly increasing level of difficulty. They passed through more brightly lit hallways and staircases than he thought the castle could hold. He took no notice of the distinct differences or directions. The only thing he saw was the charred man riding a sword three feet in front of him.

"Zapatta!" Simon shouted, flinging him to a column in front of Fyresk. He landed the scythe and turned around to sneer at his Lord.

"You cheat!" Fyresk roared. The scythe halted, and Simon kept moving forward. He caught himself before he face-planted in the dirt. Fyresk was instantly in Simon's face. "Disqualified."

"From my review?" Simon asked in outrage.

"From the first test. Your review will consist of six tests, and you must pass three. You failed the first one," Fyresk snarled.

"Why? How did I cheat?"

"In a race, you use your legs or your vehicle. No magic tricks. Come on, boy." Fyresk slipped down the closest columned hallway. It took a moment for Simon to realize he was expected to follow, but he hopped on the scythe and found Fyresk quickly.

"We could start over!" he shouted, but the Lord was done.

*     *     *

They dashed up a few staircases and landed in a beautiful courtyard. In the center were four elaborate archways fifteen feet tall with beaming vines of teal Mizik ivy lacing them together. Other magic foliage gave the place a New York's Central Park feel. The courtyard was a medium-sized square, and untamed foliage floored every inch of it. Several sprigs of weeds peaked through the cracks in the cobblestone ground. Various species of gorgeous trees were sparsely placed amongst dozens of flowerbeds. Every bud and petal glowed with Mizik's shine in neon blues, greens, and yellows. Fyresk stopped when they reached the middle.

"Your first task," he croaked, "tested your trust and courage."

"And skill," Simon spilled.

"Do not backtalk your Lord! Your test of skill will come later. Why don't you see how many laps you can get around the gazebo?"

Simon looked to his right and saw the massive gazebo made

of deteriorating planks of wood. It, too, was covered in the untamed foliage.

"What's the second task testing?" Simon asked.

"How quickly you can get as many laps as you can." He pulled out a stand with a hammer ticking a block of iron by the second. "Go!" Fyresk screeched.

Simon shot off obediently, unsure if his time started now or when he started circling the gazebo. He had never heard of this game. His playing field was Feerthel.

He knew about pacing himself, though. Simon circled the gazebo at a moderate pace as Fyresk roared insults and curses at him. He was just warming up at first. The hammer clock was ticking away, and Simon counted along.

After several minutes, just when he believed Fyresk would bust an impatient vein in his forehead, he tipped the scythe to full speed and zipped around the gazebo in seconds. With every tinny tap Simon was passing a wooden beam on the broken gazebo. This was a game of music. He pulled out the same trick he was using in the castle- using the blade to hook around the wooden beams and swing him around the gazebo. The insults stopped, and Simon could focus on the tranquility in the courtyard. He tuned out everything else in his brain and listened to the natural silence of the still day.

Fyresk eventually spoke again, but his roasted speech had a hint of defeat. "Simon! Simon! You can stop! The test is over, Simon!"

Simon heard the words, but they were swimming in his subconscious, just out of reach for him to care. He would prove once and for all that a Human from the Outside could crush any challenge in Kearlith. If Fyresk wanted to test him—

Simon was paralyzed in mid-air and brought back to the center.

"You already beat the record twenty laps ago," Fyresk sighed. "Needless to say, you passed the challenge. Endurance is key in a Collector; you certainly have much of that. On to challenge three."

*       *       *

For the third challenge, Fyresk took Simon to an obstacle course in the castle. A giant stone room with ramps, hurdles, hoops at different heights, a looping rail, and an absurd amount of fire.

"This course is open-ended. There is no start and no finish," Fyresk said as he pulled out the ticking hammer. "I'll shout the next line in the sequence, and you'll complete it. Now, the ramp to the three highest hoops." His hand gestured to the correct hoops, then he counted out four ticks and announced, "Go!"

This track was like something from the X-Games. He had played skateboarding video games all his life, but the real course was much bigger than on a tiny TV screen. From the entrance, the height of the hoops was less daunting. He tucked his knees just before the ramp and kicked off the top. As he peaked at fifteen feet, Simon noticed he overshot the hoops by several feet.

"Mulligan?" he shouted as he landed.

"Quit your backtalk. Try that again," Fyresk announced, still at the entrance.

The second time, Simon nailed the angle, and he swam through the hoops.

"The hurdles. Go!" They were harder. Simon found with every evil tick of the hammer, he was either jumping or landing. Fortunately, he made it to the end without tripping. Fyresk shouted for the tallest looping rail. Three curved steel beams surrounded the boundaries of the entire obstacle course, each set at a different angle. The scythe successfully grinded on the bar set at forty-five degrees.

The second he landed, Fyresk shouted, "The low hoops." These were closer to the fire. Simon held his breath and hugged the scythe, shooting to the other side unscathed by the licking flames. "The bars!" The scythe's assistance was over. Simon had to cross twenty feet of monkey bars. He clipped his ride on his back and swung from bar to bar like an agile ape.

This last task wore him out, but Fyresk did not let up. He continued shouting obstacle after obstacle for fifteen minutes. The hammer's tinny second mark played in Simon's head even after Fy stopped it.

"Your performance is adequate so far, Simon," he said.

Simon took a knee to catch his breath. The review was testing every muscle he had. He ached from head to toe, and he knew he was only halfway done. "By my judgment, you've passed the third task." Simon looked up and smiled, but Fyresk simply nodded. "This course was built to test a Creature's skill. I admit I'm proud to see you've proven our race's versatility and cleverness." Simon expected some sort of smile to form, but the Lord's facade was emotionless. He turned and continued. "Challenge four will not be pretty."

Instantly, the room and the hallways outside snapped to darkness. "Follow me!" he heard Fyresk roar in the distance. He still hadn't recovered from the obstacle course, but he begrudgingly mounted the scythe and slowly hovered through the black. Once his eyes adjusted, Simon noticed a hint of light coming from the hallway ahead. He chased it as quickly as his nerves allowed him, but occasionally he smashed into a column or cycloned off a corner. Fyresk's voice kept sounding farther away. "You think you can fly? You're worthless here! You're a disgrace to the Human race!"

The overwhelming blackness of everything distressed him. He tried to speed up, but every hit and skim off the columns paralyzed him. He tried to trust the path and simply focus on the flicker of dim light, but he was losing Fyresk.

The lights flashed on just for a half-second, nearly throwing Simon off the scythe. His heart-rate doubled because he saw that this room was clear. He dipped the scythe, picking up speed before the next curve. The lights flashed on again just as Simon turned the corner. He almost lost control, but he recovered and dashed into the dark distance. A few seconds later, another quicker flash revealed the true length of the room. It looked to be half the castle.

The flashes were soon accompanied by a single hit of the time-hammer, and it was getting louder. Simon was gaining on Fyresk. Every second now was marked with a tap of the hammer-clock and a flash of every lamp in the hallway. He noticed when he whipped into the next corridor or hall, there was a flicker of a shadow in front of him. Fyresk was closer than he thought.

After a few more hallways and ascending and descending staircases, Simon knew Fyresk was leading him somewhere new.

His shadow with the tinny time-hammer was less than fifteen feet in front of him, but he lost his focus on Fyresk in this new corridor. With the strobe effect, the lights revealed the heads of every kind of Creature in Feerthel and Kearlith. Their busts were stuffed and fashioned to hold menacing faces like they were in mid-taunt. Every ten feet or so, a different painting was displayed of different Creatures. Simon only caught the names of a few- Kyo, Kowlakro, Jahravel, and Lexandel.

These select Creatures, he assumed, had a more distinguished burial ground than stuffed in a hallway. The mounted heads of all the races in Feerthel lined the entire length of this corridor. Hundreds of Creatures stared at him at him every second with that hungry look in their eyes. Simon knew he was approaching insanity. He only wanted to catch up to Fyresk, finish this and the two more tasks, and go home forgetting any of this ever happened.

At the end of the Hall of Creatures, an arched doorway burst with light revealing a long hallway. Simon set the scythe to its fastest speed, and in seconds he reached the end. The shining hall blinded him after his last ten minutes in darkness. Fyresk's black blur stood with his arms folded.

"The record is eight seconds. You got nine and a half," he croaked. Simon's face dropped. "Ten is the cut-off. You passed." Simon released the tension in his shoulders with a blood-curdling sigh. He could just barely make out a smirk on Fyresk's face.

"This way," Fyresk growled.

At a decent pace, he set off on a steep, ascending staircase. The fire-lamps were lit back to blinding, but Simon found his head throbbed less if he squinted.

It allowed him to focus on his body. He was losing adrenaline at this peaceful pace, and all his pains and woes surfaced. Everything ached. His knuckles were raw from smashing into corners in pitch-black hallways; his knees were sore from constantly jumping and landing; his chest felt like his lungs had punctured and collapsed. Fyresk remained silent for quite a while. Long enough for the pain to subside and Simon's breath and strength to return.

\*       \*       \*

Just as he began to question their direction, Fyresk took a quick left, and the columned halls began holding tall slits of windows. Small fires assisted the natural lighting, but their intensity was dulled due to the Sonxlight peaking through. The ringing in his ears quit, and he felt an immense amount of pressure release from his brain. It never dawned on him how claustrophobic the castle was.

Soon the columned hallways lost their exterior until Simon found himself following Fyresk through a columned trail on the grounds outside of the castle. The trail led straight through the wall that surrounded the castle, and there were no gargoyle, Gulverbruud, or Kyejoth guards. Simon took a mental note and tried to place his location. The Rebellion could use this entrance.

The columns continued well into the Forest. Their trail snaked through, completely bypassing any normal straight and narrow Mizik path. Eventually the columns stopped, and Fyresk halted, spinning around suddenly.

"Why would the columns lead us here?" Simon asked. "This is in the middle of Feerthel."

Instead of a vocal response, Fyresk turned around and waved the columns away. They tumbled like dominoes and faded into thin air along with Simon's hopes for that secret entrance. Now they were only surrounded by indistinguishable Markers.

"Let's see how your record holds up," Fyresk half-chortled. He was definitely smirking now.

"You don't believe me?" Simon asked.

"I don't believe the Protectors. Simon, you're a talented Collector, but you've only been here a month. Jahravel, Kearlith's greatest Collector's record was—"

"Fourteen," Simon finished. "But that record was beaten." Simon couldn't stop himself quickly enough. After everything he now knew about his Lord's history with Lexandel, he did not want to make mention of his name at all.

"I know," Fyresk snarled, scowling again. "By me."

Simon tried to respond, but Fyresk took out a pebble and threw it ahead of them. He stared at the new Human for a second before, "Your task is win," and the pebble popped.

Both shot off like they were escaping an explosion. Fyresk gained the lead. The tip of his sword skimmed the dying grass, kicking up dust and dirt in Simon's teeth and eyes.

"No tricks!" Simon spat.

Simon had mastered the scythe, but Fyresk's sword technique was clearly the smarter of the two. The scythe's corners were wider and took more time than Fyresk's instantaneous inertia switches. After only a few Mizik spots, he was too far in the lead. Simon had no choice but to slam on the accelerator after every corner.

Fyresk slipped up, though. He took a right when Simon knew for a fact that the left was a shortcut for the path. He grinned as he bolted through the left, but without the constant threat of Fyresk's lead, Feerthel seemed silently taunting. The Lord surely knew the Forest better than a new Human. And he might consider this shortcut a trick. Maybe this wasn't the best idea...

The scythe shifted, and Simon sped up hoping the whipping wind would rip some of his insecurities away. He thanked the Sonx for its light. With only the beam of Mizik, Simon could never reach these speeds. In the straight paths he was topping out at sixty miles per hour.

A familiar clearing popped into view a mile in the distance. It held a circle of four giant, golden wedges like orange peels to mark the North. Hopefully there he would meet back up with Fyresk, and the scythe could pick up dust in vengeance. Once he got back on track, there was no sign of his Lord. Simon dashed ahead hoping Fyresk hadn't taken a shortcut of his own.

Sooner than Simon imagined, he reached the glass weeping willows marking the West. He had kept to the main path, but he still couldn't spot the other Human. The riot in his head started up again. How far was he behind? Or did his shortcut work? He quickly silenced the distracting thoughts and zipped through the Forest with fierce focus, taking every shortcut.

He rapidly came upon the flaming trees that marked the South. He knew his time was his best yet, and he assured himself he could beat Fyresk and whatever his record was.

"I'm only warming up, kid!" Lord Fyresk screeched from

behind him.

Simon nearly lost hold of the scythe. The outburst blew his heart-rate up, but he tightened his grip and held his speed. Fyresk was twenty feet behind him, and he was swiftly closing in the gap despite every attempt Simon made to go faster.

Fifteen feet.

Ten feet.

Five feet.

Just when Simon could almost feel Fyresk breathing down his neck, he heard two quick taps on the dirt, and Fyresk launched himself into the air. He landed on his sword with natural grace right in front of Simon and stole the lead.

They passed the East's pearly white, floating orbs, and Simon let the scythe fly him again. He put full faith in the scythe and tuned out everything but the path he needed to be taking. Fyresk was still in view, a zipping shadow roughly ten feet ahead. His starched cloak clung to his thin body. Simon focused every seed of attention on the path in front of him and slowly made progress.

Their starting point was somewhere near, and Fyresk was now less than ten feet away. To Simon's astonishment, Fyresk popped a quick one-eighty on the sword and glared at him. Simon spotted a pair of flaring posts holding a golden finish line. Fyresk cut through with his back turned. In the same conceited fashion, he hopped off his sword and sheathed it.

Simon dismounted and collapsed on the ground. The race around Feerthel robbed him of every bit of energy he had left, and he still had one more task.

"Sometimes you lose," Fyresk choked. Simon was gasping for breath. He looked up at his leader expecting to see the same contemptuous face, but he saw those blue eyes again. "No matter how hard you try to be better than everyone else, at some point you will fail. I know few real truths, Simon. But that is one of which I am certain."

"So I failed the test?" Simon asked, suddenly verging on outrage. "I have to pass the next one?"

"Indeed," Fyresk stated, losing his eyes' softness.

"Or what? You'll kill me?"

"Never," Fyresk back-handed. "I didn't kill you when we found you, and I doubt I will have any need in the future. If you fail this next task, you simply must find another profession."

Simon twitched at the audacity. "I'm one of the best Collectors Kearlith has ever seen," he declared.

"As of now," Fyresk growled through slit eyes. "After the next task you might lose the right to claim that. Get up."

His hips, knees, shoulders, and neck complained, but Simon gritted his teeth and jumped aboard the scythe once more.

*       *       *

Lord Fyresk chose a leisurely speed to travel through the Mizik paths on the way back to the castle. The soothing pace allowed Simon's limbs to rejuvenate. He calmed his temper and cooled his nerves. He flexed his fingers and stretched his neck. Without doubt this was the calm before the storm.

One more task. One more brutal test until this was all over.

Lord Fyresk waved the massive front doors open just as they were about to crash into them. He continued through the Hall of Kings and up the steep staircases and through the adorned, extensive halls of the sword castle. They continued until Simon began to think that his final test was one in endurance of boredom.

Lord Fyresk came to a stop once they reached a massive courtyard, much larger than the one previous. Tall walls surrounded the oasis of towering columns and trees which were placed throughout. Simon detected neglect in the intricate details of columns, arches, and untamed shrubberies resembling several Feerthelian Creatures. It appeared that Lord Fyresk had not hired a gardener in decades.

Simon lost his surroundings when his eyes found Lord Fyresk severely wielding his katana.

"This is your last task," he stated before he swiped at Simon from the left.

Simon quickly blocked, and Fyresk threw him a vicious slice on the other side. Simon blocked that, too, but both attacks frazzled him.

Lord Fyresk brandished his thin blade while Simon recuperated. Simon steadied his breath and controlled his temper. Fyresk was an intellectual fighter. Simon had to match his style.

Simon swung at Fyresk with a slice he knew would be deflected. The blades pinged when they met, and Simon used the force of the ricochet to sling himself into a 360.

But Lord Fyresk blocked that, too. Simon was now facing the opposite direction, and Lord Fyresk kicked him to the ground. All the air inside of him blasted away, and he sprawled across the stone floor of the courtyard, choking on his lungs.

Reflexively Simon grabbed the scythe and swirled around. From the stone floor, he blocked an indigo and orange spell. The ricocheted attack flew within inches of Lord Fyresk. Simon was quickly on his feet, and Lord Fyresk brandished his sword again, this time sending spells and hexes like machine gun bullets. This routine was getting old. Simon had to think faster. He waited for Lord Fyresk to strike from overhead, and just as he did, Simon swept at Fyresk's feet.

But he halted in mid-swing. Lord Fyresk jumped up to avoid the attack and landed right on target. Simon yanked the scythe, and his Lord was on the floor.

When Lord Fyresk opened his eyes, he was staring at Simon's extended hand. He squinted as he accepted. "You've passed, Simon," he said gravely as he dusted himself off and straightened his cloak.

"Why was that task necessary to be a Collector, Lord Fyresk?" Simon demanded.

"Collectors must be quick, clever, and fierce fighters in Feerthel Forest. I see no reason why you are not the perfect fit for the Collecting team.

"Your Mizik count is quite impressive," Fyresk continued in a manner that almost resembled defeat. "Your time on that scythe of yours is record-breaking. I'll set your quota to one hundred fifty. Your tax will remain the same. Good job today, Simon. And happy Collecting."

In an unceremonious exit, Lord Fyresk bounced on his sword

and leapt over the tall walls leaving Simon in the courtyard frozen in a state of disbelief. One hundred and fifty leaves of Mizik every day. And no pay raise.

Simon cursed the Kearlithian Lord.

## <u>Chapter 25</u>

That night, Simon woke up to a tug on his sleeve.

"Get dressed," Zahti whispered.

Simon's instinct was to moan and grumble, but he thought better of it. He got up, got dressed, yawned, and grabbed the scythe, still clinging to his slumber. Outside the shack, Zahti explained that the Elite wanted to speak to him again.

"Nice upgrade," Zahti noted. Simon yawned and nodded in response.

The shadow soldier led the scythe's way through the Forest again. Although Simon was apprehensive about another meeting with the shadow king, his half-asleep body could not care less. It barely noticed Zahti zipping him through the trees. His eyes were heavy in the night. A waning moon sporadically peaked out behind grumpy, puffy clouds. Just when he was about to doze off, his leader slowed his speed, and they passed through the shadow town. They quickly arrived at the Elite's soaring spike.

The Elite stood outside with a stance that could withstand a hurricane. "A pleasure to see you again, Simon," he said.

"Same for you, Mr... Elite."

The shadow leader chuckled. "You've been making progress in the Rebellion, I see. Although Morolith presents quite a challenge."

"I know," Simon stated. "I still have no idea how we can convert him."

"You're an intelligent and resourceful Human with a powerful set of Creatures backing you. You'll figure something out. Regardless, even if he fails to join you, your mission will succeed.

"This meeting is more than a check-up, however. We've been watching Lord Fyresk, and it seems he is hiding something within the castle. Something that is taking all the Mizik in Kearlith."

This fact woke Simon up. His eyes bulged. "What is it?" he blurted.

"That much is uncertain. The castle's lit hallways are dangerous for the Vevra. We know there is a heavily guarded room in the dungeons beneath the castle that he travels to with cases of Mizik leaves every day. The corridor to this room is armed to the teeth with lights."

"Do the Vevra get hurt in light?" Simon asked, thinking back to his escape in the caves. He was still wondering why Zahti didn't turn into his avatar when he attacked the Gulverbruud guards in the Cave.

"Low light is manageable, but the bright beams sting us unless we transition into our avatars, making us physical and exposed. In the corridor, we would certainly be noticed."

"So you need me to find out what it is. How am I supposed to get in there undetected?"

"During the attack. When the Rebellion invades the castle, you will sneak away to find this room. Everyone will be focused on the office, but you will simply find a way to break off from them."

"Simply," Simon repeated on a sigh.

"You are to gain access to that room, then clear a path for us. Then you can search for Lord Fyresk. Immediately following the attack, you are to meet me outside the castle."

"If I may be bold enough to ask, why is this secret room so important to you?"

The Elite took a deep breath before answering. "We believe that he is working on a weapon to destroy the world."

Lead dropped in Simon's stomach. He grimaced and said, "I

knew he was hiding something."

"Something powerful indeed," the Elite added. "You'll find the room at the end of a corridor four floors below the north-east wing."

"I'll figure out what it is," he said defiantly.

"Excellent. Until then, good night, Simon," the Elite said on a nod. Simon nodded, too.

"Are you ready for another ride?" Zahti asked. Once again Simon's body ripped away from his consciousness. Zahti practically threw him back to Kearlith.

\*     \*     \*

A few days later, the Sonx occasionally showed itself around large, puffy clouds, barely throwing the idea of warmth on the increasingly cooler days. Nearly every Kearlithian was gathered in Mid-City. Lord Fyresk had called a sudden gathering of every Creature in town "to discuss a major issue". He raised an earthen podium by his father's statue in order to be seen and magnified his ashy voice to be heard. Simon watched from the back of the crowd. He had a sneaking suspicion he would somehow be involved in this 'major issue', and he did not want to meet eyes with the other Human.

"Creatures of Kearlith," Fyresk began, "I'm sure I'm not the only one that has noticed the troubled times we live in. Many of you have voiced concern over my taxes. Some of you have included threats. I am well aware of the pain that has tainted this beautiful city, and she will forever be thankful for your sacrifices.

"Some have called me greedy and power-hungry, but rest assured – your Mizik and money are not wasted on me. There is a purpose for this financial drought. I will not discuss the details, for that is not your concern. However, I can assure you, soon Kearlith will prosper and thrive once more."

"How long will that take?" an irritated Vanterslove hollered. She was backed by many hurrahs.

"It is not your concern!" Lord Fyresk spat back.

"I'm concerned about when I'll start making some money!"

said a feeble, old Shintervah.

Lord Fyresk calmed himself before speaking again. "Soon enough," he said. He let his stare linger before he continued, "I have called this town meeting as a warning. I fear for the safety and well-being of Kearlith more than any of you know, and I intend to see it through the troubling times ahead. I've come to understand a truth about our founders, the Preeminents. If you've traveled through the Forest, you're well aware of some of their most harmful experiments. We've built up these people to be gods, to be glorious saints of our society, despite their misfortunes along the way to creating us.

"But they were once Humans. They were once as flawed and foolhardy as myself and Simon." Although Simon thought he was safe hiding in the back of the crowd, Lord Fyresk reached his hand out to his location in reference. Simon's cheeks flushed; his face and neck boiled. "I stand here as your Lord, the leader of Feerthel and Kearlith. I cannot demand, but I am simply asking for your support and trust.

"No one here, including myself, will deny the level of ingenuity, the perpetual inspiration of the geniuses that created us and everything we live in. I can only warn you of their mistakes. We should not treat them with such approbation."

Simon's entire face squinted, but someone lashed out for him.

"You're their own flesh and blood, you turncoat!" Morolith roared. Gasps erupted and a circle cleared around the fuming Gulverbruud.

"I will ask you to hold your temper, Morolith. As Lord of Feerthel, I could make your life very difficult."

"Ha! That'll be a change." The buffalo beast stomped out a path through the crowd. "You steal Mizik and money from us," he continued roaring as the Kearlithians darted out of his way, "you neglect telling us why, and then you denounce the Preeminents. Go ahead. Make it difficult." He snarled ever closer, but Lord Fyresk was not fazed.

"You should know my power to make things worse," Fyresk grumbled with a raised eyebrow. Morolith's face twisted, and he moved to wield his club.

"Stop!" It was Simon. He dashed up to the center of attention and ceased the battle before it began. "Fyresk is your Lord, Morolith. Creatures and Humans and turncoats aside, he is the law and the leader of our city."

Morolith huffed out his buffalo chest; his eyes widened at Simon's audacity. "He let you stay here. You, the slayer of Brobanarin. You, Simon, who gets off scotch-free from killing Creatures."

Simon was now at the front of the crowd. He bolted to face the Gulverbruud. He stepped between them so that his face was hidden from Fyresk. He winked and mouthed, "Not now."

Morolith glared but played along with, "Kowlakro would have crushed you spineless Humans." He shoved Simon out of the way and glared at Fyresk as he exited.

"As you were, Lord Fyresk," Simon said on a nod.

Fyresk's face was the one now squinting, but he quickly straightened himself and piously continued.

*       *       *

After Lord Fyresk finished his speech, the Creatures of Kearlith began to scatter from Mid-City. Simon stuck around, scouting the Kearlithians to find Morolith, but the Gulverbruud found him first. He had just passed the hardware store when Morolith's beastly hand gripped his throat and threw him against the wooden building.

"What are you planning, Human?" he growled.

"Pardon?" Simon struggled to break free, but Morolith tightened his grip.

"Don't play stupid, kid. Why do you want me in the Rebellion?"

Simon was taken aback. Morolith filled in the blanks for him. "Caylo's already hinted at an attempt to involve me in whatever you're planning, and your stunt today was clearly a part of it." Simon's face cringed. Was he that obvious? "Don't worry," Morolith continued, "Lord Fy is unaware. He's discussed with me how vexing it is not to know the identities of the rogue Kearlithians."

"So he knows there's some kind of Rebellion?" Simon asked.

"That man knows much more than you give him credit for. But as for who is involved, no, I think you're safe." Morolith released him from his death grip, but just as Simon rubbed the pain away, the Gulverbruud wielded his massive club and raised it high above his head. "From him!" he barked, swinging the club at Simon. He ducked out of the way and felt the swift wind rush past his left ear. As the buffalo-Creature recovered from his miss, Simon unclasped the scythe and stood ready.

Morolith carried the club above his head to smash Simon into the ground, but it bounced off the blade of the scythe. Morolith grunted, and Simon swung his own attack. The blade lit with flames and sliced inches in front of Morolith over and over again. He intentionally under-calibrated. The Rebellion needed Morolith in full health.

The fear tactics did little good. For a split-second Simon thought he was stepping down, but he was only judging the scythe's trail. Morolith slammed the scythe with his club and sent a wave of painful vibrations into Simon's hands. He knocked the scythe out of the way and instantly went in for the kill- a swing at his head from the right. Simon met the club with his scythe and winced through the kickback. Morolith roared.

Simon took advantage of his delay. He magnetized the scythe, and the club jumped from Morolith's hand to the blade.

"I do not wish to fight," he said.

"Me neither. I wish to kill." In a fury Morolith leapt. Simon kept still until the last second, and the Gulverbruud stumbled past him. He used the blade to sweep Morolith clear off his feet, forcing his face into the stone road. When Morolith finally lifted his head, his eyes were inches from the scythe's blade.

"You're a beast with that thing," he admitted with defeat.

"I took it easy on you," Simon gloated. "Imagine how beastly I'll be when I'm facing Fyresk."

"Your Lord?" Morolith blurted, half-chortling. "Who's to say Caylo won't get to him first?"

"No one will get to him if we don't plan for it. Morolith, if I hadn't stopped you today, you would have murdered or at the very least fiercely wounded Fyresk, and you would have had to face your bigger challenge – Kearlith. Caylo is planning the Rebellion for Kearlith in the New World."

"Caylo's no Fyresk," Morolith threatened.

"He's not trying to be. He wishes to reincorporate the Board so that all Creatures have a say in the city's decisions."

"And Humans?" he asked.

"And… Human," Simon said on a sigh.

Morolith's strong jowls actually softened. "The Board consists of seven bloody good Creatures," he said, "and one brilliant Human. You're a strong breed.

"But the Creatures should be in power. Caylo's history runs all the way back to King Kyo, the first Kyejoth. He would be the natural leader," Morolith finished after a pensive minute. "Who else is leading the Rebellion?"

"Friziv is his first-hand, and Voulderbrin is Sergeant-at-Arms."

"Not a bad line-up. Who else?"

"Nighfall will also be on our side in the attack." Simon lifted the blade from the Gulverbruud's face and offered his hand. The Creature tittered through squinted eyes and helped himself up. "Morolith, if you join us, the Board's power in the castle will be—"

"Five to three," Morolith finished. "Good strategy. When is your next meeting?"

"Tonight. The Torn Trees at Sonxdown."

"I'm committing to nothing," Morolith stated, scowling again, "but I'll be there."

*     *     *

The Sonx had begun its afternoon descent, and it was only until Simon caught sight of the brewery that he felt autumn's full chill. Adrenaline had warmed him all morning, but he was now shivering in his slow walk through Kearlith's streets. His nerves ate at his stomach today. He wanted so badly to hear Seskith's cool and caring voice, but somewhere in the conversation Fyresk's name would come up. And Simon didn't want to touch that subject with a ten-foot pole.

When he entered, Vranzic was brewing the Mizik.

"Hi, Simon," he said, his cup a little fuller today.

"Hi, Vranz."

"How was your review? I hear Fyresk and the Board can be pretty rough."

Simon's eyes narrowed. "The Board?"

"Yes," Vranzic squeaked. "The Board wasn't there?"

"No. Just Fyresk."

"That's odd," the Shintervah looked away as if calculating the irregularity.

"He kept my tax the same and demands one hundred fifty Mizik leaves a day," Simon bitterly responded. Vranzic's eyes widened.

"The madness! That's outrageous," he exclaimed, but trailed off as if apologizing for his vigor. "Fyresk has simply become merciless."

"It's fine," Simon quickly stopped him. His fury with Lord Fyresk was building up. With every passing day and event that involved that man, he found it harder to contain his anger. But he couldn't lose it here. "He knows I can do it," he said after a moment. "And I can. I just can't do anything else but Collect all night."

"And have him take almost half your share," Vranzic blurted. "The Lord's gone mad."

Just before her father finished his sentence, Seskith burst through the kitchen doors.

"Good morning, Simon," she said, smiling. "Hello, father." She crossed to the pitchers to pour a cup of Mizik, then turned around and met their eyes with hers. "So the Lord's gone mad, has he?"

"Sweetie, I'm not saying that. I shouldn't have said that. He's a good man, but—"

"My quota is one hundred fifty," Simon spouted.

Seskith's eyes snapped to slits. "What's your tax?"

"The same."

Her eyes found the ground, and she spoke to herself, "Why

would the Board allow him to—"

"The Board wasn't there," Simon said. "Only Lord Fyresk." Her golden eyes widened just like her father's. "Seskith, I'm sorry for our argument the other day. I know it's wrong to accuse the leader of Kearlith, but something about him is off. Whatever happened to him in the attack seems to have scarred his sense of morality."

"That does not sound like Lord Fyresk," Seskith said.

"This is not the same city it used to be," Vranzic uttered meekly.

"I'm aware, Dad," she spat.

Simon knew the terrible secret of the shadows and what they discovered of Fyresk's evil, but he felt it best to lie for now. He sighed as he changed his course. "Lord Fyresk seems to know what he's doing," he said. "If he doesn't want to include the rest of us, then we don't need to worry about it."

"That's the spirit," Vranzic said, calling a cheers of Mizik.

"He's always done what's best for Kearlith. He must have his reasons for demanding such an excessive Collection," Seskith said, still to herself.

It hurt to agree, but he had to, "He has more than enough experience running this city. We should simply… trust him." The last two words hit like bricks. Apparently they hit Seskith, too. She was smiling again.

"Trust is a hard thing to come by around here," she said.

Simon smiled back although his insides were screaming. "Thanks for the Mizik, Vranzic. I probably need to head home and rest. I've had a rough day."

"Still recovering from your review?" Vranzic asked.

"Something like that," Simon responded.

*       *       *

The Sonx was bidding its beautiful good-night, and the leaders of the Rebellion were meeting at the Torn Trees to prepare for the meeting.

Except for two. Simon stood in front of Roibose's home for a solid minute before knocking. Dagrio said to meet him at the glass willows of the West, but he never showed up. It was unlike the Vanterslove, specifically Dagrio, to flake out on a meeting, which meant only one thing. Dag and without doubt his entire family saw Simon's performance earlier. They must be preventing Dagrio from any meeting involving the new Human. He was in no mood for accusations.

Bucking up, he tapped on their front door. Alencia's caring grin met him and invited him inside. She offered him drinks and nourishment, which Simon passed on. Something was giving him an upset stomach, he said.

Roibose was sitting in the living room playing the equivalent of Kearlith's favorite video game- a pair of Humans fighting to the death, much like an advanced version of what Simon knew as Rock-Em, Sock-Em Robots. The controller was a small sphere that connected to one fighter. Roibose usually enjoyed the game because it allowed him to sit on his rear-end for a while, but when Simon walked in, he was standing and cheering himself on, punching and kicking the air is if it would help.

"Don't mind him," Alencia said. "This is all he does. Plays this and plans houses."

"I don't mind. It's a good match."

The AI combatant Roibose was fighting knocked his Human on the ground.

"Get up!" Roibose bellowed.

"Ten," the opponent stated. Then, "Nine."

"For the love of the Sonx, get up you worthless Human!"

"Eight. Seven. Six."

Roibose's fighter finally stood up and sent a swift punch to his opponent's credulous head, knocking him down. Roibose's fists punched the sky. He turned to Alencia and Simon and shouted, "Did you see that, honey? Simon! When did you arrive? Always good to see you, my boy."

"Good to see you, too, Roibose."

"Pardon my comment on the Human, earlier. Not all Humans are worthless, just that wooden farce of an excuse for a fighter."

Simon smiled at his sincerity. "No offense taken, sir. That

was a nice smash to the face, but I think the other guy's getting up."

"They're wooden puppets, son," Roibose dismissed. "You, my boy, are a real Human. And a brave one at that. Not one true Kearlithian stood up to Morolith today, but the new one did. I've never seen such loyalty."

"Thank you, Roibose," he said, ignoring the knots twisting his gut. It appeared these Vanterslove missed the full performance.

"This city needs loyal citizens like you, Simon," Alencia said softly. "Lord Fyresk needed that today. Reminds all the Creatures of what faithfulness and loyalty is."

He awkwardly attempted a smile.

"Simon," Dagrio spat from behind them, "are you ready?"

All three were startled, but eventually Simon spoke "Yeah, whenever you are. Thank you for your kind words, Roibose, Alencia. It was great to see you."

"Let's go," Dagrio barked. Simon swiftly followed him out the door.

*       *       *

They were soon in Feerthel; Simon on the scythe and Dagrio on an improved model of his cock-pit branch.

At first no words passed between the two. Dag was clearly upset, but he failed to give any explanation as to why. Simon finally had to ask, "Dag, why were you late?"

"You're sly, do you know that?" Dagrio asked.

"No. I always thought I was awkward and clumsy."

"None of the other Creatures seemed to notice what you whispered to Morolith after you stopped him. But I saw it clear as day."

"Are you mad at me because I helped the Rebellion, Dagrio?"

"I'm not saying anything about the Rebellion." Dagrio halted and stared at Simon. "What makes you want to kill Lord Fyresk so badly?"

"Dagrio, we've discussed this. With every meeting we learn something new about his dubious attitude and his vindictive guise.

And now—" Simon almost admitted the tiny string that would unravel the truth about the shadows. He gritted his teeth before, "Now we might have Morolith. Finally we can—"

"For the sake of this conversation, there is no Rebellion, no 'we', no Kearlith. Why do you, Simon, want to kill Lord Fyresk?" Dagrio's eyes demanded an honest answer. For a kid that was two years his junior, he held himself like a fearless hero decades older.

"I... I can't explain it. I know I never knew him before the attack, but I wish I did. I wish things had never changed in Kearlith. The way Seskith speaks about how things used to be, it sounds pure and beautiful. Kearlith is no longer that way. And I feel Lord Fyresk is the cause of it."

"Things have never been balanced. Before Fyresk, Lexandel tried to kill the true Kearlith. And before that, Kowlakro was slain by the Humans. And before that, King Kyo tried to turn everyone in Kearlith against each other. This city has a long history of heroes and villains, Simon. I'm starting to wonder which one you'll be."

Simon couldn't contain his anger. "I'm not trying to be a hero, but we both know who the villain is. For weeks now, we – you *and* I – have had the same agenda. Even outside of meetings you've told me your own reasons why you want Fyresk dead."

"I know!" Dagrio shouted on the brim of tears.

"If I was alone in my hatred for Fyresk, I would simply deal with it and let the Creatures be. But I'm not. The majority of Kearlithians want change."

"We want change! That doesn't have to mean murder!"

"Dagrio," Simon stated, holding himself a little higher, "In our first meeting with Caylo, Voulderbrin, and Nighfall, you swore to—"

"I know what I swore to!" Dagrio cried. "I know. I'm sorry, Simon. I shouldn't be mad at you. It's just... the reality of it all is sinking in. We have less than a week until we attack. Until we *kill* Lord Fyresk."

Simon sighed and sat on the scythe suspended in mid-air. "I know what you mean. It's hitting me hard, too. Back in the Outside I never believed that I was even capable, much less willing, to kill anyone. Here, I feel different. I don't feel like an Outsider. I feel like a Kearlithian. I'm just following the other Kearlithians. If at the cost of murder, we can build a just and peaceful society again, I'll do anything."

Dagrio huffed as he hopped off his floating branch and plopped on the dirt. "I should be more valiant," he said. "Honestly, I'm terrified that it will be me who finds Fyresk outside the castle. If that moment comes, I don't know who I'll be. The hero, the villain, or the coward."

"You're not a coward, Dag. You're the bravest Vanterslove I've ever met." Simon tried smiling, but it didn't take. "Besides," he continued, "I have a bad feeling I'm going to find Fyresk first. You just have to defend the castle at the gates."

"I hope this New World is worth it," Dagrio said. "Speaking of which, we have a meeting to attend."

Dagrio finally smiled at Simon and led the way to the Torn Trees.

*       *       *

Hundreds of yards away from the Rebellion's meeting spot, Simon and Dagrio heard a rumble of cries and hurrah's. As they got closer, they realized the meeting had attracted much more attention than they had imagined; the Creatures were packed into the pockets of Feerthel. They fought their way through the back of the crowd, but eventually all the Creatures caught wind of who was arriving, and they cleared a path to Caylo standing between the Trees.

"Welcome soldiers!" Caylo called without the frown. "Simon, Dagrio, there has been a turn of events. Thanks to your brawl with Morolith earlier, Simon, many Kearlithians are talking about us. We can only assume Lord Fyresk has heard the news, so we're attacking tonight."

"Tonight?" Both of them shrieked.

"Yes!" Caylo grinned. "I had hoped that we could wait one more week to prepare for the attack, but thanks to you, Simon, we have our five to three. And while Fyresk is searching for all of us, we will be infiltrating his castle."

"Let him come to us," Dagrio said with astonishment.

"Did you want this to happen, Caylo?" Simon asked.

"In a way, yes. I love the element of surprise. Creatures!" He yelled, turning his attention to the crowd without missing a beat. "Comrades! Rebellioneers! Tonight we bring justice to this city. Kearlith has had a thorn in her side for years now, and tonight we will rip that thorn away and takes its life! Tomorrow we will wake to a fresh and new world. A city that gives to its citizens instead of stealing a Creature's life away. We can all agree Lord Fyresk was in the right mindset before that terrible attack seven years ago. A noble and caring man, forthright with his agenda. The Board was proud to serve him and our beautiful home of Kearlith.

"But whatever attacked him tainted this city. I can only assume it was one of the Preeminents' creations, based on his speech today. He found something in the attack, and he's hiding it from us. The Board has been vigilant in receiving any kind of information as to what or whom he discovered, but he has persistently refused us. He's a liar, and now he's publicly denounced our founders. Tonight, he dies!"

The roared declaration brought forth hurrahs from every single Creature in the vicinity. They hollered, clapped, and hooted like Caylo was the newest rock god. On the exterior, Simon played along fervently with passionate devotion to the Rebellion. Internally, the squirrels in his head raced and crashed.

"The additional week would have allowed us to strengthen our forces," Caylo continued after the clamor died down. "But look at us. We could take on any Creature, beast, or cretin in Feerthel, let alone whatever Fyresk claims to have found. We are strong. And we're ready! Let's end his malevolent regime tonight!" Another fit of hoops and hollers followed Caylo's well planned pep talk. His red eyes lit with a fire and fury Simon had never seen before. Once Voulderbrin shushed the Rebellioneers, Caylo took the role of sergeant general again.

"We will attack in three main points of the castle. The gate, the entrance to the castle, and finally, Lord Fyresk. We expect most of you will choose to defend the gate from some of Lord Fy's most loyal. Those who wish to continue can follow myself, Voulderbrin," the owl flew in on cue and landed on the bare tree, bowing his head gracefully, "Friziv," who popped out of the trees and back-flipped on top of the mossy stump, "Nighfall, whom I'm sure most of you know," the aged Vanterslove nodded but made no move to be noticed, "and Simon," he called with a hand outstretched. Caylo paused and waited for Simon to approach the center stage.

Simon was struck with paralysis when every eye turned on him. Quickly he recovered, smirked, and leapt into the spotlight landing cleanly on his scythe. The crowd was silent for seconds before an instantaneous eruption boomed from every Creature. They roared and cheered and chanted his name. Caylo pat him on the back, but soon called for silence.

"Lord Fyresk is under the impression that his castle can save him. We know his castle. It's a tightly woven quilt of traps and few safe zones. If you choose to follow us, be warned – his castle has killed before and will definitely kill again. Keep close to us, and we will keep you safe. If you choose to defend the gate, the Rebellion salutes you. We will be forever grateful for your courage. Tonight we save Kearlith!"

## Chapter 26

The march to the castle was eerily silent. The Rebellion crept through the trees as a single unit. Each Rebellioneer made no visible recognition of the others. Eyes avoided, and fists were clenched with every free paw, hoof, and palm. Caylo led the way with his sword at the ready. Morolith held his club close in case any wild Creatures in Feerthel interrupted their assassination march. Simon, too, wielded the scythe as if Fyresk were right in front of him.

Caylo stopped them when the gargoyles at the gate were tiny blips in the distance. "We need to play this patiently. Simon, Morolith, Grelph, Kyvin, Braylius, and I will break past the gargoyle pests and continue. Enforcers and Intellects will surely begin rushing in at that point.

"After the first wave, Voulderbrin, Nighfall, Friziv, Thrax, and Kantik will catch up and meet us in the castle. As soon as they catch word, enraged Kearlithians will begin attacking. If you choose to stay, stand your ground and defend this post with your life." Caylo turned around and brandished his sword in the air.

"For the New World!" he called and charged the distance to the gates.

The gargoyles were wide awake when the Rebellion arrived. In fact, they were already swinging their staffs with fierce intimidation. Caylo thought nothing of it. He set fire to his sword and chucked it into the left gargoyle's heart. Being made of stone the piercing had no effect, but the flames persisted and engulfed the gargoyle. He collapsed off the pedestal screaming and writhing.

Caylo bolted to reclaim his sword. The other gargoyle guard dove down from his platform and squared his defensive stance against the Kyejoth. He smirked before he held out his palm and shot a stream of flames. The guard cringed, but he held his stance. Caylo slowly approached, still scorching the stone gargoyle.

The guard grit his teeth and sunk deeper into his defense until Caylo was five feet away. He cried and threw his staff straight into Caylo.

Caylo side-stepped the strike. He caught and twisted the staff as it grazed past his chest.

"Thank you," he said. He swirled the staff around and pierced the gargoyle into the ground.

Caylo nodded his head, and they continued into the castle.

Right on schedule, the Intellects ran in on long, lanky legs and sent them a thunderstorm of spells. The Rebellioneers were hundreds of feet away from the front entrance, and they were already taking cover behind the sparse trees. Simon underestimated the Intellects. Though they normally moved at a slower pace, their attacks were quick and acutely aimed. He unclasped his wand and sent a wave of magic chaos in their direction.

It slowed the Intellects for the split second the Rebellion needed to make an advance. The rebel Creatures howled and charged the tall humanoids. Morolith pointed his club, and a translucent ball burst from the end, throwing several Intellects into the air.

Out of the corner of his eye, Simon spotted one ten feet away whirling his hands around a purple sphere of fire. The Intellect snapped his hand to Simon, but the scythe deflected the spell. Dumbfounded, the Intellect's face caught the ricochet. He whirled around and landed ten feet away, his face covered in the purple flames. Simon hurried on.

*       *       *

Flaming arrows soared down from the few front windows of the castle, and the rooftops flooded with Kyejoth and more Intellects. The fire Creatures brought a blazing rainstorm, and the severely clever Intellects attempted to pick them off with spells as they were running for cover. Simon ducked and jumped far more than in his review from Lord Fyresk.

The Rebellion began the ascent up the stairs to the front entrance, but spells were flying at them from all sides.

Caylo gripped his blade and beckoned it above him. With a fierce cry, he shot a detonation into the doorway. The spell exploded into the doors with a mighty boom, but they stood completely untouched.

And then, slowly, they creaked open.

"Your Rebellion ends here," Mortimer calmly stated in an at ease position. "Follow me. And if any of you even think of retaliating, you will be sentenced to death on the spot. Test me once and see how that ends for you." The Lead Intellect began to spin around, but Caylo was quick with his wand. He snapped it out to cast a spell, but was just as instantly disarmed. "Except for you. I think Lord Fyresk would like to end you himself." Mortimer smoothly spun on his heel and began walking down the Hall of Kings. Every Rebellioneer had their eyes on Caylo and Simon. These two met eyes and nodded, silently agreeing to follow along for a while.

At the end of the hall, they descended down a steep and narrow staircase. "Are we not going to see Fyresk?" Caylo asked.

"He will come to you," Mortimer responded. "You will wait in the dungeons."

"That's preposterous, Mortimer. Lead us to Lord Fyresk this instant," Caylo stated.

The Intellect shot a quick lightning bolt at the Kyejoth's feet. "You are in no position to negotiate," he said.

Caylo's red eyes pulsed with new energy as he gave Mortimer a heavy gaze. The rest of the team moaned and followed him to a room Simon was familiar with- the same dungeon where he met the lead Rebellioneer who now walked beside him.

"I could scold you extensively for your sins against this city.

I could lecture you on patriotism and loyalty, but you are a set of idiots. Congratulations on your devious scheme. Lord Fyresk will be with you shortly." His eyelids lowered, and he vanished, slamming the iron door behind him.

Caylo, Simon, and the rest of the Rebellion collapsed on the stone floor.

"It will not end like this!" Caylo announced. "We must refocus on a new strategy."

"Will it be anything like this strategy?" said Kyvin, the Kyejoth. A snigger broke out amongst the group. Caylo fought it, but eventually he broke down and giggled a little bit.

"We have three fire Creatures here," Caylo continued. "That iron door won't be a problem. Then we have to face the guards."

"This iron door has more hexes than you can imagine," said Boffin from the open doorway. "But you could simply walk out undisturbed if it were left open."

"Boffin?" Caylo asked, flabbergasted. He snapped his head to a smiling Simon.

"Here's the deal, Caylo," Boffin swiftly said, "you can trust me and escape this cellar, or you can think me a traitor to the Rebellion and rot in here until Lord Fyresk murders each and every one of you. Your choice."

Caylo looked around at his fellow Rebellioneers, but Simon spoke for him. "How can you help us, Boffin?"

The Intellect reached into his pockets and retrieved a map. "Take this," he said, handing the map to Simon. "The current traps and safe-ways are marked. This will allow you a path directly into Fyresk's office." Caylo snatched the map from Simon and stared at it hungrily.

"He set the spiked corridor?!" he exclaimed. "And the maddening chamber!" Caylo's red eyes lit brighter with anger.

"He set them this morning, in fact," Boffin stated. "Before his humble little speech."

"Thank you, Boffin," said Simon.

"You're welcome. I do believe Fyresk is away from the castle, but when he returns, the office will be his first stop. Now hurry before any of the other guards get here. I wish you luck in your passage." Boffin bowed and exited the iron door, but he turned around. "Kearlith needs a new leader. Fyresk has become far too illogical and ill-fitted for the throne. I hope my assistance has helped clear a path to a happier Kearlith." The Intellect stood and grinned adoringly for a moment before he took off, leaving the door wide open.

The Rebellioneers bolted through the doorway and paralyzed the approaching Intellects at the end of the hall. They continued sprinting through the hallway that opened up to a tall and long chamber. Kyejoth guards were sprinting past the columns. Simon shot various spells at them, but they cleanly dodged the attacks. Soon the dozens of Kyejoth were spitting their own spells at the rebel party. The scythe back-handed several of the attacks, but Simon was dancing most of the distance to the next room.

Slowly, the Kyejoth were picked off by Morolith, Caylo, and then Simon. The downed fire Creatures moaned and cried, but made no moves to retaliate. The Rebellioneers took off to the next room.

*     *     *

They finally arrived at the front hall, and Morolith swiftly began barricading all doors save for the entrance closed. The Hall of Kings was a grand corridor with statues of every King, Queen, and heir of Kearlith. Simon took a moment in the eerie stillness to fully take in every detail of this fascinating room without flying through it at break-neck speeds. Down the main pathway lied a bold red rug that popped against the black pillars and golden statues of Jystik, Kowlakro, Hithry, Lexandel, Fyrethold, and plenty more Creatures and Humans that Simon had never heard of.

At the end of the hall opposite the entrance stood the four most magnificent sculptures in the mansion. Thomas Dirth was planted in a defensive stance. His monolithic jaw, giant biceps, and complete manner resembled his prized race. Eleanor Ocean was positioned with a psychotic grin spread across her pretty face and her hands extended into the sky as if gathering energy. Wendy Whisp floated in mid-air with her hands peacefully folded in prayer-position. Her head was placed bowed, and on one side the meticulously detailed golden hair covered her face, giving her an image of complete tranquility and innocence. On the other side her hair was pulled behind her ear revealing a deviant smirk and matching eye. Nathaniel Lantern was molded into a military at-ease position. Out of the four Preeminents, he appeared the most genuine and regal. A sleek and fearsome hilt jut out from his scabbard. Simon moved to unsheathe the sword, but Caylo's words stopped him.

"That is the Sword of Lantern. It can only be unsheathed by him."

"But he's dead," Simon retorted.

"And so it shall remain forever unsheathed. Now, onto more important matters. The next wave of the Rebellion should arrive at any moment. We'll wait in here until—"

Caylo was interrupted by the enormous front doors crashing open.

"Ah, until that," he said.

But they were not met with the other Rebellioneers. Vezlin, Mathilda, and Seskith were marching toward them on the other side of the corridor. Suddenly the Intellects looked like gerbils in comparison.

Mathilda held a unique club similar to Morolith's, but with a needle-thin end. While Simon marveled at the weapon, Seskith attacked. She shot waves of ice at the rebels, forcing them to the ground or in the air. Just when they recovered from standing up or landing, Mathilda stomped the stone floor and the rumble sent them all crashing down. The three female Creatures rushed to deal the final blows.

"I'll handle this," Morolith croaked. He pulled from his backpack Kowlakro's Harness and hurled it at the opponents. Instantly they were downed with three vicious screeches, and the Rebellion jumped up and adjusted their armor.

"Thanks, Mory," Caylo said with a humble smile. Morolith responded with a grunt and a nod.

Vezlin and Mathilda both raged under the inexorable Harness, but Seskith glared her golden eyes with laser-like precision at Simon. He wanted so badly to apologize, but this was neither the time nor the place. He ultimately met her gaze and tried to telepathically send her his condolences.

More Creatures at the door broke his concentration and the stare. Voulderbrin, Thrax, Friziv, Nighfall, and the Vanterslove named Kantik stormed in breathless and defeated.

"They're all attacking," Thrax choked out. "They're getting past our defenses."

"So we've realized," Caylo said as his eyes found the Harness. "The attack is far from over. Nighfall, Friziv, Voulderbrin, Morolith, Simon, and Thrax; we will continue into the castle. The rest of you head back to the battle outside and make sure not a single loyalist gets past that gate. And take them with you. Make sure the Harness returns to Morolith intact." He nodded to the three trapped Creatures and started off to the next corridor.

Simon intently focused on the ruby red rug in front of him to avoid any more eye contact with the Shintervah.

"You're all cowards," she snarled as they exited the Hall. Usually Seskith's bite was worse than her bark, but her remark gashed Simon.

*      *      *

The Rebellioneers rushed through the next few hallways and staircases, making the ascent up to Fyresk's office. They soon entered a room with suits of armor stationed at every marble column. Dozens of them were scattered throughout the room; the black and white checkered floor gave it the appearance of a chess match.

They remained motionless and took no notice of the Rebellioneers until the team was half-way through the chamber. Simon looked back at the entrance, and they seized with life. They clanged and clumped as they lunged to catch up to the rebels. Simon jumped on the scythe and turned his attention ahead. The statues in front of them sprang to life as well.

Simon raced around the pillars and applied his mid-air slice method to several of the metal-plated drones. They swung long swords and maces, but Simon and the other Rebellioneers dodged and evaded the onslaught. Caylo gradually advanced the team to the other end of the chamber while slicing the path in front of him.

Morolith and Friziv defended him and clubbed any armored opponents flanking them from the side. Voulderbrin and Simon were successfully drawing the guards' attention away from the rest of the rebels.

Caylo sent an explosive spell to the door to the next corridor. The door and the area around the door-frame were obliterated, and the team simultaneously dashed through the exit. Caylo, Friziv, Morolith, Voulderbrin, Thrax, and Simon all made it through, but as Caylo did a head-count, they heard Nighfall shriek. Caylo unsheathed his sword, mounted it, and bolted back into the room. He jumped off the sword just before he speared the nearest armored guard in the chest. He landed and retrieved his sword as the steel armor smashed into the concrete.

Morolith snapped into action, too. He raced off and scooped up the wounded Vanterslove. Every surviving suit of armor surrounded them. They blocked Morolith's path to the exit and grabbed at the Creatures, finally pinning Caylo to the ground. The guard with his foot on the Kyejoth's back brandished his sword in the air before the execution. Just as he brought the sword down to strike, Simon rushed in and sliced the suit of armor clean in half. Pieces of the armor suit skipped across the floor. The sword fell slack and clanked where Caylo's head had been two seconds previous.

"Simon, I..." he tried, but Simon grabbed his arm and tugged him to the next corridor.

Once every Rebellioneer cleared the door, Morolith used the debris from the explosion to block the entrance. For the time being, it worked. The clamor of steel punches and hard kicks against the cold stone echoed angrily into the dark room.

Caylo held out his palm and produced a small flame as he approached Nighfall. The fire would have illuminated more, but the air in this room seemed to suck the light away. Simon saw nothing outside the small sphere of dim, dancing illumination. "Can you continue?" Caylo asked.

The elder Vanterslove grimaced and breathed heavily through grit teeth, but he eventually stated, "I'll keep going 'til they kill me."

They smiled, and Caylo pulled out the map. "That's the good

news. The bad news is that we are now in the spiked corridor."

There was a general gasp, and Voulderbrin said, "Is there no other way around this room? I find this place particularly daunting."

"Why?" Simon asked.

On cue a needle twice the length of Simon pierced the air above them. "Look out!" Voulderbrin called. He kicked it away with his tiny talons, and it clattered into the abyss.

"Thrax!" Caylo yelled. "Please heal Nighfall swiftly, and let's get out of here."

The other Kyejoth retrieved a beaker of navy blue potion. He uncorked the bottle and poured a tad into his hand and rubbed them as if it were lotion. Then he pressed his palms against Nighfall's broken back legs, muttering unintelligible jargon. As he cast the spell, Simon's scars reminded him it had been a while since he last recharged them. He did so, but another spike fell on the party and interrupted the process.

"Swifter, Thrax!" Caylo shouted. The group suffered from an anxious silence for a few minutes in near darkness.

"Why can't we light this room?" Simon finally asked.

"Take a guess, an' ya only get one try," Friziv snapped.

"Right. Magic," he muttered through pursed lips.

"Fy hasn't activated this room since the Serlentos," Caylo said. "He knows we're coming for him."

"The devious devil," Friziv spit. "So, if I may ask, King Caylo, your 'onor, why exactly are we trustin' a map from an Intellect?"

"Simon has entrusted faith in the man. I trust his judgment." The words were kind, but his stoic stare was slightly too alarming. Simon was hoping with the rest of them that Boffin was not a turncoat, too.

He was saved from their glares by a sphere of light ten feet in diameter. Nighfall jumped in between the huddle and starting punching just in front of them.

"Come on! What are you guys waiting for?" Nighfall shouted.

Thrax was casting the sphere of light around the Rebellioneers with one hand up, and threw his other hand out to push another piercing stalactite out of the air. "I'm with the Vanterslove. Can we please continue?"

"Let's consult the map," Caylo said. The Rebellioneers gathered around him as a mid-sized spike shattered in the middle of them all. Every single one of them shrieked and went airborne. "Quickly," Caylo added.

The Creatures gathered around their new King, but Simon didn't need to see the map. "The easiest path through this hall is a zig-zagged line straight through," he said, then he dropped his voice just loud enough for the huddle to hear him. "There's a path that breaks off from the trail and leads directly into the room outside of Fyresk's office. I'll take that path and flank him from the side."

"Not a bad idea, Si," Caylo chimed in. "Where did you learn that?"

"From a book," Simon snapped.

Caylo grinned. "Voulderbrin, you lead Morolith, Friziv, Nighfall, and Thrax through this cavern and the rest of the castle with the map. Simon and I will take the shortcut. Simon, I'm sure if you're aware of the path, you understand that this is a treacherous cave." He consulted the map once more. "It is quicker, but there's a catch."

"I'm aware of the catch," Simon stated, wasting no time.

"Good," Caylo said. He took in the other Rebellioneers. "Friends, Lord Fyresk is expecting us. I was relying on the element of surprise, but it seems he is wittier than I assumed.

"His efforts will merely hinder us, not *prevent* us from bringing in the New World. We will conquer this castle and face our gracious Lord. Despite his pleadings, he will die, and we will reign in a new Kearlith."

"For the New World!" Nighfall announced again, punching the air.

The rebels stared at each other in response. Eventually each of them held a smile. They plunged their weapons to the sky and shouted, "For the New World!"

# Chapter 27

The Creatures and Simon slalomed through the thick forest of spikes. Instead of trees, the Rebellioneers were searching their way through mirror-like spikes that towered above them. The giant needles had ceased dropping from the black abyss above, but the eminent threat of them hung heavy in the air. Simon's shoulders were arched up to his ears.

At first the only sounds were distant – heavy breathing, metal clanking, and padded footsteps. Then, a drizzle of tinny chimes crept up in the near-silence. It hovered and progressed, the tones getting lower and lower.

The pack mindlessly halted and gazed above them.

"Have you all gone mad?" Voulderbrin exclaimed. "Run!"

Instantly pins and needles rained on the Rebellioneers. The Protector smashed the larger skewers and spikes before they reached the trespassers, but Simon suffered from hundreds of piercings. Soon his leather boots were slushing through needle debris. Tiny pins stabbed his feet.

Then, he remembered – he was holding a giant magnet. As he hopped on one leg, he set the scythe to cling to the thousands of needles in his boots, then he waved it around the rest of his anguished body. The needles in his skin shot out, and the blade was soon covered in a thick layer of needles and skewers. Simon hastened to catch up to the rest of the group. He held the scythe high in the air, and the rainfall of needles quickly subsided as they stuck to the blade. Triumphantly, the Creatures hurrah-ed him.

After the initial adrenaline rush, the scythe became entirely too heavy. Simon wavered his grip, and his muscles were giving out. Thin trickles of blood crept down his forearms from the tiny puncture wounds. Soon he couldn't stop shaking, and the blade dropped with a weighty thud. The shower of pins began again as the group shrieked and groaned. Thrax staggered and lost the light spell, thus complete blackness descended upon the Rebellioneers amongst the painful rainstorm. Morolith scuttled to wield the scythe. He gallantly flourished it in the air to attract every single needle, both tiny and alarmingly lethal. The light returned as Thrax burst into flame. He screamed and shot the hundreds of pins out of his body. In seconds, he lost the flames but threw a hand into the air to continue lighting the way.

"Can we please continue?" he screamed.

"Where's Voulderbrin?" Nighfall shouted.

"The break-off is just up here," Caylo announced. "We'll stop and talk there. Now go!"

The expedition tore into the slalom of spikes and arrived at the break-off point within minutes. The path opened up into a minuscule clearing. Voulderbrin had flown ahead of the group to gather millions of needles, pins, and skewers for a make-shift roof, and the Rebellion squeezed themselves under its safety.

"Can I make a suggestion to everyone?" Morolith asked.

"You may," Caylo answered.

"Duck," he said.

At first the group perplexedly stared at him, but he gripped the scythe and everyone ducked. He pulled the giant blade back and swung himself into a tornado. The surrounding spikes sliced in half.

"Great idea," Voulderbrin said. He took off to the ceiling and widened the roof to fit the space.

"Thank you, Simon," Morolith said with a stoic expression. "That blade is fierce." Without warning, he chucked it to Simon.

He faked complete terror but at the last second, he captured the staff and spun to mount the blade. "Thank you, Morolith," he said with a sincere nod.

"Mathilda make that for you?" Morolith asked with a cocked eyebrow.

"No, Dagrio made this," Simon stated proudly.

Morolith huffed in disbelief. "You're kidding me, kid. That little Bratch beetle?"

Simon was instantly enraged. "He's a genius!"

"And Bratch beetles are actually wiser than they appear," Nighfall butt in.

Caylo ended the banter. "Enough! We're on a mission here, Creatures! And Simon!" The group mumbled and huffed but eventually gave Caylo every bit of their attention. "The trails up ahead will be deceitful, unforgiving, and undoubtedly difficult. Much like our Lord.

"May I just say before we depart, that I have never seen a better set of Creatures. Simon, you don't have much competition here, but you have restored my faith in the Humans. The New World will be grand, I swear it. We will rule Kearlith for Creatures, critters, and Humans alike. Let's end this tyranny today, and awaken to a peaceful tomorrow!"

"Wait!" Morolith roared.

"What?" Caylo bellowed back.

"None of us have magnetized weapons. How can we make it through the pins without them killing us?"

The roof to the clearing clanged and broke free, and Voulderbrin floated just below wearing a heavy scowl. "Come on! I'm ready to be out of here." The roof hovered higher over them, then moved towards the exit.

"Ah," Morolith muttered. "Voulderbrin's thinking right. May we all return safely." His eyes met the rest of his crew's, and he lingered on Simon. The stare was not loathsome or disdainful; it was an unspoken acceptance of the new Human.

Then he huffed and dashed to catch up to Voulderbrin.

*       *       *

Simon toggled the scythe's magnetic powers off and shook every bit of the needle debris from the blade. He nodded to the remaining Kyejoth, held it high above them, toggled the magnet back on, and charged the downhill path to their detour. He stopped caring about Caylo. He stopped caring about the Rebellion. He stopped caring about their mission. He simply cared about getting far away from this dungeon.

And their so-called shortcut took them much deeper into the pin and needle forest. Simon ran at top speed, his legs bursting into overdrive. Despite the scythe's building density, he held it with all his might. Adrenaline and a heavy dose of Mizik pumped his blood, and he charged past the spikes with fierce intention.

"Simon!" Caylo shouted from behind. Simon twisted his head to see the Kyejoth aboard his sword holding a pin-and-skewer disk above his head like an umbrella. "Can you give me a hand with this?"

"Of course!" Simon instantly unclipped his wand and cast the levitating spell on the tiny roof of needles while Caylo gathered the raining pins and skewers and added them to the airborne pile. Simon shook the scythe off again and hopped aboard his blade as well.

Together, they created a safe-zone of roughly six feet, and they both upped their speed once they each got a firm magical grip on their roof. They trudged on for several more minutes until the spikes began to grow apart. The path grew wider and wider into a tiny tear-drop clearing.

In the middle of the clearing, a steep cave dug underground. Simon unconsciously halted, but Caylo gripped the neck of his leather vest and dragged him through the cave.

The shatter of the unattended ceiling of skewers and needles echoed down the unlit halls. The Kyejoth lit a flame in his palm, unveiling a main entrance just big enough to fit a bus through and plenty of passageways to other areas of the underground. Caylo waved his hand forward and led Simon through the main cave.

"No one really comes down here now that the Serlentos are gone."

"What happened with them, anyway?" Simon asked.

Caylo moved to speak but let out a long exhalation.

"Look, I know about the caves down here. Lexandel meticulously detailed the dungeons as well as the castle in his book. I know they used to be part of the underground system years ago before Fyresk killed them all, but that's it. What happened?"

The Kyejoth stared ahead down the narrow tunnel for minutes before he finally spoke. "They were parasites." He huffed and tried to conjure his next words carefully. "Eleanor infused the Serlentos with a lie. She said she gained power from the Sonx to craft them."

"How would she do that?" Simon asked.

"She didn't," said Caylo. "When Lord Fyrethold reigned, he revealed the truth of her ruse. He tried for years to educate all the other Creatures of their deceit. He even detonated the Cave which shot Chirth Stone clear across Feerthel. Sadly, he was beheaded before any more of his attempts caught on.

"The Serlentos were the gods of Kearlith. We were raised to praise the Sonx and fear her sons - the scorpion and razor-blade mix. The Hunters fervently obeyed their every demand for meats, and the Collectors had to deposit half their Collection to them. One of these underground caves leads to—"

"The Collection chamber on the second floor of the main hall," Simon finished.

"Indeed. Lexandel sure explicated his share of secrets."

"Well, the book is called—"

"Anyway, we were raised in rough times. Most of us barely remember Lord Fyrethold, let alone his assassination. All the while the Serlentos were fighting for their seat in this city. Almost a decade ago, Lord Fyresk made them move above ground into—"

"The Forgotten," Simon interrupted.

"Or as you call it, your neighborhood. The Serlentos were, to put it lightly, infuriated with the adjustments, and they drafted up plans to rise against him."

"That's a tough mission," Simon jested.

"They failed, Simon. Fyresk single-handedly struck down all hundred and eighty-five of the razor-backed scorpions. I mean, the Serlentos were all talk with no fight, but still..." Simon didn't know if he intended it, but Caylo slowed his speed in a pensive trance. "He's a master of magic. And that sword of his is…" Caylo couldn't continue the speech. He finally completely stopped their path. Simon halted with him and gazed at him.

"He's a Human, Caylo," he said. "There's nothing special about him. There are billions of him out there, and they can all fall."

"This isn't the Outside," Caylo said.

"I know! This is Kearlith. But like it or not, I come from the Outside. I know about the Humans."

"Those aren't Humans," Caylo spit. "Those are scum."

"Then what am I?"

Caylo waited a while before grinning and finding the ceiling with his eyes.

"You're exceptional." Simon smiled from ear to ear.

*       *       *

The pair of Rebellioneers continued gliding along the descending tunnel of the caves at a leisurely pace. The other five on the infiltration team would not reach the office for a while. The Creature and Human stood atop their weapons and strolled down the underground tunnels discussing the Serlentos, Lexandel, Fyrethold, the old Kearlith, the old Fyresk.

Occasionally, a random hole in the wall would break the path off into other caverns, but if they were anything like their infamous cave, Simon wanted to stay as close to this main channel as possible.

He was saving his detour for the end of the path.

In *A Shintervah's Secrets Revealed*, Lexandel mentioned the end of this tunnel. It was an open doorway that led into a vast room, fifty feet square with no floor. Across the span was another open doorway that opened up into two paths; one to a ladder that ascended hundreds of feet straight up to the office, and one that led underground the northeast wing of the castle, or as it was more commonly called – the Wing of the Blade. The Elite believed that whatever Fyresk was hiding was located there, and Simon had a strong sense that their burned Lord would be guarding it.

The trick to getting across the chamber before the doorway

was not simply building a fifty-foot bridge, however. Once a Creature, or in this case a new Human, passed through the doorway, gusts of winds tore and rampaged throughout the space. The floor was a deep and black abyss. Without a stable bridge and a strong hold on something, the winds would thrash the occupants against the stone walls, then pitch them down to the bottomless pit. But Simon had a plan.

"I feel I must apologize for my apprehension earlier," Caylo stated, breaking Simon's concentration and the tense silence that had built up over the last twenty minutes. "The truth of my fear of Lord Fyresk cannot escape me. He is ruthless with his blade. But together, we can overpower him. I only hope he doesn't take one of us with him."

"He's a crafty devil," Simon slithered. "But you're right. In a few minutes, we will face him, and among the seven of us we will slay him. Tonight will be the beginning of the New World," he added as a little cherry on top. He wanted to make the lies he was feeding Caylo delicious.

"We're almost to the ladder," Caylo said.

"I know. The end of the road." Simon kicked the scythe into dirt floor just behind Caylo and vaulted into the air, far in front of his Rebellion leader. When his gravity evened out, the scythe dipped, and he shot to the windy room. Caylo took two seconds to gawk, then quickly mounted the sword shouting, "Wait! That chamber is dangerous! Simon! Don't jump it!"

And yet, that's exactly what he intended to do. He slowed to the appropriate speed just before the doorway, and the scythe vaulted off the corner of the floor. As expected, the winds kicked in and thrashed and whipped him around the room. The stone walls flew at his face before he planted the blade and kicked off to continue the ride. He knew he had little time before Caylo caught up, and the winds were ripping the air from his lungs. The closer he got to the other side, the harder the gusts blew in from another direction. Simon had lost every bit of feeling in his clenched fists. At this point he had full faith that the scythe did not exist, and that he himself could simply fly.

If it weren't for these damn winds.

Caylo's shouts were echoing louder and louder, and Simon was only getting yards away from the miniscule landing on the door-sill. He had mentally prepared for these winds – Lexandel made sure he knew what he was getting into – but it was impossible to communicate the true chaos in the room and the persistent dread of the black abyss below. He caught some sort of pattern in the tumultuous cyclones. He felt for the rhythm of their thrashings. He calculated the angles from which he needed to hit the bricks in order to snap right through the doorway. With perfect form, he rapidly planted on the left corner with a deafening chink and sidled the wall until he reached the doorway, then skidded inside. The raging winds subsided.

Simon expected to simply stand up and run away, but his legs would not let him. He lay there motionless on the chilled dirt floor deep in the underground. The ladder was just ahead to his right; to his left a dark tunnel. In the middle was a statue of no particular Serlentos. The scorpion stood roughly five feet tall on two strong legs, its razor flesh a slimy forest green. It appeared to be forged out of thick iron. Its sinisterly acute tail clasped a raging torch above him.

Before Simon could truly take in the Creature's beauty, Caylo's shouts became louder and wilder. Simon flung himself to the wall holding the doorway and listened. Caylo fell to his knees just before the other threshold and shouted down into the abyss.

"Simon! I tried to tell you this castle kills! Why wouldn't you listen? Patience could have saved you! You idiot!"

With that one little word, Caylo drained out the remaining respect Simon had for him. The Creature thought he was an idiot. And Simon was just about to prove him wrong. He waited until Caylo began wailing and bolted for the left cave.

The screams continued. "You should have listened when a Creature spoke to you, you half-witted Human! Your stupidity killed you today! All your work for the Rebellion was worthless!"

That was all Simon heard before he tipped the scythe to full speed and tore to the other side of the castle. The scythe gave off a dull yellow glow thanks to another handy hex of Dagrio's. The polished stone walls of the cave reflected the straight and narrow pathway.

*     *     *

Within a few minutes, Simon turned the corner to a staircase and thanked the scythe once again for its flying abilities. He raced up the hundreds of steps to the next chamber and smashed face-first into a heavy wooden, locked door.

Gritting his teeth, he sliced the wood three times and kicked in his own cut-out door. After the low glow of his scythe, the lights in the next chamber blinded him.

The hall was extensive. The roof was far, far up, and the walls were claustrophobic and narrow. Simon's eyes adjusted to the additional lighting, illuminating an entrance at the end of the hallway. The next room was as tall and bright as this corridor, but Simon noticed something in the gap of the thin entrance.

As he rapidly approached closer, two security Gulverbruud came into focus within this giant, blindingly lit room. Simon sped through the chamber, steadily gaining a complete milieu of the enormous hall. The exterior room was hundreds of feet square and tall, with a steel vault placed in the middle, roughly fifteen feet wide and eight feet tall. The structure was a steel-plated, rectangular box with bolts that beamed the blue light of Mizik with vicious intensity.

Simon's eyes averted to the vast, white walls of the exterior room. A diamond pattern was marked with similar blue bolts across the entirety of the chamber. Every single inch of the scene was illuminated.

Simon took all this in squinting, but he blinked a few times to moisten his tired eyes; just in time to watch both Gulverbruud prepare for a fierce attack. They both locked into stances that could take the kickback from their explosive flaming assault at the intruder.

The scythe zoomed up and down and around their shots, some barely skimming the blade. He loomed closer, and they switched their elements. The right guard created vicious cyclones, each one bigger than the last, while the left Gulverbruud shot icicles and icebergs at Simon. Neither worked, although they were successful in shaking Simon up. His nerves were completely shot. He was sure he hadn't taken a breath in minutes, but somehow he or his scythe evaded every single spell from the Gulverbruud's staves.

And then a three-foot wide slab dropped down from the vault, creeping out at a snail's pace, revealing the man of the hour- the blackened Lord Fyresk.

The two Gulverbruud, both in desperate attempts to defend against defeat from a Human, stood in powerful brooding poses to gather energy, and seconds later they dislodged every ounce of it. Their spells were a direct hit, but Simon was a split second ahead of them. He shot towards the door. The Gulverbruud guards became blurs in his periphery.

His sight, his focus, his entire purpose here was the shadow of a man in the doorway. Lord Fyresk easily strolled out, recognizing Simon's little game of chicken. But Simon knew what Fyresk expected. Mere inches from Fyresk, Simon snapped into the air and landed behind his Lord with the blade of the scythe down his spine. Simon turned his hostage to the now-left Gulverbruud and shot a direct hit into the buffalo-beast. Despite the guard's size, they both tumbled and rolled.

The right guard's left eyelid twitched, and he huffed his gigantic nostrils. Simon thought he had seen the extent of the Gulverbruud's powerfully frightening appearance when he met Morolith, but this guy had gashes and years-old cuts along his face and mighty forearms. He deepened into his stance to gather magic from the castle's ground, but in one fluid movement, Simon leapt on the scythe and sliced the Gulverbruud's thick, rock-like skin. He howled and tottered backward with a thunderous plop on the stone floor.

Before he could witness his damage, Simon snapped his head to Fyresk. Already, he was rising from the crash. His eyes found Simon's before they both reached for their wands; Simon's on his vest, Fyresk's on the floor five feet in front of him. The incinerated sovereign tumbled to his stick and snapped it towards Simon the instant it found his fingertips.

But Simon shot a massive paralysis spell first. At this point, gathering magical energy was unnecessary. Magic required tremendous focus, and every thread of his attention was centered on Lord Fyresk. At the last second, the Lord met Simon's spell with one of his own, resulting in a deafening detonation that sent a shockwave through the battling Humans. Fyresk's long trench coat and even his starched collar ruffled in the whipping wind. Simon gripped his vest with his free hand despite his trust in Mathilda's strong stitch. For an instant, the two gawked in still-life fascination at the power his opponent possessed. Eventually all four eyebrows furrowed, and the battle continued.

Lord Fyresk found his blade and swung spells of all the elements at Simon. The scythe brandished in the air reflecting the attacks back at Fyresk, but the Lord didn't budge. Fyresk remained planted beside the slowly rising Gulverbruud, cutting the air in front of him with fierce rapidity. Every second he struck, thrust, sliced, or hacked at least twice. Simon grimaced as his shoulders began to cramp and weaken from the instantaneous pace. He needed a game-changer.

He swept the blade of the scythe up perpendicular to the ground, jumped, and planted his feet on the back of the blade. Using gravity as a little kick-start, he repositioned the scythe and shot away from Fyresk. Spells whooshed past his ears; they grazed his elbows and kneecaps.

The scythe danced at a quick speed, dashing in a mismatched, zig-zagged path to the vault. The solid iron door hung wide open, and Simon was anxious to lock himself inside, if only for a few soundless seconds. The flames, icicles, needles, and force attacks flew at him even faster.

Fifty feet from the entrance Simon witnessed a bizarre device inside, but one of Fyresk's acutely aimed force pushes thrust the iron door closed with a deafening, echoed clang.

There was only one option- the air. The scythe cut to the sky, mocking gravity as it sailed on a wave of nothing with Simon's feet solidly welded to its blade. Spells kept hurling at him, but his increasing distance from the Lord gave him more room to play with. Simon and the scythe danced around the four corners of the vast hall, up to the high roof. The lit diamond patterns blurred into wavy and dizzying lines.

As Simon neared the ceiling, Lord Fyresk ceased the assault, and Simon switched his attention to the floor. His knuckles tightened around the curves of the gazelle's horn. He was far, far above the vault, briefly feeling almost alone in the silent chamber. He could barely see a black blip defending the door on the floor below.

The Lord was letting him take his time. His fingertips scarcely grazed the stone ceiling. He sighed and settled his raging anger, guilt, pride, fear, and love just to have a few free seconds. He tried to stare at the diamond patterns, then the ceiling again, then the backs of his eyelids as if it would help him forget how far he was above the floor.

It didn't work. Every ounce of Simon knew that one wrong move at this point would lead to laughably certain death. The scythe softly glided along the ceiling, and Simon finally opened his eyes to face his distance. His face hardened to hold back his gut wrenching fears.

## Chapter 28

Like a pin Simon dropped from the ceiling, free falling the fifty feet with an absurd plan to weaken the Lord of Feerthel. The black blip on the floor raced closer and formed the dark outline of Lord Fyresk stalwartly guarding the vault's door. Simon was a split second away from crashing into him before he let loose a devastating blast from the scythe. His feet swiftly clung to the blade once more as he vaulted away from the explosion. He slammed a landing twenty feet from his target. Waves from the blast pushed him farther and farther away. He planted his feet on the stone floor and held tight to the scythe, using it to block and divert some of the force until it died down.

A few seconds later he dashed at top speed to find Lord Fyresk lying in the middle of the slim crater, motionless. His eyelids hid what could be dead eyes, and his face held a severely peaceful image. Simon approached slowly and lightly. He unhooked his wand and sternly aimed with his left hand, leaving his right to wield the scythe.

He crept up to Fyresk, who was becoming more convincingly dead, and rested his heavy leather boot on the Lord's hand. With this, Fyresk's blue eyes shot open, but to his dismay. His eyes stared into Simon's, failing to conceal pure astonishment and fear. In his periphery, the overwhelming peril of Simon's scythe at his throat and wand aimed at his face seemed to truly disarm the man's reality.

"What are you hiding down here?" Simon asked hysterically.

"Simon, I'm not the one you need to kill," Lord Fyresk said on a sigh.

"Why not?!" Simon shouted.

"That device in there," Fyresk pointed to the vault, but Simon knew where it was. He didn't let his eyes off the Lord. "It will save Kearlith and the rest of whatever is out there from a force more powerful than anything this city has seen. It requires thousands of Mizik leaves to even start up, and I need it to sustain for several hours."

"To fight what?" Simon asked.

Fyresk continued to hold the gaze until finally he said, "The shadows."

The cogs clicked into place, and the lies unraveled. The truth that had been dormant in the back of his mind stepped forward into the spotlight. Simon's heart dropped to the caves deep below the stone floor. His mouth dried out like he had been drinking cotton. "The... Vevra?" he said.

Lord Fyresk slimmed his eyelids and deepened his scowl. "Yes. The Vevra," he said slowly. "They have –"

Before he could continue, Caylo raged in from the entrance.

"Yes! Slay him, Simon! Make me King!" Caylo seemed pleased as he approached them, but he soon noticed Simon's hesitation. "What are you waiting for? If you can't kill the man, I'll—"

"You'll do nothing," Simon spat, turning his target to the Kyejoth. "Look, it appears we have much to discuss, but now is not the time. Fyresk, you're right, there is a force out there, but now it's here. The shadows are constantly in Kearlith and Feerthel. Caylo, you can try to kill both of us, but you'll fail. Instead, you should –"

"Fight shadows!?" Caylo shouted.

Simon tried to explain, but only a sigh came out.

"The Vevra know of Kearlith's location?" Fyresk accused.

"They know we're in this room. They're probably right outside, waiting for—"

They weren't waiting anymore. Five Vevra in their physical forms swiftly approached the Kearlithians. Zahti was the leading shadow among them, his jaw locked with severe coercion. His companions were similar shadow-people with various weapons- twin katanas, an axe, throwing daggers, double sai's, and an excessively long bow with a scythe's blade on each end. Zahti wielded an enormous sword. Its size was twice that of Simon's entire body. The Vevra held the blade as if it were made of foam, yet with an intensity that assured you it would slice like the hardest of metals. They collectively slowed to a steady march.

Fyresk was the first to attack. From the floor he shot a star directly into the cluster of shadows like a bowling ball. They scattered and sank into two dimensional shadows on the floor. They zipped large circles around the floors and walls of the vast, white chamber. Excruciating screams filled the thick air.

Fy leapt to his feet, then he, Si, and Caylo tightened their grips on their weapons and planted their stances in the auditory chaos. Their eyes were everywhere, darting from every corner of the vast room to the vault and back, with no luck keeping a true target on the Vevra.

Without a sound, a swoosh from Zahti's monstrous blade split through the triangle of defenders. The attack was aimed for Simon, but he met the weapon with the scythe and his own force. The thunderous bang deafened and echoed off the great walls as Zahti trembled from the massive recoil. Seconds later he shook it off, slitting his truly vengeful eyes at Simon.

Simon didn't let it shake him. Maybe it was the sleep deprivation and flat-out physical exhaustion that allowed him to throw away every inhibition and face the shadow soldier with nothing else to lose, and everything to gain. Three months ago, he would have run from this encounter. Whenever Kathy would threaten him with life-altering ultimatums, he would always submit. If he was backed into a corner, he would have easily surrendered.

But now he had Mizik. He had magic. He had the scythe. He had amazing Creatures around him and another Human that taught him so much more about how to live and fight and be successful than anything in the Outside. These shadows had no chance.

He slit his own eyes and shot every single fire, ice, force push, paralyze, and electrocution spell he knew. The other Vevra popped up to defend Zahti, but Caylo and Fyresk were instantly on the offense, blazing them with their best set of spells.

Though Simon faced only one opponent, Zahti's mercilessness with the gargantuan blade was proving to be the toughest challenge. It was shaped like a parallelogram, but with a sharp bite cut out of the top obtuse corner. A sword on one side and a trap on the other. Zahti played with it as if it were a childhood toy or some fake replica of the real thing, but every time it got a little too close to Simon, he knew any false move would lead to an instantaneously sliced death.

The scythe was able to bat every attack back to Zahti. Simon even threw in a few of his own stabs and sweeps. As a group, the combined Kearlithians backed the five shadow soldiers down the narrow hallway, to and through the doorway.

The shadows passed the threshold, and Fyresk swiftly slammed the door in their faces. Simon's instincts shot the blue rope to the cut-out door and returned it to its place in the bigger door. Caylo shot a welding spell the instant it slid in.

They all knew the battle wasn't over. Simon stared blankly at the door taking painfully full breaths of air. Caylo matched him; they held their weapons tightly in physical shock of the deafening silence, as if time itself had stopped. Lord Fyresk seemed to be the only one planning for the next attack. His head bowed as he shut his eyes and circled the air in front of him with his blade. He mumbled ancient jargon and planted his stance.

"Someone count down from three!" he shouted amongst the gibberish, fighting to speak and keep his deep focus. "On zero, someone else open the door."

"Three," Caylo said after a long moment. Fyresk shot his left palm up parallel to the ceiling.

"Two." Fyresk's burnt black fingertips stood solid and square. Fluidly, his hand began forming several infinity symbols.

"One." Fyresk's hand rapidly wrenched a spasm of complex shapes.

On the next beat, the door flew open before Simon could cast the spell. The shadows were ready. Before the door clamored against the wall, they shot an enormous red star straight at Fyresk. The blast was large enough to obliterate the entire castle, but Fyresk met it with his palm. He sucked the energy in a dazzling, noiseless flash.

The Lord had not lost focus since he began chanting to himself, even after the red star flashed and dissipated. As soon as the light dimmed low enough to see, Lord Fyresk bolted his eyelids open with a menacing glare. He slowed the sword to a halt when it was in line with his spinal cord, and he shoved the blade forward, erupting a massive white star ten times the size of the shadows'.

The shadow men and woman recoiled in a clumsy attempt at defense. Zahti caught the direct hit; the gargantuan star lit the shadow man upon impact and disintegrated him. The others moaned and shrieked as the light struck them, too.

They fled, and in a flash the vast hall was silent. Fyresk caught the door with his wand and slammed it shut.

*     *     *

"Questions need to be answered," he said. For the first time, Lord Fyresk slacked his shoulders and allowed his fatigue to surface on his facial features. His eyebrows softened, his stoic scowl rested into a humble frown, his eyes truly met Simon's and Caylo's. Almost in an apologetic tone, the Lord continued, "Look, I've known of this city's lack of faith in me. I know everything. I knew a rebellion was underway when Voulderbrin let Simon slip through his sights, and I had a strong theory that you were the one devising all of it, Caylo.

"My speech today was an attempt to gain some amount of faith in the truth that you two have just witnessed first-hand." He nodded to both of them.

"Not a single Kearlithian in this city knows about the Vevra other than you two. I've been trying to figure out how to destroy them before getting any Kearlithian involved. I decided the more time this city dwelled on my hiding something, the more time I devoted to fighting the shadows.

"It was my understanding that they only knew of me, which was a mistake in my judgment. The crisis is much worse than I imagined. They not only have access to Kearlith, they've found my cure." Unintentionally, he halted his speech, seemingly lost in thought of plans and courses and defense.

Caylo interrupted, "What's so frightening about the shadows? Besides the fact that they're terribly difficult to fight. With Kearlith's combined forces--"

"They wish to destroy the Sonx," said Lord Fyresk gravely.

Simon's and Caylo's jaws simultaneously dropped.

"They've apparently proven that they can exist without the Sonx. They believe they can keep the Mizik alive by themselves."

"The idiots!" Caylo shouted.

"They think with everything else wiped out, they will have free range of the world. Obviously, this is not an option. Behind me is a weapon that will thwart their plans. It will create another Sonx, and I will aim it directly into the shadow's lair, hoping to destroy it. As of yet, I have no other name than the second Sonx."

"We need to do this now," Simon blurted. "They know all about you, Fyresk. And all about Kearlith. They know something is in that room, but they don't know what it is. That's…" He found it so easy to speak before, but now he was losing his words. "Well, that's why I'm here."

"*You* brought them?" Caylo accused.

"*You* planned to kill him yourself," Simon shot back.

"Enough!" Lord Fyresk demanded. "All feuds are settled. Let's focus on the new threat. The time has come to tell Kearlith the truth."

"All feuds aren't settled," Caylo stated with a gulp. "We still have to make peace at the front gate."

Lord Fyresk spat, "For the Sonx's sake…" as he brushed past Caylo to the door.

*     *     *

A gargantuan riot had formed between the Rebellioneers and Fyresk's defenders. Hundreds of each fought tooth and nail at the gargoyle's gate. A Kyejoth wielding nun-chucks was getting ruined by a loyal Vanterslove fighting with bare hooves. Two Shintervah were dueling- one Rebellioneer with a wand, the other was Seskith's mother, holding thin sword and winning. Three loyal Gulverbruud were smashing their way through the mass of Rebellioneers, but their movements were becoming slow and forceless. Neither side was budging; you could draw a solid line across the jumble of fighting bodies along the crumbled walls of the entrance. Half of Kearlith's army vs. the other half of Kearlith's army.

"All of Kearlith!" Fyresk roared, his volume strident. "Every Kearlithian listening! Cease your attacks!" Quickly, the mass quieted. They stared in awe as their Lord fought through the crowd, followed by an ashamed Caylo and a meek and timid Simon. "The battle is over! Or, this one is at least. Look, I must admit something to all of you. We have a bigger war out there. It's the –"

"Lord Fyresk! Fyyyyyrrrrrreeeesssssk!" Dagrio screamed from the castle's front door. He dashed on all fours.

"Are you serious?" asked a Gulverbruud in the crowd.

"Fyresk, I... Everyone's... in your office... But then the... there was a guy... He's destroying us..." Dagrio couldn't speak three syllables without inhaling or exhaling.

"The Elite," Simon stated, coldly.

Fyresk met his gaze. "We're dead," he said. Simon noted a hint of accusation in Fyresk's honest, blue eyes.

"Make me louder," Simon demanded.

"What?"

"Make my voice louder." Hesitantly, Fyresk obeyed and shot a turquoise flash at Simon's neck. "City of Kearlith! We all need to move this fight to the office. Join hands and paws with those who were your foes thirty seconds ago and fight the real enemies. They are shadow Creatures called the Vevra. They can exist as tiny shadows, but in the light they must become their physical avatars. They are quick and clever, and they are attacking. Use the brightest and most illuminating spells you know. Be warned, they will be difficult. They will effortlessly slaughter you if you slip up. If you don't feel up to the task, that's fine. Return to your shacks. If you wish to save Kearlith, follow us!" Simon wrapped himself up in his speech. It boiled deep down in his gut and burned gritty determination into the back of his throat. He dashed off to the castle, paying no mind to the stunned population of Kearlith. They soon snapped out of it and followed. Every single one of them.

*       *       *

The army of more than four hundred Kearlithians moved through the halls and stairwells to the soundtrack of ruffling pants legs, low grumbling of hooves meeting the stone, the Gulverbruud sniffing or snorting, and the anxious chatter of the Creatures.

"I have to apologize, Simon," Dagrio said.

"Why?"

"I betrayed the Rebellion. I couldn't take the girls being trapped... so I let them go. With the Lifter, we went straight up to the office, and—"

"Don't even worry about it," Simon interrupted, holding his palm up. "We are way beyond betraying the Rebellion right now. It's actually great that you took them up there. I hated to see all three of them under that thing. How bad are they getting—"

"Destroyed," Dagrio said.

"Oh no."

The mob advanced through the castle swiftly, meeting no enemies or raining pins-and-needles chambers. The trick Fyresk used to travel with the columns into the middle of Feerthel began to make sense; pairs of columns fifteen feet apart created a clear pathway, despite any physical objects or walls. Within minutes they ran a straight shot to the top of the castle, not once needing to open or unlock a door.

The vitality of the battle raged even before they approached the office door. The air was filled with thick fumes and a pungent aroma of burning flesh and leather. Huge spells whizzed, spurred, and exploded every three seconds. Finally, Lord Fyresk gripped the handle to throw the door open, but the scorching metal sweltered his charred skin. He grimaced and roared, and out of his rage he ripped the ten-foot door open.

Caylo, Simon, and Lord Fyresk darted in first, wreaking havoc on the room. Simon swung the scythe and shouted every spell he could remember. Caylo mounted his sword and lit himself on fire;

then he snuck up to several of the shadow pawns and skated across their backs with his blade leaving massive gashes.

Lord Fyresk was in his realm. While he shot stars and various spells at the Vevra, he set off several gadgets and weapons in the office – seven turrets shot up out of rubble and unloaded thousands of shells of light. Four energy shields whirred to life. Hundreds of light-bulbs blinked on and zipped around the room.

The Vevran soldiers were backing down, but the Elite seemed to take it all in as battle practice. He stood on the sill of the smashed windows that were once the southwestern wall and roof, a smug grin perched below furrowed eyebrows. Occasionally, he would aim his six-foot staff and shoot off electricity or flames.

Lord Fyresk was the first to get his attention. After grounding a dozen shadows in his way, he swung his sword like a baseball bat and gave the Elite a wave of chaos to deal with.

The Elite dealt with it. He waved the spells off as if they were cotton Frisbees. With a bold sniff, he thrust the staff up like a shotgun and shot basketball-sized black holes in half-second intervals at Fyresk. The crowd gazed in terror as the room melted into slow motion in Simon's mind.

*Don't attack him*, Simon thought. *Please don't attack him. He's just trying to see how you fight.*

Fortunately, Lord Fyresk had acquired a sense of intelligent defense after his first encounter with the shadows. He drew a force-field of light around him the last second before the shadow-blasts destroyed him. But the Elite did not let up. He knew after enough damage the shield would break and Fyresk would be defenseless.

Simon knew it, too. While the Vevran Lord was in his crazed frenzy, Simon hopped on the scythe and began spinning as fast as he could. The effect was a raging tornado aimed straight at the Elite. Simon let loose a gut-wrenching roar as he unleashed the cyclone. The attack was a direct hit, and the Elite spiraled away from the castle along with a few neighboring Vevra. The other shadow soldiers had ceased their attacks to watch the spectacle, but once their leader was thrown from his perch, they fled to the windows and into the night.

The surrounding slow motion had halted to a dead stop.

Everyone present was stunned. Simon stared at Lord Fyresk, Caylo, and most of Kearlith in the silent seconds growing into full minutes. Slowly, a Gulverbruud humbly chuckled, which sparked a bit of laughter into his neighbors, and suddenly the entire office was echoing hoots and hee-haw's through the shattered glass panes of half the roof and walls of the castle's office high above the city of Kearlith.

# Chapter 29

Simon threw the front door open in hopes of awakening Raelin and Tormos, but even after shouting, "Rae! Torm! Get up! Torrrrmossss! Raaaaaeeelin!" he could barely rouse them.

In the time it took for the raccoon brothers to get up and actually wake up, Simon sketched rough designs for new armor. Mathilda had equipped him with sturdy leather bracers, gloves, calf-shields, and a chest plate, but he would have to get something to protect his raccoon Creature friends.

"What have we told you about barging through the door in the middle of the night when raccoons are sleeping," Raelin claimed once he and Tormos were a little more lucid.

"You work at night, Raelin!"

"Eh, we're taking the night off," he answered with a shrug and a yawn.

"Not today. We have work to do." Simon explained everything to the still half-asleep raccoons – the Rebellion's attack, the shadows, and Lord Fyresk's true motive for stealing Mizik. The lengthy story woke the brothers up. By the end they were hanging on every word that shot out of Simon's mouth.

But he got two different reactions-

"We will destroy them!" was Raelin's.

"Can't we simply talk them out of it?" was Tormos's.

Simon and Rae glared at his brother until finally he choked up, "Fine. Let's... kill them... dead."

"Excellent," Simon stated like a drill sergeant. He stopped, shrugged it off, and continued. "I've got some ideas for you guys." He flipped through his notebook and showed the raccoons his designs for helmets, torso and leg armor, and weapons- Rae with a whip, and Tormos with a bow and arrow. Tormos sniffed and tittered at the idea.

"You need not worry about me and weapons, mate. I can handle my own," Tormos cooed as he sat back with a smug smile.

"You'll fight them unarmed?"

"He's best at that," Rae said, shrugging. "I myself like the idea of a whip, but I have my own means of defense." He scampered off to the shabby wooden cabinet in the corner. Simon and even Tormos were literally on the edge of their seats in anticipation. Raelin kept stopping and over-zealously stealing glances just to increase the suspension. Finally he produced with a "Tah-dahhh!", two raccoon-sized swords connected by a short link-chain screwed in at the bottoms of the hilts.

Raelin made a dazzling spectacle, complete with a helicopter simulation in which he actually went mid-air, a juggling routine involving the single pan in the shack and a mug, and a whipping routine that nearly caused them to have heart attacks. For the finale, Raelin planted a back paw on the stump lamp and hoisted himself in the air. He barely grazed the eight-foot ceiling as he performed a perfect three-sixty with two back-flips, nailing the landing poised and ready to attack. His eyes were disturbingly menacing. Slowly, Simon and Tormos began clapping. A slow clap was better than none at all under the eyes of a raccoon with sword nun-chucks.

"Okay, so I don't need to worry about a weapon for you, either," Simon remarked. "At least tell me what you think about the armor. These are just sketches, but we'll need to talk to Mathilda about getting you two something a little sturdier than shaggy shirts."

Tormos snatched the notebook from Simon's lap before his brother could get to it, but Raelin was quickly atop the footboard next to Tormos. Each raccoon fought to have more of the notebook in front of him, which most Creatures just assumed was impossible, but not these stubborn brothers.

"Forget it!" Simon yelled to break up the fight before it began. "We can talk about it later. We need to get to Mid-City."

                    *        *        *


The entire population of Kearlith and some interested Feerthelians were gathered again at the statue of the beheaded Lord Fyrethold; every Shintervah, Vanterslove, Kyejoth, Gulverbruud, Gullen, Biffleflenn, and Intellect. Lord Fyresk was not present yet. The crowd of well over six hundred Creatures packed themselves into the plaza at Mid-City, lowly humming and whispering quick conversations, inquiring the newest gossip.

After the battle in the office, just long enough for the victorious Kearlithians to celebrate, Lord Fyresk held up a palm to silence the crowd. Like magic, this simple act attracted the attention of every Kearlithian in the office. He shifted and slimmed his eyelids, scanning the victorious mob. He immediately turned his administration into overdrive and forced everyone to evacuate the castle. The immense wave of relief was cut short, and the saviors of the day relinquished out of the premises before testing Lord Fyresk's limits. As they began to scramble through the office door, he announced, "Gather the city of Kearlith, every Creature you can find. I'll hold a meeting at Mid-City in a couple of hours. If you know of any Creatures out in the Forest, invite them. Any and all families, friends, and house-pets. I want *everyone* in that plaza!"

And now the soldiers and all their families were standing around Mid-City in their pajamas or armor in a thick, grumbling murmur. The clearing usually seemed enormous and doused with firelight, but with this amount of Creatures, it reeked of sweat, breath, and worst of all- shadows. Simon stood at the back of the crowd with a raccoon on each shoulder.

Just as Simon thought it, Tormos tugged on his ear and asked, "How much do you know about what he's going to say, Simon?"

He was blindsided, and he noticed that the question caught the attention of dozens of Creatures around him. "Um," he started. "... Everything." The crowd gasped, but Simon hastily continued, "But I want you to hear it from him. Believe me, he's about to reveal the truth. And I don't want to try and explain it. Let your Lord do it."

All the Creatures in the ten-foot vicinity were staring at him, the front few harassing him with inquiries and fighting amongst themselves over the more appealing questions. He had never felt like a celebrity before and was always belligerently against them, but he had to admit, the attention was flattering. He denied every bit of the senseless chatter and simply stated, "I'll let Lord Fyresk explain."

As if to save him, Fyresk coughed through his amplified voice. Every Creature's head snapped to the statue- Fyresk was strongly standing atop his father's shoulders. "Tonight, you will hear no lies. I will begin by admitting I have been hiding something from all of you. To my justification, I wanted to build a better defense before seeing any of you involved. I am truly remorseful for my actions, and we can plan for requital later, but first we all must face a mighty obstacle. The Vevra.

"They are a race of shadows that were created by the Preeminents over a century ago. They were originally regarded as harmless, but they seem to have evolved. Our four leaders shed them off far in the East and prayed to the Sonx to never see them again. Now they are back with an absolute plan to destroy the Sonx.

"This is why I've been using immeasurable amounts of Mizik. I've been developing a second Sonx – a weapon that will create another star not nearly to scale, but large enough to flatten any and all establishments in their lair.

"They will be prepared for an attack. They will be ready and waiting for us to strike if they do not attack us first, but we will fight as an invulnerable army and save Kearlith, and the Outside, from the fate of certain death.

"The date of our attack will be released later. For now, buy or forge your armor, work your muscles at least twice a day, and prepare for the biggest battle this city has ever faced. May this be a reminder to us all that we have much to fear past the reaches of Feerthel."

The Lord leapt off his father's shoulders abruptly, resulting in a unanimous gasp on the front rows. He disappeared from view from the rest of the Creatures, but he soon popped through the crowd in front of the other Human.

"My. Office," he said.

Simon slumped in an overdramatic whoosh, but he obeyed. He knew very well when to do so. Fyresk was quickly off on his sword, making a notorious Kearlithian exit. The other Kearlithians were all staring at him, but none of them made any more movements to bombard him. Simon gazed at them all and made his laggard exit.

Simon decided to walk the distance to the office. As much as his body ached and begged for rest, he needed the quiet time. Without Fyresk. Without Caylo. Without Vezlin. Without Seskith.

Just some calm, tranquility, and undisturbed peace in the little amount of time he'd been given. In the Outside, the events of the last twenty-four hours would have mentally crippled him. But he trusted Lord Fyresk now. Fyresk should have killed him and Caylo both after they defeated the shadows, and he had only grimaced a tiny hint of disappointment. The rest of the façade was his usual broodiness.

The edges of Simon's brain and gut were still hesitant to hop aboard the trust-Fyresk train. This could all be some part of a master plan, and maybe Lord Fyresk was smarter and more evil than he could ever imagine.

But something was different about those blue eyes. They exuded the truth, and now he was letting the Creatures see it. It could not be forgotten that they were facing an excessively more difficult enemy now, but they gained a powerful ally. With Lord Fyresk and Kearlith's combined abilities, the Vevra would undoubtedly surrender or die.

*    *    *

The door to the office was closed when Simon finally drew near, but only the top half was still hanging on its hinges. Because of this, and possibly because of sleep deprivation, Simon cackled and yelped like a little kid. The fact that Lord Fyresk took the time to close the top half of the door was the funniest thing in Feerthel at that moment. It started out as a simple giggle, but the release fed a wave of unyielding laughter.

Just as he began to coo and contain his hilarity, he caught a glimpse of the demolished wall above the doorframe exposing the top half of the office, and he lost it again. Every knot and tight muscle in his gut released with every cackle. He wasn't afraid anymore. Not of Lord Fyresk or the Vevra or anything else within Feerthel. Anything past that, maybe, but that did not dampen his current fit of giddiness.

Lord Fyresk leisurely creaked the door open with his best scowl on, which only fueled the fire. Simon was soon grounded in the fit, fists pounding the stone floor, hearing the wild howls of his own mirth echoing off what was left of the walls. He expected Lord Fyresk to take action any second now. He knew Fyresk would strike wrath upon his head, but he could not care less. His insides were dancing, and he was too weak to contain them.

Simon slowed to a steady breath eventually, although occasionally a little more relief would sputter out. He met Fyresk's eyes, still stuck in that same accusatory slant, his jaws still locking the scowl- but the corner was twitching. Minuscule dimples formed atop his coal-black cheeks. A grin formed, and he coughed up a slow chuckle. He, too, was captured by the hilarity of the moment.

The moment was quick, and Lord Fyresk fought off the strong urges to continue much faster than Simon could. He found a strong stance and straightened his cuffs and shoulders. His mouth found not a scowl, but a smile-like cousin of one.

"That was not how I intended this meeting to begin," he stated.

"I'm full of surprises," Simon said.

Fyresk huffed. "Indeed. As you proved in this very office." Fyresk spun around and marched into the room that remained after the battle.

"There are two men to fear in the Vevra race," Lord Fyresk started, wasting no more time. "Last night we faced both of them. The Elite and Zahti. Thank the Sonx we ended Zahti. Simon—"

"You've met them before, haven't you?" he asked. His eyes

found Fyresk's hands, then the rest of the charred man.

"Yes," Lord Fyresk stated, understanding the gesture. "I've met the Vevra. And yes. That's how…" His eyes averted. Simon had pieced the two together, but he failed to resist bawking in astonishment. This may be the first time in history Lord Fyresk failed to hold his stake in the conversation. "Their magic is powerful. I have no doubt that if their plan works, they have the potential to destroy the world."

"Fyresk, I'm sorry," Simon blurted. "They were really nice to me, and…"

"They helped you escape," Fyresk continued for him.

Simon sighed. "Yeah."

Fy again found a small smile and a huff of laughter. "I knew you couldn't possibly escape Serlentos Cave by yourself. I never connected the dots until you informed me they knew of Kearlith's location."

"I just followed the whispers. Apparently it was Zahti that led me out of the Cave and fought off all the Gulverbruud. One night, he came to the shack and took me to the lair. That's where I met the Elite and all the other Vevra."

"It's a death trap," Fyresk announced. He looked around as if someone else had said it, then nodded for Simon to continue.

"Yeah. Bloody Sonx it is—"

"Simon!" Fyresk spat.

"Sorry, sir," he said, eating his cheek. "He… Zahti… took me to the lair. It is horrifying, Fyresk. I don't know if these Creatures know what they're getting into."

"Kearlithians will fight to their death even if the safest thing to do for everyone is run." Fyresk sighed and dropped his gaze a bit. "But I've seen it, too, and you're right. The Creatures will lose the majority of their valor in the Vevra's territory."

This affirmation took several minutes to soak in the heavy air of the demolished office. Clouds of dust still persisted in the corners as if mocking the presence of the shadows. Simon started a light stroll around the debris. Lord Fyresk simply held his stance, examining and evaluating him.

There was a calm in the thick, dense air for once, and Simon found the peace and tranquility again. His own affirmations of his recent achievements poured in, and standing on the highest point in Feerthel Forest, Simon felt on top of the world. He gazed out of the gaping hole in the walls and ceiling, breathing in the full view of Kearlith. He valiantly stepped inches away from the edges of the blast, letting the fantasy of immortality sink in. He gazed far down at Kearlith from the lofty office. He had conquered this castle. He had conquered Kearlith.

And he could have effortlessly sliced the life out of Lord Fyresk.

He turned around and smiled as if the Lord were reading his thoughts. As if to say, "It's okay now, though. Right?"

The winds suddenly kicked in across the treetops. Simon saw the leaves ruffle just before the winds hit the castle which gave him no time to step back. A mighty gust shoved him over the edge. Fyresk shouted from behind him, but Simon turned around and sneered as he leapt away from the ledge. His heart jumped into his throat; his gut replaced its spot in his chest. Amongst the chaos of his flapping clothing and armor and the nerves in his brain screaming at him for this decision, he heard Fyresk call his name again and again.

The side of Simon that was frail, and weak, and scared, and an idiot, accepted his fate in the cosmos and splattered across the earth beneath him. But a new Human survived that fall. The new Simon snapped the scythe off his back and rode the waves of the wind, just enough to plant a good landing on the nearest rooftop and take to the air again, back to the remnants of the office.

Once Simon reached the top, he gracefully parked the scythe in mid-air and stepped off. Carefully he returned the scythe to its place on his back.

Lord Fyresk's face gave no indication of his temper- the corners of his mouth drooped, but his lips were pursed, and his eyebrows were as far away from his slit eyes as they could get. Simon bashfully kicked some debris off the ledge just to hear it land several seconds later. "What can I say? I'm—"

"Yeah, yeah. Full of surprises. I get it," Lord Fyresk said, finding his composure.

Simon laughed to himself and took a seat on the edge of the

office floor, letting his legs hang and dangle in the wind. He looked
back at the bits of debris still floating in the corners, and he noticed-
the shadows were dying. The Sonx was rising.

Lord Fyresk found a place next to Simon. Silently they
watched the light bring in the day. Blue, red, and golden hues swept
through the sky, landing in navy and violet splashes on the few thin
clouds. Kearlith's true beauty petrified and burned. The Sonx soon
showed herself, and the wavy blanket of treetops was swathed with
color and vibrancy. The image ached. Simon wanted to capture it
and keep it forever – the portrait of this beautiful little hidden city
surrounded by the magical and dangerous Forest, illuminated by
dozens of bold shades of gold, violet, amber, orange, and navy. For
the first time in over a month, Simon wanted something from the
Outside - he should have brought his camera.

He tried to find the darkness of the Vevra's realm out in the
distance of the mountainous Outside, but to no avail. Somehow,
Fyresk caught on. "You can't see them from here," he said. "Trust
me, I've tried. They have a visual dome above them like Kearlith.
And the Preeminents buried them far away. I truly thought we were
far enough away that they were oblivious to Kearlith's location."

"What else is past the perimeters of Feerthel? Is it more than
just the world of the Humans?"

Lord Fyresk abruptly sniffed and held his face seriously,
"I've heard legends. Rumors. But they're all stories. Right now, I'm
focusing on Kearlith." He waved his hand across their view. "What I
can see."

Simon found himself grinning. "Good strategy."

"I've seen much of the Outside," Fyresk admitted. "The
outer banks. And the Lake is a frequent getaway."

"They don't kill you?" Simon asked in astonishment.

"I'm *Lord* Fyresk, Simon," he said. "Anyway, most of it is
just trees. No direction, no paths. I don't mean to deceive you; even
without the Vevra, there are things past Feerthel that we need to be
on the lookout for. I keep everyone inside Feerthel for a reason."
With that, he took in one last massive inhalation of the fresh air and
found his legs. He offered his hand to Simon, who smiled at it for a
moment before accepting it.

They both made their way to the door, but Simon snuck one last look at the picturesque view of his beautiful city.

# Chapter 30

Consciousness found Simon late the next day, but Raelin and Tormos decided now was the perfect time to deliver payback for Simon's exciting wake-up call in the middle of the night. They burst through the door clinging and clanging a set of chimes and cymbals on wheels with a Ziggokeif's Joke Shop price tag on it. They sang and whooped, intentionally off-tempo from the bongos they were playing.

"How in Kearlith could you steal this?" Simon shouted across the noise.

"Carefully!" Raelin shouted. "It's all about technique."

"What did we say about Tormos joining in on your career, Raelin?" Simon demanded.

"Relax, King Uptight. He just wanted in on this one job of revenge," Rae was sneering now.

"Fine. Do what you want." Simon turned his cold shoulder on the bed and tried to find sleep again, but the raccoons got his brain stirring. Fortunately, they got the message and silenced the contraption before throwing it in the corner, but the damage was done. Simon was awake.

He lay there pretending to be asleep, but his brain was reeling the playback of the preceding day and night. It got caught on the events in the main hall. Like a broken record, the image of Seskith's glare played on repeat. "You're all cowards," she said.

He would have to face her today. And he wanted to see her. He wanted to apologize and make everything okay, but he knew Seskith would be in no mood to accept him again. She hated him. After all his repentance, all his deep transformations, he knew a simple "I'm sorry" wouldn't cut it. Knowing the Shintervah's reputation for intellectual stubbornness and this one's in particular, she would procure a complex series of crazy challenges to prove his worthiness.

By the time Simon finally got bored of lying down, Raelin and Tormos were snoozing in their respective spots- Rae on the armchair, Torm at the foot of the bed. He briefly struggled with the urge to bust out the bicycle of cymbals, but that would only start a war. A noisy and sleep depriving war. And he was already planning on facing one of those.

Simon groggily got dressed, heightening his spirits as much as possible. Seskith failed to see much of his talent in the castle, but maybe she saw him get rid of the Elite. Maybe she was impressed enough to forgive him. Maybe she no longer saw him as a coward. Or maybe she still hated him. Simon lazily threw on his only pair of jeans- shabby and patched together. His shirt somehow found itself on him. He sat on his bed and stared at the ceiling, unconsciously shifting between chewing his cheek and gritting his teeth.

He sighed and shook his head. He was thinking like the old Simon. The one from the Outside. The one that splattered on the castle's floor early that morning. The new Simon would march right into that brewery and woo Seskith with his charm and charismatic presence. She *should* be impressed with his skills in the office battle. He shot himself up and straightened his shoulders, stretched his neck. He kicked on his boots and over-zealously laced the strings. "Bye, guys," Simon threw at the napping raccoons as he marched out the front door.

Seskith was not herself when Simon made it to the brewery. First off, her eyes were flaring with hatred and vehemence. Second, she was throwing every ingredient and tool in the vicinity at Simon- only because her knife and Rutroot ammunition had run out. Simon yelled things like, "Seskith, stop!" and "I just want to talk about—ahh!" in between the times he wasn't jumping or ducking from pain.

"You need to leave. Out that door you can walk in silence. Inside here will be chaos for you," she said, momentarily ceasing fire.

"Seskith, I—" he tried, but she fired again.

Soon she was only throwing sugar packets and scones at him, so he boldly found a stance in the line of fire. Though the ammo was light, her power behind the pitches packed the slightest amount of a sting.

Then the attacks suddenly stopped again. Simon kept his eyes closed and his head down, but for a full minute nothing happened. Eventually he craned his neck up and snuck a peak at his attacker. He gulped as he gazed into her slit eye down the shaft of a ready arrow. She had the bow pulled back to a U position rather than a slim C. Her ferocity shook her aim, but at this close range, her likelihood of missing was slim to none.

"Please… Don't shoot…"

"Give my one good reason why I shouldn't!" she demanded.

"Um… Because you love me?"

The arrow snapped off the string. Simon zipped back to the wall behind him, captured by a punctured sleeve. The arrow nicked the base of his neck which at first went unnoticed, but after the rush this slight wound pounded and forced grunts and screams out of him.

Seskith's face was harder than stone, a look of foul stench. She gradually meandered over to Simon trapped on the wall. Her lips and sharp teeth came within inches of his. She looked into his eyes as if she were trying to mentally break in and smash every thought, fact, idea, and belief. "Your audacity is not flattering."

She kicked the bow up and brought it to Simon's neck, ceasing his ability to breathe or speak. He panicked and felt the wall behind him. Maybe if he could focus, he could set off the repel hex on the scythe. As Simon's terror progressed, his consciousness decreased.

He was barely able to walk his hand across the stones to the scythe. The second he did so, Seskith and her bow blasted away from him.

The scythe was instantly at the ready, and the battle was on. Seskith took no time recovering and countering. Her bow was beautiful and cunningly lethal- in melee combat, the bow was a simple wooden staff. At a range, though, she pulled a hidden string from the wood and fired off arrow after arrow.

Hundreds of arrows ricocheted off the scythe. At first, he set the scythe to magnetize the arrows, but Seskith was smart; the hex had no effect. Somehow her bow negated the magnetism. Simon sweated through the disbelief that he was still breathing. He was in no place to attack, but so far, his defense was stellar. At a snail's pace, he advanced within striking distance of the menacing Shintervah.

Seskith showed absolutely no fear or restraint. Once Simon was close enough, she alternated sweeps and torso-strikes. She mercilessly bashed him with every inch of her bow, giving him no window of opportunity to strike.

But Simon was patient. He fought off a smug smile as he paced himself in his defense- efficiently blocking with the scythe in anticipation of her next moves. Vezlin made damn sure he had upper body strength. Her Tarzan challenges forged his biceps and forearms into sleek but strong steel. In addition, Simon barely put the scythe down except to sleep. Every spare second he was practicing, waiting for a moment such as this. Even when Seskith began to weaken and tire out, Simon kept his smirk to himself.

She suddenly shouted and sent a piercing jab to his gut. Simon easily stepped aside and hooked the bow with the blade of the scythe. Thanks to inertia, she stumbled forward, and thanks to a slight kick to the back from Simon, she fell flat on her face.

Simon had seen many things after eighteen years of life, many disapproving faces and loathing eyes. None stung quite as deep as Seskith's dead glare from the floor.

The sickness in Simon's stomach almost collapsed him, but he trusted his intentions. He stood his ground.

"I'm sorry," he said. "I just want to talk. No weapons." Meeting her gaze, he tossed the scythe and the bow aside. They bounced and slid across the stone floor.

"We have nothing to discuss. I wish to surround myself with

Creatures I consider loyal. You meet neither of those criteria."

From the floor, Seskith leapt at his throat. Her thin fingers grasped his neck and her thumbs closed in on his wind pipe.

"I would warn you about what would happen the next time you kicked me, but it won't matter. Today, Kearlith will be rid of the other filthy Human."

Simon's vision began to darken around the edges. He felt himself losing life. Everything ached more and more as the darkness increased. The last image he saw was a tearful Shintervah with broken eyes and a quivering set of sharp teeth. The last thing he heard was the twinkling of the doorbell.

*     *     *

When Simon awoke, he stared at the brewery for a moment with full vision. He tried to take a deep breath, but his trachea burned as if he had inhaled acid. He coughed until he thought he would pass out again, but Vranzic popped up next to him and patted his back.

"Easy there, son. Seskith has a mighty grip. That throat will be sore for a while."

"Where... the hell... is she?" Simon sputtered out.

"Here," she said. She waltzed into his field of vision, arms crossed but eyes soft and tearful.

"Seskith..." he tried. "Seskith, I'm sorry. I only kicked you... to save both of us."

Instead of responding, she simply turned her head and began to walk away. Vranzic spoke up and shot out his hand to halt her. "Everyone in this city knows the dreadful and appalling news of last night's events, if they weren't involved in them themselves. But the truth is out now, and we must face that. We must not place blame," Vranzic gave a heavy nod and piercing stare to his daughter.

"He is building a weapon, dad!" Seskith shouted.

"I know, Seskith. So are they," he smoothly said.

"He's leading us to war," she finished.

"Sweetheart, the Vevra are bringing war to Kearlith," Vranzic cooed. His typically frantic behavior took a break, and the father-daughter relationship was restored. Vranzic solemnly tilted his head, and Seskith yielded.

"Look, I'm aware of how little my opinions of loyalty mean right now," Simon started, "but I will fight with Lord Fyresk. He and I have made our peace. He's even forgiven Caylo, Morolith, and the rest of the Rebellion. The Vevra are very real, and they need to be stopped. The second Sonx is the only way to get rid of them before they destroy all of us."

"Lord Fyresk is a fool," Seskith stated, stunning both Simon and her father.

"Wait a minute," Simon accused, "weren't you the one lecturing me on my loyalty to our Lord?"

"I trusted him. I had no idea what he was using our Mizik for, but I knew he would never use it for selfish gain," she retorted. "I never imagined this."

"Well this is what is happening, Seskith." Simon stood up and met Seskith's eyes as a man. Not as a kid or a boy or a new Human. "The Vevra will attack us in who knows how many hours, so we need to attack them before they destroy the Sonx. You can lie to yourself and live in the old Kearlith if you want to. Meanwhile, the rest of us will be fighting shadows in the black abyss of their fortress.

"Thank you for saving me, Vranzic. I'm sure I'll see you again soon." Simon gave Seskith one last glance before making his exit.

He had just passed the threshold of the doorway when she finally called out, "I did, by the way."

"What?" Simon asked as he stopped.

"I... L-- I answered your question," she finally said, sauntering over to the doorway.

"Which one?" Simon was dumbfounded.

"The one from earlier. Yes, I did." She gave a pained grin before slamming the door to the brewery.

She loved him. It clicked in his brain along with the door.

Simon stood in front of the closed door with his shoulders slumped heavily to the left. His mouth drooped and his head began to follow. Passing Kearlithians witnessed and gossiped about the stunned Simon. He had completely zoned out, mentally slapping himself for not catching on to her answer quicker. She did. She loved him.

His body became nonexistent; his brain became all reality, and he replayed her simple grin as she closed the door. He watched it over and over, but every time he felt as if it were a dream or a movie. The memory would fade away, and he ached of emptiness until he realized that this picturesque scene was real.

Eventually, he snapped out of it. He shook his head and stretched his back. He beamed as he waltzed down the street, practically skipping. Simon's stance was new to him. He stepped with vigor and tenacity while slightly arching his back to straighten himself. No more slump-backed Simon. Simon the Kearlithian held himself with pride, honor, and a complete lack of inhibitions.

His target was Mathilda's. If there ever was a time to switch back into her good graces, it was now.

*       *       *

Her door was closed and the lanterns in her shop were out when he arrived. Her oversized rocking chair sat empty and motionless. Simon knocked on the door four times, but there was no answer. He knocked again. No answer. He sighed as he started off back down the path.

"Simon?" Mathilda yelled from inside the shack. Simon froze. That voice sounded outrageously angry. He was confident in his progress in combat, especially after the castle and the brewery, but much early on he made a billboard-sized mental note and triple underlined it in bold red ink- NEVER PISS OFF MATHILDA.

He turned the buffalo horn that substituted a doorknob and carefully stepped inside the shack. Light from the Sonx pierced golden ribbons through the dim space. Behind the rays, Mathilda sat in her chair at the cash register, snarling and gritting her teeth. A single candle was lit on the counter that splashed her left side in dim golden flares, but it failed to compete with the Sonxlight that washed the leather shop with a low glow.

"You abandoned this city," she started, attempting to come

off as calm.

"Fyresk and I—"

"*Lord* Fyresk will *not* be a part of this conversation," she snapped. "Crysis and his wicked Scythe will."

"I know all about him and the Scythe. I read about them in Lexandel's book."

"Simon. Those are Kearlith's wounds. And last night you acted as a prodigy to both demons with a scythe of your own. Today, you're boasting about your loyalty to *Lord* Fyresk."

"So now we can talk about him?" Simon snapped. From the echoed silence of her response came the slow and droning pound of her club hitting the tough sandpaper of her palm.

"Listen, worm- I'm not sure how forgiving you Humans are on the Outside, but if life in Kearlith has taught me anything, it's to rarely forgive and never forget."

"Forgive me, Mathilda!" Simon shouted. "*Lord* Fyresk has! Since I've been here, I've wanted to save and assist this city in any way I could. At first I thought I'd be useless and end up living on the streets begging for fish or Duzuks.

"And last night I helped in unveiling a horrible truth. The time for blaming and petty anger will come later, but now we must focus on the Vevra."

The pounding stopped. "Petty?"

"How will your anger with me assist Kearlith, Mathilda?"

She moved as if to bark, but held back. She was speechless.

"Exactly. Look, I'm truly sorry about everything. I should not have lied. I should have released the Harness. And I know we can't just go back to the way things were after we defeat the Vevra, but if it's any consolation, I was relieved when I heard Dagrio set you three free."

"You should leave," she spat through gritted teeth.

"I spared Lord Fyresk, Mathilda! I made sure to get to him first before Caylo or Morolith or Voulderbrin because I *knew* they would have killed him on sight. I forced the truth out of him."

"And you'll mark that down as noble," she huffed.

"I was never going to kill him."

"Rog dung. You've just found yourself on the wrong side of

the fence and managed to climb over before it burned up. Go enjoy your ride of lies. I'll have no part in it. Mind you, I will be a key factor in bringing Kearlith victory against the Vevra, but you'll be fighting beside me. Not with me. Now, leave!" She roared the last word and bolted up from her seat, charging at Simon.

Instinctively, Simon found himself outside the shop, slamming the door closed, just in time for it to catch her attack. The smash rammed Simon into the dirt road. He fumbled and stumbled on top of his scythe and shot away from the raging Gulverbruud.

# Chapter 31

In the early morning of the next day, Simon and the raccoons awoke to a steady and rapid tapping on the door. Raelin roused first. He yelled, "This home is not vacant! Come back in... two... or... twenty..." and ended with a snore. The knocking did not stop or slow down. Simon finally shot out of bed and ripped the door open.

"What?" he shouted. He knew it was Vezlin.

"You and I have much to discuss," she said sweetly, hiding the anger that was without doubt present and raging.

"I already know what you're going to say, so I'll save us some time. You're disappointed. You're angry. I should learn my lesson of loyalty. You never want to see me again.

"I would try and defend myself, but we both know how that would end. Look, I'm very, very, *very* sorry to you and every other Kearlithian whom I've hurt. I really am. In the little amount of time I've spent here, I've screwed a lot of things up. I've pissed a lot of peop—Creatures off. I've made new friends and lost most of them. I'm aware of my place here, Vezlin." During the speech, his face became stone cold, darkened. "From now on I'm just going to Collect all night and find other things to do with my time during the day. That is, if there will be a day again."

He sighed before he finished, "I have a battle to prepare for."

"That was the main topic of discussion," she said, holding her sincere smile. "Simon, I am hurt. You kept many terrible secrets from me. From all of us. On the other hand, I was almost astounded to see you in that hallway. Almost.

"But we must set aside our emotions. As you've said, we have a battle to prepare for. Get dressed and meet me at my house in an hour." She gave a short nod that matched the bizarre image of a pleasant and courteous Vezlin.

Simon was too boggled to respond. She matched her nod with a short bow and walked backwards, making a rare but casual exit.

The brother raccoons were still snoozing in their positions. He debated on starting his day early, hitting the streets of Kearlith and seeing the town on what might be his last day. But after a swift review of his current image in the city, he decided to lay low for a bit. He carefully climbed into the bed as to not wake the snoring raccoons.

"You were right, you know," Raelin said through the snoring. "You have screwed a lot of things up."

Simon pinched his closed eyes as if it would relieve some of the mental strain. He begged for sleep to find him. He wished to skip the next ten hours until the Sonx died. Possibly for eternity. Even if they did somehow manage to defeat the Vevra, his reputation in the city had tarnished into rust. He had faith that his city would live to see another day, one that was victorious against the Vevra, but he just wanted it all over with. He just wanted to Collect and live a simple life.

Tonight he would Collect. Vezlin had challenged him to a few all-nighters before, but he was pacing himself then. His current record was a strong three hundred. Tonight, he would certainly smash that record. Every Kearlithian in the city would awe at his Collection. And the second Sonx would have all the more power to destroy the Vevra.

The train of this thought was short lived, for sleep soon found him again.

*        *        *

And again, incessant tapping interrupted everyone's slumber. Tormos spoke up this time, "Simon, if you don't tell her to shut up, I will personally go over there and —"

"Shuuut up, Torm. You won't do anything. But really, Simon. Make it stop," Raelin added.

Finally, Simon shook off his vague dreams and ripped the door open again.

"*That* is why I hate knocking," Vezlin said. "You're late. Come on." She marched away from the door, but he stopped her this time.

"Vezlin!" he called out. "Let me put on pants."

She scoffed and crossed her arms, waiting with one raised eyebrow. Simon threw on a cleaner shirt and a pair of pants, not forgetting to grab his vest and scythe. Vezlin returned to her scolding face as he hustled out of the shack.

"You're late, *and* you made me wait."

"I had a rough night," Simon jested pleadingly.

"I'll give you that. Let's go."

The black dress captured her again. Her feet grew together and sharpened into talons. Her fingertips elongated and multiplied up her arms, forming them into wings. The red markings transformed into glowing feathers across her body and strands of feathers in the wings. She was a massive, mysterious, beautiful hawk.

She gave him just enough time to admire her before she took to the sky. Simon had grown accustomed to being baffled in Kearlith, so he hopped on the scythe and took off through the trees on auto-pilot, still in awe of the Creature.

\*       \*       \*

The door was open when he got there. Vezlin was standing at her Mizik mini-bar, brewing a cup of Mizik that was so strong he smelled it before he walked in.

"Would you like a brew?" she asked.

"Um... Yes," he said begrudgingly. He was still acquiring a taste for the bitter Mizik – Vezlin drank it thick and concentrated like the double espressos he remembered from the café – but he couldn't turn down a free cup of magic. He took a seat at the simple café table sitting in her breakfast nook.

Vezlin poured the blue hue of black liquid into the mug with her back turned to Simon. The anticipation of her next moves made him uneasy. Finally, after the silence began to linger a little too long, she turned to him with his brew. She walked over to the breakfast nook and took a seat after she handed him the tiny mug. "You could have killed me." She stared him in the eyes.

"I could never kill you, Vezlin. I could defend myself, but—"

"I believe you," she said, stopping him. "Simon, since you've been here I've always thought of you as a novice, a young student. Clearly, you've learned. You've exceeded my teachings and become quite a fierce fighter. I've never been afraid of you before. After you blew away the Vevran lord, I was truly in shock."

Simon was speechless. No one had ever been afraid of him before. They both sipped their Mizik in the awkward silence.

"I guarantee you the Vevra have no chance of survival," Vezlin finally said. "Not with all our talents combined."

"Not a chance," he said absently. "Vezlin, why are you not screaming at me right now? Seskith and Mathilda both want to murder me. Why don't you?"

She cocked an eyebrow before responding, "You're impressive." Simon was struck dumb again, but Vezlin quickly picked back up. "Look, you learned your lesson. I trust Lord Fyresk, and he trusts you. It's all behind us. So let's focus on the battle.

"The second Sonx will destroy their base, but it will not eliminate their population. The Vevra are quick and crafty, and they will not go down without killing many, if not all, of us."

"I'm aware," he said. "I've known about the Vevra since I've lived here."

Vezlin took him in for a moment with pensive eyes and the thinnest of smiles, then she continued, "Then you know what we're up against. After the battle in the office I never want to see another shadow again. They'll haunt me for eternity. But despite our fears, we must put an end to the Vevra."

"The Vevran soldiers that attacked the office were a mere

handful of their population," Simon said. "Their base is swarming with thousands of shadows."

"Do you know when they'll attack?" she asked.

"Not a clue," he admitted. "But I'm sure they won't wait long. Right now, they're building their ranks and gathering magic, strategizing and planning the right time and methods. They're like champion chess players."

"What's chess?" Vezlin asked.

"It's a—. Nevermind," Simon said. "Vezlin, this attack could destroy all of us."

"I know, Simon." Her face melted into a somber expression. For once, Vezlin appeared afraid.

"The office attack was only a sneak preview," Simon mumbled. "If we invade their base first, our numbers will quickly deplete. And if they invade Kearlith first, it's the same story."

"They will never get Kearlith," Vezlin stated. "I'm still on the fence on whether we can destroy their territory, but they will never take this city."

"Well they have until tomorrow. Fyresk plans to attack at dusk."

"May the Sonx save us," Vezlin said as she sipped her Mizik.

"Both of them," Simon said as he did the same.

They conversed more about the battle in the office and how incredible Kearlithian soldiers were, until the emblem on Vezlin's door ignited red. Interrupting the conversation with propitious timing, a familiar face entered Vezlin's shack.

"Hello, Caylo," Vezlin cooed after she waved the door open.

"Hi, Vezlin, Simon. Sorry to barge in, but Lord Fyresk wishes to see Simon at the castle. He has called an immediate Board meeting." He held his hand to his chest and softened his eyes. For the first time, Caylo appeared amenable and honestly apologetic.

"Then why does he need me there?" Simon asked.

"You're on the Board now, Si," Caylo answered.

Simon's eyes widened. He looked to Vezlin. She glared at the other Kyejoth with a twitching eye.

Slowly, Simon responded, "Oh."

"It actually begins in a few minutes. I've been searching all over the city for you. Again, I apologize for interrupting, but we need to hurry."

"As Lord Fyresk wishes," Vezlin said, switching her shocked expression to her stern scowl.

*       *       *

The two ex-Rebellioneers walked side-by-side in silence through the streets of Kearlith. The monotony of the simple exercise allowed them to gather their thoughts. After they started the march up to the castle, Simon finally asked, "How did you know to go to the vault instead of going to the office?"

Caylo flashed him a grin. "You're not as sly as you think, Si."

"Hm," Simon said.

A heavy pause passed, then Caylo spoke up. "You never intended to kill him, did you?"

Simon's eyes found the ground for a while, then the trees, then the sky, and then Caylo. Finally he breathed, "No. Not even for a second."

"Even when you led the Vevra—"

"Yup," Simon interrupted.

"Hm," Caylo said.

The two continued in silence up the path to the castle.

Simon kept all his questions to himself about why Lord Fyresk wanted him on the Board. He knew Caylo would have his comments and theories, but right now, Simon didn't want to hear any of them. All he could focus on was the fact that the Lord of Kearlith wished to know his input before making any city-wide decisions. Simon was now a key member of the population of Kearlith.

And Caylo was still on the Board. The Creature who was dead-set on killing the man last week was now walking with his accomplice to the castle. Simon studied the Kyejoth. Normally he waltzed as if everything were beneath him, but a great deal of charisma would let you know he's okay with it. Now, he slightly slumped as if a little more weight of the world were atop his shoulders. Simon knew this meeting would be much worse for him. Caylo was the one who started the Rebellion, after serving as Lord

Fyresk's right-hand man for three years. The Lord turned out to be a very forgiving man, but the darkness persisted in his demeanor. They both seemed to wonder how much of that darkness would be present at the meeting.

The gargoyles were back at their posts when the pair arrived – their stances stoic, frozen in their terrifying positions. Without the gargoyle guards budging an inch, the gates opened on their own accord. Simon cast his eyes up to see the damage of the office, but it looked as pristine as it was three days previous.

Caylo lethargically led the way to the back wing of the castle where all the Board meetings were held. Until this point, Simon had never stepped foot in the back wing, although he might have raced through it on the scythe at some point. He had been various places on both of the side wings of the giant sword, but never the Wing of the Blade. Lexandel had written extensively about the layout of this area, mostly conference rooms and dining halls fit for hundreds, but he mentioned various training quarters that Simon was on the look-out for – rooms with cloners for targets and enemies, a room with a healing fountain, the ancient weapons hall, the gym, a room with hundreds of metal pieces that could form thousands of race tracks. Unfortunately, most of the doors were shut throughout the halls, but he definitely heard some rumbles, explosions, and roars coming from a couple of the rooms. Fighting his interest to explore, he trudged on to the Board's conference room.

*      *      *

The rest of the party was present and staring at them when they entered. They sat in extravagant, silver chairs with red velvet pads around an immense steel table. Portraits of famous Kearlithians with stern faces lined the walls. Lord Fyresk gave a wave of his hand, and the monstrous doors slammed shut. After a pause, his hand gestured them to their seats as if he were surprised he had to coax them into sitting down.

The new Board consisted of its previous members- Mortimer, Caylo, Chrysaetos, Friziv, Morolith, Nighfall, and Voulderbrin, but seven new faces sat at the table now- a miniature, demonic looking

Gulverbruud, a young, burnt golden Gullen, a long and lanky kid with blond hair puffing out of a black bowler, a girl with blazing red, pixie-cut hair and a cute smile, and a tiny black owl that seemed to be snoozing. Then Simon saw two faces he recognized- Dagrio and Seskith.

"Thank you all for attending this meeting under such short notice," Fyresk began. "I've decided to expand the Board to allow seats for the future leaders of Kearlith. Each race will now be represented by two Creatures – one seasoned Board member and one outstanding youth. In the future, this decision will be voted on by Kearlith, but based on recent events, I've brought in the eight of you. I doubt I will face much discrepancy." He looked around the room at everyone's eyes. Without hesitation, they all shook their heads. Not one Creature disagreed that Simon was one of the outstanding.

Fyresk's demeanor softened. "Although I have felt justified in my decision to guard this city against the truth of the Vevra's existence, the time has clearly come for all of you to find out. It has pained me to keep this secret from Kearlith. After my initial contact with the Vevra, after the attack seven years ago, I never wanted to face them again. I knew, eventually, they would find us, but I thought I could come up with a solution by now." His royal blue eyes found Simon's. "I swear by my sword and my throne if we survive this war, this city will prosper and thrive in the absence of the Vevra.

"Together, this new Board will devise our offense and defense to best the Vevra," he continued. "Their attack on the office was a modest prequel. I'm near certain they will leave us be until nightfall tomorrow, preparing a massive ambush at their base. It is my honest belief that they want us to attack them."

"Why would you lead us straight into a trap?" the chubby Gulverbruud kid snarled. Lord Fyresk snapped him a look of such malice, the Creature crumpled up into a fetal position in his chair, barely fitting his fat calves on the edge of the seat.

"We can set off the trap," said Fyresk, slowly. "Look," he persisted as he took a breath, "if we all try to fight these demons outright, we will all die. We first need to distract them while we find the Elite. Once he's located, we will set off the second Sonx. Then, fighting them will be much easier. After he's dead and their base is destroyed, we can easily deplete the rest of their numbers."

"The Elite will be at the main base, Lord Fyresk," Simon suggested. "The center spike. It's the tallest one. We'll wait until he comes out, then aim the star right where his heart would be."

"We need the star above the trees, Si."

"The new Human's got a point, however, Lord Fy," said the tall blonde in the bowler. "The Elite will doubtlessly be protecting the most significant structure on the site. Shooting the star above him would be the most logical answer."

"Indeed. The star will shatter the main base if we keep it just above the treetops. Soon after the surrounding spikes and structures will dissolve, and the land will be an open battlefield.

Lord Fyresk took a moment to scan the room, pensively staring at each member of the new Board. "We will split into three teams- a decoy team, a scouting team, and a defense team. The decoy team will strike first. Then the scouting team will sneak into the base and locate the Elite. Once I shoot the star, the defense team will step in, and we will all fight for our lives.

"The decoy team will be Mortimer, Nighfall, Chrysaetos, Yahnvry and Kirbirin." Both the bowler-hat kid and the young golden eagle slumped in desolation. "Voulderbrin, Seskith, Caylo, Neeva, and Simon, you will be the scouting team." Out of the corner of his eye, he saw the young Kyejoth flash him another cute grin. He was staring at Seskith, though. She gave him no in. In fact, she gave him as little attention as she was giving this meeting. "And that leaves Morolith, Friziv, Gulfred, Marilio, and Dagrio on defense. The rest of our soldiers will not strike until they see the star."

"What about the rest of Kearlith? There are plenty more that want to fight," said Neeva.

"Circle them around the perimeter of the Vevra's base once the decoy team sets off the trap," said a rich, ominous voice coming from Marilio, the prodigy Protector. The tiny, black Biffleflenn still appeared to be snoozing. "Then, when the star goes off, they'll be fighting on all sides. The scouting team can fight from the inside out. We should set a team of other Kearlithian soldiers to scout the scouters after the war begins."

"Great plan, Marilio," was all Fyresk said. The Lord appeared dumbfounded.

\*        \*        \*

After the meeting was over, Simon took one step every two seconds on the path back home. He took everything in. The tall, blindingly bright stone walls throughout the giant sword's halls. The intricately decorated bowls of blue flames in the corners. The glorious Hall of Kings with perfectly golden-cast statues of bold and noble people and Creatures. Outside he could see his breath, but he didn't care. He kept his snail pace. The red splashes amongst amber and yellow leaves. The dim light from the city that barely brushed the bellies of the clouds. The crippled and refurbished shacks built with flat boulders and varnished scraps of wood standing high and low on the grid of the streets.

He pushed the door to his home open and collapsed straight on the bed. He didn't plan to sleep; adrenaline and straight terror wouldn't allow it. He simply needed to not be moving anymore. The Sonx was dying in a few hours; then he would Collect. Until then, he wasn't budging.

The raccoons hardly noticed him entering. They muttered hello's and continued snoring. Simon quickly mimicked them, but he never fell asleep.

Once the Sonx began to die, Raelin and Tormos roused, and they tried many times to test if Simon was awake. After the tenth ear tug, they gave up and left for the night. He was still in the sprawled out position, but he was wide awake- obsessed with a challenge. He was waiting for the night, waiting for the Mizik to start sparking.

He was mere nanoseconds from beating the record in the race around Feerthel. Tonight, he would beat the record of the biggest Collection, from dusk 'til dawn. Lexandel's greatest was five hundred thirty-two Mizik leaves; Seskith's was four hundred ninety-eight. After several attempts of this quest, Simon's record sat at three hundred and sixteen.

The last of the Sonx's rays burnt out of the sky, and he shot into Feerthel. The first few Mizik leaves were Collected within the first five minutes. Simon made no time for error. In the race around Feerthel he had to focus on speed; in this race he had to focus on placement and direction. Simon was resolute on being the King Collector.

# Chapter 32

Simon's head hit the pillow just after the Sonx sang its radiant "Good morning" to the city of Kearlith. He awoke in the afternoon the next day fully rested and confident, despite only a few hours' sleep and the dread of the pending night's events. Maybe it was because all the fuses in his brain were shot; maybe it was because he had already accepted death and his fate. For whatever reason, he hopped out of bed, dressed himself, and performed a lengthy warm-up without the pangs of fear or the tightly wound apprehension. There was no more uncertainty – tonight he would either live or die. Simple as that.

He had all day to prepare for the night, and he decided to try and share it with Seskith. Without his usual hesitation he strode down to the brewery. He knew she was probably furious with him still, but he had a plan that might be just intriguing enough to get back into her good graces.

Upon his entrance, he was greeted by a cheers-ing Vranzic. Simon's disappointment was slight; he did like her father, even on those glass-half-empty days, but he ached to see Seskith again. Vranzic instantly bombarded him with strategies and schemes- all of them sounding like complex chess moves not even he could understand, much less the Gulverbruud. Simon tuned most of it out and began imagining the battle in his head to imitate and create his own tactics.

The free Mizik brew was nice, though. And all the scones, cookies, and cakes were fresh, since the previous batches were... disposed of.

Just when Vranzic started on a tangent about the value of a good defense, Seskith sailed through the front door and halted once she saw their sole customer.

"Hello, Simon," she slithered.

"Hi," he said on a breath. Her arms were full of shopping bags. Simon's instincts to offer assistance kicked in, but he decided to sit still. "I'm here to talk strategy. I know you don't really want to talk to me right now, but I think we must."

"I think I'll leave you two alone," Vranzic said as he wiped his hands of the Guaraberries he was chopping.

"No, Dad. You should stay." She was still glaring at Simon, then she lunged the load of groceries through the back doors. Simon and Vranzic shared look of confusion for a few minutes before Seskith came back.

"One thing I am certain of," she said as she returned. She poured a cup of Mizik and took a seat at the bar on the other side of her father. Simon tried to shut her up before she revealed too much that the Vevra could overhear if they happened to be hiding in the shadows. "We should not split up. Our odds of escaping will drastically increase with the five of us combined."

"I agree," he said. "If we split up, one of us, if not all, will die. Listen Seskith, we shouldn't talk about this here. We can discuss it later. I have a little surprise." Simon's eyes tried to find Seskith's. "That is, if you would like to go on what might be our one last adventure."

Their eyes matched, and she smirked.

*     *     *

They all finished their cups of Mizik, and Simon started leading Seskith to her surprise- the view from on top of the office. Her temper had cooled after her brew, but a few yards down the path, she snapped.

"Why. Did. You. Not. Shut. Me. Up?" Seskith screeched, punching him on every word.

"I'm sorry, I—Ow! I didn't want to be... ow... rude."

"Well great. Now the Vevra know we're going to stick together when we invade!" She was still screaming, even though Simon was desperately waving his hands.

"Sh!" he finally said, but she winked. "What? What is-- Ohhh. But, we *have* to stick together, Seskith," Simon yelled, catching on. "Even if the Vevra know. And also, ow. That still hurts."

"Sorry," she said meekly.

Though the tension between them had been high strung since the Rebellion's attack, their promenade up to the castle proved to be relaxing and light-hearted. They discussed Kearlith after the attack on the Vevra, old Kearlith again, and Seskith even inquired about Simon's home in the Outside. He didn't explain much. They were a few paces before the gargoyle's gate when he stopped them.

"What's so exciting about the castle?" Seskith asked.

"It's a giant sword! What about that isn't exciting?"

"True. But it's not surprise. You promised a surprise."

Instead of responding, he smiled and handed her a blindfold. Her face dropped.

"No," she said. His smile widened, and she eventually gave in.

"Now hop on the scythe," he said as she finished tying her blindfold.

"What?" she asked, but Simon didn't explain. He gripped her hand and planted her on the back of the scythe's blade. Sensations similar to those he experienced in his dreams pinged through every muscle in his body. He kept a tight grip around her waist and tried to shake off any distractions of yellow blurs. Then he shot straight up to the office.

The wind was whipping on top of the highest point in Feerthel. Seskith and Simon took a seat near the edge. They tried to have a conversation, but few words can pass through chattering teeth and raging winds. Seskith rolled her eyes and began rubbing her palms together, murmuring Kearlith's ancient language. She thrust her palms up, and a sphere of warmth and tranquility surrounded them.

Simon smiled at her for a moment, then looked out on the city. Irony grabbed the air, for the two could not find two words to say to each other. After chattering through frozen teeth, this calm, warm bubble still possessed a tinge of dread like a needle was placed inches away ready to pop it.

Simon tuned out his mental images and focused on the view. "How much of this was different when you were a kid?" he asked after a while, gazing at Seskith now instead of the city.

She kept her attention on Kearlith. "Most of it. It used to shine. Creatures really cared about the condition of their shacks. I know it's silly, but I picture these pretty pastel watercolors when I imagine what it used to be like. Now it feels like everything is a continuous, charcoal sketch. I've heard before I was born, when the Humans were still here, we lived in a time of abundance. Plenty of jobs, plenty of money, plenty of Mizik. Kearlith has never seen a time of true peace, but I will always think times were better back then."

"It will never be perfect, Seskith. We'll never return to the way things were when Humans were around. I'll probably be the last one here, and..." Simon trailed off.

"True," Seskith said, finally looking Simon in the eyes. "But Kearlith can be better. She's weak right now."

"We'll make her stronger. *Almost* like she used to be."

"We will," Seskith agreed without her smirk. Her simple smile emanated candor. "Look," she said as she looked back at Kearlith, "I'm sorry for my anger earlier. And for trying to kill you. I know this war is inevitable. I just feel bombarded by it all. I wish Fyresk told us sooner. I never thought he would keep a lie like this. The secrets just swept me off my feet."

"While we're apologizing – I'm sorry I joined the Rebellion," Simon muttered. "I never wanted to kill him. I just wanted the truth. I figured teaming up with them was my best shot at demanding answers. I wanted to do my part and be—"

"The hero," Seskith finished.

"Yeah," Simon agreed.

"I think you succeeded," she said, smiling.

For a while the two sat in pensive silence and watched the breeze brush the treetops across Feerthel.

\*       \*       \*

After Simon's attention drifted from the beauty of the Forest, he looked again to Seskith. Simon knew enough time had passed. He and Seskith had made their peace. She had already admitted it to him in a vague and suave way. All he had to do was admit it back.

He just had to say the words. That's all he had to do.

He had plenty of chances. An hour passed, and he could count the amount of words he said during that time and the three words he wanted to say on one hand.

"Seskith," he finally started.

"So now we have to split up," she said at the same time.

"What? Oh, Right. No, not necessarily. Even if the Vevra know we'll stick together, we're still much stronger than if we split up."

"But even our strength combined could not conquer them. If there are two groups of scouters and one gets captured, the other can continue to scout. There's five of us- two in one, three in the other."

"That's true. The Vevra won't know how many scouters there will be. How would we split it up?" Simon asked.

"You and I will take Voulderbrin. He'll be our lookout. Caylo and Neeva can handle their own."

"That's smart. Two Kyejoth can back them off with their flames. I still don't know how we'll be able to sneak into the Vevra's fortress, even with Voulderbrin's help."

"It helps when you're black as the night." Lord Fyresk's voice startled them from behind.

Although still shaken, Simon took a stab, "Yes, but few have that advantage. We're yellow and pale. We'll definitely stick out."

"My fur happens to be golden," Seskith said with mock anger.

Simon hoped for seclusion on the roof of the office, but he took advantage of Fyresk's company. "I have something for you,

Lord Fy," he said as he pulled out his Mizik wallet, building the anticipation as he slowly unclasped the hinge. He retrieved a handful of leaves and passed them over. He grinned as if his Collection contained thousands of leaves. Lord Fyresk fashioned a perplexed façade as he accepted the leaves. Simon repeated the process over and over until Fy's bewilderment grew into actual giddiness. "I Collected all night. Five hundred forty-three leaves of Mizik."

Both Lord Fyresk and Seskith shared a wide-eyed look. They stammered their responses, but finally Seskith muttered, "Wow."

Simon shot his eyebrows up with a grin, "Impressed?"

"You're uncanny," said Lord Fyresk. He took a seat and joined the pair on the edge of the office's glass roof.

*     *     *

They killed a couple hours gazing out on the city and discussing more strategies. Their Lord had spent many a night since the attack seven years ago formulating their best moves, hence the chaos of the office. Simon peeked down through the glass and saw that everything was in its rightful place again. Now that there was nothing to do but wait, Lord Fyresk apparently had time to tidy up. Simon's distraction from the conversation reeled back when he heard Fyresk ask the question, "Would you two like to see the second Sonx?"

Simon shot up, willing to jump right off the roof of the highest point in Feerthel. Fy had to stop him. "Not again!" he shouted with the return of his scowl.

Seskith was not as pleased, but she hesitantly followed them through the hatch window into the office. Simon eagerly led the way down the staircase. The instant they hit level ground, Simon mounted his scythe, and Lord Fyresk mounted his sword. Seskith dropped on all fours and sprinted close behind. Simon's avidity bulged out of his eyes. Neither Lord Fyresk nor his scythe could go fast enough. The wait was unbearable. He looked back to Seskith who kept a stern face, even with her rapid running.

Despite Simon's impatience, they traveled through the castle quickly thanks to Fyresk's column trick. All three of them were on alert. At any second, the Vevra might kick off the war with a skirmish. The entire city of Kearlith was on alert, and the castle had been on full lock-down since the attack. Even in the vast white chamber with the second Sonx, their eyes were shifting to the corners and walls looking for shadows.

Lord Fyresk halted them and stepped forward, lifting his hand up to the steel wall of the vault. He pulled back and twisted as if tugging an invisible rope. A thin door just Fyresk's height and width cut out of the wall and slowly folded flat on the floor. Lord Fy entered first, Seskith followed, and Simon squeezed in just as the door began to fold up again.

A dim blue glow lit the vault, emanating from a UFO-shaped disc hovering over a thick metal well – five feet in diameter. In silence, the three gazed at the bowl of Kearlith's Collection of Mizik, thousands of leaves pulsing their blue glow. Their light and energy seemed to feed the disc; its dull hum echoed off the steel walls as it leisurely spun inches above the metal framing.

"How does it work?" Simon asked

"Kearlithians have been asking that question for years, Si. None have formulated the perfect theory to magic, but – "

"I meant the second Sonx," Simon blurted.

"I know," Lord Fyresk coolly replied. "No Creature can tell you how it works. Do not expect *me* to." The statement returned the room to silence, except for the dull hum of the disc.

Out of the lull, Seskith cried, "How could you keep this a secret?"

Fyresk didn't meet her tear-stricken eyes. "For Kearlith's safety. If the Creatures had known what happened to me, they would have blindly battled the Vevra, and the city of Kearlith would have no more population."

"You Humans," she slightly spat, "you underestimate us. We could have taken them out then. But now the shadows have gained their strength and an entrance into Kearlith."

"I'm aware, Seskith," Lord Fyresk stated as she turned away. "Your anger and pride is precisely why I've kept them concealed. I know full well what Creatures are capable of. Even if I had a horde of Humans and Creatures fighting with me, I would be hesitant to start a war with the Vevra. It was in my best interest – and Kearlith's – to keep this a secret and tend to them myself until they invaded Feerthel."

"And now they have. Along with Kearlith." Seskith would not stop.

"You underestimate the Vevra." It was Simon this time. Both Fyresk and Seskith snapped their heads to him. "After I met them, the last thing I wanted to do was talk about them. I wanted to forget they ever existed. But they found me, and basically kidnapped me to their territory. You should cut Lord Fyresk some slack, Seskith. Dealing with the Vevra is like nothing I've dealt with before."

"Human," was all she said, but her smirk returned.

"He's right. If we survive—"

"When!" she interrupted.

"Right. *When* we survive, those who aren't dead or mortally wounded will be scarred from the mental terror of the Vevra."

"We will destroy them," Seskith said. They all nodded in accord and stared at the pit of endless Mizik leaves. The disc softly spun above the metal railing, allowing Simon to see every last hex on it. The scars on the disc pulsed with light in the same rhythm of the Mizik leaves below.

*        *        *

Simon led the path down to Mid-City. Through the castle, through the gates, through the streets and neighborhoods and shops of Kearlith. Seskith and Lord Fyresk followed behind. Both appeared curious to see where they were going. Simon couldn't explain why, but the statue of Lord Fyrethold seemed to be the right place to sit and await the fate of war. Others seemed to catch on- more Kearlithians than usual were aimlessly roaming the plaza, taking in every detail as if it were their last.

He gazed upon the statue in the same fashion. Seskith and Lord Fyresk flanked him, doing the same. They basked in the strength, the unwavering courage of the beheaded man, standing as if the weight of Kearlith were atop his shoulders rather than a cranium.

More and more Creatures flocked to the statue. An unspoken calling of Lord Fyrethold's legend persisted throughout the air. Eventually, Vezlin and Dagrio walked up and joined the crowd slowly forming around the statue. Their eyes met, but no words passed between them. No words needed to be said. They all knew why they were here.

"Hey hero. Are you up for a duel?" It was Seskith who offered the challenge. She clipped the bow off her backpack and wielded a ready stance, squaring towards Simon. With a grin Simon wielded his scythe and prepared a stance to match Seskith's challenge. He locked into position. She immediately started with a wide overhead, which he parried with the component stance and kicked the attack back. He jabbed to the chest and sliced to the right, a favorite attack by his mentor Lexandel. She consequently stepped back and brought her bow up to block him, then spun around in a cyclone to throw off his guard. She ended with a low-ground swipe that Simon successfully leapt and avoided.

Their duel incited a riot. Throughout the plaza, the rest of the Creatures broke out into mini-battles, every Creature practicing their best tactics and battle strategies. They sliced and slashed, hacked and stabbed, tucked and rolled. Their anticipation could not be contained.

Vezlin observed Simon and Seskith's battle. She stood a safe distance away with an arm crossed and the other pensively stroking her chin. Five minutes later, however, she hunched into an attack stance, and double-teamed against Simon. The scythe successfully blocked both of their attacks for a while. Then in a flash, Seskith cartwheel-ed backwards and landed with a ready arrow squarely aimed at Simon. Before he could process the spectacle, she shot him right between the eyes.

Simon saw the arrow release and felt his eyes cross as they watched its path. Just before it made contact, he winced.

But nothing happened. When he opened his eyes again, the arrow was frozen in mid-air maybe an inch away. His eyes refocused on the Shintervah beaming in the background. Simon grinned back in relief. In fact, he started laughing. Seskith joined in, and eventually Vezlin melted into hilarity, too.

As his laughter subsided, Simon gazed at the scene on the plaza- cheetahs wielding maces and fighting gazelles, buffaloes with axes and staves fighting guys with flaming swords, eagles and owls popping in on the various battles. It was brutal, vicious, and beautiful.

\*     \*     \*

By the time the Sonx began to die, the Creatures were sprawled out in Mid-City. There was a low lull of conversation, but most of them were resting their bodies and minds for the actual battle.

They rested for quite a while. Some began snoring in the midst of the distant and rare mutters. As if in meditation the Kearlithians became perfectly still and fully, absolutely alive. They watched the Sonx start its descent past the treetops, becoming calmer as warm rays were replaced by the biting cold shadows. The last sliver of light died out over the horizon, and the Creatures began to get restless. They stood up and stretched, still in their states of absolute presence, patiently waiting for Lord Fyresk to make his appearance. All of them in their own heads, oblivious to one another, fervent to find out how the battle would end tonight.

Simon stood among them, performing simple jumping jacks to warm up his body. Surrounding him were Vezlin, Seskith, Dagrio, and Caylo, each doing similar exercises. All their peace treaties were signed in the silence. They gazed at each other with trust and honest respect.

Lord Fyresk appeared out of the shadows instantly. "Do not look at me or acknowledge me. Just listen," he whispered as he subtly passed them small, pewter pebbles. They froze at his sudden entrance, but obeyed and continued exercising. "The decoy team will deploy in five minutes. In two minutes, every Kearlithian will be circling the plaza. The rock I've just given you will shake when you are to meet at your designated area and set off for the Vevra's lair. Simon, Seskith, Caylo- you're meeting at the gates of the castle. Dagrio, you're meeting Vezlin in Kyo's Park. Do not follow each other. Wind your way to your destinations, and at all times- be. On.

Your. Guard." He practically coughed the last part out before he cut through the crowd of Kearlithians.

They kept exercising as if the last minute were not filled with orders for their death quest.

As instructed, the crowd populating Mid-City's plaza began winding and twisting their way through each other. There were hundreds of bumps and sorry's and excuse-me's, but no one minded the quiet chaos. They mindlessly wandered in every direction until the little rocks in their pockets shook. Their grave faces never met eyes.

Though Simon was traveling at a strolling pace, his heart was beating out of his chest. The anticipation of waiting for any movement from the rock dragged the seconds into hours. Several times he thought he felt it shake, but when he checked, it sat dormant. Five seconds later he was checking it again.

When it finally thrashed in his pocket, there was no doubt it was time; the rock smashed and dug into his leg. He slowly strolled a curvy path towards the castle.

# Chapter 33

Fortunately, the path to Kearlith's castle was almost a straight shot past the Shintervah and Kyejoth territories. The slim moon cast little light, and Fyresk had dimmed the street fires as if to tease the Vevra. Simon's hands fiercely gripped the scythe, but he did not dare enchant it to light his way. He swiftly power-walked up the path in his best attempt at silence. Though Fyresk felt confident the Vevra would hold their attacks, that was not guaranteed. Simon's eyes were wide open.

As he neared the bend in the road that forked into the Kyejoth's territory, he couldn't tell if it was magic or his mind that made the shadows dance and come alive. His eyes would straighten and focus, revealing a still trail lined by stationary trees and shadows, but out of the corner of his eyes, the shadows splashed into action.

He trained his eyes to the ground and picked up the pace.

When he arrived at the gates, the gargoyle guards were stoic. Simon looked around to see if any of the other four had beaten him there, but he appeared to be alone.

Soon after, Simon witnessed a silhouetted figure dashing up the path. It was Neeva, grinning from ear to ear. Her features were sharp and attractive. She wore a flowy, mauve shirt with tight black jeans.

"How did I know you'd be the fastest one here?" she asked.

"Um… I don't know," he squeaked.

"Well, I bet—" she started.

Simon stopped her, "Look, we really can't be talking right now. We don't want to give away our positions."

"If the Vevra want to find us, they will," she spat. "If they want to *kill* us, they will."

Suddenly, Seskith snuck up behind Neeva whispering, "But we don't want to be a barking target." Neeva shot back with an exaggerated scoff. Seskith's eyes found Simon's, and they grinned.

Not a minute later, Caylo arrived followed by Voulderbrin.

"I thought we weren't supposed to follow each other," Neeva accused.

"I followed the treetops, and we met at the bend back there," Voulderbrin said through a scowl. "Now, shh."

Caylo and Voulderbrin made eyes and nodded to each other, then cast their arms and wings out to their sides, muttering jargon and random syllables. Together, they built a dome of translucent, pastel-colored spells. It grew to encompass them all, and then slowly faded as the two original Board members brought their focus back to the group. Simon was dumbfounded, but Seskith and Neeva simply nodded in an accord, committing to the quest.

Caylo led the path around the castle and through Feerthel. Simon silently glided the scythe through the air behind Seskith with Neeva and Voulderbrin somewhere behind him. They were spaced out just enough to sense each other's presence. Simon couldn't exactly see Seskith, but he impulsively knew where to go.

The scouting team was crawling through the Forest. The decoy team was set to travel faster, and once the scouting team heard the uproar, they could bolt into the darkness. Until then, the scouts moved agonizingly slow.

Simon's mind had just begun to wander off when he barely noticed a shadow in the path up ahead, steadily increasing in size. His veins instantly froze up, and every muscle tensed.

The silhouetted form belonged to Lord Fyresk riding his katana. "We're almost out of Feerthel," he whispered. "If you can remember, the Vevra are still a bit farther. Are you prepared for this, Simon?"

Simon stared Lord Fyresk dead in his bold, blue eyes and nodded. "Yes," he said.

Through the darkness he swore he could see Fyresk smile, but he couldn't be sure. The Lord vanished just as quickly as he appeared.

Simon refocused on the path ahead. Now that they were about to leave the vicinity of Feerthel, the trail became subtle and hidden. He needed to catch up. He kept Seskith in his sights, but trailed back enough so that she was a dim, golden blur in the surrounding darkness. They were all speeding up. Simon heard the whirrs of the trees as he rushed past him. Without the straight and narrow line of flight, the forest outside of Feerthel was much less forgiving on the corners and hooks.

He knew they had to be close. He was starting to wonder whether the decoy team had already been attacked and eliminated, since he heard nothing but the whooshes of the trees.

But then he heard it. The instantaneous screams and heinous cries of Kearlithians and shadows left no doubt- the war had begun.

*     *     *

The scouts bolted into action. They raced farther away from Feerthel and closer to the terror, disregarding the trees with blatant naivety.

Swiftly they found the outskirts of the Vevra's realm; the tall shadow spikes pierced the black air. Simon couldn't tell where the spikes ended and the night sky began. He spotted no Vevra, but he kept his eyes on the closest spikes.

Caylo slowed to a halt, his eyes dashing to every spike as if he saw a Vevra atop every one. He held up a hand and gave the official signal for "move forward". He knew this meant only Simon, Seskith, and Voulderbrin. The two Kyejoth were going to skate the outskirts before entering.

The overexposure of the dark, open clearing was violating. Simon felt like a shadow could pop out in front of him and maul him within seconds. The scythe was wielded, cocked, and ready to swing. Simon and Seskith crept next to each other – Simon watching their left side, Seskith watching their right – while Voulderbrin floated and flapped his wings inches above their heads.

They approached the first shadow spike. It was taller than most of the inferior spikes in the area at roughly fifteen feet, but miniature compared to the five colossal shadows towering in the background. The other closest spike coiled up into a sharp point. All the spikes oozed black smoke like dry ice. They came within a few feet of the structure, but no Vevra leapt out. They crept on, taking a zig-zagged path to the middle towers. The shadow spikes closer to the five main towers started to take on height. Deeper into the middle of the Vevra's territory, the spikes were twenty, thirty, forty feet high. Simon knew any second now, one Vevra would take form and start a commotion, ringing the bell for another battle.

But the grounds remained quiet, the kind of silence that pierced Simon's anxiety. The chill existed everywhere. Simon felt it in his bones, in his veins. The office battle alone had hosted hundreds of Vevran soldiers, and yet the towers appeared to be deserted. He felt all their eyes on him.

Simon was leading the way to the main tower, but he stopped them once they reached the border of spikes. The five focal shadow towers stood alone in a large clearing. The closest tower stood twenty feet away; their target was fifty. Simon, Seskith, and Voulderbrin gazed at the image, captured by its mystical ferocity. The main spike was hundreds of feet tall, and it exuded the black smoke as if the entire structure were a frozen solid shadow.

Simon turned around to his partners and met their eyes. They all nodded one last time in agreement, offering grunts in obligation.

*This is it,* Simon thought.

Simon looked around as if crossing the street, and he zoomed towards the main spike. Every muscle in his body cringed as he passed the closest spike, but he zipped by unscathed. The gargantuan smoky tower was twenty feet away. The spike loomed ever closer.

Then the Elite's massive image emerged with a haunting grin and a maniacal laugh. Simon moved to snap the scythe off his back, but the Elite leisurely raised his hand, still cackling, and Simon lost all sight and consciousness.

*      *      *

Once Simon could see again and stand on stable ground, a dim and grave image was before him- four pillar candles tucked in the corners, lighting the shadowy surfaces beneath their feet, the walls, and the ceiling of a bare, black room. Everything oozed the same black smoke. Caylo and Neeva stood in the center of the room with their hands strapped behind their backs.

The Elite kicked the remaining scouts into the room, his maniacal cackling intensifying, adding to the insanity of the situation. He ripped the scythe out of Simon's hand and gazed at it, taking in every detail.

"Dagrio is a spectacular mastermind of design," he noted as if this conversation were being held over a morning brew of Mizik. Simon was speechless. The Elite simply hummed and crept through the shadowy walls. The five Kearlithians were left alone, although they felt completely exposed to countless Vevran eyes.

And Simon was without his scythe.

"What happened?" he screamed to the ceiling.

"We all got caught," said Caylo without an ounce of his beaming self-esteem.

"We underestimated them," Neeva said, winning her a scowling glare from the group.

"They haven't killed us yet. They want us alive," said Seskith who was testing out the endurance of the smoky black walls. The wisps of shadows were deceitful; the walls appeared to be stone solid. The muted thud of her paws slamming their barriers barely echoed in the tiny room.

"They only want to drive us to insanity," Neeva said. "If I get don't get out of here, I'll—"

"You'll survive," Seskith stopped her.

Simon zoned out of the conversation and fully took in his environment. The Vevra's trick worked; this room was maddening. There was no indication to where they were. The top of the tower? Underground? On another planet? He was simply in a room that looked to be closing in with blackness. The smoky walls agonizingly feigned claustrophobic dread.

The maniacal laughter returned along with the Elite's voice, but the five remained alone in the black chamber. "I've waited all *week* for this, and the way you five crawled through the Forest- I nearly died with eagerness. But now I have you. Trapped and helpless. There is nowhere to run. Nowhere to hide." With this, he showed his face. He stepped through the shadowy wall and joined them like he was the host of the party. "I must say, your efforts to escape us were quite impressive. We lost track of several of you after you left Mid-City. But I fear Neeva was correct in her assumption- you underestimated us."

This cut a deep gash into the hearts of the Kearlithians. They couldn't bring themselves to admit defeat, especially an intellectual one.

"Where have you brought us?" Seskith demanded.

"To the shadow chamber located deep within the first Vevran tower."

"How far underground?" Voulderbrin asked as if calculating the caves in his head.

"We're not underground," the Elite said with slight huff of laughter.

"Then where are we?" Simon shouted again. His anger and the excruciating room were unbearable.

"You're above ground, Simon. Just not exactly in your normal dimensions," said the Elite. "And you will stay here for eternity. *Unless* you tell me one little detail." His eyelids lowered as he grinned wide. "Where is Lord Fyresk?"

"He's writing your eulogy," Seskith spat.

"You know, young Seskith, you are in no position to threaten my authority here. You are my prisoner, after all," the Elite said with too much zeal. "Tell me where he is, and I will let you free. But you've made me wait this long. I have absolutely no desire to end this too soon. I'll let you and your putrid friends rot in here for as long as it takes."

"We don't know where he is," Caylo said. "He kept his whereabouts from us intentionally. Torture us all you want, but you'll never get your answer. Not before Lord Fyresk himself shows up and pays his vengeance."

Caylo swiped the Elite with a quick left kick, knocking the shadow Lord into a stunned state for a moment. He shook his head and swung Simon's scythe at the bold Kyejoth.

The blade bounced off the barrier of rippling pastel multi-colors inches away from Caylo's shoulder.

"Ah! Thank the spells," Voulderbrin shouted.

Caylo held a suave stance and allowed him another swing. The infuriated Elite quickly recovered from his astonishment, shaking his head and grimacing through his pearly white teeth. He took advantage of Caylo's submission with a mid-section slice. Without flinching, Caylo watched the blade ricochet off the pastel barrier.

"Where is your Lord?" the Elite roared. "I warn you, do not challenge me- you *will* rot in here until you inform me of his location. That shield spell will not protect you from the slow death of starvation." The Elite was fuming. Veins protruded and pulsed from his biceps as he tightened his grip around the scythe. His arrogant giddiness had crumbled into malevolent vehemence. He received no answer, and he lunged for Caylo.

But the scene was interrupted by two new prisoners in the shadow cell. Raelin and Tormos shot in from the middle of the wall, slashing and clawing at the Elite's face. Wendy Whisp's locket dangled from Raelin's right fist. Tormos cleanly landed on the floor and was instantly airborne again with a round-house kick to his knees, sending the Elite crashing down.

Several Vevran soldiers followed the raccoons into the overpopulated cell and fought to keep them grounded. The raccoons jumped across the Vevra's shoulders. One guard hit them both with a force-push spell, flinging them on the floor. Another guard hexed their paws, and they meshed into the floor.

The commotion allowed everyone's focus to remain on the rampant raccoons, so Simon snuck over to the Elite and grabbed his scythe. Instantly, he felt complete again. He took a swing at the rising Elite, but the shadow Lord caught the blade in his hand.

The Elite spun the blade, causing the handle to twist out of

Simon's possession. Just before he lost it, Simon hexed the scythe to explode with flames. The Elite hissed and let the blade clang and scrape against the shadowy floor. Simon smiled as he picked his scythe back up and brought every attack he had upon the Elite- slashes, overheads, lunges, side-sweeps. The Elite remarkably blocked every single one, but Simon wasn't going to let him get an attack in, even if he was protected by the multicolored barrier.

Seskith, Neeva, Voulderbrin, and Caylo also commenced in their own separate battles. Handfuls of the Vevran guards were pouring in from the walls while the rest of the scouts backed up Simon's battle with the Elite. Seskith pulled out bundles of Fyrovine and lit them all to give the room extra light, but Neeva cleared her throat before she raised her palms up to the guards and threw a river of flames into their faces. She smirked at Seskith as she kicked the smoldering shadows. Seskith simply narrowed her eyes, readied her bow, and shot over Neeva's shoulder. The arrow landed between the eyes of a Vevran soldier with an ax in mid-swing.

More guards were swarming the smoky cell, and the Elite started to get his groove back. Simon's slices were now being blocked and countered by backhands and undercuts. The shadow Lord anticipated Simon's moves before he performed them. He was turning this into a dance.

The Elite swung with an abrupt rage, a powerful overhead strike that should have split Simon in two. The rippling pastels returned and ricocheted the Elite's blade into the ground. Simon noticed that the barrier was weakening. The colors were fading and the ripples were stirring quicker. Soon, the Elite's sword would cut through.

The Elite knew it, too. He sliced at Simon in a frenzy until the pastel multi-colors were no more, and Simon was deflecting the Elite's attacks with the enhanced scythe and his own strength. The clangs became painful. Every single blocked slice shot hundreds of pounds of pressure through his wrists and into his shoulders. The Elite was smirking again, systematically judging his every move. He swung a stream of overhead strikes that almost forced Simon to the ground, but he managed to fend off the storm of attacks. The Elite left his legs and mid-section defenseless. Simon took it as the perfect opportunity to make a strike.

But the Elite caught the scythe and easily ripped it out of Simon's hands. Maybe it was because Simon truly felt as if he had lost his mind, but the Vevran lord and the shadow chamber halted to half-speed. The Elite had his sword directed towards Simon's neck, and his balmy smile inched closer to Simon's.

"This will be rewarding," the Elite seethed. And he set his sword to strike.

Simon didn't wince. He didn't flinch or recoil. He watched the blade rise in the air, and he heard the thunderous chamber fade to silence. Like a baseball player, the Elite swung his mighty sword with demonic force. Still in slow motion, Simon waited patiently, still watching his guillotine creep towards him. His body pleaded for the relief, the liberation from its many aches, pains, and sore muscles.

*      *      *

Then Lord Fyresk's blade pierced through the shadows surrounding the Elite. Simon couldn't see Lord Fyresk for obvious reasons, but the blade emitted a blue glow that persisted through Simon's fading vision. With a swift slash despite the surrounding half-speed, Kearlith's Lord brought his own wrath down upon the Elite.

Fyresk at least stunned the shadow-man, if only for a quick second. He did not hesitate before he gripped Simon by the wrist.

"Grab the others!" he roared. Simon had forgotten that the room consisted of anyone else other than the Elite, Fyresk, and him, but he scrambled to retrieve his scythe, then he turned to his right and lunged for Seskith's wrist. She in turn grabbed Caylo, who grabbed Neeva, who grabbed Voulderbrin. As Raelin and Tormos wrapped themselves around Caylo and Seskith's arms, Lord Fyresk cast a spell on the bond between Simon and him that continued down the line and fastened them all together.

Simon's vision was swept with darkness. He was being harshly tugged through complete black. He felt wispy like his soul was being ripped out of his body and into absolute nothingness. The fact that he was feeling anything kept him sane. The haunting, fleeting feeling was nothing compared to the terror he felt battling the Vevra. His breath escaped him, and a numbing, paralyzing sensation poured into his limbs.

When he finally caught his breath, Simon fought for it on the cool earth back in the dimensions he was used to. He and the other scouts were curled up on the dirt a few feet away from the middle smoky spike, and Lord Fyresk wielded a ready sword protecting them.

The majority of Kearlith was here, all of them fighting the Vevran soldiers' avatars. The second Sonx was blazing above them, forcing the Vevra on the battlefield into their physical forms, and diminishing the dark towers' size by the minute. Already, the ground was full of collapsed Creatures – seriously wounded or dead.

After he could feel his limbs again and shake away the feelings of numbness, Simon vaulted himself into an attack position, flailing the scythe at the surrounding Vevra. Quickly, the Elite emerged from the shadow spike with his eyes on Lord Fyresk. Simon tried to step in, but the Elite swatted him away as if he were an insignificant housefly. Lord Fyresk and his sword were ready. The clinging and clanging of the Lords' great blades echoed across the Vevran territory. The surrounding duels took a brief halt and marveled at the spectacle. Within seconds, all the Creatures realized they were in mid-war and began hacking and slashing at each other again.

Simon's attackers were relentless. There were three of them; four if you counted the swordsman that was switching between Mathilda and him. Mathilda stood a few yards away blasting the Vevra with the heavy side of her club like a shotgun, while Simon was picking off the few that missed the onslaught of deadly spells. One was double wielding sai's, another had a scimitar, and the third had a massive mace. Simon was performing huge sweeps with his scythe that seemed to keep the attacking Vevra at bay. He kept making quick glances at Mathilda to see if she was noticing his valor, his protection and support. She did not. Her eyes darted from soldier to soldier, almost intentionally blocking Simon out. He defended her anyway.

Especially when she dropped her club. Without warning, her arms fell slack, and the club toppled and bounced on the dirt. She appeared to be stunned, although Simon didn't see a spell or hex attack her. He leapt in front of her to block the Vevra's attacks.

Then he saw him, too. A strapping and scarred Shintervah with a long, black, braided ponytail was spinning and slicing a path through the Vevran soldiers. He kicked and punched with classic Kung-Fu finesse.

Shastlin had returned for Mathilda.

He nimbly leapt into the circle that Simon was clearing around her. She shook herself out of her paralysis and picked up her club to deal more damage to the countless Vevra. Mathilda, Shastlin, and Simon stood in a triangular form, rotating in a circle to attack the soldiers with each of their strengths. A wide circle of falling Vevra was clearing around the three Kearlithians. The local Kearlithian soldiers noticed, thus they soon found their way surrounding the triangle.

## Chapter 34

Hordes of shadow soldiers were filling Simon's peripheral vision. Although the second Sonx cut an immense amount of light through the dark territory, the shadows held a large majority to the battling Kearlithians, swarming the field with a blackness that felt eerily similar to the shadowy prison cell he just escaped from. Simon witnessed at least one of every race slaughtered by the Vevra.

Despite their lack of numbers, the surviving Kearlithians were terrorizing the Vevra. Simon was impressed to see his fellow soldiers wreaking such havoc on a place that had haunted his thoughts for weeks now. He continued fighting off the Vevran soldiers that dared to assault the triangular formation. The scythe was flaming now and swiping the shadow attackers. He couldn't see the Elite or Lord Fyresk anymore, only the fallen bodies of Kearlithian Creatures and puddles of dead Vevra.

He could see Dagrio and Morolith battling on the outskirts of the circle they had cleared. Morolith was making wide sweeps with his massive club, knocking the Vevran avatars to their dead shadow puddles in one hit. Dagrio was duel-wielding wands; his right was being used solely for ice and fire strikes while his left was performing multiple spells and hexes on other Vevran enemies. He was single-handedly warding off more than ten shadow soldiers. The two fought back to back, holding a strong defense for the relentless fighting triangle. Morolith didn't seem to notice Shastlin's presence.

Simon's attention snapped to the sky – Thrax was soaring through the air on a fishhook branch assisted by the screeching Axolotls on hand-gliders and the roaring Goyliguin riding logs like surfboards. The battles momentarily halted as everyone gazed up at the sight. Simon noticed other Creatures of the Forest surrounding the Axolotls and the Goyliguin. They skimmed across the shadow spikes that surrounded the five in the middle, and on their landing, they literally hit the ground running. The sleek iguana grizzly bears brought massive axes and hammers. They were destroying dozens of Vevra in single swipes and ground-pounds but were constantly being bombarded with wave after wave of more shadows. The Axolotls leapt from Vevra to Vevra, clawing some in the face while spitting lava or poison at others in mid-air. Feerthel Forest had arrived with powerful reinforcements.

The triangular formation was holding strong. Simon, Mathilda, and Shastlin were a perfect trio of offense and defense. Simon was now making ice and fire swings with his scythe, shooting waves of icicles and flames at the onslaught of Vevran soldiers. Instead of the satisfying sizzle of a hit, the shadow men and women would simply expand and explode before oozing into miniature black holes on the floor. Still, Simon was satisfied with every Vevran death he caused.

His body was now on its seventh or eighth wind, and he fought like he was invincible. His arms were swinging the scythe on auto-pilot, and his legs were mechanically pivoting around the circle.

*       *       *

Then a window opened up in the sea of shadows, and Simon saw a horrible scene. The Elite was boldly marching up to Lord Fyresk who was obliviously battling six other Vevra. His blade hit three different blades every single second while his wand danced around his peripheral vision and defended against the magical obliteration that surrounded his battle. The Elite grinned with the maliciousness of a back-stabbing assassin as he strolled up behind Fyresk's back.

Suddenly, Seskith leapt in the middle of the path between the Elite and Lord Fyresk.

Simon tried to break away from the triangle. He lunged for the window, but it closed in with angry Vevra slashing various bladed weapons. With every last push of adrenaline, magic, and energy he had left, he demolished the window back open, just in time to see the Elite cast a spell that countered Seskith's block. The spell stunned her and flew her backwards several feet. The Elite wasted no time in casting the deadly spell. A flash of black lightning immediately bolted out of the shadow Lord's fingers and encircled the Shintervah.

Simon was too far away. He shuffled to mount the scythe, but the Vevran soldiers grabbed at him and forced his weapon into a blocking position. He saw Seskith's hands find her face writhing in pain. She involuntarily shook and courageously tried to meet the Elite's eyes with hers. But the Elite intensified the spell and cast her away into the sea of shadowy warfare.

The attack caught the attention of Lord Fyresk. He spun around and began countering the spells and hexes that the Elite was now shooting. Lord Fyresk's blue eyes held a hint of insanity. He had just witnessed the death of Seskith.

Simon saw it, too. He wickedly mauled the surrounding Vevran soldiers and mounted the scythe, regardless of their reaching and grabbing for him. He bolted into the air to the location of the scene. His body executed his moves while his brain drowned in an ocean of disbelief. As if she were just any other Creature, Seskith the Hero was thrown into the pile of casualties in the Vevran war.

Like theatre masks, the Elite's face held a wild smile and Lord Fyresk's face held an agonizing grimace. Both of them were creating a rave show with their multi-colored neon explosions, each creeping slower towards the other in a battle of audacity. They reached a three-foot distance and commenced a bladed tête-á-tête

Lord Fyresk was forced to defend from a storm of sword slashes from the Elite. In fact, the shadow Lord was so focused that he almost didn't notice Lord Fyresk raising his wand with the hand that wasn't flailing the sword in various parries.

Almost.

Lord Fyresk struck with his wand, but the Elite cast the black lightning again, deadening Lord Fyresk's wrist. Fyresk writhed with pain and fell back. When he looked up, he was gazing down the Elite's steel blade. He watched the Elite's boot squash the hand that was holding his sword. Then, the Elite stabbed his steel blade into Lord Fyresk's chest. Despite layers of sturdy armor, thick, red blood gushed out, glimmering in the second Sonx-light.

Simon knew he only had one shot. After all his training, after every one of Vezlin's challenges, after his duels with Dagrio and... Seskith... He had to make this count.

As Simon approached the scene of the massacre, time melted to half-speed again, and Simon smoothly executed his specialty move. He vaulted off the scythe with his hands in a reverse position, then spun a smooth three-sixty, creating a cyclone with the scythe. The Vevran and Kearlithian soldiers were thrown back with a vicious wave of winds.

The Elite was cleanly beheaded. His body and head whirled away in separate directions and melted into pools of shadow.

Every Creature in the vicinity – Kearlithian and Vevran – halted and gawked at the sight. Simon stood hunched and breathless, his arms limp and the blade of his scythe resting on the ground.

Thrax and Vezlin were the first to move. They immediately dashed to Lord Fyresk and began the healing process, mumbling more jargon and rubbing the giant gash in his chest.

The Kearlithians turned to their still-astounded Vevran opponents, and unleashed the last bit of their anger, honor, and pride.

They faced no dispute; the Vevra were giving in. They were all melting to the puddles of shadow that now flooded the area.

Five minutes later, the shadowy pools and spikes vanished, and the Kearlithians stood breathless in an empty clearing with the bright light of the second Sonx above them. Simon could barely hold himself up. He heaved as he fought to catch his breath and hold back the agonizing sobs that were threatening to erupt. This was his moment of strength and courage. He took a massive sigh and blindly mounted the scythe.

He knew exactly where she was. The image of her golden body flying limp and lifeless through the air would surely reappear in future nightmares as a shadowy golden blur. He only had to pay attention to her landing during one of the many times the scene flashed back in his head like a broken record.

Roughly two hundred feet away he found her. Seskith had no visible wounds. Her Shintervan body would be preserved in its natural pristine state. Simon kissed her forehead as he gently stroked her dreadlocks. His fingers interlaced hers.

"There will never be another like her." It was Dagrio's soft voice behind Simon's shoulder.

"I will be," Simon said. "I will try to be, at least. She believed in honor. In trust. In courage. I will never be the Creature she was, but I will try."

"She died a hero," Dagrio noted.

Simon turned and impassively stared at Dagrio through watery eyes.

A brush of a woman's smooth hand found Simon's shoulder.

"Simon," Vezlin tried, but no words followed his name. She lightly rested her beautiful hand on his shoulder for support as they all listened to the crickets chirping and the locusts singing in the far distance.

*       *       *

Soon after, Voulderbrin and the other Protectors swarmed the sky and began shooing the Kearlithians back into the borders of Feerthel. The war was sure to stir attention, and the Protectors would be cleaning up this mess for months.

Simon kissed the back of Seskith's hand and rubbed her chin despite the hushed roars around him. "We're out of Feerthel!" and "We must rush back to Feerthel without the Humans seeing us!" sounded dull and distant.

"I will always remember you, Seskith," he said. "And I loved you, too."

A hazy mist encased Simon's vision and thoughts. He rode the scythe back through the untamed forest in an auto-pilot daze. He couldn't shake himself of Seskith's death, her powerless body twisting and contorting under the spell of the black bolts of lightning. The scene remained playing in his head the entire silent trip back to Kearlith. Other Creatures would pass him and pat him on the back in consolation, but Simon hardly noticed. He thoughtlessly repositioned the scythe to keep from falling, and the scene would start again.

*     *     *

The silent and tense atmosphere in the city of Kearlith erupted in a wave of whoops, hollers, and cries when the victorious Kearlithians returned. A few entered more sullenly, cursed with the knowledge of bad news on the battlefield. The remaining population that was not present for the battle was eagerly waiting the heroes' return. Dozens of family members were scattered across the outskirts of the city leading up to the castle.

Shastlin and Mathilda were waiting for Simon. Their hands were clasped together, but their faces possessed utter solemnity. Simon abruptly embraced Mathilda and held on to her like a life-jacket. His tears soaked the shirt under her leather armor, but he didn't care. Hugging her felt right.

She gingerly patted his head as they both mourned the loss of a fine Kearlithian.

"Kearlith will always remember Seskith the Shintervah," she said through quivering lips.

"The Hero," Simon added.

Mathilda nodded and rubbed Simon's head. "Thank you for saving this city, Simon," she said.

Their embrace lasted decades, until another eruption of yelps and roars broke out in the crowd. Lord Fyresk had returned from the battle. He remained conscious, even if he was woozy and half-asleep. White bandages with blood seeping through wrapped his torso. Two Enforcers were carrying him on a stretcher. They halted in the middle of the horde with disapproving faces.

One of them announced, "Lord Fyresk must return to the castle's hospital! Everyone gather and get a good look at his health, then we must hurry off to—"

"Oh, pipe down, Yarel," Lord Fyresk spat. He tried to sit up while the other Enforcer tried to suppress him. After a daring glare from Fyresk, the Kyejoth allowed the Lord to sit up. "Kearlithians! Today we celebrate victory!" His whispered roar carried throughout the crowd. Lord Fyresk let the citizens of Kearlith rejoice in their pride and triumph. Despite their losses, he allowed one moment to truly honor their achievements. The Vevra and the Elite were no more.

Eventually, Lord Fyresk managed to silence them with a raised palm. "We must remember our success. In the years to come, we will remember that if it weren't for a pack of Creatures so courageously brutal, so dreadfully clever, the Vevra would have remembered this day in our wake. All of you, every single Kearlithian present, contributed to Kearlith's victory today."

Fy took a moment to catch his breath. The Enforcer named Yarel quickly knelt by his side to assist him, but Fyresk batted her away. "But success must be assisted by failure," he finally continued. "Tonight, we lost several Kearlithians. Some, who probably saved my life."

Simon was gazing at the mass of proud and saddened Creatures surrounding him. With this, he looked and found Lord Fyresk's bold, tearful, blue eyes staring right at him. Lord Fy held the gaze for far too long, and the crowd eagerly lingered on the next lines of his speech. Fyresk gave a slight sniff and slowly found them. "As we remember our triumph, we must remember the fallen. If your family has not returned tonight, I give you my sincere condolences. I can assure you, I share in your loss." With this, Lord Fyresk collapsed again. He tried batting the Kyejoth away, but finally they suppressed him. As they waved their hands in a friendly fashion with grave faces, they flew Lord Fyresk to the castle.

Simon stood still, the loss of Seskith weighing heavy on his shoulders, ripping his trachea to shreds. His throat was raspy. He fought for his breath although the battle was over. His eyes were begging to release tears, but his clenched teeth kept them in.

Just then, a heavy hand clapped his shoulder blades. "Well, when one door closes, another one opens. Isn't that right?" asked

Caylo.

Simon glared at him in attempts to mimic Lord Fyresk, but Caylo didn't take it. He continued in his signature polished manner, "Life in Kearlith includes many hardships, Simon. Those who can withstand may call themselves Kearlithians."

"Then call me a Kearlithian," Simon backhanded as he turned a cold shoulder to Caylo and marched off to his humble shack.

# Chapter 35

The Sonx rose again the next morning, bringing about a new day with a fresh start. Simon was curled up in his Mizik blanket attempting to shield himself from all of it. The events of the past week kept him in a sleep-with-one-eye-open state. He was now shifting into mostly conscious, but he couldn't bring his body to stand. The fetal position under a warm blanket was much more comfortable. And even if he stood up and started his day and walked out that door, he still wouldn't see Seskith.

At least when he was half asleep, he could still see her smirking face.

An annoying tap at the door interrupted Simon's broody thoughts. "Come in!" he called. But the tapping continued. Simon cried a strident "Ugh!" and rummaged to put his pants and boots on.

"What?" he declared as he tore open the front door.

A meek and timid Gullen jumped back. "Lord Fyresk is holding a ceremony tonight. In the Courtyard of the Castle at the last forty-five," Terlinthia squeaked, giving a fearful nod before she flew off.

"I'm sorry, Terlinthia! I didn't mean to…" but she was gone.

Simon huffed and found his previous curled up position on the bed. He didn't mean to yell. He wondered how long this ache would last. How long before he got used to the emptiness he felt. How long before he could smile and feel good things again. More than anything, he wanted to be proud of himself. Of his city. Of their triumph. Their glorious call to arms. Instead, he was filled with dense blackness as if he were made of the shadowy material that imprisoned him just a few hours ago.

His eyelids were only closed for five minutes before Raelin burst through the front door.

"Have you heard?!" he shouted. "Lord Fyresk is throwing a ceremony!"

"We've heard, Rae!" Tormos shouted from his curled up position at the foot of the bed. "It's tonight!"

"Well, we must prepare," said Raelin as he lugged a couple of clinging bags inside. Suddenly, Simon and Tormos were intrigued and awake.

"Hey Raelin?" asked Simon nonchalantly.

"Yes, Simon?" Raelin asked.

"Where did you get those bags?"

Raelin grinned, revealing his many sharp teeth. "You don't want to know."

"Yes, he does," Tormos blurted. "Or I do, at least,"

"Well," Raelin began, lingering for anticipation, "our parents."

"What?" Tormos cried. His hands slapped his face, and he began circling the shack. "No, no, no, no, no. Tell me they're not coming to the ceremony."

Raelin's grin continued.

"Noooo!" Tormos cried.

"I had to, Tormos! I wanted to look my best for today. Plus, they're our parents. And last night was just as much a victory for Feerthel as it was for Kearlith. They deserve to celebrate with us!"

"You just want to laugh at them being idiots," Tormos accused.

"Well, that *was* the main reason, but do you blame me?" he asked bewildered.

Simon tried to find sleep again, but Raelin was soon on his back, scratching his ears and nose. "Come on, guys. Let's go have a day on the town in pre-celebration. It'll be great!"

"I can't celebrate," Simon announced, dropping the temperature in the room a few degrees. Raelin jumped in front of Simon's face and nudged his shoulder until they were eye to eye.

"Simon, look at me." Raelin's jovial tone was suddenly stone serious. "Seskith's death was a great loss to this city. We all know that, and we all grieve for her. But her loss cannot cause the loss of you. You must pick up and continue her fight for Kearlith."

Raelin's words struck deep. Simon pondered the statement, then pushed the Mizik blanket away and stood up. He was right. Simon survived the war. In fact, Simon won the war.

"That's the spirit!" Raelin announced as if he were reading Simon's thoughts. Tormos groggily grabbed his clothes and got dressed while Simon layered up for the chilling winds. Winter was moving in early.

Soon, all the boys were ready to hit the town, and Simon opened the door, revealing Dagrio in mid-knock. He moved to talk but was rendered speechless once he saw them.

"Hi, Dag," Simon said.

"Hi, Si," he said.

"What did you need?"

"Well, I," Dagrio began. "I was wondering if… I mean, I know it's weird to ask, but… if maybe you could help me shop."

Simon shot his hands to the raccoons' mouths to stifle their laughter.

Luckily, Dagrio didn't notice. His eyes were squeamishly watching the sky. "It's just that… well, I… don't know how good I look. And it's not that I think you would, it's just…"

Simon interrupted with an unintended, slight huff of laughter, "It's fine, Dagrio. You can tag along with Raelin and Tormos. We were just about to head to town."

The Vanterslove gave a squinted glance to the raccoons standing behind Simon.

"What?" Tormos asked, still trying to hold his giggles in.

Dagrio shook his head, then looked to Simon and wordlessly nodded his head. Simon managed to find a bit more laughter and led the way to the city.

For a while the boys strolled in silence, simply taking in the beauty of a tranquil and serene Kearlith. Most of the Creatures were still snoozing, but some of the shops were open as if it were a casual Tuesday. Simon found himself automatically eyeing the shadows and realizing he had nothing to fear. This occurred at least twice every ten minutes, and every time he felt the subtle, brief wave of relief.

But the occurrence always concluded the same – maybe while he was in town, he could celebrate his victory at the brewery. Oh wait...

He continued pretending to be okay. He smiled and waved at the early-rising Kearlithians, and threw in a comment whenever Tormos and Raelin were bickering too loudly.

Dagrio brought him out of his head, "I know you don't want to talk about it, Simon. But I'm really sorry about... you know."

"Yeah, me too," Simon admitted.

"This city really won't be the same without her. You're going to have a lot of slack to pick up as a Collector." Simon faked a smile, but no words. He kept walking and unwillingly presenting himself as pleasant.

*       *       *

Eventually, they made it to their first stop – Fine Threads N Things. This shop looked posher than the one where Simon bought his Mizik blanket. The three female Intellects at the counter were yapping and politely criticizing each other's decisions on tonight's gowns. When they saw the four boys, they whooshed to their assistance and quickly began taking measurements. "My, my, how skinny!" said one. "And this is the one that supposedly beheaded the Elite," said another.

Simon was going to bark a comeback, but the comment was lost in the gabble. He decided to let it go. He allowed them to twist and mold his arms while they hastily shoved their tape measures into him and his friends. Finally, they all stepped back, taking a long gaze in unison and shuffled to retrieve their finest suits.

The tailors failed to ask for their preferences. Simon, Dagrio,

Raelin, and Tormos all stood with their faces contorted in confusion, feeling rather small compared to the towering Intellects.

The half-humans swiftly returned and began handing them various pants, shirts, jackets, and cravats. "Just get dressed back there in the curtains, dears. Then come out, and we'll be the judges," they demanded.

Simon and his friends did as directed, making sure not to trip over or even touch any the gaudy dresses and robes. They found the quaint dressing rooms tucked in a back corner of the shop.

He had to admit – he looked rather dashing in the suit. It was jet black with metallic blue pinstripes, complete with a silky silver undershirt and cobalt blue cravat. The Intellects had overestimated how much Simon was willing to spend for the celebration – especially when he wouldn't be celebrating – but for the moment, Simon enjoyed looking like a handsome and wealthy hero.

He wore the suit out, and as soon as he unclasped the hooks of the curtain, the three aged Intellects were applauding and giggling like schoolgirls.

"That's the one!" one of them shouted.

"Yes, that's it!" another agreed.

Dagrio emerged from his dressing room as the ladies were gawking and gobbling about Simon's suit. Immediately, their faces dropped.

"Nope. We'll try again." One of the Intellects sighed as she went to retrieve more options. Dagrio sighed too as he returned to the dressing room.

"Um, I don't think I can afford this," Simon admitted to the Intellect that looked most like a manager.

"Don't worry about it, Simon," she said, bringing back one of his first memories of Seskith.

"No, really, I can't take something this expensive."

"You saved this city, Simon. You can have the suit," she said with a smile.

Simon was taken aback based on their comments from earlier, but he gradually found the dressing room and changed back into his clothes in stunned silence.

\*     \*     \*

Simon waited ages for the raccoons and Dagrio to try on five or six more options, but eventually they all walked out of Fine Threads N Things and continued up the streets of Kearlith with four bundles of handsome and debonair attire. Simon had a little more bounce in his step along with his friends. Maybe the ceremony wouldn't be so bad now that he felt a little more dapper.

For their next destination, Dagrio wanted to stop by Flarehva's Trinkets. Simon doubted she had any new inventory since their last visit, but he agreed it would be good to see her again. The raccoons agreed to the adventure.

They passed the red ribbons disregarding gravity, and again Simon was mesmerized. He momentarily paused as their formless dance engrossed him.

"Hey hero!" Flarehva called from her stoop. Seskith instantly invaded Simon's brain again. Although Flarehva said it, he only heard Seskith's voice. There was no escape.

"Ah, Simon!" Caylo called as well.

Simon grimaced at the situation. What did Caylo want with Flarehva?

He wasted no time in asking. "What are you doing here, Caylo?"

"I was simply chatting with a fellow Kyejoth, Si. What's gotten you so edgy?" he asked.

Simon knew Caylo wasn't to blame for the death of Seskith, but his blasé attitude was like salt in the wound.

"Yeah, Simon," Flarehva agreed. "You of all Kearlithians should be jumping for joy today. You brought an end to the Vevra."

"You sliced off the Elite's head!" Caylo exclaimed.

"Seskith is dead," Simon stated as if the fact had been painstakingly overlooked.

"I know," said Caylo. "And nothing will bring her back. Kearlith lost a great citizen last night. But you must not forget, in recent months she's gained an incredible one." Simon slit his eyes in suspicion, and Caylo continued with that slight, suave smile, "Yes, Simon. You. No one will ever replace Seskith, but I think Kearlith will be happy that at least you moved in."

Still through slit eyes, Simon shot, "How did I get here? Why did Voulderbrin let me in?"

Caylo glanced at Flarehva, then at Dagrio, and finally at the raccoons, fully taking them in for the first time. He shrugged as he carried on, "I guess it's no big secret anymore. You were called. To my best guess, I can only imagine you found interest in a single, perfectly circular Altostratus cloud, correct?"

Slowly, Simon answered, "Yes."

Caylo's grin grew wider as he walked up to Simon and put his arm around him like they were still two peas in the same rebellious pod. "Voulderbrin and I devised a plan to launch certain signals, hoping some curious Human like yourself would defy the Outside and seek shelter in this city. We were hoping – on an extremely risky presumption – that Lord Fyresk would spare you.

"You see, ever since the Vevra's attack several years ago, I've presumed Lord Fyresk to hunger for a future, to cling to Mizik like it was his last hope. Voulderbrin, myself, and the rest of the Rebellion seemed to agree that it was time to bring it to him."

"How did you pull it off without him seeing it?"

"We simply planned it. Voulderbrin has control of the sky, and we kept our eyes out for Lord Fyresk. As soon as he was deep within the castle, we signaled. Finally, you showed up."

Caylo took a moment to pat his back and relieve a sigh. "Thank the Sonx, right? Well, it was great seeing you again, Flarehva. Dagrio. Simon. Raccoons..." He tipped an imaginary hat to all of them and strolled down the street.

The group of shopping men followed Flarehva inside. Dagrio chit-chatted with Flarehva about the battle while Raelin and Tormos attempted to suppress themselves around all the tiny little knick-knacks they could steal.

Simon aimlessly wandered the aisles, reading the names and descriptions but processing none of them. He made a point to touch as many gadgets and gizmos as he could, hoping the sense of tactility would rejuvenate interest, but it was no use. His mind was in other places, in far dimensions of shadows.

*       *       *

Even when they bid their good-byes to Flarehva, Simon did so without noticing or putting an ounce of effort into it. He couldn't escape the emptiness of Seskith. There was only one place that might come close to healing his true wounds.

"I'll meet back up with you guys in a little while," he said.

"We were just about to go to Ziggokeif's Joke Shop!" Raelin whined. "I was going to get something to prank my parents tonight!"

"Sorry, Rae. I'll only be a few minutes. There's just someone I need to talk to."

Raelin seemed to understand. He shrugged and nodded and jumped on Dagrio's back. "See you in a while, Simon." They all said separately.

Simon nodded in response and started off on the path the brewery.

Earlier he had wanted to avoid the Mizik Brew and its absence of Seskith for the rest of his life, but after Caylo's detached conversation and Raelin's enthusiastic attitude, he needed someone to remember her like he did.

A glass-completely-drained Vranzic sat at the counter and mindlessly waved him in once the door-chimes sounded. Simon quietly sauntered over and found a seat at the empty bar in the dull silence of the café.

"Hi, Vranz," Simon finally said.

The tearful Shintervah turned his eyes and nodded to Simon.

"Hi, Simon," he muttered. For a moment, the two sat in the silence, save for Vranzic's occasional sniff. Simon tapped the bar with his fingers for a while until he noticed the annoying, repetitious echo. He had zoned out again on Seskith's absence, still expecting her to walk up at any second and ask if he'd like a refill.

"Would you like a brew?" said Vranzic, interrupting the silence and bringing Simon back to the real room. The one without Seskith.

"Yeah. Thanks." Simon sighed and tried to think of something else to talk about first. He needed small talk. Maybe something about how the birds sound great this morning. Or how the brewery is looking rather clean today...

"I miss her already, Simon," Vranzic said, cutting right to the chase as he passed Simon his Mizik brew. "I feel like she's gonna walk right through that door at any minute."

Simon's mouth moved to respond but found once again that he failed to release speech. He ended with a tiny grin and took his first sip of Mizik. As always, the bitter bite punched his throat and coated his veins with the slow pulse of energy. This had become such a routine that Simon barely noticed it anymore.

Today, he noticed. With a fresh sense of appreciation, he noticed everything. He started taking in tiny details about the brewery as if it were his first day here – the smoothly curved, cedar wood bar, the hundreds of tiny fire-lit lamps hanging from the ceiling, each emitting small beams of dull golden light like stars.

Then he noticed he hadn't said anything yet.

"I do, too, Vranzic. And everyone keeps saying that she will be severely missed. I know she will. But no amount of Creatures missing her, no amount of words can bring her back."

"I know what you mean, Si," said Vranzic. "No matter what anyone says, it seems to widen the wound. They all want to understand, to sympathize, but they don't. They can't."

"They'll be over her death by Tuesday," said Simon.

Vranzic had tear debris in his eye, but he was smirking. "I hope you're aware of how much she liked you, Simon."

"I know," Simon said. And he did. He looked away to hide the pain that struck when he remembered that he never got to tell her when she was alive just how much he liked her.

*      *      *

Raelin had only pinned the last button on his collar before Simon grabbed him by the hand and practically flung him out the door of their shack. They were already late to the ceremony. Tormos had a hard enough time getting into his suit – the Intellects fit it a bit too tight as if to give him a hint – so Raelin relaxed and laughed the entire time Simon and Dagrio argued with Tormos. It wasn't until he started buttoning his own suit before he realized the Intellects fit him a little tight, too.

Simon and Dagrio stood and pouted the entire time. They were dressed and ready, though both of them seemed a bit grim to be attending a celebration.

Now they were rushing out of the shack. "Come on! Let's get this over with," Simon barked as he returned Raelin to his legs, and they hustled up the path to Kearlith.

"Come on, Si," Dagrio said, glancing back to the raccoons and pulling out his compact cockpit. He traced one of the hexes on the two-foot-long canister, and his vehicle began to form – legs and arms popped out on both sides, and the canister itself unraveled into a shield.

Simon glanced back to the raccoons as well, then he unclipped the scythe. He nodded in response, and they both took off towards the castle, leaving Raelin and Tormos in their dust.

In the peaceful, familiar action of riding his scythe on the smooth terrain of air, Simon began to wonder what the Courtyard of the Castle was going to look like when it was packed with Creatures. He had only seen it a few times in passing – one of those in the duel with Lord Fyresk – and it never seemed to impress him. It sat above the Hall of Kings at the bottom of the hilt, with its own tower hosting a grand view of Kearlith that was open to the public. The columns and foliage were laced with meticulous, intricate detail. Though during the day the Sonx constantly washed the vast space, the lights always appeared off. There never appeared to be any good reasons to go to the Courtyard.

Lexandel dotingly referred to it as 'the Court'. In his childhood apparently Creatures and Humans alike would attend galas, ceremonies, tributes, and celebrations held there. Several times throughout the history lessons of the book, the Shintervah referenced 'the Court'.

The demon Lexandel.

Simon sped up to rid his brain of any Shintervan thoughts. Luckily, Dagrio caught on, and they quickly found themselves at the Court. The Creatures of Kearlith filled the space so tightly that Simon could hardly find a spot to get close enough to see anything. Instead, he saw the backs of many cheetahs, buffalo, owls, golden eagles, gazelles, tall people, and fire-people.

Some of them turned around and noticed his presence. They suddenly opened a gap in the crowd and vigorously waved him to the front. With a quizzical face, Simon looked to Dagrio, who simply shrugged.

"Lord Fy wants you up there," a Gullen spat, pointing his darkly golden wing to the tower Simon could now see in the clear path. Lord Fyresk was giving him another menacing glare from atop a short balcony. Still perplexed, he ran through the crowd.

As he walked onto the stage, Simon noticed the true beauty in the Courtyard of the Castle. Below the tower two grand stair-cases led up to a small terrace jutting out from the base. At each corner of the stage, four highly decorated columns stole Simon's eyesight. Each displayed a separate theme of each revered race – Shintervah, Gulverbruud, Kyejoth, and Serlentos. Simon took too long gazing at the Shintervan column. Some danced, others played hide and seek. He looked away to Lord Fyresk, who stood in the middle of the platform with arms crossed and a strong hold on his menacing glare.

"You're late," he seethed.

"I know. I'm sorry," Simon whispered. "I have these raccoons, and they were getting dressed and—never mind. I'm sorry." He looked out to see every Creature, every Intellect, every citizen of Kearlith, staring at him and the Lord of his new city. Were they waiting on him to start?

Lord Fyresk cleared his throat before, "Creatures of Kearlith, forgive me for the delay, but the hero of the hour has arrived." He paused and waited for it to begin – the instantaneous uproar of paws, hands, and hooves clapping. Simon's raging pessimism tried to hold back a beaming smile, but the ovation of every single Creature and Intellect in Kearlith forced his pride and ego to the surface. In gratitude he nodded and threw his hand in a waving gesture. He thought about bowing, but he didn't know if they did that here.

He looked to Lord Fyresk who was sporting a smile of his own. Fyresk threw his hand in a silencing gesture, and the city fell quiet. He began again and called out to the crowd, "Noble Kearlithians, last night this city achieved a great deed for itself, and for whatever lies past Feerthel in the Outside. We have defeated the shadow demons, the Vevra, all thanks to your heroism, Feerthel's Mizik, and this man named Simon." Lord Fyresk held out his hand, palm to the sky, and referenced the new Human sheepishly standing next to him. Again, the crowd in the Court erupted in applause and hollers.

And again, Lord Fyresk silenced them after a moment. "We have purged the world of haunted shadows. I now see my error in failing to trust you with the task of ending the Vevra's dark reign of terror.

"Today we celebrate our victory in the war, but we must honor those who sacrificed their lives so that we could live in a Vevra-free city. Kearlith lost many soldiers of every race last night. Though the cost was great, their atonement shall be remembered for eternity. Tomorrow in the graveyard, we will hold a mass funeral to remember and bury the bodies of those that were recovered from the battlefield.

"If not for Simon and the castle's hospital staff, I would have joined the ranks of the deceased last night, but I managed to survive. The doctors have saved me with a hexed chest and a tranquilizing amount of painkillers." Lord Fyresk looked down as did the rest of the Kearlith, though there was no need; his iconic black suit covered the unsightly gashes on his chest.

"The Elite has cursed me with more than physical wounds, however. He has illuminated a humbling lesson – we all will fall. My end was extended last night, but time will end me as it does all things.

"In light of this revelation, I have decided to pass along many of the duties of my title. I will remain Lord, ruling over Feerthel and everything within, but Kearlith will have a new King." Lord Fyresk held out his hand to Simon again as if referencing him, but Simon looked around. Lord Fyresk had to continue, "Creatures and Intellects of Kearlith, I present to you – King Simon."

The Kearlithian crowd gave perplexed, audible gasps and half-comments, each of them looking to others in a questioning manner. Simon fashioned the same contorted face. "Lord Fyresk, you can't be serious!"

"Oh, I am, Simon," Lord Fyresk whispered.

"But why? Why me of all people? Or Creatures?"

"You unarmed me, then spared me. You wanted answers, not blood on your hands. Mercy, tolerance, and a thirst for truth are traits not commonly found in Humans, even in Kearlith. You're the type of man I'd like to see as King." Lord Fyresk let loose a subtle wink, and he continued his speech before the Kearlithians began rioting with questions, comments, and disapprovals. "I have contemplated this decision to every extent, and I think Simon will bring grand things to the city of Kearlith.

"But he and I will not be leading alone. I have also instated a new Board. As I call your name, please come up and join us on the terrace. Chrysaetos. Morolith. Caylo…" As Lord Fyresk slowly listed off the Board member's names, Simon's gaze found the Kearlithians' eyes. They were all glaring at him, not in outright fury or suspicion, but in utter puzzlement. As the Board members took the stage, they, too, eyed him with disbelief. The pre-established Board members were all standing on the platform now, all holding the same glare. Simon's shoulders were stuck shrugging in defense. Lord Fyresk began naming the new Board members. "Yahnvry. Dagrio. Neeva. Kirbirin. Gulfred. Marilio…"

Just then, Dagrio shuffled up the grand staircase and hurried over to Simon. He punched his shoulder and quietly exclaimed, "My best friend is King!"

Simon smiled and allowed the comment to fill him with pride.

"And Kahvly," Lord Fyresk finished.

Simon had never heard of Kahvly, but apparently Kearlith had. They gasped in unison and silenced themselves as they awaited the newest member of the Board to take the stage. Slowly, a young, meek Shintervah crept up the stairs. The hair on his head was golden, short, and spiky, much like Vranzic's, only somehow more disheveled. He had heavy, dark violet bags under his eyes. He nervously rubbed his hands together as he gave a slight nod to the crowd of astonished Kearlithians.

Lord Fyresk continued, "For those of you that are too young to remember or," his eyes looked to Simon, "were not present for the events, an infamous Shintervah named Lexandel once rose to power and briefly held the title of King of Kearlith. Before Simon he was the last one to hold this title.

"This devious Creature was able to kill off every Human in Kearlith, save for two, along with various other Creatures that stood in his path of devastation – including his own brother. Lexandel's father and his nephew fled into the deep pockets of Feerthel, isolating themselves in fear of his wrath.

"After my father banished Lexandel, he took the title of Lord to peacefully weave the barrier between Feerthel Forest and the city of Kearlith. He attempted many times to locate the elder Shintervah and his grandson, but they were never found.

"Ever since I eradicated the world of Lexandel, I have tried numerous times to locate them myself. Today, I am proud to announce that I have made peace with the family of a Creature Kearlith would assuredly like to forget until the end of time."

There was a slow-rising rumble amongst the crowd of Kearlithians. Lord Fyresk jerked his hand as if to silence them but let the roars linger for a little longer.

"In the time since the fateful events surrounding Lexandel's rise and fall from power, these two Shintervah have built up a collection of Creatures that escaped the atrocities and wished for a life of freedom and isolation in Feerthel. I have been able to coax Ruvy and his grandson Kahvly into staying in Kearlith, and for Kahvly to serve as a member of the new Board.

"As all of you are aware, I hope, I listen intently to the opinions of the Board. Though my say is final, I profoundly depend on my advising staff to make decisions that favor the progression of a fair and unbiased Kearlith. I will take every consideration the new Board has to offer as I have done in my years of ruling Kearlith." Lord Fyresk waited for a round of applause that did not occur.

He cleared his throat before he continued, "It is my best belief that this new Board will serve as an ethical, honest, and virtuous hand in the ruling of Kearlith. With this new regime, I deduce absolute freedom from corruption and deceit." With this, the crowd of Kearlithians found enough to applaud for. They clapped and yelled in uproarious passion.

"Faithful Kearlithians," Lord Fyresk concluded with his own

passion, "may today mark the biggest conquest this city has seen in decades!" The Lord waved for the appropriate amount of time before he nodded and made his exit.

Simon was left on the platform as King of the city with the Board of his new advisers. He would have stared awkwardly at the faces of the Kearlithians, but their attention was elsewhere.

The rest of the Kearlithians chaotically filed out of the Court in attempts to be first seated at the Dining Hall. According to Lexandel the Dining Hall *always* followed the Courtyard. There was *always* a plethora of food and seating, so all the scuttle was for nothing. Simon waited until every Creature had left the Courtyard before he allowed the reality to sink in. The stillness of the moment became picturesque, as if all of this were some photograph he had found on some website while he was surfing the internet in a half-asleep state.

But this was real. Simon was now the King of Kearlith. The King of this Courtyard and its skillfully decorated stage and columns.

# <u>Chapter 36</u>

Slowly in uniform fashion, Simon put one foot in front of the other as he made his way to the Dining Hall. He had always hated the cafeteria at school; thus, he was apprehensive of a community dinner in Kearlith. He never seemed to belong in any clique, so he always picked the last table, usually the broken one in the corner.

In the Dining Hall, every table was appropriately dressed with a heap of food, and every table looked the exact same. Dozens of circular tables filled the space of the vast hall. Beaming blue Mizik lamps hung on the tall walls, illuminating the room with a white glow holding a golden tint. The lighting effect was surreal. Simon had only to sit anywhere and enjoy himself in his dazzlingly adorned castle.

"Hey King!" he heard Dagrio exclaim from the middle of the hall. Simon eased into the seat next to him surrounded by a score of inquisitive Kearlithians. "Let the King eat in peace!" Dagrio announced, taking on the role as Simon's personal bodyguard.

Simon subtly smiled at the gesture and plated a large amount of mashed potatoes, grilled Voxus patties, and some type of delectable-looking yellow dish. The yellow dish turned out to be a custard with such light and sweet complexity that it won the entrée of the night, despite the scrumptious runners-up that followed.

Simon tasted a little bit of everything from the various serving trays in front of him.

He was licking his fingers of something purple – he had stopped asking the names of things after the second course – when the back of his collar tugged him to the floor. His throat erupted a "Yiah! Hmph!" as his body smashed into the floor with a thud. Two raccoons leapt on top of him and started bombarding him with questions, "So you're the new Human? And you're King! Did you really kill the Elite? How? You're so skinny!"

Raelin and Tormos quickly rushed to the site of the action, pulling their parents off Simon. The two new animated raccoons kicked and flailed to get out of the grasps of their sons. Once Simon stood up and dusted himself off, Rae and Torm let their parents loose, and they scurried to the bench, the table, and Simon's dining neighbors, striving with such determination to get on the same level with Simon. Dagrio managed to grab their father and throw him on the ground, but he quickly rebounded and prepared a pouncing stance on the floor.

"I talked them out of their prank," Dagrio whispered with a smirk. "The way those two talk, I made them realize their presence would be enough of an embarrassment."

Simon managed to smile as he reclaimed his seat at the table. "Thanks, Dagrio," he said.

*     *     *

The raccoons weren't the only ones in Kearlith that wished to say a word or two to Simon. He lost count of how many Creatures came up and tapped him on the back, disrupting his second, third, and fourth courses. Simon could only take two bites before he was answering questions and offering thanks and shaking hands. Every time a new Creature stepped up, Simon's stomach reminded him how little he had eaten in the past week.

Finally, Simon was stuffed with a miserable amount of anonymous victuals, followed by an immediate lack of movement and inhibitions. He simply wanted to sit there and hibernate in the fifty pounds he had gained over the course of the hour, but the parade of incessant comments and curious Creatures never died down. During one of the rare and quick breaks, Simon tried to slink past the seated Creatures in the Dining Hall, but naturally, someone noticed. They called his name and begged him to stop. Simon hurried on without looking back.

By the time he made it out of the Dining Hall, Simon was near sprinting. He took a quick right and followed through the chambers and halls that surrounded the vast cafeteria, hoping his adherents would assume he was running away from the castle.

Simon halted once he heard voices coming from a room up ahead. Caylo and Lord Fyresk.

"There is nothing to discuss."

"I thought we had made our peace, Lord Fyresk. You've forgiven me. Why would you not name me King?"

"I never led you to believe your actions would be overlooked. I offered forgiveness, not a clean slate," Lord Fyresk spat before he noticed the other Human. Simon tried to duck behind the doorway, only to be stopped by Caylo's voice.

"Why him?" he asked.

Lord Fyresk gazed at Caylo for a few moments. His face was a stone scowl. "*That* is none of your concern."

"You've lost your mind, Lord Fyresk," Caylo said, throwing the comment away as if he were ridiculing his attire.

Lord Fyresk simply gazed at Caylo. "Think what you will. I know my truth, Caylo. Do you know yours?"

Caylo moved to speak but failed. He gruffly straightened his chest and sniffed. He glared at Lord Fyresk as he marched past him, complete with an almost comedic shoulder shove.

Fyresk scoffed, but he looked to Simon, and they both shared a smirk.

"So, I'm King now," Simon said as he approached Lord Fyresk.

"Yes, Simon."

"And you're sure?"

"Yes, Simon. Do not challenge me. I have made my decision."

"Okay. I'll trust you," Simon muttered. He looked at his feet, then at the blank stone wall across from them. "Was Seskith recovered and returned safely?"

"Yes. The fairies delivered her after the Kearlithians headed back to the city."

Simon's eyes widened as he looked back at Fyresk. "The fairies?! You know about the—"

"I'm *Lord* Fyresk, Si. Who do you think introduced her to the fairies and Lahdavehr?" he asked with a wink. "I know all about Lahdavehr and the woman she used to be."

Yet again, Simon's brain blew a fuse. "Who?"

Lord Fyresk only smiled.

King Simon sighed. "Fine. No further questions about that. But I want to know one other thing. Why did you let me live when I first got here? Why did you not slay me like the other Humans who broke through to Kearlith?"

Lord Fyresk gazed at Simon for what felt to be an eternity before responding. "I have much to regret and be thankful for in my history with Humans from the Outside. I know full well they are not to be trusted. But something from my gut screamed that you were different from the rest of them. I still haven't been able to put my finger on it. I guess we can call it intuition.

"After I'm gone, this city will cease to have a bloodline connected to the Preeminents, but I will save it from a complete absence of Humans altogether. Who knows what the future holds for Kearlith. I trust you will rule it with integrity." Lord Fyresk tipped his head and slit his eyes. "Do not disappoint," he said. Then he smirked.

\*      \*      \*

Simon breathed in every bit of the city's crisp, secure air on the trip back to his old shack. He took in every detail – the badly designed shop signs, the scrambled patches of mismatched lumber, the rough boulders jutting out into the sidewalks, the wide roads, the narrow alleys, the deep cracks within the poorly cemented sidewalks, the empty fire posts awaiting the night, the street debris gathering in the corners of the intersections, the hand-carved street signs barely tacked onto posts, and the general sense of sluggish progression.

Some of the Kearlithians had rushed back to their shops after dinner to prepare for the night's market. They stopped and waved at their new King as he passed them on the streets. King Simon modestly waved back.

Although Mid-City was slightly out of his way, Simon felt it was an appropriate time to pay his respects to Lord Fyrethold. He slowly approached the headless statue when he arrived. Something about the presence and the energy in the man's stance made it appear as if he could wield the frightful sword he was resting his hand on in a split second, and behead you himself in the next.

"Hi, Lord Fyrethold," Simon squeaked. "I know we've never talked before, and this isn't exactly a conversation right now, but I wanted to say thank you. Thank you for saving your son, and this city. I'm sure you were an incredible man, and a courageously honest Lord. I hope I can continue yours, Fyresk's, and Kearlith's legacy." He nodded awkwardly and started on the path to his shack.

An eerie silence filled the space of the empty shack, as if it knew it would soon become desolate. In the same fashion as his walk back from the castle, Simon breathed in the stale and familiar air of his former habitat. The effect was humbling; Simon still felt like a new Human, not the King. He cast his wand to the stump lamp, and it instantly raged a comfy fire, throwing light onto the sparse furnishings – the dusty sofa and matching chairs, the rusty sink, the Mizik blanket-covered bed with poorly welded legs, the nook of Tormos and Raelin's belongings in the corner.

Just then, his raccoon pet crept the door open.

"So I guess it will just be me and Torm from now on," he said, bashfully.

"Don't be crazy, Raelin. You guys are moving into the castle with me."

Raelin waved his paws as his eyebrows shot up. "We couldn't possibly…"

"Oh, but you could. And you will," Simon stated. "And once I take the throne and we all get settled, you'll be finding another job. I cannot in good conscience allow one of my best friends to be a thief in my city."

Raelin gave an ever so slight huff before responding. "I guess you're right, Simon." He paused as his eyes gazed out the window of their humble shack. He looked back to Simon before he admitted, "That would not be in good conscience of the King."

## KEARLITHIAN WORDS

### - Money in Kearlith -

**Duzuk**- bronze pebble.

**Dillian**- silver pebble worth 50 Duzuks.

**Doth**- gold pebble worth 50 Dillians.

**Daxer**- black pebble worth 100 Doths.

### - Glossary -

**Axolotl**- Enlarged, magical axolotls. Protectors of the Axolotl Lake and its rivers.

**Biffleflenn**- Owl Creatures. Protectors of Kearlith and Feerthel.

**Bratch beetle**- Bronze and teal beetles found in Feerthel Forest.

**Chirth Stone**- A huge boulder located in Feerthel Forest. It once covered Serlentos Cave.

**Clauderban**- Rock-Creature. Could easily be mistaken for a clump of rocks.

**Cuffersha**- Rabbit-like Creature.

**Feerthel Forest**- The magically constructed, forested region outside of Kearlith. Roughly eight miles in diameter.

**Flervana**- Jellyfish that swim in the treetops of Feerthel Forest.

**Goyliguin**- Iguana-Grizzly bears. Found in Southeast Feerthel.

**Guaraberry**- Berries found on the Guara Bush- a strand of Mizik-based plants. Sweetly sour in taste, but dense in magic.

**Gullen**- Golden Eagle Creatures. Keepers of Kearlith.

**Gulverbruud**- Buffalo-Rock Creatures. Hunters and Enforcers in Kearlith. Created by Thomas Dirth.

**Intellects**- A tall and lanky humanoid race. Their brains have been magically enhanced, but they are not dependent on Mizik like Creatures are.

**Kearlith**- The city located in Feerthel Forest.

**Kratikoi**- Enlarged praying mantis Creatures.

**Kyejoth**- Human Creatures enhanced with fire-power. They, unlike Intellects, are fully Creature and dependent on Mizik. Created by Nathaniel Lantern.

**Rog**- Red-skinned hogs.

**Rutroot**- Root of the Rut tree. Builds endurance and heals.

**Sengli**- Penguin-swan Creatures.

**Serlentos**- Scorpion-razorblade Creatures. Created by Eleanor Ocean with intentions to make them superior as Sons of the Sonx.

**Shintervah**- Cheetah-air Creatures. Usually Mizik Collectors in Kearlith. Created by Wendy Whisp.

**Sonx**- The Sun.

**Tobbly**- Chameleon squirrels Lexandel trained to despise and attack Humans.

**Vanterslove**- Magical gazelles. Builders of Kearlith.

**Vevra**- Shadow people. Harmed by the Sonx unless they take form of a physical avatar.

**Voxus**- Fox-like Creature.

**Zelph**- Salamander snakes. Found in Southeast Feerthel.

## - Spells-

**Anahvy**- The magnetic/fetching spell.

**Craesoffe**- The detonation spell.

**Extervoso**- Extinguishes a small flame.

**Flifferfin**- The fluffy spell.

**Flindervosa**- The ember spell. Sparks a small fire.

**Gravro-rull**- Increases gravity ten times.

**Iceveral**- Spouts a flow of ice.

**Invosis**- The enlarging spell.

**Kiliivna**- Instantly sets every cell in the body on fire.

**Kilito**- Sends a beam of physical force.

**Zapatta**- The zip-line spell.

## KEARLITHIANS-

## THE PREEMINENTS-

**Thomas Dirth**- The Brute. Created the Gulverbruud. Married to Eleanor Ocean.

**Eleanor Ocean**- The Beauty. Created the Serlentos. Married to Thomas Dirth.

**Nathaniel Lantern**- The Brain. Created the Kyejoth. Married to Wendy Whisp.

**Wendy Whisp**- The Brave. Created the Shintervah. Married to Nathaniel Lantern.

## KEARLITHIANS (continued)

**Alencia**- Vanterslove. Wife of Roibose. Mother of Dagrio.

**Bentavi**- Vanterslove. Sister of Dagrio. Mathematical mastermind.

**Blirbeck**- Fairy. Overcompensates for his fairy femininity.

**Boffin**- Intellect. The wand-shop owner.

**Caylo**- Kyejoth. Fyresk's right hand man. Lead Enforcer for the Board.

**Chrysaetos**- Gullen. Lead Keeper for the Board.

**Crysis**- Human. Younger brother of Jystik and Kyo.

**Dagrio**- Vanterslove. Son of Roibose. Mastermind with gadgets.

**Delezi**- Shintervah. Son of Lexandel. Brother of Vranzic.

**Flarehva**- Kyejoth. Owner of the trinket store.

**Friziv**- Shintervah. Lead Collector for the Board and employee of Ziggokeif's Joke Shop.

**Fyresk**- Human. The Lord of Kearlith and Feerthel. Son of Lord Fyrethold.

**Fyrethold**- Human. Father of Fyresk. Killed by Lexandel.

**Gulfred**- Gulverbruud. New member of the Board.

**Hithry**- Intellect. Named King after Kowlakro and before Lexandel.

**Jahravel**- Shintervah- The fastest Collector until Lexandel years later.

**Jystik**- Human. Older brother of Crysis and Kyo. Becomes the first King of Kearlith after the Preeminents give up power.

**Kahvly**- Shintervah. Son of Lexandel's brother. Great-nephew of Ruvy.

**Kellabane**- Vanterslove. Sister of Dagrio.

**Kirbirin**- Gullen. New member of the Board.

**Kowlakro**- Gulverbruud. The Creature King. He served a time when peace between Humans and Creatures was at its peak.

**Kyo**- Kyejoth. The first Kyejoth. Younger brother of Jystik. Older brother of Crysis.

**Lagelle**- Vanterslove. Builder.

**Lahdavehr**- The Mother Tree and keeper of the fairies.

**Lexandel**- Shintervah. Originally Collector, then King. The leader of Kearlith preceding Fyrethold.

**Marilio**- Biffleflenn. New member of the Board.

**Mathilda**- Gulverbruud. Morolith's sister. Wife of Shastlin.

**Morolith**- Gulverbruud. Lead Hunter for the Board. Brother of Mathilda.

**Mortimer**- Intellect. Lead Intellect for the Board. Simon's history teacher.

**Neeva**- Kyejoth. New member of the Board.

**Nighfall**- Vanterslove. Lead Builder for the Board.

**Raelin**- Raccoon. Roommate of Simon. Brother of Tormos.

**Roibose**- Vanterslove. Head Housing Builder. Father of Dagrio. Husband of Alencia.

**Ruvy**- Shintervah. Father of Lexandel. Great uncle of Kahvly.

**Seskith**- Shintervah. Collector and employee of the Mid-City Mizik Brew. Daughter of Vranzic.

**Shalice**- Vanterslove. Builder.

**Shastlin**- Shintervah. Husband of Mathilda.

**Soiko**- Vanterslove. Sister of Dagrio. Master Builder.

**Terlinthia**- Gullen. Greeter at the Mizik bank.

**The Elite**- Vevra. The King of the Vevra.

**Thimethian**- The talking, burnt orange house-cat of the castle.

**Thrax**- Kyejoth. Owner of the potion shop.

**Tormos**- Raccoon. Brother of Raelin.

**Vezlin**- Kyejoth. Formerly Enforcer; currently Collector. Simon's Collecting trainer.

**Voulderbrin**- Biffleflenn. Lead Protector for the Board.

**Vranzic**- Shintervah. Owner of The Brewery. Seskith's father. Lexandel's son.

**Xivian**- Fairy.

**Yahnvry**- Intellect. New member of the Board.

**Zahti**- Vevra. The Elite's right-hand man.

**Ziggokeif**- Vanterslove. Joke shop owner.

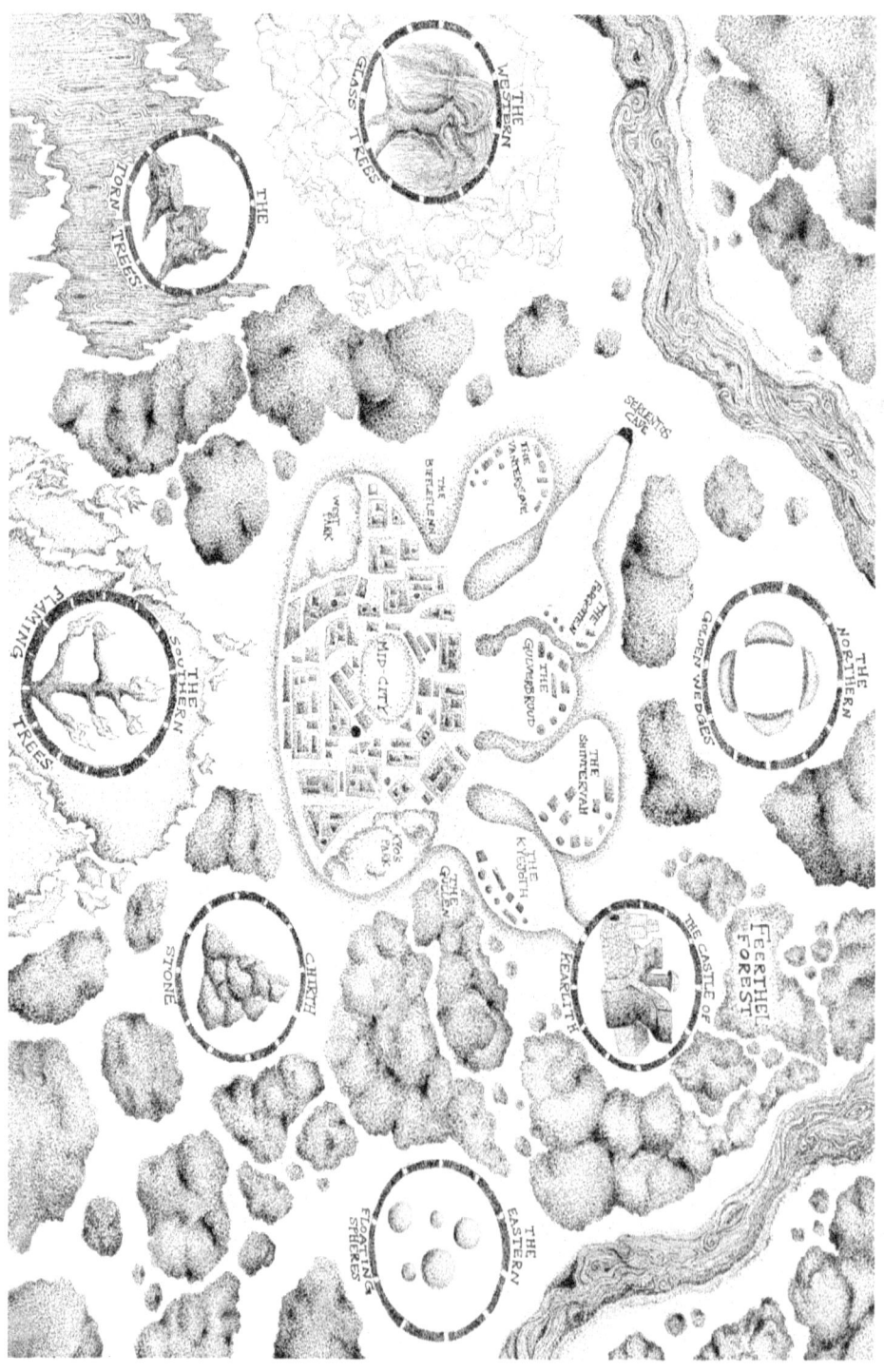